The
Drinking
Gourd

The
Drinking
Gourd

A Casey Cavendish Mystery

Katherine Fast

LEVEL
BEST BOOKS

First published by Level Best Books 2022

This novel is entirely a work of fiction. The names, characters and incidents portrayed in it are the work of the author's imagination. Any resemblance to actual persons, living or dead, events or localities is entirely coincidental.

Author Photo Credit: Jocelyn Finlay

First edition

ISBN: 978-1-68512-116-7

Cover art by Level Best Designs

This book was professionally typeset on Reedsy.
Find out more at reedsy.com

Dedicated to Jeffrey Fast

Praise for THE DRINKING GOURD

"A confident and compelling debut by an author to watch! Timely and thought-provoking, *The Drinking Gourd* combines a solid mystery with a riveting and brave look at the tensions of history, and the way the past haunts us—until we face it. Main character Casey Cavendish is tough and wonderful—and we root for her all the way. Do not miss this!"—Hank Phillippi Ryan. *USA Today* Bestselling Author of *Her Perfect Life*

"*The Drinking Gourd* resonates with vivid characters ensnared in a web of love, betrayal, and greed that roils just below the surface of a sleepy college town. Wrongly sent to prison for dealing cocaine, Casey, the hero-rebel-victim, fights to clear her name before she's framed a second time, this time for murder. Fast, a fresh new voice in the crime fiction world, offers a twist on the damaged heroine and a powerful sense of place with echoes from the Underground Railroad."—Kate Flora, award-winning author of the Joe Burgess series

"Two compelling characters, one an ex-con, the other a cop, take you on a wild ride as they untangle the mysteries that haunt the past, shatter the present, and threaten the future. I couldn't turn the pages fast enough."—Barbara Ross, Author of the Maine Clambake Mysteries and the Jane Darrowfield Mysteries

Prologue

1964 Oberlin, Ohio

Casey Cavendish had dawdled and daydreamed and now was late for the last Sociology class before spring break. She mounted her bike and raced down West College Street, riding too fast to avoid the pothole, a remnant from winter snow. The bike lurched and the wheel buckled, pitching her off to the side. The frame was bent and the front tire flat. Unhurt but angry, she grabbed her book bag and ran. She'd never make it in time.

As she passed a freshman dormitory, she cast a thieving townie eye on a shiny new Raleigh. Unlocked. She glanced around and then took advantage of a time-honored local tradition of "borrowing" a college student's bicycle. Townies didn't consider it stealing, just rearranging the location of some foolish student's transportation.

She approached the gothic spires of Peters Hall just before the hour. She flung the bike toward the end of the bike rack, seized her bag, and took the stone steps two at a time. Inside she dashed across the atrium and up the stairs leading to the classrooms.

Breathless, she slipped into the last row of seats next to another townie and her best friend, Jules, who gave her a mock scold for her last-minute entrance. Casey was too excited to concentrate on the lecture, her mind racing in anticipation of picking up her boyfriend, George, who was arriving from Yale that afternoon. The only reason she'd come to class at all was to turn in her term paper. She rummaged in her book bag, withdrew the paper and slid it across to Jules. She mimed handing it in, and please.

The professor paced back and forth across the front of the room, hands clasped behind his back, droning his erudite take on something or other. When he made his turn, Casey ducked out the door. She flew down the stairs and across to the door. Outside, she hesitated a second, casting about until she spied her ride.

A voice called her name from across the street. Charley Crockett, the high school student she tutored in history, waved wildly for her attention. She waved back but wasn't going to stop for him this morning. She dumped her book bag into a saddlebag and mounted the bike.

From behind, sirens wailed and lights flashed. She turned and a cruiser cut her off as she reached the road, skidding to a halt a few feet from her. A bullhorn blared, "Off the bike! Now!" Doors slammed and two officers approached. One grabbed the handlebars and the second yanked her hands behind her back. "You're under arrest."

For borrowing a bike? Casey's heart pounded wildly. She tried to speak but no sound came out. As one officer cuffed her, the other opened the leather flap of a pack under the bike seat and retrieved a package.

A second cruiser screamed down the street and jumped the curb, chasing Charlie across the college green. He was fast, but on foot he was no match for the car. He turned his head to look back and stumbled.

"No!" Casey screamed as the cruiser smashed into him.

Chapter One

Ten years later, 1974, Oberlin, Ohio

C asey edged her bike into a rack beside the stone steps of Peters Hall and listened to the night quiet of the small college town. A half moon dipped in and out of scudding clouds, making the shadows of the building's gothic spires dance in diamonds of dew on the freshly mown grass.

She forced a deep breath to quell the growing tightness in her chest, but she couldn't fend off the images that flooded over her. Right here, a decade before, she'd run down these stone steps and jumped on a bike. Sirens screamed, a bullhorn voice ordered her off the bike, and her world collapsed. She was arrested and charged with dealing cocaine a month before graduation.

She shuddered and drew a curtain over the memory, although she knew it would only be temporary. Breathe in; breathe out, she told herself. Calm down. She was out of prison on a lovely spring evening, free to go anywhere she chose. She'd signed up for an evening adult education class in handwriting analysis to keep from going crazy.

At the sound of approaching footsteps, she instinctively ducked into the shadows. In her student camouflage of jeans and navy sweatshirt, she hoped she was invisible.

A tall woman with a low voice approached. "No light. No sign. I'm supposed to *divine* the location?" She dressed like a gypsy in flowing peasant skirt, silky blouse, and a man's satin vest. A harlequin scarf knotted her wild mane of gray hair. She dumped a cardboard box on the sidewalk and held up a rumpled paper. "Peters Hall, Room 205." She turned in a circle, frowning at the constellation of college buildings surrounding her.

Casey rubbed a long scar on her forearm. Relax. No threat. No one wanted to hurt her. Matter of fact, no one wanted anything to do with her. The woman had to be the handwriting instructor, Barbara Roman. Casey stepped into the light. "This is Peters."

"Good Lord!" The woman jumped and backed up.

"Sorry. Didn't mean to scare you." Casey suppressed a smile. She hefted the box onto her shoulder, grabbed her book bag in her other hand, and led the way up the stone steps.

Inside they walked into a brightly lit, airy, central court dominated by an enormous stone fireplace. Before them a graceful staircase rose to a landing and then branched, leading to a balcony that overlooked the two-story atrium.

Casey's shoes squeaked on wide oak floorboards buffed to a mirror shine. They approached a long table in the center of the space covered with a white cloth. A sign with a fat, yellow happy face read, "Welcome. Please sign in."

"If you're here for adult education, you're early," a disembodied voice challenged from under the table. Despite the intervening years, Casey recognized the high metallic whine of Mrs. Swain.

From shoulder height Casey dumped the box of materials on the end of the table.

Mrs. Swain banged her head as she materialized from below. When she saw Casey, her smile tightened and her nose twitched. "You'll have to wait outside until I'm ready."

"Nonsense." Barbara Roman stepped forward. "Miss Cavendish and I need to set up Room 205."

For a split second, Casey wondered how the woman knew her name. But they'd all recognize her. Oberlin was a small town with a long memory.

Mrs. Swain grabbed a plastic garbage bag and a door sign and stomped up the stairs. By the time she entered the classroom, she'd lost her breath but regained her composure. Casey placed the box on the floor and listened to Mrs. Swain spit instructions.

"Leave the room exactly as you find it. No food or drink." She handed the garbage bag to Casey, spun on her heel, and tripped over the box. Instinctively, Casey grabbed Mrs. Swain's arm to break her fall and gasped as the woman's wig sailed past. Mrs. Swain shook off Casey's helping hand and snatched her errant hairpiece from the floor. "Clean the boards if you use them." The door slammed behind her.

Casey covered her mouth and struggled for control. She stole a glance at the instructor and they both doubled over laughing. It was the first time Casey had laughed in a long time. It felt wonderful.

The feeling didn't last.

She sat in an amphitheater-style classroom where she'd taken Sociology ten years ago. Now, with only one final paper left to submit for American History to finish her degree, she'd decided to join the handwriting class that had begun earlier. No problem to make up lessons. She'd taken correspondence courses while she was in prison. The subject both fascinated and baffled her.

When she'd come home, she was determined to find out who had betrayed her, railroaded her into prison, and made her pay for a crime she didn't commit. But no one remembered anything, or wanted to remember. Many of the players from ten years past had moved on. The police officers involved were either dead or retired to other locations. She had no legal access to old records. Frustrated and bitter, she'd vowed to make a fresh start. Maybe this handwriting course would distract her from her troubles.

When the class began filing in, Casey forced herself to sit tall. As they passed her seat, a few rubbernecked and whispered, but no one spoke to her.

Unlike the college courses, locals taking an adult education course would know her, or of her. Before she was convicted, she was the pride of the locals, a townie who'd gone on to the college. Now she was a pariah, the prodigal whose return was not welcome. For the better part of the last year, she'd avoided townsfolk by living in her own shadowland. She'd nearly driven herself around the bend completing the lonely circuit from a room in her great aunt's house, to the library, to classes and back. She was ready to break out.

But she wasn't ready when Barbara called the class to order and asked Casey to introduce herself.

Silence. Old wooden chairs creaked as students turned toward her. Casey's pride was the only thing between her and the door. She gritted her teeth. *Dammit, you have every right to be here.* She met the stare of each student in turn, recognizing a few of the older ones. *Why worry what these people thought of her? She already knew. She had nothing to lose. She'd goddam lost it all.*

"I'm Casey Cavendish. I spent the last ten years in the Ohio Reformatory for Women." Ignoring the collective intake of breath, she forged on. "When I was in prison, I got letters from outside. I learned as much from the handwriting as I did from the content. I took a correspondence course inside, and now I want to learn more." The class exhaled.

Good thing I kept it short, or they'd have passed out. No big deal. No fireworks, no bloodshed. She'd scaled the first hurdle, but her nightmare wasn't over. She was still surrounded by a gray aura of shame. She might be free, but now she was shut out rather than shut in.

Toward the end of the class, Barbara gave an assignment. The primary focus would be on their own writing, but they were also to assemble samples of writing from friends that they'd known over a long period of time. During the course, they'd examine changes in the writings to see if they could link the changes to corresponding shifts in personality.

Casey didn't have a circle of friends. Never did. Always a loner, she'd had only one best friend, Julietta Loveland, Jules. Now Mrs. George Kenworthy. Jules Kenworthy. Just thinking of the two names linked together made Casey want to spit. *She* should be Mrs. Kenworthy, faculty wife, and mother of an adorable little girl. She unclenched her fist and forced herself to listen to the closing of the lesson.

As Casey waited for the class to file out, she watched Barbara struggle to impose order on the materials scattered around the front of the room. She wanted to ask her about Martha's too-perfect handwriting, but it was late. *Just go.* She grabbed her book bag and headed toward the door. One of the old floorboards squeaked.

"Casey! Talk with me while I clean up." Barbara's lecture voice changed to a more inviting tone. "Unless you're in a hurry, of course." She didn't wait for a response. "Organization is not my strong point." A pile of handwriting samples slid off the desk into a wastebasket. She waved at the papers and laughed. "Sit for a moment. What's on your mind?"

Casey helped collect Barbara's materials while she explained her dilemma. "The only handwriting samples I have are letters from my great aunt, my brother, his wife Martha, and a convict in Marysville." She watched Barbara's face for her reaction. Despite Barbara's kindness, Casey felt scrutinized, as if she still wore prison orange. "My brother is a recovering alcoholic. He wouldn't appreciate me airing his addictive traits in public. And I only have one sample from Marysville. I don't even have examples of my own writing."

"No scrapbooks, old papers, notes?"

"No. When Martha married my brother and moved into our old apartment, she cleaned out my room."

Barbara nodded and was quiet for a moment. "It must be hard for you in this town. Why did you come back?"

Barbara's bluntness surprised Casey. No one else had dared ask how it felt to be an ex con. She shrugged. "My aunt's old and frail. She offered me a room in exchange for cooking and cleaning while I finished up my last semester of college."

"There are lots of colleges in Ohio. Couldn't your brother and his wife take care of your aunt?"

"They have full time jobs at a restaurant here in town. And Aunt Mae would never live with them—Mae would drive Martha nuts." Casey paused with a small smile. She rather liked the prospect of driving Martha nuts.

"How long have you known Martha?" Barbara asked.

"Since we were kids. I've never been one of her friends. You met Martha's mother, Mrs. Swain—the lady with the flying wig. She's no fan, either. I could use a letter Martha wrote to me in Marysville, but I can't make any sense of it. The only reason she wrote was to tell me my old love had married my best friend."

"That's the writing you brought with you?"

Casey frowned and looked to the side. She didn't like being so easily read.

Barbara laughed. "Don't worry, I'm not a witch. When people linger after class, they usually have questions about a writing."

Casey rummaged in her book bag for Martha's letter. "Her writing's regular and even, but she's a slob." Casey hesitated and then amended, "Well, she's organized at work. She delights in cleaning up after everyone else, but her home is a sty. I can't tell anything about her from this." She handed the letter to Barbara.

Barbara took her time, slowly rubbing the paper between her thumb and forefinger. She turned the page upside down and studied it some more. "Maybe she doesn't want you to know anything," she mused. "Do you see any personal touches in the writing? Any signs of originality?"

Casey shook her head. "No."

Barbara rubbed her fingers over the indentations on the paper once more. "Heavy pressure is the only trait that distinguishes this from perfect copybook. It feels as if she carved the writing into the paper. Otherwise, it's studied—exact—written slowly for maximum control." She glanced up at Casey. "We call this a 'persona' handwriting. The writer adopts an outer shell, or persona, of admirable qualities, to hide more vulnerable or embarrassing traits. The shell is what we see here."

"So, what can you tell from a persona handwriting?"

"Not much. It's a calculated façade. Do you have any idea what she's so afraid to show the world?" As Barbara spoke she drew her fingers through narrow funnels of empty spaces that ran down the page.

Casey cocked her head. If she colored in the funnels, they'd resemble chutes from the children's game, *Chutes and Ladders*. "What do the funnels mean?"

Barbara frowned. "They're called 'chimneys.' Not a positive trait."

Casey waited for Barbara to say more, but instead she handed the paper back. "Do you have other samples of her writing? Something written in haste or under pressure?" Barbara looked directly at Casey. "Or, even better, writing from an earlier point in time, before she took cover?" Her voice trailed off, but her gaze remained intent.

No, but I know where I can get one. Casey met Barbara's gaze. "I'll see what I can dig up. Thanks." She put the writing back in her book bag and rose to leave.

"Take care with this woman, Casey. She's a pressure cooker, and she's very, very angry."

Casey turned and met Barbara's eyes. She nodded but didn't speak.

So am I.

Chapter Two

Casey ran down the stairs, across the atrium, pushed open the front door, and came to an abrupt halt, overwhelmed by a flash of *déjà vu*. Her chest tightened. The walls swayed and began to close in. *No! No! No!* Her fingernails dug crescents in the palms of her hands. She shouldered through the door and dashed down the steps to the bike rack. Gasping as if she had just run a mile, she slung her book bag into the rear basket of her aunt's old bike and pushed it forward, not trusting herself to ride. But she'd made it. Determination. No, anger. Anger was the key. Well, she had plenty of that.

As she walked the bike along a diagonal footpath that students had worn between buildings, a large oak swallowed her in deep shadow. She fumbled with the light on the handlebars. Aunt Mae's ancient bicycle had fat tires, a light, and a bell to warn pedestrians, squirrels, and slow-moving dogs they were about to die. Casey's mouth turned up at the corners picturing Mae, a brick of a woman, riding her "wheel" down the center of the road followed by a caravan of impatient cars. The bike had one speed, forward, and locking foot brakes. No need for gears. The last glacier had pancaked the northern Ohio terrain.

A sample of Martha's writing was in a filing cabinet in the cellar of the Drinking Gourd, the antebellum inn where she and Jules had grown up. Problem was access. Her brother Art and Martha lived in the same rooms over the restaurant that Casey's family had rented when she was a girl. Now Art ran the bar, and Martha managed the restaurant. Martha would rather chew off an arm than help Casey. On Monday night the restaurant and bar closed, and Art and Martha would be at Aunt Mae's for dinner.

George and Jules Kenworthy lived in the fancy owner's quarters where Jules had grown up, while Casey was stuffed into a back room at her great aunt's house. The Kenworthy family attended the college concert series on Monday nights.

So, no one home at the Gourd, and the only way to get Martha's writing was to take it. The Westminster chimes of Finney Chapel rang the hour. Nine o'clock. Casey mounted and rode past a classroom building and cut across to the street. The dormitories were lit up but quiet. Cramming for final exams.

Half a mile later she approached the Gourd from the rear. All lights were out except for a dim glow in the restaurant kitchen. From behind, the old inn formed the base of a U-shape, bordered on the left by a new wing that had been added by Jules' parents while Casey was gone, and on the right side, although not attached, by a large barn. In the hollow of the U was a wide cobblestone patio with a well in the center.

As she glanced up at the window to her old room on the second floor, a wave of sadness engulfed her. This was the last place she'd been truly happy. As girls, she and Jules had plumbed the mysteries of the inn and coopted a coal bin in the cellar for their Bloody Cats Eyes clubhouse.

When Jules' ancestor, Abe Loveland, built the inn during Abolition, Oberlin was a station on the Underground Railroad. Loveland created a number of ways for slaves to escape bounty hunters who tracked them, including a secret passageway between rooms, a pole they could ride like firemen and an underground tunnel.

He named the inn after a slave song, "Follow the Drinking Gourd," that contained encoded messages instructing fugitive slaves how to navigate by stars in the Big Dipper, which they called the Drinking Gourd, on their nocturnal journey north to freedom.

Casey stashed Mae's wheel out of sight on the far side of the barn and walked to the well in the center of the patio. The Kenworthy's back door was on the left. The rear entrance to both the kitchen and to the Cavendish apartment above the restaurant was on the right. Casey approached a bulkhead located in the center that provided direct access to the cellar where she could find Martha's writing.

She hauled open the heavy metal door and brushed the air to clear away cobwebs before stepping down stairs to the cellar door. She lifted an old wrought-iron latch and entered.

A high thin tone pierced the air and a red strobe flashed overhead. She had sixty seconds. She patted the wall to her right until she felt the keypad. Holding her breath, she pictured the number and letter combinations on the pad. J was a 5 and 5 was in the middle of the second row of buttons. With painstaking care, she entered "JULES" followed by the pound key, bottom row right.

The red warning light continued to flash, and the high keening note persisted. She re-entered the numbers. No change. The police would arrive in less than five minutes. With a shaking hand, she entered 58537 again, hesitated, and pressed the asterisk key. Silence. She closed her eyes and exhaled. Close.

Inside she paused to let her eyes adjust to the dim light. The moon sent beams through a small coal chute window at ground level, revealing the behemoth of an old furnace in the center of the room. She groped overhead for the metal wire she and Jules had strung the length of the cellar. Yes! Still there. She followed it past the indistinct forms of two huge soapstone washtubs and an ancient circular washing machine with a mangle wringer. On the left, she sensed, but couldn't see, four coal bins. She walked to the last bin tucked into the corner, the little room she and Jules had used as their clubhouse.

When she'd asked Art if the clubhouse had been cleared out and put to some new use, his reply surprised her. He said that Jules wouldn't let anyone touch it and, besides, it was such an awkward space under the stairwell that led up to the Kenworthy kitchen that it would be more trouble than it was worth to fix up.

She tried the door latch. Locked from the inside. She smiled. She located the trip cord that snaked under the stairs and gently pulled it until she felt the interior latch rise. Securing the line on a nail, she pushed open the wooden door. Inside she groped forward until she bumped into a desk. Inside the pencil drawer, she found a candle and a box of wooden matches.

When she lit the candle, the room illuminated. Martha's handwritten Bloody Cats Eyes oath would be in the file cabinet to the right of the desk. *But first.* With her palm up, her fingers probed inside the drawer until they touched a wallet-sized packet taped to the underside of the desktop. With a few careful tugs, she retrieved a small picture frame.

She ran her fingers over the ornately tooled leather case, unhinged the tiny brass clasp, and opened the frame. Carved maroon velvet on the left panel protected the photograph on the right. The exquisite workmanship was squandered on what was arguably the homeliest couple ever to take wedding vows. A tall skinny man with scarecrow outcroppings at the sides of his pointed head looked pleased with himself and a tad foolish. Next to him, a short, squat woman with a slash of a mouth and downcast eyes assumed an expression of impending martyrdom.

Generations of Jules' family claimed that a bounty hunter pursuing two fugitive slaves had died in the Drinking Gourd. The proof of the claim was this picture and the letter tucked behind the frame. Casey slid her nail underneath the picture until she felt the resistance of the letter.

She closed and latched the frame. For years no one had been able to find the picture. She put it in her pocket. After all, it was hers. She'd snagged and hidden it when Jules' father planned to sell it to an antique dealer.

Now, for Martha's handwriting. Casey tugged on the handle of the file cabinet drawer. Locked! Damn! So much for…

Unless. Would it still be there? Casey turned to a battered wooden sword hanging on the wall, the Sword of the Spirit from Lutheran Bible School. The sword was covered with Bible citations for passages she had memorized before she was kicked out. Next to it hung an equally battered Shield of Faith featuring the symbols of the Apostles. Oh, the battles they'd waged! Those with fancy swords and shields were Crusaders. Infidels like Jules had to fight with sticks and garbage can lids. Martha had ratted them out when Jules bashed her. Sometimes Jules went too far. Then again, Martha was a nasty, whiny kid.

11

Casey eased the sword off the nails holding it, unscrewed the hilt, and shook a small key into her hand. Her luck was holding. The lock popped out and the file drawer rolled open.

Before her were the official records of the Bloody Cats Eyes Club. She remembered how Art, in his infinite, older-brother wisdom, had asked if "Cats Eyes" was meant to be singular or plural possessive. It was his thesis, as resident pain in the ass, that the name needed an apostrophe.

Behind five or six newer spiral notebooks, she found the yellowed, un-apostrophed club records including detailed maps of obstacle courses she and Jules had run, a list of potential club members, and a series of diabolical initiation rites that the same candidates had never passed. Most of the pages were written in Jules' unmistakable bold flair, a few in Casey's smaller writing.

"And here it is," she whispered, opening a folder with the tab "Pig Face." Inside was a single sheet of paper. She drew her fingers across the back of Martha's oath and was amazed to feel the indentations made so many years before. Heavy pressure, just as Barbara Roman had said. But this writing wasn't perfect. Not by a long shot. Not even nice. Muddy smudges, ticks of irritation, and grasping hooks carved into the page.

Well, Martha had been very angry when she wrote it. Casey and Jules had just subjected her to an initiation ceremony that she was destined to fail. In candlelight, dressed in hoods and choir robes "borrowed" from the church, they'd circled and canted bogus Latin phrases: *Agonies Dei cum laude in excelsius digitalis cul de sac quasimodo obligado.*

Casey glanced at a symbol on the back of the clubhouse door: a cat's eye and three drops of blood. The first two drops were from a blood oath she and Jules swore to each other to be best friends forever. The third was Martha's. After Martha passed the first tests where they led her around blindfolded and dripped hot wax on the back of her hand, Jules jabbed her finger with a needle and smeared her blood on the door.

Desperate to keep her from their club, Casey made Martha kneel and recite the Cats Eyes oath and then write it, while Jules disappeared to prepare the final test. Upon return, she produced a tin cup filled with a potion she called "nectar of Cats Eye." When Casey realized what was in the cup, she tried to keep it from Martha, but Martha grabbed it and chugged a mix of Lemon Fresh Pine-Sol and Tilex. It was a nasty trick. Martha retched and heaved like a dog and swore revenge.

As she was closing the filing cabinet drawer, Casey noticed dates on the cover of the first spiral notebook. The script looked like Jules' writing but was smaller and more fluid. Of course, Jules' writing had changed as she matured. The date on the second notebook took up where the first ended, like a check register. The last notebook began in April and didn't have an ending date.

She opened the first notebook. Jules was keeping a journal.

Put it back. Why ask for trouble? But she was curious.

The Kenworthy garage door opened with a loud mechanical jolt.

Casey tore out a middle page and jammed it in her pocket beside Martha's writing. She re-filed the notebook, rolled the door closed, and punched in the lock. Car doors slammed. She snuffed the flame and put the candle and matches in the drawer. In the dark, her hands shook as she replaced the key in the hilt of the sword and hung it on the wall.

Footsteps entered the Kenworthy kitchen directly overhead—heavy, then lighter high heels, followed by the patter of small feet.

"Daddy, read me a story." A little girl's voice. Gabby.

"I can't hear you," George replied in a teasing, singsong voice.

"Daddy, *please* read me a story," Gabby corrected.

Casey closed and lowered the latch to the clubhouse door.

"That's better, honey. Brush your teeth and put on your jammies. I'll be up in a sec."

Another wave of yearning and regret broke over Casey. She was wrong. She had more to lose. Gabby was George and Jules' little treasure and would forever link the two. She cursed the tears that streamed down her cheeks and the knot in her throat. Get out. She grabbed the guidewire and picked her way across the cellar.

"Where are *you* going?" George demanded.

Casey froze.

"As if I didn't know." George answered his own question.

High heels tapped across the wooden floor. Casey exhaled. He was talking to Jules.

Halfway to the old furnace, light from a bare bulb in the center of the cellar flooded the room. Jules' footsteps descended the stairs from the kitchen. Casey stood like a statue next to the furnace. If Jules looked her way, she couldn't miss her, but she veered off and walked directly to the second coal bin.

"What the hell do you care?" Jules shot back at George. She fumbled with a lock and entered. Casey heard the clink of bottles from inside the bin. The wine cellar. Casey dashed behind a soapstone washtub and waited while Jules re-crossed the cellar, climbed the stairs to the kitchen, and turned off the light.

Casey followed the wire to the bulkhead door and skidded to a halt at the sound of approaching voices outside in the patio.

"Next time, we drive. My feet are killing me." Martha's distinct whine pierced the air.

"Maybe you should wear more sensible shoes. We weren't going to the opera," Art responded.

The couple crossed the patio heading toward the Cavendish back door. Casey ducked behind the washtubs.

"I dress up for our *one* evening out with your doddering old aunt and look at the appreciation I get. You only have eyes for the drunken slut next door. I could be invisible for all you—"

"Invisible if you were silent. Hold your tongue. The Kenworthys are home."

"You left the bulkhead open. I thought I told you to close it."

"I closed it before we left."

The voices drew nearer. Trapped.

"It's probably Jules sneaking out with another bottle."

"The Kenworthys have internal stairs to the cellar, m'dear. She doesn't need to sneak in through the bulkhead."

"I've watched her. She thinks she's fooling everybody. She goes for a 'walk'

14

out the back door, enters the cellar through the bulkhead, swipes a bottle and retires through the kitchen to the bar."

Casey climbed into the closest washtub and held her breath just as Martha's high heels appeared in the bulkhead opening.

"Martha, get back here!" Art hissed. "And keep your voice down. What Jules does is none of your business. You already got us thrown out of Mae's tonight. If you're not careful, you'll be out of a job."

"I'll say what I please. You know it's the truth." Martha didn't lower her volume.

"Christ Almighty, I refuse to listen to your poison." The door to the Cavendish entrance opened and closed. Although the voices were muted, Casey could still follow the argument.

"Aren't you going to close the bulkhead?"

"I wouldn't want to lock Mrs. Kenworthy out of her own home."

"Then come upstairs to bed."

"Why would I do that?"

"Why not stop in at the bar for a bottle? After Jules, that's your second love, isn't it? Ever think of how I feel with you mooning and sniffing after her?"

When all was quiet, Casey struggled out of the washtub. She made herself into a shadow and slipped outside to the barn.

Riding home, she chastised herself for the close calls. When the adrenalin subsided, her thoughts turned to Art's miserable situation. As a boy, he'd been an egghead and a piano prodigy who was totally besotted with Jules. Probably still was. A nasty accident ruined his hand and musical ambitions, and Jules never looked his way. Somehow, he ended up with Martha Swain.

Growing up Martha had worshipped and tried to be just like Jules. She despised Casey because Jules chose her to be her best friend. Casey even felt a little sorry for Martha. But not Jules. Jules had earned her pain.

So, there was trouble in paradise.

Don't be a fool. George is a married man with a family, and he's already betrayed you once.

15

Chapter Three

C hief Crockett punched the steering wheel. He backed the cruiser into a driveway and parked behind a stand of lilac bushes tall enough to hide a tank. Dousing the lights, he hung his head out the window, taking in great gulps of cool night air.

Yesterday, Eugene Connolly, the Town Manager and Crockett's boss, had barged into the Monday staff meeting and publicly dressed him down for his handling of a failed drug raid over the weekend. His words belched up like a cud that needed more chewing.

"Your lack of discretion turned a private college problem into a matter of public record. Frankly, I thought you knew better. That's why I championed you for our first black Chief of Police."

When he took the job, Crockett hadn't realized how hard it would be to walk the tightrope between town and gown, balancing the conflicting demands of the two. Serve and protect. But if he served one master, he couldn't protect the other. If he did his job, he'd be fired. If he didn't, he'd be fired. Only option left was a half-assed job.

"Let it go, JoJo," he whispered. He got out and stretched his long legs, picked a few lilacs, and buried his nose in the blossoms. When he'd worked in the bowels of Cleveland, he'd dreamt about the fragrance of lilacs and newly mown grass, the graceful canopy of tree-lined streets, and the night quiet of Oberlin. No dirty halo of city lights to mute the heavens. Crockett searched the sky until he found the Big Dipper.

A cyclist whipped by. Crockett measured his progress down the street by a chain of dogs that erupted one after the other as he passed. He even knew the names of the dogs.

Despite Connolly's words, Crockett felt more connected and appreciated in Oberlin than he ever had as a detective on the Cleveland force. Oberlin wasn't just a small town; it was *his* small town. When he heard a siren, someone he knew was in trouble or on fire. Despite the daily tedium, what he did made a difference. Best of all, it was a great place for his family.

He pulled out and made a circuit around the town. Streetlights punctuated the slate sidewalks at regular intervals. Not a creature was stirring except for a car two blocks ahead, stopped at one of the town's four traffic lights that marked the corners of Tappan Square, a thirteen-acre tract of land in the center of town. The town hadn't changed much since Crockett left to play football at Ohio State. College buildings surrounded the square on three sides. On the south side, most of the stores carried the same names, and, some said, the very same merchandise they'd offered a decade before.

College maintenance had cleaned off one of the huge memorial boulders on the square that the students had decorated last week. Too bad. The painted rock face had borne an uncanny resemblance to the Dean of Students whom the students called Dapper Dean Drucker.

The driver of a sleek BMW glanced repeatedly into his rearview mirror. Couldn't blame him. Big, black policeman in a cop car following him at night. When the light changed, the law-abiding citizen flicked on his turn signal and crawled through the intersection. Crockett flashed his strobes and pulled the BMW to the curb.

"Right rear tire's low, Ron," Crockett called through the open window. He smiled wide, but the smile didn't reach his eyes. Passing the BMW, he inched along five miles below the speed limit toward the Drinking Gourd, where he suspected Ronald Goodrich Swain was headed.

How many people used three names? Franklin Delano Roosevelt. John Fitzgerald Kennedy. Martin Luther King. As a kid, he'd asked Ron about it. Ron was full of himself even then, saying he was destined to be "Good and Rich" someday.

As he drove by college dorms, Crockett noted the lights of college students burning the midnight oil. Must be masochists to select a college sporting the fun-packed motto, *Learning and Labor*. No fraternities or sororities. No cars. No booze. The only distraction from books and conservatory practice rooms was an anti-war demonstration. Decade after decade of Oberlin students assumed the burden of saving the world from itself, earning a reputation for doing good, but not always doing well. Few got rich saving souls, tilting at windmills or practicing grace notes in the conservatory, but many became excellent scholars and musicians. If they didn't overdose. *That* was the problem.

Less than a mile farther west, Crockett noted familiar beat up cars and pickups in the parking lot across the street from the Gourd. Diehards were throwing back one last pop before closing time. On an antique sign hanging from a post at the front of the inn, stars in the Big Dipper which fugitive slaves called the Drinking Gourd pointed to the north star and freedom. Small blinking lights behind the stars added twentieth-century kitsch to the sign.

Crockett was proud to the core of the inn and Oberlin's role during Abolition, but he feared that developers, like Swain in the Beemer behind him, wouldn't care if the inn was historic and would tear it down in a heartbeat.

The old inn intrigued him, and he'd hate to see it razed. Besides, what would town folk do without the local watering hole? In the spirit of temperance, yet another college cause, the town was technically dry. But one glance at a map showed that the town had the shape of an artist's palette, with the Gourd in the thumb indentation. The town line bisected the building. The inn, tavern, and parking lot belonged to the county, and were exempt from the town's liquor laws, while the newer residential addition fell within the town of Oberlin.

Located on the northwest boundary, the Gourd was as far as it could be from the black section in the southeast quadrant. Fugitive slaves might have found shelter at the inn, but few of their descendants sat at the bar at closing time.

Soft light emanated from the downstairs front room of the owner's residence. George was working late in his study, which probably meant that Jules was perched on a barstool nursing a glass of wine.

As Crockett turned back toward town, he glanced in his rearview mirror and watched the red taillights of the BMW enter the Gourd parking lot. Crockett had frequented the Gourd in his drinking days, a black face in a sea of white, mostly to keep an eye on his younger brother Charley, who went there to stir up trouble.

Enough. It was spring. Crockett picked up speed. He was heading home to the finest woman in the universe and the cutest little girl that ever lived. He was back in Oberlin, a town he mostly loved and would always call home. After college graduation, he could bask in three months of relative calm. Right now, he had a job to keep.

Crockett jumped, startled by the crackling of the radio.

"Watson, here, Chief. Got a 911. Overdose in Barrows Hall."

"On my way. Call Connolly." Crockett stepped on the gas, hitting the strobes but not the siren. He could be discreet.

As the cruiser rocketed toward campus, the scream of a siren ripped the air. Crockett grabbed his radio. "Choke it, Watson! Get back to the station. Don't need a battalion for an overdose." The high-pitched wail dropped an octave, whooped twice in defiance, and sputtered out. Captain Watson didn't acknowledge his order. Watson had been in the meeting with Connolly yesterday and knew better than to use the siren. He also knew that Crockett would take the heat for being indiscreet. Watson was a sly one.

In his rearview mirror, Crockett caught the rotating strobes of an ambulance. Good response. Cruiser and ambulance sped in tandem toward a men's dorm on the north end of campus.

Crockett and two Emergency Medical Technicians converged on the rear entrance. "In the laundry room. Downstairs." The elderly dorm supervisor's voice quavered and his hand shook as he pointed to stairs at the end of the hall. Crockett and the EMTs barreled down the steps to the basement.

Four students surrounded the body in a protective circle. The lead EMT pushed past students whose bare feet seemed glued to the cement floor. Kneeling by the inert form, he barked directions to his assistant.

"Okay, fellas, give us some room." Crockett gently herded the students toward the door. They were reluctant to end their vigil, as if standing over their friend could protect him from what had already happened.

Crockett swallowed hard to dispel the metallic taste in his mouth. The young ones were the hardest. The precious spark of life was so fragile, so easy to crush. Kids were oblivious to danger, as if their hormones had driven their survival instincts into remission.

"We got a pulse. *Go! Go!*" the EMT yelled. He continued to attend to the boy, while his assistant ran for a stretcher.

Crockett took a pad from his shirt pocket and approached the dorm supervisor. "Need the boy's name to check him into the hospital, sir."

"Cam. Cameron Stewart Erickson the Third."

From the looks of the paraphernalia surrounding Cam, he'd been free-basing cocaine. Sunken eyes in dark sockets contrasted sharply with the transparent pallor of his skin. Naked to the waist, his ribs jutted from his thin, hairless chest. Low-slung, filthy jeans revealed a puff of pubic hair where underwear should have been. Cameron Stewart Erickson the Second would not be pleased by his son's appearance. Maybe that was the point.

A thin, tormented wail pierced the air. Crockett followed the sound to a figure in the corner hidden beside an industrial-sized dryer. With his arms locked around his knees, the boy rocked back and forth, vacant eyes staring straight ahead through bottle-glass lenses.

Crockett knelt and checked the boy's vital signs. At his touch, the boy quieted, but continued to rock.

"He's Cam's roommate, Jonathan Phillips, but everyone calls him Philly." The dorm supervisor had followed Crockett, his curiosity momentarily stronger than his fear.

In stark contrast to his roommate, Philly wore a starched shirt tucked into a new pair of corduroy slacks. His torso was thin and reedy like a plant stem raised in artificial light. Crockett asked the dorm supervisor about the boy's waxen complexion.

"Philly spends his life glued to his books. Sometimes he doesn't emerge for days, and Cam has to drag him to the dining hall. Despite their differences, they are...were...are..." His voice trailed off as he backed toward the door.

The EMTs lifted Cam onto the stretcher and wheeled him into the hall. A second later, Crockett heard muffled curses in the hallway as Dr. Clyde Drucker, the Dapper Dean, barely avoided a collision with the stretcher. Connolly must have alerted him to the overdose. The EMTs shoved past Drucker as a unit and ran with the stretcher up the stairs.

"Oh, Jesus! Is he—?"

"Lucky to be alive." Crockett half-pulled, half-lifted Philly to his feet.

Drucker stepped forward. "Good work, Crockett. I can take it from here."

Crockett put his arm around Philly whose wobbly legs threatened to buckle, steering him into the elevator. He pushed the button and locked eyes with the Dean. The staring contest ended when Drucker had to reach out to keep the elevator door from closing. "You hear the man yesterday?"

"I heard." Evidently, most of the western world had heard of Connolly's tongue lashing. "You do your job, Dr. Dean. I'll do mine. Philly and I will escort the ambulance. Discreetly." Crockett punched the door-close button. "Calm down the students. You find anything, *anything at all*, about the dealer, call me."

As the doors began to close a second time, Crockett noticed Drucker's rigid posture and stunned expression. The man was afraid of facing the students. This time Crockett stuck his hand between the closing doors.

"You'll be fine. Just talk with them. 'Bout anything. 'Bout nothing. Keep them talking until they get normal voices back. They just looked into the eyes of death. They're scared and angry. Slow down. Breathe deep. And call for backup."

Chapter Four

Crockett rose with Leila and their five-year-old daughter, Jackie, at the crack of dawn. He cherished the early morning hours with his family around the breakfast table. He watched his wife Leila scoop oatmeal into Jackie's bowl.

She was a big-boned woman, slightly over six feet. When she wore heels, she looked him straight in the eye. Her short hair and long, graceful neck gave her the proud bearing of an African queen. He wished they could have spent more time in bed. Time to go. He tousled Jackie's head and kissed his wife a little longer than goodbye.

Crockett greeted the dispatch officer who was finishing the graveyard shift, grabbed a cup of coffee, and entered his office without switching on the lights. He sank into a large, swivel chair. These were the rare, quiet moments when he could think and plan.

He sipped his coffee while editing his "To do" list. It had two columns: "Bombs" and "Snowballs." Bombs were critical, time-sensitive tasks requiring immediate action. Anything else was a snowball, because he knew full well there wasn't a snowball's chance of getting to them before graduation week.

The chimes of Finney Chapel rang the three-quarter hour. After reviewing the log of activity from the night before, he pushed aside a growth of forms and folders, unlocked a gray, military-issue filing cabinet, and withdrew a thick manila file with the tab, "Crockett, Charles."

Crockett stared at a picture of his younger brother, Charley. Sure was one handsome manchild. Crockett smiled at the cocky face. Charley had been the funniest, the brainiest, and the most talented of the Crockett children. He could run faster and jump higher than any kid on the block. Just once he jumped the wrong way. Just once. What a goddamn waste.

Crockett was startled by a monumental belch. Watson grunted his way up the stairs to the station's rear entrance. Crockett still had a minute before Watson discovered him reading with the lights off.

Wrong. Watson barged through the door, mouth ablab. "Stopped at the hospital on the way—"

"Hold it, Captain. Try again." Crockett spoke without looking up, careful to keep his voice neutral. Watson had no sense of other people's space. No walking around sense, for that matter.

Watson opened his mouth to object, thought better of it, and retreated. Crockett slid Charley's file under a stack of papers.

When he took over as acting Chief a year ago, Connolly advised him that Watson had expected to be tapped for Chief and was seriously bent out of shape. Crockett had given him the better part of the year to make an attitude adjustment but was running out of patience.

A chastened Watson knocked before re-entering. At Crockett's nod, he spoke. "Good morning, Chief. I have an update on Cameron and his roommate. Cam was airlifted to a detox in upstate New York before dawn, listed in 'critical but stable' condition. Helicopter. Gotta be loaded.'"

"And Philly?"

"Sedated. His parents fly in this afternoon to take him back east to some nut house outside Boston." Watson flipped through his notes. "McLean Hospital. No way to know when the parents or kids will talk to us."

"Good work. Keep on it," Crockett replied, but he knew that by evening the boys' dorm rooms would be picked clean. Watson's calls would never be returned. "Three weeks to go. They almost made it."

Watson shrugged, hiked his pants, and returned to the outer office.

Crockett opened an *Oberlin News Tribune* folder. The local weekly published a "Police News" column based on Crockett's notes. He reported all calls to 911, and summarized other, non-emergency calls as he saw fit. College incidents rarely appeared in the paper, but last night's call from

Barrows was a 911. Crockett thought for a moment and then wrote:

Police and Rescue responded to a 911 call from Barrows Hall. Situation quickly stabilized. Two students taken to hospital for observation and later released.

For the past three quarters of a year, he and the town manager had worked without friction, but as Jenny, the dispatch and office manager, had explained to him, Connolly underwent a personality change every year around college graduation. She likened him to a helium balloon—full of gas and likely to explode under pressure. Crockett avoided any mention of drugs. No reason to ignite Connolly.

Connolly wasn't the only one feeling pre-graduation jitters. The whole town would heave a collective sigh of relief when the college closed down for the summer. But first they had to get through Illumination Night, when Japanese lanterns lit Tappan Square, and the college band played everything but traditional band music for the assembled multitudes. And then baccalaureate and graduation, and a score of weddings.

Oberlin would be clogged with proud parents and distinguished alumni returning for their class cluster reunions. Some visiting dignitary would make an appearance, exhort graduates to champion lofty ideals, and collect an honorary degree. Nothing bad could happen that week.

Then blissful quiet. Townie kids would reclaim the Arboretum, the college forest, take swimming lessons in Crane pool, and hit tennis balls on the college courts. Their parents would barbecue and raise world-class tomatoes in backyard victory gardens. Old ladies would gossip and tat on front porch swings, sipping iced tea with fresh mint. You could hear a neighbor hammering two blocks away.

Summer was the town's catatonia following a manic episode: a time to heal, to catch one's breath, to gather strength and resolve before the next onslaught in the fall. By then, the town would welcome the electric shock of student energy, the lifeblood of Oberlin.

In the meantime he had work to do. Crockett gathered his notebook and a file labeled "1974 Commencement Prep" and headed for the staff meeting in the conference room.

Half an hour later, Eugene Connolly barreled into the station conference room, slamming the door with enough force to endanger the opaque glass pane. Crockett, Watson, and Jenny spun in unison. Connolly often made cameo appearances during their morning staff meetings. Crockett glanced at the clock and noted the exact minute of Connolly's entrance.

"Mornin', Euge." Crockett didn't stand upon his superior's entrance, knowing the man's sensitivity about height. Even wearing elevator shoes, the fleshy pod of Connolly's nose just reached the second button of Crockett's uniform. Connolly's crueler detractors called him Stump. His only growth spurts after puberty had been lateral.

Despite the cool morning temperature, perspiration beaded Connolly's forehead, as if his brain were boiling over. He threw his suit coat on the back of a chair, rolled up his sleeves, and hauled the chair to the table, wedging himself between Crockett and Jenny. He pushed aside their papers to make room for his leather portfolio. Jenny shrank from his encroaching elbows and stared at the sweat prints his fingers left on his portfolio.

"Coffee?" Crockett suggested to no one in particular.

"Two sugars, no cream." Connolly was in no mood for banter.

Jenny shoved back with an attitude and shot Crockett a look designed to castrate. Moments later she slammed a tray of coffee mugs on the table. Crockett smiled inwardly, admiring the way she turned such a simple action into a reproach. Jenny, a tiny woman by any standards, was dwarfed but not intimidated by the oversized men in the room. He caught her eye and patted the table, silently suggesting she change her seat to the empty chair on his left. With an apologetic smile, she took the proffered seat.

Just as Connolly leaned forward, Crockett dug into his pants pocket and slapped a handful of coins onto the table. He isolated a quarter and slid it across the table to Watson. Connolly cleared his throat for attention, but now Jenny created a distraction, rooting about in a large purse. She retrieved a billfold and sighed. "Mind making change?" she asked Watson. Watson nodded, took her dollar, and pushed three quarters back.

"Thought it was free," groused Connolly, flipping a quarter onto the table.

"Thanks." Watson was in a good mood, having just won the betting pool by guessing the time closest to Connolly's entrance. He scooped up the take and Connolly's unwitting contribution.

Enough fun and games, thought Crockett. "Unless you have other pressing matters, we were discussing traffic control for graduation week and the possible disruption of another anti-war demonstration."

"Well, as a matter of fact, I *do* have a few pressing things on my mind." Connolly flipped open his portfolio and jabbed his finger at a newspaper page with lines highlighted in fluorescent yellow. "Like, who is the 'reliable source within the Oberlin Police Department' quoted in this article?"

The spotlight article, "Drugs on Campus," in the morning edition of *Cleveland Plain Dealer* was the latest in a series of investigative pieces about escalating drug use on college campuses. The journalist cited recent incidents at Oberlin and other schools as evidence that Ohio's small liberal arts colleges might not be the safe haven parents thought them to be.

"How does this guy know about Sunday's botched raid? Who's feeding him information?"

"I don't know," Crockett answered.

"You don't know? You don't *know*?" Connolly banged the table with his fist making the coffee mugs jump. "Articles like these can destroy the reputation of a small college like ours. Oberlin offers a unique combination of small-town ambience and the intellectual and cultural influences of academia."

Connolly only had three or four set-pieces. Crockett recognized lines from the speech Connolly had made when he announced Crockett's appointment.

"Other schools offer four years of football, beer parties, and incidental education. But Oberlin is *different*. It is a *liberal*, liberal arts college."

Crockett tilted his chair back and lowered his eyelids. Although open, his lidded eyes were impossible to track, leaving his mind free to roam. He knew the party line, but depending upon a person's political persuasion, Oberlin was either a liberal Mecca or the devil's own mistake.

Watson shifted in his seat, hitching his pants, a sure sign that he had something to say. Crockett caught his eye and shook his head. Watson shrugged and began to clean his nails with a Swiss Army knife.

Crockett recognized the chip on Watson's shoulder. Dougie Watson grew up convinced that everyone from the college saw him as townie white trash. Truth was, no one saw him at all until he ate his way to local fame and could serve a useful purpose on the football team. He specialized in falling forward consistently, creating sizable holes in the opposing defensive line for Ronald Goodrich Swain to run through. He and Swain were town bullies growing up and were still friends.

Connolly continued his rant. "College students are crazy. They jump off balconies thinking they can fly. Slit their wrists to see if they bleed. Hell, they even hang themselves from pajama cords for more intense orgasms. It's tragic, but if no one dies, these incidents are best handled as *college matters*. Yesterday I told you to be discreet. Now I'm ordering you to stay away from the dorms and out of the press."

Watson couldn't stand it any longer. "Last week you said we could pussyfoot around the library reading room and watch students turn pages, but not to enter the stacks where the little pansies snort and get off. Now you're saying we gotta have permission to enter a dorm?"

Crockett wrote "stacks" on his Bombs list.

"I think you've finally got the picture, Captain." Connolly spoke to Watson as if he were mentally challenged and then turned to Crockett.

Crockett sat forward and pushed aside Connolly's portfolio. With his face inches from Connolly's, Crockett spoke, his voice lower and slower than Connolly's. "We got a 911. Boy's life was in danger. He needed immediate help."

Connolly shoved back from the table. "I have no problem with your response to a 911. That's your job, but I have a big problem with the siren last night and with this." He jabbed his fat forefinger at the newspaper article.

Crockett's eyelids returned to half-mast. Images of Stump jumping off a balcony, slitting his wrists, and hanging from a pajama cord danced behind his eyelids.

"Consider this your last warning. You must be discreet about college matters. And discretion means—"

"No press." Crockett rose from his chair. He understood. Hush, hush.

No mess. No press. He circled the table, eyeing the startled Stump. "That's what this is all about, isn't it? Press. I told you. I don't know who leaked the story." A dangerous edge crept into his voice.

"Then you better damn well find out. This is *not* just about press." Connolly shrugged into his suit coat, gathered his portfolio, and stalked to the door. "If you can't keep a lid on drugs, you will be pounding the pavement—somewhere else." He slammed the door, ensuring himself the last word.

Crockett returned to his office and closed the door to discourage a staff recap of Connolly's rant. Problem was, Connolly was right. The Oberlin Police had failed to stem the recent tide of drugs pouring into the town and college. Two attempted busts at the college had only yielded unfavorable publicity. Not for the first time, Crockett wondered who was feeding the press.

He underlined "stacks" on his Bomb's list. The stacks of Carnegie Library were touted by Oberlin Admissions Reps as the repository of one of the most comprehensive book collections in the nation. Floors and floors, some said miles and miles, of dimly lit corridors of books could be the perfect, clandestine maze for dealing and drugging.

Crockett didn't have any first-hand knowledge of the stacks, but Casey shelved books there a few evenings a week for extra money. She was the last person Crockett wanted to ask about drugs. Even if she were innocent, as she claimed to be, she had been there during the bust when his brother Charley was run over by a redneck cop. Whatever the truth was, she'd done time. Keep it light. Invite her to lunch. Reluctantly, he picked up the telephone. He'd ask her to keep her eyes open for any suspicious activity and then pray to God she'd forgive him for using her.

Chapter Five

C asey kept one ear tuned to the voices in the conference room of the police station while she snooped around Crockett's office. She was waiting for him to finish dressing down Dougie so she and Crockett could go to lunch. Casey smiled. She liked calling Captain Watson "Dougie." It infuriated him.

Dougie's voice rose as he defended himself, but Casey couldn't make out individual words. She continued her tour of Crockett's office, trying to convince herself she had no reason to be nervous. Although Crockett might be an old friend, he was the law, and she was an ex-con.

She sat in his oversized leather chair and twirled about once. She was early. A breeze wafted from a window, lifting the edges of neatly stacked papers anchored by a paperweight a child had painted. A blinking red telephone light announced waiting calls.

The top drawer of the file cabinet to the left of the desk was open. She ruffled her fingers across the tops of the exposed files. A number of them were lifted higher, as placeholders for others that had been temporarily withdrawn. Names on the folders were organized alphabetically. She looked closer. Nothing for Cavendish, Cassandra.

Someone was watching her. Looking up, she met the eyes of Crockett's wife Leila, gazing at her from a family portrait on top of the filing cabinet. Next to Leila were pictures of his daughter Jacqui and an older picture of Crockett's parents.

Casey stood and continued her survey on the far side of the room, swiping her fingers in the dust along the bookcase. She stopped mid-swipe before a high school picture at the far end. Charley Crockett's eyes smoldered, challenging the cameraman. He was a handsome kid, built like his older brother JoJo, but two or three sizes smaller, as if cigarettes had stunted his early promise. His mouth turned down in a sardonic, street-cool pose.

The volume of Crockett's voice increased as he approached the door. Casey slipped into a chair in front of the desk and watched the doorknob turn as he got in his last licks before entering.

"Discover anything on your little tour?" Crockett asked as he sauntered to his chair.

"Nah." Casey flicked dust off her fingers, making a mental note about Crockett's powers of observation.

"How's your course?"

"I just submitted my last term paper. I'll graduate in a few weeks."

"I meant the handwriting course."

How do you know about—

"Relax, Casey. I stopped for a word with Art and Martha walking down West College last night. He said you ducked out of dinner at your aunt's by crashing a handwriting course in adult ed. I know Barbara Roman. She and I go back a long way. Met her working a forgery case in Cleveland years ago."

"Did she ever analyze your writing, Chief?"

"Cut the 'Chief' business. 'JoJo' or 'Crockett,' okay?" He offered one of his engaging, light bulb smiles before continuing. "Yeah, Barbara did mine once. She said I was private, methodical. Keenly observant. Liked my pleasures. Had some addictive tendencies, and a temper." Crockett paused and shook his head. "Pretty well nailed my ass."

"Speak of nailing, you pretty well pounded Frederick Douglass into the ground."

"Frederick Douglass. Almost forgot Watson's first name. Remind me how he got it."

"C'mon, you know the story." Casey suspected he could tell the tale to the last detail, but decided to humor him to ease the tension. She began in a dramatic voice, as if she were reading to a child.

"Once upon a time on a cold winter's eve, in a dilapidated trailer just outside town, a babe was born to Harriet and Wilbur Watson. Missy, a young, black midwife, delivered the baby. Wilbur was off on a toot, and Harriet was pissed. According to Missy, Harriet was also drunk, which complicated the delivery. She'd forget to breathe or to push, or would try to do both at once and pass out. But in the wee hours, she finally delivered a chunky baby boy."

Casey's voice softened to represent Missy. "What will you name the chile, ma'am?"

Crockett grinned in anticipation. Encouraged, Casey changed her voice to speak for Harriet. "I was gonna call him after his dad, Wilbur. But 'Willie Watson' sounds kinda faggy, don't it?"

"Um. What others did you think on?"

"He needs a name folks'll respect." Casey hesitated and then continued in Harriet's voice. "Got any ideas? I'm so pooped I can't think on anyone 'ceptin' George Warshington, and Elvis Presley."

"Let's see. There's Abraham Lincoln, and Benjamin Franklin, Frederick Douglass, Babe Ruth—"

"'Frederick Douglass.' Now, that's handsome. Ain't so common. Was he famous like them others? I mean, would townfolk reca'nize the name?"

"Oh, yes, ma'am," Casey mimed. She turned to Crockett. "And so, little redneck baby Watson was named after a famed black abolitionist."

Crockett chuckled. "You're a natural, Casey girl."

"Somehow I don't think you asked me here to tell old stories, did you, Crockett?"

"No, ma'am. I asked you for lunch. C'mon. Get there in five, we won't have to wait." Crockett jumped up and ushered Casey out the door. She collected her bike and pushed it beside him down Main Street toward the Campus Restaurant. "Actually, I called you to pick your little brain. You see the article in *The Plain Dealer* about drugs on college campuses?"

Casey nodded.

"Had another incident last night. Kid freebasing in the laundry room in Barrows. Boy's parents whisked him away to some ritzy rehab in New York.

31

His roommate's under observation in a mental hospital."

As they walked into the restaurant, Casey scanned the room for potential threats. *Stop it!* None of these nice old ladies is going to jump you for cigarettes. They waited in silence while a waitress wiped down a table. Casey glanced at Crockett. What's he want? The mention of drugs put her on high alert. Old friend or not, ten years on the Inside made her leery of any truck with the law.

As they slid into opposite sides of the booth, Crockett leaned forward and spoke in a low voice. "Got a real problem with this drug thing. Twice I thought I had my quarry set up. First time was in the college Rathskeller. Roommate of the guy who went off the deep end in the fall came forward. Wanted to help. He'd already made a connection and bought some stuff. We got him to set up for a second buy. Dealer never showed. Kid left school the following weekend. Someone got to him.

"The second setup was a girl whose roommate was using. Didn't want to get in trouble with drugs found in their room. We arranged a raid. Nothing. Not even talcum powder." Crockett stopped his monologue when the waitress approached. They both ordered the burger special.

Casey watched Crockett fidget with a saltshaker. *Here it comes.*

"I was hoping you'd help me identify likely spots where college kids could make a drug connection—"

Casey pushed back and challenged Crockett with her eyes. "Like, maybe, Peters Hall?"

Crockett winced.

Serves you right. Casey struggled to control her anger. It was the classic scenario: lawman squeezes ex-con to become a stoolie.

Crockett plowed on. "No. I'm thinking a more private place where you could deal without attracting attention. Occurred to me you'd have a unique perspective as a townie and a college student."

Casey glared at Crockett. "You mean the unique perspective of a townie college student convicted for possession with intent to sell."

Before he could respond, the waitress returned with cheeseburgers, fries, and pickles. Casey and Crockett fell silent with the welcome distraction of food.

So, the meeting wasn't about her; it was about Crockett. He needed information, and he was willing to use her to get it. She thought for a moment. A private place college kids frequent, like the lounge of Wilder Hall, or the bar at the Gourd, the basement of the Co-op bookstore, or the library. Of course. That's it. The library. They were like the catacombs. Whole generations of Oberlin students had been conceived in the stacks of the library, and she shelved returned books in the stacks. "Why do you think the action's in the library?"

Crockett acknowledged her quick take. "Friend of the boy who died last fall described him as anti-social, troubled. Said he ate, slept, went to an occasional class, but spent most of his waking hours in the stacks."

"Sounds like ninety-nine percent of the student body."

"I'm not asking you to do anything, Casey. Just to keep your eyes open."

"Okay, *Chief*. But I don't get to the stacks much now. Although they'd deny it to the public, the librarians have parked me on the first floor in baby books." Casey looked at her watch. "Uh oh, I'm late. Gotta get back before the old fossils miss me." Rising quickly, she abandoned her burger, took a five-dollar bill from her wallet, and placed it in the center of the table. Halfway to the door she turned and pointed to her eyes but she didn't smile.

Chapter Six

Friday morning Casey propped open a window in the Children's Room to give the long black cat Bookend room to sprawl on the sill. Early morning light warmed the cat's fur and caught stray dust motes floating in the air. Bookend responded to her strokes with a languid, rusty purr, exposing parts he wanted scratched.

The public part of Carnegie Library occupied the front half of the first floor consisting of an adult room and a children's room and the library's administrative offices in the back. A wide staircase led up to the college reference library and a huge open-air reading room lined with bookshelves and long wooden tables designed for student study. Beyond was the entrance to the stacks—a labyrinth of low-ceiling rooms packed with thousands upon thousands of books.

The Children's Room was Casey's favorite place in the library. The smell of waxed floors and old books brought back memories of simpler times, childhood days of innocence, and exploration. Every Friday morning she prepared the room for the Saturday onslaught of children participating in the reading program. The other librarians thought her job was idiot work. The Scowlies, as she secretly called them, much preferred to support faculty scholars, and, if pressed, the occasional brilliant student, in the heady pursuit of knowledge.

Casey knew when she applied for work at the library that she faced an uphill battle. Few employers welcomed an ex-con, and all of Casey's library training and experience had been behind bars. Fortunately, the college was committed to an experimental rehabilitation program, one of its newest causes. Casey helped fill the employment quota that guaranteed grant money for the program. Although their frown lines deepened, the Scowlies were stuck with her.

In the fall, she'd sorted and shelved books, and stamped date due cards by the hundreds. Whole weeks of her life were lost in the bowels of the library, pushing a metal cart laden with books through the narrow aisles of the stacks.

It wasn't until January that Casey spotted her opportunity. Ever the pariah, she was sitting by herself in the lunchroom when she overheard Mrs. Palmer, La Scowlie Prima, whine about having to read stories to a horde of filthy townie brats. Casey had kept her head down, but tuned her ears to Scowlie frequency.

As tireless guardians of the written word, the Scowlie triumvirate toiled to protect their sacred trust from irresponsible students and clueless new faculty. Every book on a shelf was safe; every one checked out, in peril. Children topped the list of book enemies: the smaller the child, the greater the threat.

Casey studied the women at the next table as she eavesdropped. Even sitting, Mrs. Palmer, who was over six feet tall in her stocking feet, assumed the overbearing posture of a raised hatchet. Evangelical eyes burned beneath black eyebrows, and a hairnet confined any stray gray hairs that dared escape the bun knotted at her neck. She would make an ugly man, and a surly horse.

Next to Mrs. Palmer, Circulation had the puffy, mottled complexion of an aging cauliflower. Although not appetizing, she looked benign, but Casey knew everything that came out of her mouth was rancid, especially her breath. Finally, with her back to Casey, Reference sat ramrod straight as if her anorexic body had been impaled on a broomstick. All three wore mid-calf, boxy suits from the fifties, and sensible, rubber-soled, lace-up shoes.

Every month, one of the librarians rotated to Children's Room duty. They hated it, and they especially resented the Saturday morning reading program for the younger children. They were professionals serving academia, not babysitters.

Early the following Saturday morning, Casey showed up uninvited and volunteered to help Mrs. Palmer arrange the Children's Room for the reading. As she moved chairs and tables, she raved about how she'd loved the program as a child. What a worthwhile program it was. Could she stay and help with the children? Weren't they just adorable?

For the first time, Casey witnessed a fissure of a smile crack the wily old librarian's face.

Mrs. Palmer even thought it was her idea to create a new bottom rung in the library pecking order with the tacit understanding that Casey wouldn't be in line for promotion to higher echelon positions. Although the Scowlies remained nominally in charge, Casey assumed responsibility for the room, meaning no other librarians need lift a pinkie.

The Children's Room was the perfect, out-of-the-way place to park the embarrassing employee. Due to Scowlie neglect, the children's reading program had declined for three years running. Now Mrs. Palmer could fulfill her obligations to the college rehab program, and, with the same stroke, blame the reading program's failure on Casey. Whenever a parent appeared, Casey faded into the background.

Bookend rolled to direct her strokes. Animals, plants, and children all responded to her. It was the adult world that shunned her. Saturday morning reading had become the highlight of her week. The kids held their breath when her voice threatened and trembled when she cackled. They giggled at her silliness, and, best of all, squealed with delight when she surprised them.

She took great care not to let the Scowlies know how much she enjoyed her new job. They'd be happier picturing her mopping drool and scraping gum off the undersides of tables.

The past week she'd been surprised and secretly pleased at the number of children who came for the reading. She wondered if Gabby would come again. What a terrific little kid. And what a terrific name, Gabriella. Her face was too thin to be as beautiful as Jules, but that might be a blessing. Jules was too pretty for her own good.

The door to the main entrance opened. Probably La Scowlie Prima.

Casey rushed to her desk and picked up a returned book, the image of early morning industry. She pictured Mrs. Palmer marching straight through the foyer past the door to the Children's Room, following the blade of her nose to the double doors that led to the second floor. She listened for the sound of doors opening and closing, signifying that Mrs. Palmer had passed by once more without giving her the time of day. Nothing.

Casey looked up and gasped. She dropped the book and her knees gave way, forcing her to sit abruptly.

"Casey, are you all right? I didn't mean to surprise you." George Kenworthy stood above her. She pushed back, fixing her eyes on the desk. Second semester he'd replaced the ailing faculty member that taught her American history course, but the huge class was held in Hall Auditorium, and she was confident he didn't know she was there. She'd avoided face-to-face contact with George since his return, although she watched him from afar.

She fought for equilibrium and drew in a long, slow breath before speaking. "How may I help you, Professor?"

"I'd like a quiet word with you."

Casey began sorting and stacking the books that had been pushed into the Return slot overnight. "We have no 'quiet words' left to say." *Leave me alone!* "Unless you have a specific request, I've got lots to do."

"I can see that. You and the cat."

She felt the heat of his presence towering motionless over the desk. She willed her eyes to scan the return date on the card before her.

"So now you send out the dreaded notices: 'Pay your library fees by Friday noon or we'll use your diploma to line rat cages in the Psych Department!'"

Against her will, the outer corners of her mouth turned upward. "No, the librarians upstairs are the ones who threaten mutilation. I only deal with the little tykes."

"Good to see your smile again. One little tyke I know says you're super. I wanted to tell you how—"

"Please," Casey interrupted. She couldn't bear to hear his lame excuses, his apologies, his pleas to make amends, or his attempts to pretend nothing had ever happened. Most of all, she didn't want to hear herself forgive him. "Please leave."

"It's a small town, Casey. At least we can be civil."

A flash of anger gave Casey the strength to look up. Although he was thirty-five, he hadn't changed much since college. Laugh lines etched by the sun rimmed his eyes. Sandy hair, a little too long in front, gave him a boyish look. *Damn you.*

"I had nowhere else to go. Mae gave me a room, and the library supports a program for ex-cons. You, on the other hand, are golden. You and your bride can go anywhere you please."

"They made me an offer I couldn't resist, and I wanted to come back—"

"*Another* offer you couldn't resist." Casey didn't bother to disguise her bitterness. "Again, unless you have a specific request—"

"Actually, I do. The reference librarian upstairs was swamped and suggested you could help me locate a few books that are either lost or mis-shelved." He hesitated. "Casey, it's been so long—"

"Which books?" How dare he waltz in and expect her to chase down books for him?

George ignored her curtness. "I need to find a few source books for a paper I'm writing. You might be interested. It's about the role of the Drinking Gourd in the Underground Railroad." He pulled a rumpled paper from the inside pocket of his tweed jacket, smoothed it out, and placed it on the desk in front of her.

Such beautiful hands. Long fingers, a bit bony, with little tufts of blonde hair on top. She'd dreamt of these hands, even drawn a picture of them once in prison.

"…wonder if you would check the stacks."

George raised his finger and gently stroked her cheek. She turned her head aside and backed her chair out of reach.

"I'm so sorry, Casey. For all of us, believe me, I'm sorry. I made a terrible, terrible mistake."

She didn't look up as he slowly walked out the door.

Bookend jumped up onto the desk and butted her with his head. She buried her face in his fur and sobbed. George had meant the world to her once. After another wave of tears, Casey rose to close the Children's Room door. She didn't want the Scowlies or some tyke to interrupt her while she bawled her eyes out.

She cursed him for coming and cursed herself for caring. Casey slammed the door hard enough to rattle the pebbled windowpane. Startled, Bookie leaped to the top of the bookcase and peered down at her.

"Sorry, Bookie. I'm not mad at you. Just the universe." Well, she could narrow that down a bit. George. "'So sorry, I made a terrible mistake,'" she muttered as she walked around the room rearranging displays.

He'd invaded her safe haven. She'd lived here like a mole, visited by small children and on rare occasions, a librarian. Parents of children dropped off their charges, but usually didn't come into the room. Her room.

"Which terrible mistake was it, George?" Casey returned to her desk and picked up the list that he'd left. The first title was a little blurred by tears, but she could make out the rest of the familiar writing. "I'm so sorry," she mimicked.

"Well, I'm sorry, too. Sorry that you didn't call me or see me at the station after I was arrested. Sorry you didn't visit me in jail while I awaited trial. Sorry you couldn't lift a pen and write to me for ten years. And so, so sorry you married my best friend."

She wadded George's list into a tight ball and snapped it with her thumb and forefinger, sending it sailing across the room.

A flying wad of paper was more than Bookend could ignore. He dove for it, batted it, and chased it skittering across the floor, rearing on his hind legs, charging, dancing sidewise, capturing it, and punishing it with his back paws. His performance ended with the paper ball positioned directly in front of his cat food dish. He sniffed at the empty dish and looked up at her.

Casey couldn't help but laugh. "Good show." She removed the first few volumes of the children's encyclopedia, retrieved a can of Friskies, and fed him. She hid his food because Mrs. Palmer hated cats. She'd staged a cat pogrom against the strays that lived in the stacks. Bookie was the last one standing, but she couldn't corner him. Casey lured him downstairs, named him, and vowed to keep him safe.

She picked up the ball to toss it into the wastepaper basket, but instead returned to her desk and unfolded it. Reference had sent him to her for help and would expect her to locate the books.

Would he have come to see me otherwise? Was there a chance that he really was sorry?

She smoothed out the paper. Act like a professional, not a bitter, jilted lover. The past was past. They could be civil, but that was all, sorry or not.

Chapter Seven

Sixteen children between five and seven years old sat on little mats in a semi-circle, their wide eyes glued to Casey as she finished reading the first chapters of *The Wizard of Oz*. Although they clamored to continue, Casey left them in suspense, eager for more the following week. She distracted them by announcing a surprise. The week before she'd taken a picture of each child with her brother's camera. She created a "Children's Library" card for each one by pasting their pictures and names below the title and then laminating the cards at the Oberlin Co-op.

Now she asked the children to line up alphabetically by last name. The chaos of sixteen children trying to sort themselves by letter kept them busy for a good five minutes. When they were in order, Casey solemnly handed each child a personalized card.

As each selected a book to take home, Casey punched a hole in the card. "When you return the book in good condition, I'll use a different punch to change the hole to a star. When you have three stars, I'll put your name on a large star that glows in the dark and pin it to the ceiling."

While she was punching cards, Mrs. Palmer stormed into the room, pursing her lips at the noise and confusion. A few children shrank from her, possibly due to her resemblance to the Wicked Witch of the West. Mrs. Palmer picked up one of the laminated cards. "How much did this cost?" Even her voice crackled.

"Good morning, Mrs. Palmer, and Mr.—?" Casey nodded to a tall figure with camera equipment trailing in Mrs. Palmer's wake.

"Photographer," muttered Mrs. Palmer.

"Harris," said the photographer, simultaneously.

"Pleased to meet you, Mr. Harris." Casey gave Mrs. Palmer her sweetest smile, and her hand to Mr. Harris. "The cards were free. I used my brother's camera, and Mr. Lee at the Co-op laminated them *gratis*. His daughter Elsie is in the reading program." Casey nodded toward a towhead on the other side of the room.

"Set up over there by the window where it's not so cluttered," Mrs. Palmer ordered the photographer. She turned to Casey. "Round up five children with their cards. Include Elsie."

Casey dutifully selected and lined up five children in front of the window. The littlest angel, Gabby, was first. At the photographer's direction, the children proudly held up their library cards.

"When I count to three, say 'Cheese.' One. Two—"

"Wait just one moment, young man." Mrs. Palmer inserted herself into the center of the picture, stooping to reach an equal plane with the children. Casey heard an ominous growl followed by a spitting sound. Bookend crouched on the windowsill behind the ivy planter, ears flattened, tail lashing. Before Mrs. Palmer could locate the source of the noise, Casey rushed forward.

"Excellent idea! Wonderful!" she gushed. "Children, look up at Mrs. Palmer, hold up your cards, and smile. You can smile, too, Mrs. Palmer," she added, curious to see if the fissure in the woman's mouth would reoccur.

"Say 'Cheese!'"

It wasn't pretty, but Mrs. Palmer pulled her lips taut against her gums. Casey glanced at the windowsill. Bookend was gone.

"One more," the photographer suggested. "Have the little girl hand Mrs. Palmer a book. That's it. Hold it. Cheese, pretty please."

Mrs. Palmer had a harder time manufacturing a smile this time, because Gabby touched her hand when she gave her the book. The instant the shutter clicked, Mrs. Palmer wiped her hands on a tissue. "Children are such little Petri dishes of disease."

Mrs. Palmer regained her composure enough to greet the parents as they arrived to pick up their children, while Casey rolled up the mats. In ten minutes, all the children had gone except Gabby, who sat in a little chair clutching this week's book, waiting for her mother. Her mouth drooped at the corners. Her worried eyes flew expectantly to the door each time it opened, only to look away when it closed.

Mrs. Palmer glanced at her watch, turned on her heel, and left, her public duties satisfied for another week.

Casey had been surprised when Gabby said her mother would come for her instead of her grandmother. Although Casey'd caught an occasional glimpse of Jules, they hadn't come face to face. Her jaw tightened at the prospect. *Keep cool.*

Bookend climbed the tree outside the window and jumped onto the windowsill with a feather touch. He was a ratty old cat with many stories to tell if only his tattered ears could bear witness. Long, graceful black whiskers hinted of an earlier day when he was a handsome tom about town. He'd trained Casey to feed, pet, and play with him.

Casey tousled Bookie's head, and he responded with a rattling purr that Gabby heard clear across the room. Her eyes lit at the sight of the cat, and her mouth formed a perfect "O." Casey pulled a small stool over to the window for her to stand on.

"Bookend, meet my friend, Gabby. Gabby, this is Bookend. If you move slowly, he'll let you pet him."

"Booken'," she whispered, climbing up on the stool. Slowly she copied Casey's strokes while Bookie purred and postured. The child was mesmerized by the cat, and, to Casey's surprise, Bookend nuzzled Gabby's hand, insinuating his big head under her fingers. She giggled with delight as he taught her the best moves. Casey reached for her sketchpad and a pencil to capture the scene. A bulb flashed, and all three of them jumped.

"Sorry. Didn't mean to startle you. I just couldn't resist the picture. Thanks for your help with Mrs. Palmer." The photographer apologized and was out the door before Casey could say a word.

Movement across the street caught Casey's eye. Ron Swain, trailed by two construction foremen, inspected the access ramp his crew was building for the old science building. During the week, she'd seen the Swain

Construction truck come and go. In idle moments, she'd sketched the scene and some of the laborers in action.

She'd half expected Ron's muscular torso to gravitate to a paunch, but Ron had kept himself in good shape. He reminded her of a well-fed mastiff, sleek and powerful, with a fine head of short-cropped hair. But still, in all, a dog. He clipped and lit a cigar. That was new.

"Mr. Ron," said Gabby, also looking out the window.

"You know Mr. Ron?" Casey realized it was a silly question.

"Yup."

A yellow roadster pulled in behind the Swain Construction truck. A few seconds later, Jules emerged, striding confidently down the street like a model on a runway.

"Mommy!"

Yes, indeed. Goddam mommy. Jules looked more beautiful than she had ten years and a child ago. Casey eyed the slim lines that emphasized Jules' long legs. She must have poured herself into those jeans. A white peasant blouse gathered along a low neckline accentuated her ample bosom and made her seem buttermilk wholesome at the same time. Masterful. The work crew whistled their appreciation when Jules gave Ron a welcoming hug and kiss on the cheek.

Déjà vu. In high school, Jules stunned Casey any number of times when she'd chosen to go out with Ron instead of George. Casey had asked Jules outright what she saw in Ron. Jules mooned over his insolent black eyes and his slow, knowing smile that dripped with suggestion. Posturing astride his Harley with muscles bulging and hair slicked back in a fifties' DA, Ron had been the epitome of every mother's worst nightmare. "Baaad," Jules would say, drawing out the word with a wicked grin of her own.

Jules had continued to trade off between George and Ron during the first two years when she and Casey were coeds at Oberlin. Jules would date George when he was home on break from graduate studies at Yale, and go out with Ron when George returned to school.

At the end of their sophomore year, Jules told Casey that she'd broken up with George because he was so boring. "I wanted to go to a party, but, no, he needed to paw around in some dusty old relics in an attic. I told him to lighten up. He told me to grow up if I wanted to marry him. Huh? What a deal. His nose is either in a book, or he wants to go to some gravesite or museum to look at bones and bayonets and old letters."

"Actually, that sounds pretty interesting," Casey had admitted.

"Well, you want him, he's all yours. He'll be on his own this weekend, 'cause I'm off with Ron. Now, there's a guy who knows how to show a girl a good time. He makes things. Works with his hands. Oh man, what he does with his hands." Jules rolled her eyes and pretended to swoon. And here she was again, ten years married to George and the mother of a little girl, all kissy-face with Ron.

Jules turned and spoke to someone behind her. Casey shifted for a better view. She'd dubbed Ron's two foremen the "Swain goons." She flipped back a few pages in her sketchbook to pictures of them she'd drawn earlier in the week.

The goon closest to Ron shuffled and lumbered along like an enormous teddy bear with massive shoulders and arms covered by a mat of short black fur. He had an incongruous round, button nose and a cupid's-bow mouth fixed in a permanent smile. Even at a distance his flat, hard eyes and glassy stare made the smile sinister. A quiet, slow-moving, lethal teddy bear.

The second man fidgeted, coughed, and rubbed his nose. He shoved his hands into the pockets of his jeans, shifting his weight from foot to foot. A close-cropped buzz cut emphasized the oversized ears jutting from his head.

"Bear and Dumbo," giggled Gabby, a mischievous look on her face. "That's what Mommy calls them, but she says I mustn't. Bear's okay, if you give him treats."

But evidently not Dumbo, thought Casey, noting the omission. She watched Jules speak to Dumbo before turning back to Ron. Dumbo shrugged and walked toward the library with the practiced gait of a high school hood, adding an extra lift at the end of each step.

Gabby stroked Bookie one last time and jumped down from the stool. She collected her book and marched toward the door. At the last moment, she turned and gave Casey a radiant smile.

Dumbo opened the door and beckoned to Gabby. Acne erupted in open sores from his cheeks down his neck and shoulders spreading like boils mounding under his thin T-shirt. A band of blackheads rimmed his forehead where he usually wore a cap.

Gabby sighed, her smile displaced by the protrusion of her lower lip. She ignored the hand Dumbo thrust at her and dawdled behind him as they left the library. Seconds later, Casey heard her high-pitched squeal, "Mommy! Mommy!" as she ran to Jules.

"There's my little girl!" Jules sang out, loud and clear from across the street, as if she were projecting her voice for the stage. Or for Casey.

Casey moved from the window, but her mind's eye completed the embrace of mother and child. Her sudden motion knocked the sketchbook to the floor. As she picked it up, she studied her portrait of Dumbo.

"The ears are too small." She spoke aloud to drown out voices from the street.

She surveyed the room before returning the tables to their regular places. "The open area in the center of the room worked much better." She nodded as if answering herself. Earlier, she had worried that the younger children wouldn't be able to follow the storyline and that the older ones would be bored stiff, but all of them were caught up the instant the tornado swooped up Dorothy's house. Casey smiled, remembering how Gabby's jaw dropped and her eyes popped when the house landed on the witch.

Stop it! Think about how the morning went and what you can learn from it. Sure. Don't think about a pink elephant. Don't see Jules scoop her little bundle of joy into her outstretched arms and smother her with kisses. Think of something delicious. Like ice cream. But images of Gabby foiled her ice cream ploy, popping up at random like targets in a firing range.

"Mocha almond." Sometimes it helped to be more explicit. Car doors slammed. The high whine of the roadster joined the deeper purr of Ron's BMW. Casey peeked out the window just as the van door rolled shut and the goons drove off behind their master.

"Butter pecan."

Mrs. P's appearance at the photo op was perfect. The program would get a boost without casting Casey into the public eye. She'd worked hard to be invisible. That reminded her. The photographer. He'd been flirting with her through the lens of his camera. He was baby-face cute, but painfully shy. Would that be so bad? What would they do together, stamp library cards? Sort negatives? He wasn't exactly her type.

Casey laughed. Her type. Right. Anyone who was her type would evaporate like air freshener the moment he found out she was an ex-con. She'd had a whole scrapbook full of admirers in college, but she'd cast them aside for George. *Stop. Stop. Stop.*

Casey locked up and rode across Tappan Square to Gibson's Bakery. She'd earned a treat today. Concentrate on the little joys that make life worthwhile.

She ordered one scoop of mocha almond, and a second of butter pecan on a sugar cone. Riding down the street she steered Mae's ponderous wheel with one hand and held the cone in the other, licking and concentrating on positive thoughts. She didn't see the pothole until it was too late. She slammed back on the archaic foot brakes, bringing the bicycle to a shuddering halt. The mocha almond scoop sailed over the handlebars and splattered on the pavement. She stared at the melting ice cream. With a flick of her wrist, she jettisoned the butter pecan. Watching it hit the road, she tossed the cone and rode home.

Chapter Eight

Casey glared with death-ray concentration at the clock on her dresser that buzzed like a mechanical mosquito. The Children's Room was closed on Mondays. She'd hoped to sleep in but had forgotten to turn off the alarm. She cocked her arm, took aim, and lofted a pillow toward the dresser, relishing the muffled impact and the ensuing silence. She snuggled under the covers, blotting out the early morning light.

It was no use. A cool breeze wafted through the open window, carrying the scent of moist spring promise. She'd have preferred a gloomy, soul-dampening drizzle. A single maple leaf caught a thermal draft and danced and waved all by itself, full of the joy of life. Or sap. Casey waved back with a wimpy gesture that would make Queen Elizabeth proud. George would call it a Glory Day.

Last Monday she'd risen with the sun, eager to catch the morning light in watercolor. She'd sung in the shower until Mae had pounded her cane in protest. She had her own room with kitchen privileges. No roll call. No searches, barbed wire, or guards. She could slam the screen door, jump on Mae's bike and ride. Anywhere she pleased. Today she didn't please.

A fool's paradise. She'd been dancing alone, like the leaf.

She'd taped some of her pictures to the wall. Amateur. Below the pictures were two piles, materials she was collecting for her handwriting class, and a notebook and text for American history. With all her might, Casey winged her other pillow at the piles and watched them slide off the desk in slow motion.

The loud thud of the text drew fire from Mae, who thumped her cane from the front room. Casey smiled despite herself and pounded her fist on the wall, sassing Mae.

She tore down the picture of George's hands and destroyed a series of quick sketches she'd done of him lecturing. At times she'd replayed favorite scenes from the past, and even allowed occasional daydreams of a future with George. *Who was I kidding?* There was no future with a married man with a family.

But for a while, she'd had the next best thing. Daydreams. So much more rewarding than reality. Observing from a distance, she'd memorized his teaching schedule, days, times, classrooms. She watched for his car in the faculty parking lot, a little black Civic with a child's seat in the back and dog hair on the floor. She knew his office hours in the King Building and the location of his mail slot.

She stared at her pale reflection in the bathroom mirror, a far cry from the wild and free spirit of yesteryear. Her daydreams might be in Technicolor, but her life was a winter landscape of dull ochre and grays, without a focal point or perspective. She needed to color herself in bold, vibrant colors.

She should have transferred into another course when George took over the American history class second semester. But she'd been curious, and the class was huge. She'd felt safe tucked into the last row of the large auditorium packed with students where George couldn't see her. Research assistants graded the tests, so there was a chance he didn't know she was taking the class.

Thump! Thump! Pause. *Thump! Thump!* Pause. Amazing how Mae could make that cane speak.

When Casey went to class, she wore ratty student clothes but took care with her makeup and hair, in case anyone took a closer look. *Anyone?* With the back of her hand, she swept a pathetic collection of beauty products into the wastebasket. She vowed to avoid George and stop tracking his progress about town.

Clump, shuffle. Clump, shuffle. Now Mae inched down the hallway, storming the kitchen with her aluminum walker. Pots rattled and crashed.

"OK, OK! I'm coming." Casey sighed and pulled on a pair of scrofulous blue jeans and an old sweatshirt. When she reached the kitchen, Mae greeted her with a small smile from the breakfast nook where she awaited service. "I thought you had class on Mondays."

"I'm not going."

"No tea for me. I'll just take juice this morning," said Mae. Casey raised the ceramic pot and saw the burnt out bottom. Without a word, she heated water in a saucepan and made her aunt a cup of tea. "Those teapots are colorful, but they don't make them very strong. How 'bout I get us one with a whistle?" Earlier in the week, she'd found a large box amidst other clutter where Mae had hidden five other ruined teapots.

Mae grumped her approval between slurps. "Why aren't you going to class?"

"It's my day off. I decided to sleep in—or at least, I *tried* to sleep in."

"The way you're going, you'll sleep through your own graduation. Just a couple of weeks to go, and you're cutting classes. Are you going to jeopardize a college degree just because you're angry at George Kenworthy?"

Casey stared at her. She hadn't said a word about George's visit to the library. She shuddered at the closeness of the town and its shared knowledge.

"Seniors with a B+ or higher in a class can write a paper and blow off the exam. I'm home free with an A, and I've already submitted the paper."

A cagey expression crossed Mae's face. "The girls say George is *hot.*" The "girls," Mae's network of crones, had bat ears. They knew everything that had ever happened in Oberlin, and a few things that hadn't. "Cat got your tongue? If you can't help yourself, at least fix my cereal."

Casey poured cereal and milk into a bowl.

"Felt a tad sorry for yourself this weekend, did you?"

"What would you know about how I feel?" Casey regretted the words the second they left her mouth.

Mae let the silence hang for a while before replying. "You mean, what would a withered old maid know about love?" Mae's hawk eyes fastened on Casey.

Casey squirmed. That was exactly what she meant. "OK, I was sad because it was Mother's Day," Casey admitted.

Mae gnawed at a crusty piece of toast, gave up, and dunked it in her tea. When it was gummable, she stuffed it in her mouth. "So, you miss your mother, or you're not a mother, or both. Trust me, I understand." Mae gave Casey a bitter smile. "But moping around won't bring your mother back or get you a husband and family. You're young. Consider your options."

"Options? I don't have options. What I need is peace and quiet, and a little sleep."

"What you need is a shower."

Casey glanced at the clock. She could still make it to class.

She streaked across Tappan Square, her legs pumping the pedals of Mac's wheel like pistons. The undulating, white marble façade of Hall Auditorium loomed before her. Compared to the gothic monument of Peters Hall, the ultra-modern building looked like a beached whale. Detractors called it Moby-Dick.

She jammed her bicycle into a rack, grabbed her book bag, and slid into the auditorium behind two other tardy students. Class had already begun. Students leaned forward in their seats to capture the new Assistant Professor's interpretation of events leading to the Civil War. George was much better than Jameson, the ailing fossil he'd replaced, whom students had dubbed "Short Naps." Jameson had lectured from the podium with the subtlety and drone of a bagpipe. By contrast, George was in constant motion, walking and gesturing as he spoke.

He must be aware of his effect on students, especially the sweet young groupies in the first row. When had he become such a performer? He was a different person from the brainy, quiet jock she—*Just stop it!* Mae was right to scold her for being a misery.

Laughter startled her from her reverie. Students loved the juicy bits George salted into his lecture, asides rarely found in texts. He culled his material from old recorded interviews of Civil War veterans, from songs and art of the era, and from all manner of Civil War paraphernalia.

Casey knew firsthand how he found his material. During the Christmas vacation of her sophomore year in college, she and George had roamed across lonely, frozen graveyards searching for headstones from the mid-1800s, and attended a Civil War show. She shuddered, remembering hideous bayonets with deep grooves in the blades designed for efficient blood drainage.

Lights in the auditorium dimmed for a film clip featuring the Weavers at Carnegie Hall. George first explained that Pete Seeger was a folk and protest singer whom the John Birch Society had branded the "Canary of the Communists." Seeger led the Weavers in a spirited rendition of the old slave song, "Follow the Drinking Gourd." At one point, Seeger invited his audience to sing along, and to Casey's surprise, students around her picked up the strain and sang with the audience in Carnegie Hall.

Her mind roamed back in time, seduced by the haunting melody, remembering the last time she'd sung it after the final high school football game when Oberlin High won the conference championship. The team and exuberant fans had formed a conga line of cars, honking and hooting through the town and then through the cemetery where they careened around the curving lanes in a motorized version of crack the whip.

As was the custom after victories, Ron Swain led the procession on his Harley. Usually, George, Jules, Art, and Casey would pile into George's family sedan and putt along as trail sweep. But that night Jules jumped on the motorcycle behind Ron. Art and Martha paired off in the Swain's car, leaving George and Casey alone at the back of the line.

George should have been on top of the world. He'd just been named Most Valuable Player and had already received early admission to Yale, but he drove behind the parade in silence, distracted and remote.

"This is really stupid." George yanked the wheel and pulled over at the back of the cemetery. "I'm sick of playing games. Especially driving this pig. Mind walking?"

Some memories have a deeper texture, an added dimension etched into the brain. Casey could still see the headlights of retreating cars wash over gravestones, featuring each stone as the caravan faded from view.

They walked in silence until they came across a rectangular slab, one of the cemetery's few aboveground coffins. Carved into the side in large letters was the name, "Loveland." Nothing more. Not "Abe Loveland," or "Abraham Loveland." No dates or epigraph. Just "Loveland," as if the prescient patriarch had foreseen generations of young lovers rejoicing in the privacy of his monument.

The stars were so close Casey could pluck them out of the sky. She pointed to the Big Dipper. "There's the Drinking Gourd." She followed the line of stars in the bowl of the dipper, "And the North star."

George looked down at her with the first smile she'd seen all evening. "How do you know that?"

"Oh, you know. From the old slave song."

They sat leaning against the Loveland monument. Although Casey had known George ever since she could remember, she found herself with a stranger, alone, under the heavens. She'd allowed herself an occasional daydream about George, but had always known he was for Jules. She couldn't construct a simple sentence.

"Sing it for me."

"*Sing?* Oh no. Why ruin—"

"Humor me. I've heard you sing with Jules. You've got a lovely voice. Please."

After a few false starts, Casey launched into the plaintive tune.
When the sun comes back and the first quail cries,
Follow the Drinking Gourd.
For the old man is awaitin' for to carry you to freedom,
Follow the Drinking Gourd.

George stretched out on his back in the moist grass, gazing up at the constellation. He took her hand and held it against his chest. "More," he demanded. Casey nestled next to him. Despite the mortal remains surrounding her, she'd never felt so alive. She sang the second stanza.
The river bank'll make a mighty fine road,
The dead trees will show you the way.
Left foot, peg foot, traveling on,
Follow the Drinking Gourd.

"Lovely. What does 'Left foot, peg foot,' mean?"

"Peg Leg Joe was a freeman with a wooden leg who guided slaves along the river banks at night. When they reached the southern banks of the Ohio, Peg Leg—" Suddenly, Casey stopped, mortified. "C'mon! You know this!"

George laughed, but he wouldn't let go when she tried to pull away, and when she shivered in the night chill, he drew her under his jacket. Again, she snuggled against him, grateful and excited by his warmth and nearness.

He cradled her head against his chest, and his breath warmed her hair. She felt the reverberation of his voice in his chest. "Beautiful," he said, as he raised her face to his. He traced the outside of her lips with his forefinger. It tickled, and Casey laughed and rubbed the spot.

"Here, let me do that." Their first kiss was a self-conscious collision, but soon they surrendered to sensation. Casey could still smell the grass, moist with early evening dew, and feel George stretched alongside her. He brushed the hair from her face, kissing her eyes and cheeks and lips while his hands explored. They both laughed nervously when he couldn't undo the zipper on her jacket.

"Let's start over," he whispered huskily, much of his earlier tenderness lost to urgency. "I don't want to crush you." When he pulled her on top of him, Casey felt the arousal of parts she had only imagined before. His hand kneaded her sweater, gently at first, but then more firmly.

As he caressed her, a wave of sensation washed upward from her breast to the roof of her mouth and then back down to her navel and below. With his other hand, George stroked the small of her back, and then pressed her hips against him.

Suddenly, he froze.

Casey heard a popping sound, like tires rolling over gravel. George rolled her aside and sat bolt upright, brushing off his clothes.

Ron fired up his Harley directly before them. The engine screamed as the one-eyed machine captured them in its spotlight. Casey raised her arm to shield her eyes.

Ron sat astride the motorcycle in a black leather jacket. With the visor of the helmet pulled down, he looked like the Black Knight in a jousting match.

Jules rode behind him. They flipped up their visors in a single, synchronized motion.

"Thought I'd find you here, Kenworthy." Ron sneered down at the compromised White Knight. "You sure know how to show a girl a good time. There's a lot more privacy in that little house over there." Ron jerked his head toward the Loveland mausoleum across the cinder path. "Ask Jules. Maybe she'll lend you the key." Ron turned and gave Jules a knowing smile.

As he spoke, the caravan of fans caught up with him. The drivers slowed to a halt when Ron held up his hand and turned off their engines with the downward gesture of his arm.

"Gotta get your butt down to the Rec Center for a photo op."

George stood, but didn't respond. He stared at Jules. Jules leaned into Ron, tightening her grip around his waist. She met George's eyes with a haughty glare.

"Wha'samatter, Kenworthy? Pussy got your tongue?"

George spoke directly to Jules. "It's not what you—"

Casey wanted to scream *"Oh yes it is! It's exactly what you think!"* but she was stunned by George's lie and shocked at the raw emotion on Jules' face.

"Riiiight," Ron interrupted. "You got ten minutes to get to the Center. Ought to be enough time for Tinkerbell to grant your wish." He flipped down his visor. "Let's go, babe. Who knows, maybe you'll get Mr. Lucky tonight."

Casey stared at Jules with her arm circling Ron's waist. *Unbelievable.* Was Jules sleeping with Ron? When they were younger, Ron's sister Martha had confided that he named his privates "Mr. Lucky."

"Gentlemen, start your engines!" Motors roared and revved in response to Ron's command and uplifted hand. Jules' eyes passed through Casey and skewered George with a withering glare before the caravan moved on.

"I don't understand," said Casey. "Who is Mr. Lucky?"

When George didn't respond, Casey repeated, "Who's—"

"I heard you," George growled. "Mr. Lucky is Ron's penis. Swain calls his dick 'Mr. Lucky.'"

The image faded as the auditorium lights rose. Students packed up while

George gave the reading assignment for the last class of the semester.

Casey bolted for the door. Outside, temporarily blinded by the sun, it took her a moment to locate Mae's wheel.

"Casey, wait!"

Omigod. She cast a thieving eye upon a newer bike close to her, but she wasn't fast enough.

"Miss Cavendish! A word, if you please," George called out. Students turned and Casey's face heated to medium-rare. There was nothing she could do.

George caught up with her and lowered his voice. "I hope you've enjoyed the class." When she didn't reply, he continued. "Come on. Let me walk you to the library."

"Thanks, but today is my day off."

"I know."

"You do?"

"Yes. But I—" The great verbal gymnast was speechless. With a self-deprecating laugh, he finally muttered, "How about I walk you to the library anyway?" They continued in silence. She pushed her bike over the uneven brick pathway, while he walked alongside carrying a leather satchel bulging with papers.

"I was hoping you'd come again today. And that I'd catch you this time, before you spirited away." She flinched at his touch as he reached out to stop her. Looking down to escape his eyes, she tried to push on. But he stopped her again, this time with the pain in his voice. "Casey, please. I need to talk with you." He placed his hand on her arm and willed her to meet his gaze. "I've missed you so. It's been torture. It's a Glory Day. Stay with me awhile."

Casey forced her eyes to disengage and begged her mind to rule. She wasn't sure what his intentions were, but *any* intentions with her would lead to disaster. "I really enjoyed the course—"

"Casey, I'm talking about you and me."

"You're married with a family. The only 'you and me' is in the past where it belongs."

"You're right. I'm married, but I won't be for long. Maybe we can't be together in the present, but at least let me dream about the future."

But I won't be for long? Casey didn't trust herself to answer.

"Friends for now?" George asked softly.

Casey nodded. "For now," she whispered.

Chapter Nine

After closing the Children's Room Tuesday evening, Casey climbed the stairs to the student reading room and stacks. All day, George's words had replayed in a continuous loop: "I'm married, but I won't be for long," and "...at least let me dream about the future." With her mind deadlocked between hope and fear, she opted for action. She'd find the books on George's list without compromising her pride.

During her lunch hour, she'd located two of the four books, but two others listed as "available" had eluded her. Tonight, she'd make a book-by-book search in the American history rows of the stacks in hopes that the books were mis-shelved but still within the general vicinity of their correct location.

In the reading room with its high ceilings and long wooden tables, students hunched over books, deep in concentration. The only movement was the occasional turn of a page, but she sensed the harmonics of hormones playing over the chords of scholarship. She caught herself searching for familiar faces. As if she would know any students now.

As she surveyed the room, she felt another pair of eyes watching her. Scowlie Reference. Casey whirled about and glowered at the sour old bat and then strode to the door to the stacks.

Inside the netherworld of the library, she waited for her eyes to adjust to the dim corridors. Naked bulbs hung from the ceiling on long cords at the end of every other row providing just enough light to read the spines of books. Her sneakers squeaked on the translucent glass floor tiles, breaking the silence as she wound through narrow passageways connecting room after room of floor-to-ceiling bookshelves. Each room in the literary labyrinth contained a silent crypt of Dewey's subject matter categories.

She jumped at an explosion behind her. A student cloistered in a study carrel at the end of the aisle sniffed twice and sneezed again.

"Bless you!" Casey's disembodied voice floated in the air.

This time, the student jumped. As she tiptoed away, she imagined the soft padding and panting of a dog trotting behind her, a dog that would mutate into a werewolf with razor-sharp fangs and burning red eyes. Casey smiled. She was a friend of the dark.

The Scowlies refused to enter the stacks at night, so with the exception of an occasional student, the place was hers. She slowed her pace when she reached the room with the call letters and numbers for American history. In the third row, she found several books that were out of place, but not the two on the list. Continuing slowly down the row of books on slavery and abolition, she read every title, looking for Soubrette, *The Underground Railroad from Slavery to Freedom.* Just as she was about to give up, she spied the book under the T's. The other book by Buckmaster eluded her.

She dawdled on, entering the next aisle, hoping to discover other sources George might find useful. She knelt to examine a pile of derelict books stacked on the bottom shelf. She sank to the floor, leaning against a strut in the opposing bookcase. Half an hour later she found a likely prospect: *Oberlin, the Colony and the College, 1833-1883,* by James Fairchild, an early college president. The cover was loosely connected to the text by a few threads. The last date stamp on the card in the back pocket was March 14, 1938. This could be a find!

The Exit door opened and closed. Rubber-soles squeaked to a stop in the next aisle. Peering through spaces in the bottom row of books, she saw thick black hair curling around bare ankles stuffed into worn sneakers. The student shifted from foot to foot. Either he had to go to the bathroom, or he was nervous.

Dirty sneaker odor assaulted her. Quickly, Casey gathered her books and rose to leave. At eye level, she glanced through the row of books and was mesmerized by a three-carat blackhead on the back of the student's neck.

She imagined squeezing it and shuddered involuntarily.

Sneakers withdrew a slip of paper from his back pocket. What was wrong with his hands? Nothing. He was wearing white surgical gloves. After consulting the paper, he reached up and selected a black volume from the top shelf. Instead of opening it, he looked quickly to the left and right, offering Casey a clear profile. One she'd drawn before. Dumbo. How would a worker on Ron's construction crew get into the stacks of Carnegie Library?

If he turned, he'd see her. If she moved, he'd hear her. She held her breath. Dumbo's gloved hand removed a wad of bills from a hollowed-out square inside the book. He counted the money, folded it, and stuffed it into his back pocket. Squatting he retrieved something from a small backpack on the floor. He stood up, replaced the book, and walked down the aisle. The Exit door closed.

She exhaled. Close, but he hadn't seen her. She crossed herself for good measure. She wasn't Catholic, but why take chances? The guy wasn't wearing surgical gloves to protect himself from germs. *Get out!*

She jammed the books for George into her book bag and turned to leave. The Exit door re-opened. She ducked into her aisle. The backlit silhouette filling the doorway was pudgy with lots of hair. He moved slowly down Dumbo's aisle. He stood still as if listening. A moment later, he reached up and selected the black book on the top row. He glanced down his row and back at the Exit, before opening the book and tucking something into his jeans. He closed the book and replaced it and within seconds was out the door.

Casey walked quickly in the opposite direction. As soon as she was confident of her knees, she broke into a trot and then a full-out sprint, back through the maze toward the main reading room.

"What the fug?"

Casey barreled into Sneezy who was juggling books and a box of tissues. She staggered forward, barely keeping her balance. From the crashing and cursing behind her, he wasn't as lucky.

She loped on, her hard breathing and the rapid patter of her sneakers echoing through the corridors, rekindling the earlier werewolf image. She stopped short. Slow down. Walk like a student. *Hell, I am a student!* She didn't want anyone to remember the crazed, panting female in the stacks.

When her eyes acclimated to the bright lights of the main reading room, she made a beeline for the stairs. She wanted to put as much distance between herself and the drug deal as fast as she could.

Scowlie Reference raised her hand like a traffic cop and beckoned to her with the curl of a yellowed talon. *What does she want?* Casey inched toward the Reference desk. Her mind raced with last-minute exit ploys: throw up and race to the Ladies' Room, yell, "Fire!" or, better yet, "It's a bust!" Half the students would dive under the tables to avoid the other half bolting for the door.

A putrid smile washed over the Scowlie's face. As the woman's lips moved, Casey struggled to make sense of her words.

"I've got you now, my pretty!"

Casey stared in stunned silence. Reference waited for her to speak. "Pardon?"

"I said, 'I told you not to feed the kitty.' Yesterday, I found a dish on your windowsill reeking of fish," Reference said with a self-satisfied, gotcha grimace. "And, you need to sign out any books you've got in that bag. After all, this *is* a library."

"Oh. Sorry. Sure." Casey dumped the books on the counter and gave Reference her student ID. As soon as the books were checked out, Casey walked to the Reading Room exit. The instant the doors closed behind her, she bounded down the stairs to the first floor, past the Children's Room, and out of the library.

Free! She dashed toward Mae's wheel, but skidded to a stop at the last moment, her eyes fixed on the leather riding pack behind the seat. The strap was unfastened. When had she last used the pack? She backed away and glanced around. She was alone. Could she have left the pack open? Not likely, but possible.

Casey reasoned with herself to allay her mounting panic. The scene in the stacks had nothing to do with her. For all she knew, there could be transactions going down in every third aisle. *But she would have buckled the strap.*

Disjointed images from the drug bust ten years ago crashed into her mind: Charley Crockett hollering to her from across the street and then running across Tappan Square, the siren screaming as the cop car jumped the curb in pursuit. Charley's unmoving body on the grass. And the large packet of cocaine in the leather pouch under her bicycle seat.

Casey forced long breaths. Although the scene in the stacks had nothing to do with her, the hollowed-out book bothered her. She and Jules had passed notes, gum, and even money in a hollowed-out biology text in high school. Her sense of foreboding ratcheted up a notch.

No! A black and white cruiser approached the library. Make a run for it across Tappan Square? The cruiser would mow her down, just like Charley. She prayed that Crockett was driving. The reflection of the streetlights against the windshield made it impossible to see the driver. Headlights swept across her. Casey closed her eyes.

The cruiser accelerated and passed by. Casey watched it turn at the next corner and continue along the far side of Tappan Square. She waited until it reached the center of town before she approached Mae's bicycle. She lifted the open flap and peered inside. Empty.

She buckled the strap with shaky fingers and threw her book bag into a rear saddlebag. Once again, she walked the bike slowly for a few paces, waiting for the confidence to return to her queasy knees before hopping on.

Then she turned on her headlamp just like a law-abiding citizen and rode toward home. The instant she walked in the door, she dialed Crockett's direct number. She'd just witnessed a drug deal. She hadn't done anything wrong, but someone else had, and she'd been there.

"You have reached two-one-six—" Crockett's answering machine. "If this is an emergency, press zero for immediate assistance." No way she'd talk to anyone else. "Crockett, it's Casey. It's Tuesday night. I may have something for you."

By Wednesday mid-morning Casey had finished all her work, re-arranged the Children's Room furniture, and watered the plants. Why hadn't Crockett called? She paced the room to ward off thoughts about the scene in the stacks.

The demons of the night had tortured her sleep. The last dream was the worst. It began with her walking home from the library enjoying the balmy spring evening, but ended with her sprinting across Tappan Square, chased by a police car. It was futile; there was no escape. She raised her arms in surrender and turned into the headlights. The chrome bumper curled into a sneer, and the car leapt forward. There was no driver. Casey screamed and fell before the oncoming tires. And woke up.

She leafed through her sketchbook until she found the picture of Dumbo, the skinny man with huge ears on Ron's construction crew. What if someone found out she was present during a drug deal? Sneezy might be able to identify her, although the light was dim. Bookend jumped up on the desk and lay down on her sketchbook with a rattling purr. Casey stroked him absently. And Reference. Reference wouldn't forget Casey's performance last night. Not good.

Bookend wasn't interested in low-grade attention. He abandoned his lovey ploy and jumped to the floor. With tail switching and ears back, he stomped toward his dish.

She popped open a tin of cat food while Bookie circled like a shark. "We need a new place to feed you. Reference is onto us." She cast about for a moment until she spotted the perfect place. Dragging a chair with one hand and carrying Bookend's dish in the other, she walked to a tall bookcase against the back wall.

She stood on the chair, placed the cat's bowl on top, and jumped down to survey the effect. It looked like a cat dish on top of a bookcase. She grabbed the pot of English ivy from the windowsill and placed it in front of the dish.

Bookend leaped from floor to chair to his new feeding place in one fluid motion. Perfect. Except for the long tail draping over the end of the bookcase. She rearranged the ivy for camouflage. It would have to do for now.

The phone rang. Casey answered on the second ring. "Carnegie Library, Children's—"

"Crockett here, Casey. Sorry, can't talk. Meet me—"

Bookend coughed. Casey glanced up at the cat gulping down his chicken and liver entrée as if it were his Last Supper.

"Slow down. You'll choke."

"What?"

"Sorry. I was talking to my cat."

"Campus Restaurant in a half-hour?"

"Sure, Chief. I'll be—" But he'd hung up.

Crockett would think she was daft talking to a ratty old cat. But Bookie was much better company than the Scowlies. Sometimes he'd talk back, punctuating her pauses and finishing her sentences. She straightened her desk before going to lunch. Why did she care about them anyway? They'd probably die off before she could win them over. And what for? They were about as much fun as prison guards. But even prison guards were company. She'd been so lonely since coming home. Casey cut off her train of thought. What had she expected? No use dragging her toenails.

Chapter Ten

From the last booth at the rear of the restaurant, Crockett waved to catch Casey's attention. She waved back, but her jaunty smile was missing. With her hair pulled back in a tight band, dressed in gray and black, she bore little resemblance to the Casey he knew in high school, or even the Casey who visited his office the week before. Then her cheeks were pink from riding, her hair bounced when she walked, and her eyes sparkled with a glint of her old mischief. Much as he hated to pressure her, he had a job to do. He realized that he was staring and shifted focus to his coffee.

"It can't be as bad as the sludge at the station," she said with a tentative smile as she slid into the booth opposite him.

"Nothing approaches Watson's coffee," Crockett agreed.

His comment dropped into dead space between them.

"I ordered bagels." Crockett signaled to the waitress.

"You're in a hurry, then." It wasn't a question.

"Nah. Just practicing my winning ways on the new waitress." Crockett forced himself to lean back in the booth. "Thanks for meeting me on short notice. Good to get away from the station. Graduation. Connolly's undergoing a personality change, just as Jenny predicted."

Again Casey nodded. They fell silent as a svelte black teenager brought place settings, coffee, and bagels to the table. After serving them, the waitress gazed into Crockett's eyes. "Let me know if you need anything."

Crockett responded with a slow, half-smile and an appraising look.

"Anything else, that is," she backed into the empty table behind her. "Oh, golly! Sorry," she apologized, escaping to the kitchen.

Casey awarded Crockett her first genuine smile of the day. "'Oh, *golly?*' You still have the magic, old man."

"Look, but don't touch. Jail bait for sure." Crockett bit off half of his bagel before he realized what he'd said.

Casey's grin evaporated. She waved off his mute apology, but her posture stiffened.

He looked around before leaning forward, speaking in a hushed voice. "Whatcha got?"

Casey mirrored his posture and toyed with a saltshaker as she told him about the Swain goons outside the library window, giving particular emphasis to the jumpy one Gabby called Dumbo.

"Jumpy one'd be Danny McPhee. Don't know the other's name. Seen them trailing after Ron."

"I saw a drug deal go down last night." Casey described the scene in the stacks. "The guy who took the money looked like Dumbo."

No wonder she was nervous. The big guy Bear'd be too obvious for a college drop. But a nervous little guy with a face full of zits'd fit right in. "You'd swear it was McPhee?"

Casey backed off. "I don't want to swear to anything."

Crockett eased up. "Pretty scary after all you been through. *Really* appreciate this, Casey. May be the tip we need." He leaned forward for a better angle on her plate, smiled, and swiped half of her uneaten bagel. "No wonder you're a shrimp. Eat like a bird. Still shelving books for those nasty old ladies?"

Casey hesitated. "Actually, I think I told you last week about finishing up my American History course. I had to check a few footnote references for the last paper." Casey withdrew a rumpled paper from her jeans pocket and pointed out the call numbers for the books to identify the drug aisle.

"You need this?" Crockett asked.

"I made a copy. What are you going to do, Crockett?"

"Set me a little trap." Crockett grabbed the other half of her bagel. "Stay out of the stacks, okay? And mum's the word. Not even your cat."

"You've got a wire on my cat?"

They both laughed, but it wasn't an easy laugh.

Outside Crockett watched her wait for the light and walk her bike across the street to Tappan Square before mounting and riding off. Guess that was the difference. Before, she'd ride against the light, challenging traffic like any self-respecting student. Now, he was watching. He was a friend, but he was also the law.

A friend, but how much did he really know about her? They met when he was protecting her brother Art from school bullies Ron Swain and Dougie Watson. Later, she sat next to him in world history. She was quiet, a loner. Lived in her own world, sometimes by her own rules.

Jules had been her only friend. Odd combo. Jules growing up with a silver spoon, Casey in the servants' quarters. Crockett walked slowly down Main Street, not eager to return to the station. He hoped his friendship with Casey could survive the events of the intervening years. He wanted to believe she was cooperating, but she closed down last week when he asked for help. A week later, she did a one-eighty and squealed on a drug deal.

Why? She was scared. Thought someone spotted her. What were the odds? Thousands and thousands of books, and she just happened to be in the same aisle looking at the same books the druggies were using. Possible. But he didn't believe in coincidence.

But why? She just got out.

Drugs. It all came back to drugs. And it was probably his little brother, Charley, who introduced her to them. Crockett had reviewed the evidence from the trial. Despite her denials, the case against Casey was convincing. Was there some thin chance she could be telling the truth? He hadn't seen any signs of drug use, but then, she'd have to be crazy to meet with the Chief of Police stoned.

Another thing worried him. She'd lied. A little lie, but a lie nonetheless. Last week she said she'd submitted her American history paper. Today, she was still checking footnotes. He pushed open the door to the station, marched to his office, and closed the door. He added Daniel McPhee and Bear to the Bombs list under "Stacks." Then, reluctantly, he added "CC" on the next line.

A few telephone calls later, Crockett had arranged his trap. Later in the afternoon, a police officer dressed in an Oberlin College Buildings and Grounds uniform would install a surveillance camera at the end of the row where Casey had seen the exchange.

Chapter Eleven

T he chimes of Finney Chapel rang the half-hour. Eleven thirty.
George's faculty meeting didn't get out until noon on Thursdays.
She'd drop off the books in his office in Rice Hall and then go
home for lunch. That way she wouldn't appear too eager to make contact.
She stuffed the books into her book bag and glanced around the Children's
Room to make certain all was in order. Rats. She'd forgotten to switch the
picture. She wouldn't want to disappoint her viewing public.

Casey strode to the children's *World Book Encyclopedia* and retrieved an
envelope from the back of the "S" volume. Sifting through a group of photos,
she selected one of her favorites, a swarthy Israeli soldier in full commando
gear who had signed, "Love, Boaz" across the bottom. She opened the
shallow center drawer of her desk and replaced a photo of a blonde Adonis
with the new photo.

She returned Adonis to the cache in the encyclopedia. She'd chosen the
letter "S" in honor of the Scowlies, the beneficiaries of her project. This
photo would set their tongues awag. Casey had been bending their minds
ever since she realized that Scowlie Circulation routinely rifled her desk
and her mail slot.

Five minutes later, Casey parked her bicycle outside Rice Hall, the faculty
office building, a heavy Romanesque pile of stones that once had elaborate
turrets and spires. Architects had scalped the roof in an attempt to make it
a less incongruous annex to a modern classroom building.

Inside, she made a pretense of checking the marquee before taking the
stairway down to George's basement office. She knocked on the door. No

answer. She flipped the sign on his door from "Please come in" to "Please do not disturb," and closed the door behind her.

A large oak desk and swivel chair dominated George's spare cubicle. Above, a high window provided a view of passing feet at ground level. A tall bookcase crowded the single straight-backed chair that faced the desk.

Casey had never seen a faculty office so devoid of books and papers. No learned tomes in the bookcase. Even the walls were bare. His desk had a telephone and a two-tier metal file. The bottom layer, labeled "Out," was empty. The top "In" tier was full of old leaflets and directories and a stack of pink While-You-Were-Out telephone messages.

She knew George worked at home a lot, but she assumed that he used his office once in a while. Maybe he wouldn't find the books. She'd leave him a note in his faculty mailbox. She wasn't about to deliver books to the Gourd.

Problem solved, she sat in the swivel chair and twirled, first to the left, and then to the right. When she stopped spinning, she came face to face with a small picture that had been hidden by the inbox. Casey wilted. A radiant Jules proudly holding her little girl. Gabby looked to be about two years old. Casey tore her eyes from the photograph. It didn't matter. She was just doing a favor for an old friend. She positioned the books next to the telephone messages where he couldn't miss them.

The name on the top message caught her eye. Renee. Casey looked closer. "Renee called," 5/14 at 8:30 AM. The second message at 9:00 AM was also from Renee. Casey sifted through the stack. All from Renee.

The door swung open. Casey's hand flew to her mouth as if she had burned her fingers. Her face blushed crimson as she looked into George's startled eyes.

After his initial shock, George laughed. "If it isn't my favorite coed. Make yourself at home, Miss Cavendish." He closed the door and gave her a quizzical look.

He's taunting me. He knows the effect he has on me. She walked to the front of the desk. "Caught me. Your chair has a good twirl," she said in her most offhand manner. "I thought you'd be in a meeting." *Oh damn! Now he knows that I've got his schedule.*

"Humphries sang." Humphries IV was the latest in a long line of basset hounds that students lured to class with choice bits from the dining hall. It was an unwritten college "policy" that when Humphries crooned during a lecture, class was dismissed. "To my knowledge, this is the first time he's performed in a faculty meeting. The place emptied in seconds."

Casey shoved her book bag into his hands. "I located one book that will be sent back from a borrowing library next week. Another will have to be replaced. The Soubrette had been mis-shelved. You also might be interested in the one by Fairchild. I still haven't located Buckmaster's *Flight to Freedom*."

George took the book bag but held on to her hands. Casey jumped at his touch as if she'd been zapped by an electric current. She blushed again, afraid to look at him. She was so transparent. Her face must be maroon. She tried to pull away, but he drew her closer.

"Thanks for finding the books, Casey. If I'd known you were here, I would have brought the old hound a T-bone steak." He spoke with such tenderness Casey dared a glance. She drew in a quick breath at the intensity in his eyes and tried to back off a second time, determined not to melt into a puddle at his feet.

Abruptly he released her hands. "I'm sorry." He laughed, but his tone was deprecatory. "Lord, it seems 'I'm sorry' is all I say to you. I don't want to put you on the spot..." He stopped mid-sentence and turned, but now he was the one with averted eyes.

"That's not true. I *do* want to put you on the spot. But not if you don't want..." His voice trailed off, and he hesitated, waiting for her to speak. When she didn't respond, he flung his arms in the air. "Oh, hell, Casey. You haunt my dreams." His voice broke. "I look for you everywhere." He was quiet for a few moments before speaking again. "Where from here?" he asked softly.

Casey's confusion at the ambiguity of his question must have been written all over her face. To her relief and disappointment, George helped her out. "Home? To the library?"

"Home, I guess." Brilliant. Jules would never be this flustered. Casey glared at the photo on his desk.

"Or would you take a walk with an old friend who promises to be better behaved?" George gave her a wry smile during the split second it took her to decide. He scooped up his messages and then nodded toward the picture of Jules and Gabby. "I use that picture like a cross to ward off student groupies. And chew lots of garlic." His laugh eased the tension as he opened the door.

Casey couldn't believe she and George were walking down the street having a conversation about the economic causes of the Civil War. Well, he was having a conversation. She caught enough words to follow his train of thought and to murmur encouragement. She pushed her bike alongside, just as she had a lifetime ago when he returned during college breaks.

Walking with George was terrifying, natural, and very public. She was surprised to feel guilty. She hadn't done anything wrong. But she *would*, had she her druthers. It wouldn't matter. In a small-town morality play, Casey would be cast as the evil temptress. She didn't slow her pace or blink an eye when they passed Mae's house.

At the next corner, George stopped "How about a stroll around the cemetery for old time's sake?"

Her mind reeled, but she managed to mutter, "Sure." Maybe he only wanted to walk in a more private place. His eyes had followed every car that passed by. As if it mattered. Word of their stroll would already be warming the wires.

Tension drained from George's face as they strolled along the gently curving lanes. "Where are you, Casey? I seem to have lost you." George had finally realized that he was talking to himself.

"Sorry. I couldn't help but remember how the earth moved in Loveland," Casey admitted.

A smile played around the edges of George's mouth. "You sang 'Follow the Drinking Gourd.' Remember? But I interrupted. You were remembering how the earth moved."

"Yes, when Ron and the caravan came back." Quickly she added, "I was thinking about the expression on Jules' face." Casey waited for a response, but George chose not to answer.

When they reached Abe Loveland's monument, he took her bicycle and leaned it against a tree. Without a word, he drew her to him for the second time, and this time she didn't resist.

"Come on, if the earth is going to move, I'd rather be on the far side of Loveland, away from that monstrosity." George glanced across the road at the Loveland mausoleum. Two enormous riding mowers were parked beside the building. "Looks like the grounds crew is out to lunch."

George caressed her hand as they sat in the grass and leaned against the large stone slab, listening to the water splash over rocks in Plum Creek.

"Would you like me to sing the song again?" This scene played out much more easily in her dreams

"No, Case." He kissed the back of her hand. "Don't worry. I won't bite. Not very hard anyway." He touched her lips with his forefinger to quiet her and then kissed her gently. He drew back and looked into her eyes for permission. The second kiss lingered, and by the third, Casey shuddered and responded.

"Damn!" George's sudden motion left her spinning. "Company. *Again.*"

The nose of a little yellow roadster turned the bend, heading directly for them. Jules! Jules wouldn't see them as she drove past, but Mae's wheel was in plain view.

The car stopped and seconds later a car door closed. They waited. Nothing.

Then clinking followed by metal scraping on concrete. Silence.

"She's in the mausoleum," Casey whispered. After waiting for what seemed like an eternity, Casey braved a peek to confirm her hunch. Just then, Jules emerged from the building carrying a bag. Casey shrank back, almost toppling George directly behind her. Neither moved until the purr of the engine faded from earshot.

"What was she doing?" George asked.

"I have no idea." *She's hiding something.*

They lapsed into silence, defeated once again by the omnipresent Jules.

George took her hand. "You know, everyone assumed we were meant for each other." His voice bespoke a vulnerability he hadn't shown before. Casey

73

smiled encouragement, and he continued. "There was never a question in my mind how the play would end. The script was solid. It was just our acting that fell short. We were so young."

Casey nodded and leaned against him.

"But at some point, we began testing each other. She thought I took her for granted. I probably did. Nobody, but nobody, took her for granted."

Casey's mind reeled. *She? Her?* He was talking about Jules! Casey stiffened and her mind screamed. *What about me?*

"You and I were so much better suited for each other. I just couldn't see it then." George stroked Casey's arm absently as he spoke.

Casey relaxed and nestled against his shoulder again.

"You asked why Jules gave me that awful look years ago. We were just beginning to play our hurtful games. Neither one of us knew how to be wrong or how to apologize. She rode with Ron that night to punish me, because I stood her up earlier in the week. When she saw the two of us together, she knew I'd one-upped her. She was jealous and maybe even a little hurt. I hoped so."

Casey stared at George, unable to speak. For years she'd cherished that magical evening, but it had been about Jules. He'd just been using her. Always, Jules. *Goddamn Jules.* Casey shrugged herself from George's arms and jumped to her feet. "So, I was just a foil?" Her voice rose. "Is that what this is about, George? Jules-baiting?"

She glared at the road where the roadster had disappeared. When she spoke again, her voice was controlled and her jaw clenched. "I like the idea of punishing Jules. But when I do, I'll act on my own behalf, not as your tool."

George stood and faced her. "Come on, Case. You haven't been listening. It's *over* with Jules. Let's not argue."

"So, who's Renee?" Casey couldn't believe her own words.

George recoiled. He paused as if he were composing his next lines.

"Never mind," she said before he could respond. She didn't want to hear the lie he was constructing. Hadn't he said she haunted his dreams, and what a fool he'd been? What more did she want?

74

"No, it's all right," George replied. "You're wondering about the telephone messages. Renee is the pain in the ass editor who's making me re-check all the goddamned footnotes."

Casey turned to hide her shame. She'd just accused him of an affair with his editor.

George turned her gently back toward him. He bowed his head to hers, forcing her to look into his eyes. "Case, can we back up a little and start over?"

She watched their fingers entwine, her mind a battlefield. It could never work. He'd be a fool to leave Jules. Neither would leave Gabby. And Jules had it made in Oberlin. But he was fool enough to be seen with Casey. He had everything to lose; she, nothing at all, except her pride. The town would never accept her. She'd always be the sly ex-con who wrecked the golden couple. Then again, he'd left town once. Maybe he'd leave again.

With his other hand, George raised her chin to look into her eyes. "I'm willing to go on if you are."

She returned his gaze and smiled. "I—" Her words were drowned out by the sudden roar of the mowers across the road. They both jumped and then laughed.

"I guess lunch break is over," he said.

Chapter Twelve

Friday morning Casey cloistered herself in the Children's Room, afraid that her face would broadcast her thoughts as clearly as a television screen tuned to a romance. She blushed, and then laughed at herself. She should either turn down the volume, or switch channels before one of the Scowlies caught her grinning at a blank wall.

This morning the world seemed cleansed. Colors pulsed with energy and light. Her dark lens had lifted, but along with it, her protective shield, leaving her puzzled. Should she shout for joy or crawl under her desk? Any action would be better than the deadening inertia that had sapped her energy and threatened her spirit. She set about the paperwork that the Scowlies had left in her in-box. Today, even their mind-numbing tasks couldn't touch her mood.

The ring of the telephone practically lifted Casey out of her seat. *Get a grip.* She let it ring a second time before answering, "Carnegie Library, Children's Room."

"Hello, Casey."

George! Casey looked to the door to make sure she was alone.

"Hello?"

"Yes, hi. Sorry. I was—" She stopped mid-sentence. *Thinking of you.*

"I just read your term paper. Excellent job!" When Casey didn't respond, George continued, oblivious to her silence. "I was especially interested in the story of Vernon Bathory. What was your source? There wasn't a footnote or a reference." The last comment had a slight professorial scold that helped Casey gather her thoughts.

"It's not in a book. It's from a picture Jules and I found at the Gourd. The letter was tucked behind the picture."

"Unbelievable! Do you have it? Is the letter still with it?"

"The picture's on the mantel at Mae's house." Casey didn't mention that Jules' father had taken the picture from them with the intention of selling it, and that she had stolen it back and hidden it in the clubhouse. Or that she had recently re-stolen it when she took Martha's handwritten oath.

"Could I stop by on my way home to take a look at it? Say, around seven o'clock?"

Casey smiled, but then realized he couldn't see a smile over the phone. "Sure." She didn't like the "home" part, but "stop by" held promise.

By six-thirty Casey and Mae had eaten, and Mae had retired to her room to snore at the television. When George arrived a half-hour later, Casey beckoned toward the porch swing instead of inviting him in. "Mind sitting out here? It's a bit noisy inside." She nodded to the telltale flickering of a television behind the nylon curtains in the front room.

"Outside is fine." George dropped the books Casey had found for him on the floor next to the swing, sat, and held his hand out to her. The spring twilight and the rocking motion lulled her spirits and eased the conversation. A long flower box filled with pansies that Casey had planted the week before shielded them from the street. She listened to his voice rise and fall above the laugh track on the TV. An occasional car passed, but otherwise, they had the world to themselves. George stroked her fingers absently while he talked about his dreams, how he wanted to raise Gabby in a small town, and how much Oberlin and the Drinking Gourd meant to him.

"Is that why you are so interested in the picture?" Relief flooded over George's face. He wanted to talk about the picture, but didn't want to bring it up.

"Well, with your permission, of course, I might be able to use the story to spice up my manuscript." He looked slightly embarrassed. "Readers relate to concrete examples, especially if the example involves a tragic tale of love and loss with a bit of gratuitous gore thrown in.

"If the picture and letter can be authenticated, it's a dream come true. The story has it all—a newlywed bounty hunter leaves his wife to chase a desperate slave family and dies a mysterious death at the Drinking Gourd." George paused and took a brochure from his jacket pocket and handed it to Casey. "This is why I asked to come by at such short notice. Experts at a Civil War conference I'm going to this weekend can look at the picture and the letter."

The front of the brochure highlighted conference keynote speakers. Inside, Casey scanned a list of topics and vendors who would display their wares. She flipped to the back. A handwritten note was scrawled over a description of facilities and registration details: "Dear George, Please take care of Gabby this afternoon. Nana has a cold. Off to the dentist, Jules."

George spied the note and reached for the brochure, but Casey held onto it. "Nana?"

"For 'Grandma.' That's what Gabby calls Jules' mother."

Casey jumped up and headed for the front door. "Wait a sec, while I get the picture. The program looks interesting, but I'd rather read about it later," she called over her shoulder. Moments later she returned with the photograph.

"Perfect!" George gasped as he stared at the ugly newlyweds. "That's Bathory all right!" He explained what Casey already knew, that Vernon Bathory's exploits as a bounty hunter were well documented. He was last spotted in Oberlin, but he never returned or was heard from again.

Carefully George eased the letter from the back of the old leather frame. Casey watched him read and re-read the letter Hilda had written to Vernon. Casey knew the letter by heart. Hilda begged Vernon to stay clear of the Drinking Gourd, where folks suspected Abe Loveland harbored the fugitives Vernon was hunting. She said Oberlin was a nest of rabid abolitionists and advised him to intercept the slaves when they made the run for Lake Erie.

George was ecstatic. "Just what I need! I just hope it'll be in time."

"In time?"

George's euphoria flagged. "We inherited a lot of debt. Instead of paying off the construction costs for the new Gourd addition, Jules' parents poured all of their money into a retirement community. Frankly, I don't know how we made the last few payments."

"How would this help?"

"If the Gourd is declared a national historic site, we can apply for a restoration grant and special tax advantages to keep us afloat. A listing in the National Register of Historic Places amounts to free advertising. Best of all, the Gourd would be off-limits for developers."

But Casey had stopped listening, stuck on the words *"we"* and *"us."* Once again the domestic realities of George's life intervened. *"They"* were still making plans.

George took Casey's hand. "What is it, Casey?"

"'We.' 'Us.'"

George drew his finger across her cheek. "Be patient, Case. It takes time to iron out all the pronouns." He kissed her gently. "I've got to go now, but I'll call. And thanks." He patted the leather picture frame in his pocket and headed for the porch stairs. "Would you mind returning the books for me?" he asked.

Casey nodded. She offered a brave smile and then turned away so she wouldn't have to watch him leave. As she reached the door, George intercepted her, kissing her with a hunger that would make her dreams shudder. When he finally pulled away, all he could say was, "Soon."

Chapter Thirteen

Early Friday evening, Ron pulled his BMW into a parking slot in front of Merrill's Jewelry. Ron would be late for cocktail hour, but if he arrived bearing gifts, his wife would forgive him.

"Good evening, Mr. Swain. The pearls are lovely. Merrill produced a narrow box with a string of large Tahitian black pearls and a smaller box of matching earrings. Elegant. Perfect for Mariko's slender neck. He slid a credit card across the counter.

"Would you like them giftwrapped, sir?" Merrill waved to three long rolls of wrapping paper hanging behind the cash register.

"Absolutely." Ron selected the creamy beige paper and matching ribbon. Mariko loved gift-wrapped surprises.

Ron had once asked Mariko why she spent so much time wrapping gifts when they would just be ripped open. She explained that, in Japan, a present wasn't complete unless it was wrapped. Wrapping honored the occasion and increased the value of the gift. The covering could be an exquisite work of art or an inexpensive tissue, depending upon the value of the gift and the stature of the recipient.

As he watched Merrill's deft fingers twist the ribbon into a graceful bow, Ron imagined Mariko's onyx eyes dancing in anticipation. A tidy little package, just right for Mariko. And Mariko was a tidy little package, just right for Ron. He ran his fingers through his hair and smiled. He loved his little package, but once in a while, he appreciated the other gifts life had to offer. Jules had been unbelievable this evening. He could be rough with her, and he didn't have to worry about hurting her. Good thing he and Mariko

80

were going out for dinner with the Watsons. Mr. Lucky would have time to recover.

He signed the charge with a long, bold flourish. Walking down the street to the pharmacy, he tucked the necklace in his breast pocket and the earrings in his trousers. Mariko could discover them. When he paid for Mariko's prescription, he admired his signature once again. Ronald Goodrich Swain.

Ron unlocked the BMW and slid into the leather seat. He stuffed the prescription in the glove compartment and then checked out his tie in the rearview mirror. A little six o'clock shadow. Jules would have whisker burn. Tonight it had been hard to keep her attention long enough to nail her. He laughed but his mood shifted as he headed toward home. She was becoming a problem. His smile dissolved to a grim line. He couldn't let pleasure interfere with business. Slowing down, he willed his mind to replace Jules with Mariko.

As he waved to the guard at the entrance to the new, gated community, the knots of tension in his shoulders began to relax. He turned into his driveway and gazed at the lovely home he'd built for Mariko. Who would have ever thought he would marry the woman of his dreams, and live in the finest home in town?

The first time he'd seen Mariko, he was gambling in Vegas, on R & R from the Marine Corps. The dealer greeted the players with a polite bow and a soft Asian accent. When her black almond eyes met his, he was paralyzed. He couldn't recall playing the hand, just the overwhelming magnetic pull when her eyes locked briefly with his. Although she looked away demurely, he sensed her heightened awareness of him when she cleared the board and replaced the chips.

From that moment on, she played him like a harp. Not that she was an angel. Her delicate fingers knew the full spectrum of erotic melodies, and her eyes, wide with innocence one moment, would be sultry and ripe with promise the next. She drove him wild.

"You okay, Ron-san?"

Ron jumped, surprised to see Mariko at the car door watching him. He gave her a sheepish grin and cut the ignition. How long had he been idling in the driveway? He shifted the earring box in his trousers a little closer to Mr. Lucky. He patted his breast pocket. "Surprises tonight," he teased, leading the way to the door.

Chapter Fourteen

Friday nights were always busy at the Gourd, and tonight was no exception. Art lit a cigarette behind the bar during a lull in orders. The long evening had started early when the after-work, blue collar crowd dropped in for a few pops. They were a boisterous group, calling back and forth between booths, joking and heckling.

By five o'clock, the rough-and-ready drinkers were replaced by clutches of office workers, eager for gossip and a few risqué jokes. Whisper, whisper, whisper, and then a booth erupted at a punch line or a destroyed reputation.

Jules entered and ordered white wine at the bar. She wore a starched cotton blouse and a short skirt, with low heels, the picture of a wholesome Midwestern American beauty queen. She flashed Art a dazzling smile and winked for payment, and then, to his surprise and disappointment, left. Usually, she sat on a barstool and chatted with him for at least one or two glasses.

Throughout the evening, diners sat at the bar with pre-dinner cocktails waiting for tables to clear in the restaurant. Between eleven and twelve o'clock, the hardcore crowd settled down to earnest drinking. A few couples not ready to call it a night cuddled and groped in the privacy of the booths along the walls. A thin cloud of smoke hovered over the singles along the bar, mesmerized by the flickering images of a TV. Art tossed a tip into a tin cup next to the register, wiped down the bar, and began washing glasses in preparation for last call.

Elmer Duffey twisted around on his stool toward the kitchen. "Here comes trouble," he announced. He swiveled back to the bar and hunched protectively over his drink, sliding an ashtray closer for ergonomic smoking. Every Friday night he sat on the same stool, wearing the same clothes and drinking the same Scotch.

Jules had returned for the curtain call. He turned to watch her entrance. Trouble indeed. The stark light behind her accentuated Jules' curves and transformed her hair into a caramel aura. She'd changed into a tight black leather skirt, fishnet stockings, and a short-sleeved, blue angora sweater that hugged her torso. Art took a drag on the cigarette he kept lit behind the bar and poured her a glass of wine. As she climbed on the barstool, he noticed a nasty bruise on her cheek.

"Evening, Jules."

"Where's everybody?" she asked brightly, a little too loud for the established ambience.

"Well, I'm right here," grunted Elmer. He laughed and wheezed.

Jules smiled, "Sorry, Elmer. Didn't see you there."

"Hard to miss," he wheezed again, ending in a productive smoker's cough, swallowing when he couldn't spit.

Jules rolled her eyes, then surveyed the players at the end of the bar, an English instructor and his boyfriend.

"Mind if I play some music?" She held out her hand for change for the jukebox. Time for the sad songs. Art retrieved a handful of quarters from the tin cup of stored tips. He reached out as if to give her the coins, but at the last moment gently turned her face with his forefinger, studying the swelling on her cheek.

"What happened?" he asked quietly.

"I fell and hit my head on the doorjamb." Art felt her warmth on his fingers and the scent of her favorite *L'Air du Temps* perfume. When she looked up into his eyes and smiled, he caught his breath. Her changeable eyes were deep lavender, melding with the cornflower blue of her sweater and the smoky shadows of the bar. He snapped an imaginary mental shutter to capture the moment for eternity.

She uncurled his fingers. "Honest," she added over her shoulder as she walked to the jukebox.

"Was the doorjamb named 'Ron'?" Art instantly regretted his words.

"Actually, the doorjamb was George." She slotted coins and pushed the letter and number combinations of her favorites.

Art frowned. George? George was off to some conference. That's why she was on the prowl. She was covering for Ron. Art had seen his black BMW in the lot earlier.

He lit another cigarette and watched Jules lean over the jukebox. It didn't look like she had anything on under that skirt, but he couldn't tell for sure in the haze. He tore his eyes away, poured another brew for the instructor, and topped off Elmer's Scotch.

He made a last-call tour of the booths, taking orders from the couples still upright, averting his eyes as he passed the clutch in the corner. The slow lament of Patsy Cline singing "Crazy" broke over him as he cleared and wiped off a table.

"Anybody wanna dance?" Jules called out from the jukebox. A few heads turned, but no one responded.

"What'samatter with the men in this town? C'mon, Elmer. Dance with me."

"Jesus, Jules. Leave him alone. Time to pack it in." Although Elmer was smiling, Art knew he was sensitive about his prosthetic leg.

"Then you dance with me, Artie," begged Jules.

"Go home, Jules. I've got to clean up here." He escaped behind the bar before she could intercept him. Nothing he would love more than to hold her in his arms and slowly circle the floor, but he wasn't a total masochist.

"Crazy," Jules crooned along with Patsy. She held up her arms and danced with an imaginary partner, gliding slowly around the room.

Art followed her graceful movements and listened to her voice break and cry along with Patsy. "Sorry about that, Elmer."

"No problem. Good thing she don't have to drive. She's a handful, that one." He laughed and threw back his Scotch.

Jules twirled for the finale, bumped into a chair, and lurched against a table.

"Oh, Lord!" Art rushed around the bar. "Let's go." She clung to him as he walked toward the kitchen. He opened the door and called to the galley for Jim the cook to close the bar.

He carried Jules out the kitchen door and down three steps, reluctantly putting her down on the cobblestones. He glanced upward and caught sight of Martha in the kitchen window glaring down at them.

Jules lurched sideways and then threw her arms around his neck, nuzzling her face between his chin and chest. "Omigod, Jules," Art objected, but he didn't extricate himself from her embrace.

She'd left the back door to the Kenworthy apartment wide open. Art sat her at the kitchen table and made a quick circuit of the house to make certain there weren't any unexpected visitors. As he opened the door to the master bedroom, he smelled the acrid stench of cigar. He flipped on the lights. Jules' early evening, all-Ohio outfit was piled in a heap at the base of a rumpled, unmade bed. He slammed the door and stopped checking rooms. *Damn her to hell.*

When he got back to the kitchen, Jules was bent low over the kitchen table, a single-edged razor blade poised in her right hand. "No! Jules, don't!" he cried, seizing her hand as she lowered the razor.

Jules laughed, raising a cloud of white powder. "Damn. Now I'll have to start over."

But Art wasn't paying attention. His eyes were riveted on a stunning aquamarine ring on Jules' right hand.

"What are you doing with *that?*"

"Snorting it, silly. What do you think I'm—"

"*This.*" Art clamped his hand around her wrist and drew her hand level with her eyes.

"Oh." She looked up slowly without moving her head, giving him her most endearing smile. He watched her eyes harden when she realized he was having none of her turn-on routine.

"Let me go." She pulled her hand away and rose to refill her wine glass.

He blocked her path.

She sagged back into her chair and looked at the ring. "Casey gave it to me after your mother died."

"Nice try. Casey told me that Mom was cremated in her blue suit, wearing her aquamarine ring."

"I doubt that you'll ever understand this…" she began.

"Try me."

"Your mother was like a second mother to me. A real one. My mother hated my guts. She wouldn't even talk to me after—"

"The ring." He was beyond caring about Jules' family problems.

"When your mother died, Casey was a mess and you got so drunk Casey had to tell you about the service." Jules stared at him in an attempt to regain moral ground.

"Go on."

"Casey asked me to help select clothes for your mother to wear in the casket. We made it through the clothing, the jewelry and her glasses. But then Casey broke down looking at shoes. I held her for a while and we both cried. Later, I told Casey I'd deliver the clothes to the funeral home."

"And you kept the ring."

"She was going to be cremated," Jules wailed. "Casey was dressing her up to be cremated. Don't you understand?" she sobbed. "I wanted to keep something of hers with me." Jules put her head in her hands on the table and cried.

He walked to the door, confused and furious. "So, you've had the ring all this time. How come I never saw it before?"

"I kept it in a safe deposit box. When I saw it this morning, I couldn't bear to leave it behind. I never thought you'd…please, please, don't go," she cried as he opened the door. He turned to see her face streaming with mascara tears. "Help me, Art. Don't leave. Everyone wants part of me, but no one but you wants the whole thing." Her voice broke as she cried and spoke at the same time. She reached for the wine bottle, but he was faster. "You and Casey were the only ones who ever loved me, and she hates me now. You did love me, didn't you?"

Art held the half-full wine bottle to the light and then raised it to his lips and drained it. It was the only thing he could do to help her. "I'll always love you."

At this, she broke down completely. Her whole body wracked with long, heaving sobs. He cradled her head against his midriff, rocking her slowly, stroking her hair, and talking to her in soft tones as if he were gentling a skittish horse. "Time to call it a night."

She rose as if to obey, but then stopped at the counter and took a plastic packet out of a canister.

His compassion whiplashed to anger. He was on dangerous emotional ground, and the wine wasn't helping. "How long have you been doing that?"

"Since school. Everybody did it. Except Casey. I got her to try it once, but she didn't like it. 'It'll kill you, Jules,' she said. But she's the one who went to prison. Served her right."

She laughed and hiccupped and then broke into sobs again. "I told them Charley made a mistake, but no one believed me. Casey set me up, but Charley got the wrong bike."

"Charley?" Art probed. Jules wasn't making sense, but then, he was surprised that she could even speak. She pushed back from the table and waited a second before trying to stand. He caught her as her knees gave way. "Enough talking. Let's get you to bed, sweetheart."

Chapter Fifteen

Jules sat on the floor in the corner of a small room. Above her, the walls expanded and collapsed. The ceiling spiraled, slowly at first but then faster and faster. Her stomach rushed to her throat. She thrust her head between her knees, sucking in long gasps of musty air, forcing back the insistent bile.

The wave passed. Straightening, she leaned against the wall. But something was wrong. The wall was breathing. Jules lurched forward, dry heaves silencing her scream. Everything went black.

When she regained consciousness, warm arms surrounded her from behind, propping her up.

"Where am I? Turn ona light." Her words slurred. Her tongue was a swollen cotton pad fouled with vomit and wine. So thirsty. Dizzy.

"In the cellar."

Twisting toward the voice behind her, Jules lost her balance, but helping hands immediately righted her.

"Steady now. Drink this."

One hand gently tilted her head back and another pressed cool metal against her parched lips. A heavenly stream of nectar washed over her tongue and down her throat. Velvety smooth, like coconut milk in a piña colada. She drank greedily until she had to stop to breathe.

"Thanks," she said. She leaned back against the warm body.

"But you're not finished."

Again the cup pressed against her lips. This time she drank slowly, draining the cup.

"That's better."

Must be dreaming. Or stoned. Had to wake up. She shook her head. Lightning bolts pierced her skull. Moaning, she pressed her fingers against the throbbing veins in her temples.

"Here, let me." Fingers gently massaged the sides of her head in a slow, circular motion.

Jules closed her eyes savoring the rhythmic pressure. Her head wobbled like a bowling ball. The weight behind her shifted. She heard liquid pouring.

"Just a little more."

"No." She turned her head aside like a petulant child, crying out as new spikes shot through her skull. She pushed the cup away, spilling liquid down her front. "Damn! All over my…" But these weren't her clothes. The material felt scratchy, coarse. Too tired to worry about it. "Lemme sleep."

"Sleep? All right."

Hands rolled her over slowly until a blanket enveloped her like a cocoon. So blessedly warm. An arm cradled her head, while fingers caressed her cheek and stroked her hair. Jules closed her eyes and burrowed into the blanket.

"Oh! There's still a little more in the cup."

A hand grabbed her hair and yanked her head back. A rough object jammed between her teeth, forcing her jaw open. She struggled in her cocoon, but couldn't move. Her final scream drowned in a choking gurgle as nectar flooded her throat.

Chapter Sixteen

At six-thirty Saturday morning, Crockett angled his cruiser behind the ambulance at the Gourd. He jogged around to the courtyard and met Watson at the Kenworthy back door.

"Find George?" Crockett asked.

"Nope. Faculty office is locked, and his car's not in the parking lot. Jenny checked Highway Patrol. No accidents with a Civic." They followed the sound of voices to the basement door. Watson led Crockett down the stairs and stopped at the bottom step. "You don't need to be here. I got it under control."

"Lord, it stinks in here! Open that little window up there and help me get her out of this blanket. She's a mess." Martha's nasal nag shattered the air.

Crockett pushed past Watson. A bare bulb lit his way across the uneven floor, past a mammoth furnace toward a row of coal bins. He ducked under the lintel of a corner room with Watson hot on his heels. A group of crime scene experts milled around in the tiny space, talking in clusters. Looked like a cocktail party. In the corner, a photographer perched precariously with one foot on a chair and the other on an old desk, angling for an overhead shot.

"Watson, clear the room!"

Silence. Everyone stopped in freeze-frame. Crockett lowered his voice but didn't conceal his anger. "Everyone out but you, Watson." When no one moved, Crockett flung his arm toward the door. "Now!" he bellowed. As a unit, they jumped and reluctantly obeyed. All but Martha who remained bent over Jules.

"Martha, get away from her! Upstairs!"

Martha rose, her eyes sliding over Crockett as if he were an oil spill. She threw a dishcloth on the floor and followed her jaw out of the room.

Crockett knelt beside Jules who was wrapped in a blanket on the floor, willing her body to move, to sit up and laugh in her teasing way. Bruised and dirty, she looked like a discarded doll, her unblinking, bloodshot eyes staring at the ceiling.

Even in disarray, she was a beauty. But her energy was gone. Only a vacant shell remained. Crockett swallowed hard and looked away, his anger temporarily abated by the travesty before him. He rose and surveyed the photo equipment, jackets, and medical bags strewn across the floor. "Secure the scene," he ordered. As he turned away from the corpse, his foot tipped over a bottle of all-purpose spray cleaner. "Un-fuckin'-believable! Few minutes more, Martha would've washed and waxed the floor."

"Whaddya all blown up about...sir?" Watson whined.

"Anyone with her when she died?"

"No. Jim—you know, the cook—found her when he came down for supplies. He called Martha. She called us."

"Where's Art?"

Watson shrugged.

"Know what to do at an unattended death, Captain?"

"Yeah, sure. But this is an overdose."

Crockett turned toward Watson, his eyes lidded. When he spoke his voice was slow and dangerously gentle. "We have to investigate an unattended death. Can you *prove* Mrs. Kenworthy was an overdose? Could she be a suicide? How about foul play? One piece of evidence might tell the story. Anything left that could help us figure what happened?"

"Yeah. Matter of fact I found this under the kitchen table upstairs." Watson pulled a plastic baggie from his back pocket and tossed it to Crockett.

Instinctively, Crockett caught it, adding his fingerprints to the bag. He swore and glowered at Watson. "Every piece of evidence touched or cleaned up? High profile police fuck-up two weeks before graduation. Connolly'll split a gut."

"Guess I'm glad you're here after all, *Chief*. Wouldn't want to take all the heat alone."

In his mind's eye, Crockett's hands circled Watson's throat, squeezing harder and harder until his weasel eyes popped to the floor. Satisfying, but he wasn't going to wreck his career strangling Dougie Watson.

"OK. OK. We shouldn't have touched stuff." Watson nodded at the baggie in Crockett's hand, including Crockett in the "we." "No big deal. Don't have to prove a thing. Medical Examiner will say she was loaded with drugs and booze."

Crockett shook his head to dispel his anger. This tragedy was not about Watson. "Got to learn respect for the dead, Captain."

Watson squared his shoulders and hitched his belt. "Why respect her dead? Didn't respect her living. She was a mess! Ask Martha. Ask anyone." Watson warmed to his own defense. "No reason to march in here and make a scene in front of everybody."

Crockett turned back to Jules. "Why not suicide?"

"Martha said it had to be an accidental overdose 'cause Jules was too vain to be found looking such a mess. Made sense to me. Suicide, overdose, she's still dead. What's it matter?"

What's it matter? Crockett didn't respond. It mattered a hell of a lot to those left behind. Now George and Gabby, maybe even Casey, would be saddled with questions, nagging doubts, unfinished business, and guilt.

Crockett studied Jules, forcing himself to take in the details of her ruin. "Overdose. That all? Beautiful woman, young wife, mother. Cold and alone in the cellar, rolled up in a blanket. You talk like she was a piece of meat gone bad."

"Well, she was a well-known piece. And she was baaad." Watson chuckled. "Half the town saw her drunk last night, and the other half probably slept with her."

Crockett's fist splintered the pine boards inches from Watson's head.

"Jesus!" Watson threw up his arms to ward off another blow.

Crockett rubbed his knuckles, forcing his anger inward.

"Crockett! Get up here. We've got a problem!" Martha hollered down the

93

stairwell.

No shit.

"Gabby's missing!"

Chapter Seventeen

"No!" Casey woke up on the floor in a cold sweat fighting with her sheets. She sat up and turned on the bedside light to dispel the hideous images populating her brain. This morning she could easily identify the catalysts for her nightmare: seeing Jules in the cemetery, Gabby racing into Jules' welcoming embrace, and the Wicked Witch from *OZ*.

She glanced at the clock over the refrigerator: seven o'clock. She pulled on a robe and crept down the hallway to the kitchen. In the early morning, she had the place to herself. Rummaging behind the toaster oven she found Mae's secret stash of ginger snaps and took a carton of milk from the refrigerator.

The prison psychologist made a distinction between her "gothic novel" dreams and her "revenge" dreams. Gothic dreams were romantic daydreams she could summon and dismiss at will. In prison, these dreams ran unchecked like background music beneath the hard, outer patina she wore for protection. Late at night, she'd invite the past to creep over her, replaying her favorites, embellishing them with finales that found her in George's arms.

Her revenge dreams were so repressed that they only surfaced in night-mares. In these dreams, Jules was killed in an automobile accident, stricken by a hideously deforming disease, or, in a recurring dream, took her own life. Regardless of the horror inflicted, George was free.

The psychologist asked Casey why she rained death and destruction on Jules, while sparing George, when both had betrayed her. Casey explained that Jules had never loved George. She'd used him and railroaded him into a reluctant marriage.

"Oh, poor George," the counselor clucked. "Everything happened so fast. He must have been confused. He had to get back to Yale. He was too busy to pick up the phone or walk to the police station. Too busy being seduced by your best friend."

Casey had bridled at his sarcasm, but the counselor advised her to ask why George had abandoned her to face the charges alone, and how it had come to pass that he married Jules within months of her arrest.

Anxiety tightened in her chest as her thoughts began spinning. Just as she dismissed one negative thought, two more popped up in its place, multiplying and dividing like crazed amoebae. She paced the kitchen, her frustration mounting with each turn. She fought the temptation to cry by draining the carton of milk. She'd cried enough. "Soon," she whispered softly. Soon she'd have her turn.

Strange. She cocked an ear at a faint knocking. It sounded like someone was at the front door, but when she walked to the door and looked through the pane, no one was there. Just her overworked imagination. As she turned away, she recognized the creak of hinges from the front porch swing.

Her brother Art sat in the swing with his head in his hands. She smelled the alcohol from ten feet away.

"Art?" Casey rushed to him. "What's wrong?" She sat on the swing and put her arm around his shoulder. "What happened?"

He moaned and tried to speak, but his words slurred and didn't make sense. She stroked his hair and waited until he could talk.

"I killed her," he whispered between sobs.

Killed? He killed Martha? No. Impossible. He wasn't a violent drunk; he passed out when he'd had too much.

Art raised his head, his ruined eyes staring at nothing at all. "Cold. Her skin was so cold. She didn't blink. All wrapped up in a blanket."

"Come on inside. I'll make some coffee."

"Sober me up?" Art gave a deprecating laugh. "That's what Martha said." He looked at Casey. "Why would I want to do that?"

"Martha?" Art wasn't making sense.

"She threw me out when I refused coffee. She didn't want the police... didn't want them to see me drunk." Art swallowed hard. "God, I loved her. Couldn't help it. I don't want to see another day. I came here because you're the only other person who really loved her. Once."

"Jules," Casey whispered.

Art nodded, unable to continue.

"Art, you're not making sense. You could never kill Jules."

"I tried to help her. She was so unhappy." Art lurched to his feet.

"Where are you going?"

"To crawl under a log with this bottle." He patted his jacket. "You can't help me now, sis. I'm sorry."

Casey watched him walk away, knowing he didn't want her to follow. She shivered and rocked back and forth on the swing trying to remember his exact words. "Cold," he'd said. "Her skin was so cold." "I killed her."

Jules was dead. Casey's mind was paralyzed by shock, hope, and guilt. George was free. She'd wished Jules dead so many times. She was so easy to hate. But now there was an empty place in the world where Jules should be. Art was right. She'd loved Jules. Casey wiped away an unexpected tear and swallowed hard, betrayed by a growing lump in her throat.

They'd shared secrets and lies, failures, crushes, and dreams. But neither her best friend nor the love of her life had helped Casey when she needed them most. They married and trotted off to Yale and had a darling little baby girl while she rotted in a cell for ten years burning with anger and hate.

The last time she'd seen Jules, she sashayed down the street, gorgeous, reckless, and full of life, giving Ron Swain a kiss and waiting for Dumbo to collect Gabby. Casey's eyes refilled thinking of the little girl, now a motherless child. She wondered if she'd miss hating Jules as much as she'd missed loving her.

The phone rang inside. Casey rose to answer it, but then sank back on the swing and let it ring. She couldn't talk now. What if it were George? Did he know? He said he'd call her.

Thump. Thump.

Oh, no. Casey passed Mae in the hallway and picked up on the fifth ring.

"Casey? It's Crockett. Afraid I have bad news. Martha found Jules in the cellar early this morning. Looks like she overdosed." Crockett paused. "Sorry, Casey. Watson took the call. She was dead when he arrived."

"Oh, no," was all Casey could manage.

"Casey, I need your help."

"Help?"

"That's why I'm calling. Gabby's missing. She may be hiding. George and Art are out somewhere. Martha says you know this place inside out."

"On my way." She hung up, raced to her room, and dressed. On the way out the door, she told Mae that Jules had overdosed and Gabby was missing. Before Mae could ask questions, Casey jumped on her bike and was gone.

Chapter Eighteen

Casey jumped the curb and ploughed across the pasture to the back of the Gourd. Poor Gabby! Had she seen her mother? Why else would she hide? Her wheels skidded over the wet cobblestones of the courtyard. Ditching the bike by the well, she ran to the Kenworthy back door. Crockett met her in the kitchen.

"Find her?" panted Casey.

"Nope. Looked everywhere. She's gone."

The cellar door swung open and Martha grumbled in. She hiked up the hem of a ratty terrycloth bathrobe to clear the threshold. Casey stared. Without makeup, Martha's face looked like a ball of pastry before it was rolled out.

"I just checked the cellar again." Martha addressed Casey without greeting, the same way she talked on the telephone.

"Thought you locked her in her room after you found Jules." Crockett turned to Casey. "Come upstairs. Maybe you can figure it out." He led the way to Gabby's room above the kitchen. "Locked from the outside." Crockett gestured to a skeleton key still in the lock. A tray with a half-eaten frozen dinner and a juice cup sat on a child's table.

"Have you seen her little pack anywhere? The one with the yellow ducks and purple bunnies she hauls everywhere?" Casey asked.

Martha shook her head.

"Where's Ralphie?"

"Ralphie?" Crockett was confused.

"Gabby's little dog," explained Martha. She fiddled with a curler that had escaped from beneath a pink plastic cap. "He ran out of Gabby's room when I looked in on her this morning. Haven't seen him since."

Casey forced herself to concentrate. Could Gabby have used the passageway under the eaves? She skirted the bed and bent down under the sloping ceiling to unlatch the door to a storage area. She and Jules crawled through the storage way that connected between rooms as kids.

"We already looked in there. The door on the other side is blocked with a heavy dresser."

Casey approached a tall antique armoire.

"That's the first place we looked. We've been over this room with a fine-tooth comb. C'mon downstairs, I'll make coffee."

Crockett and Martha left the room, but Casey stayed behind. She opened the double doors of the armoire. Inside, Gabby's clothes hung on a low rod. Casey pushed them aside and reached deep inside to the back panel. She tapped from left to right. Tap. Tap. Tap. Nothing. No resistance.

"Damn!" An adult couldn't squeeze past the waist-high rod, but Gabby wouldn't have a problem. Casey dumped the clothing on the floor and wrenched the rod from its sockets. The backboard inside the armoire had been painted black to disguise a panel door that slid sideways. It was open.

Crockett pounded up the stairs. Casey stepped into the armoire, groped for the metal pole she knew was beyond the panel, and jumped. She hugged the pole like a fireman and dropped straight down. Too fast! She squeezed the pole to slow her descent, but it was like skydiving in the dark without a parachute. She hoped no one had sealed off the trap door on the first floor. Fine time to think—

Her feet hit planks that buckled under her weight, giving way on both sides of the pole. Slowed by the trap door, she made a perfect landing on the clubhouse floor below. Above her, heavy springs pulled the planks back up to their original position.

Casey looked around the old clubhouse, wishing to God that it hadn't come to this. She'd hated Jules for ten years, but she'd loved her far longer. Unbelievable. Jules was gone. Later. She'd be dead for a long time. Right now Casey had to find Gabby.

Dropping to her hands and knees, she crawled under the desk to the wall. Something moved under her hand! She jumped and banged her head. Groping around, her fingers found a round, metallic object. Omigod. She jammed a small tin cup into her jacket pocket. What was Art's little cup doing down here?

"Please God, no," she prayed as she raised a piece of rough burlap covering a section of the wall. The slats that should have blocked the entrance to the tunnel leaned against the wall.

"*Gabby?*" she cried.

Casey backed away and broke the police tape as she dashed from the clubhouse, up the stairs, through the kitchen, out the back door, and across the patio to the well.

A large pot of flowers sat on the wooden cover that protected the mouth of the well. She sent the pot crashing to the ground and lifted up one side of the hinged cover.

"Gabby, can you hear me? Gabby! Answer me, please," Casey begged. She cocked her head, listening. Nothing. She peered into the darkness and called again. No answer. *If she fell in*—Casey stifled the thought. *But if she didn't...*

Casey ran to the barn and threw her weight against the oversized door, riding it as it rolled sideways on metal runners. Inside it was dark and quiet. She held her breath listening, waiting for her eyes to adjust before walking down the central planking between the stalls that lined both sides of the barn.

"Gabby," she called softly, forcing her voice to calm. "Don't be afraid. Just stay where you are." Silence. She continued to talk while closing in on a far corner stall. "I just want to make sure you and Ralphie are okay." As she got closer, she heard a light, rhythmic thumping.

She pushed open the Dutch door. A straw mound in the corner wiggled and whimpered. Ralphie's black tail emerged and beat a shy welcome against the wall, raising motes of dust and straw.

"Hi, guys." Casey kept her voice low and soft, talking to the mound as she approached. She knelt and brushed pieces of dirt and straw from Gabby's upturned face. Gabby quivered, hugging Ralphie. Her eyes were enormous orbs, like a baby owl in a nest.

Gabby reached out to her and began to sob. Casey gathered girl and dog into her arms and rocked them, slowly, back and forth, making gentling sounds. Tears of relief streamed down her face.

"Casey? Casey! Where the hell are you?" Crockett's voice thundered through the barn. Gabby's body stiffened.

"It's OK, Gabby. That's Crockett. He's my friend."

"Noooooo." Gabby squirmed to break loose, but Casey instinctively tightened her hold. "Really, he's nice. Look. Ralphie isn't scared." But Ralphie, sensing Gabby's fear, began a low, warning growl as Crockett's heavy footsteps neared the stall.

"Hush, Crockett. Gabby's scared," Casey called, but her warning came too late. Crockett's bulk filled the doorway.

Gabby screamed.

Startled, Crockett scowled and backed away. He slid down the side of the stall into the straw, turning sideways to make himself look smaller. Casey hugged the hysterical child to her, stroking her hair and rocking until the sobs turned to sniffles. Gabby stopped struggling, but remained tense. Her eyes never left Crockett's face.

Crockett's eyelids lowered. Casey reached over and touched his shoulder. "Sorry, Crockett," but nothing she could say would erase the terror in Gabby's eyes.

Shifting attention back to Gabby, she made the introductions. "Gabby, meet Crockett." She pushed a stray curl from Gabby's forehead. "He's a very nice man. He's a friend of mine." She rolled her eyes at Crockett and prayed that he'd understand. "Crockett, this is Gabby and her dog, Ralphie."

Crockett was silent for a long moment. Then he spoke to Gabby in a soft voice. "Actually, Crockett's my big person name. Most kids call me JoJo. Always have. You can call me JoJo, too." He looked away to give Gabby time to study him.

A hush came over the child as she watched him woo her dog by wiggling his fingers and making encouraging clucking sounds. Ralphie sniffed his hand warily and then gave a tentative wag as the big fingers caressed the magic place behind his ears.

"JoJo," whispered Gabby.

Crockett's face broke into a slow smile.

Chapter Nineteen

After Gabby left with Grandma Loveland, Casey joined Crockett at the breakfast table in the Kenworthys' kitchen. At first Gabby had been reluctant to leave, but she changed her mind when she was told that her grandmother had chocolate ice cream, and the alternative was a nap.

"She okay?" Crockett asked, worry wrinkling his brow.

"Hard to tell. She hasn't asked for her mother again. She must know that something's dreadfully wrong."

"Got to get hold of George. Martha said he left last night for a Civil War conference. Jenny reached the conference headquarters. He hasn't registered for any sessions yet. State Police don't have anything."

Martha entered, drawing stares from Crockett and Casey. Soft brunette curls framed her face. Dark lashes and eyebrows contrasted dramatically with her delicate, china-doll complexion. She had sculpted her mouth with lipstick pencil and filled it in with complementary layers of mauve lipstick. Her entrance was preceded by the light touch of floral perfume. Martha had transformed herself into classic perfection in beige slacks and matching sweater set. *Daytime elegance*, thought Casey, aware of her own crummy jeans and sneakers.

"You can quit gawking any time." Martha measured ground coffee into a filter. "I closed the Gourd for business. We had a reception scheduled, and a bunch of dinner reservations." With a deep sigh, she poured water into the coffee maker, and then looked up with a mournful smile that would do a funeral director proud.

Martha prattled on, her nervous energy filling in the silent spaces left by Casey and Crockett. "No one ever sees me without makeup. Not you. Not Gabby." She pushed the button to start the coffee. "Not even Art. The only time he saw my morning face, he said it was grounds for divorce."

Crockett interrupted her chatter. "Martha. Casey, too. Sorry to add to your burden. Art was drinking in the bar when Jim came to work early this morning. Jim tried to talk with him, but Art grabbed a bottle and left."

After a moment's silence, Casey stole a look sideways at Martha. The earlier animation drained from her face, leaving a resigned, all-suffering expression. "He isn't back yet. He was pretty upset to see Jules and needed to be alone."

Casey couldn't tell if Martha was experiencing a genuine emotion or putting on one of her finer performances. Seconds later mascara tears eroded Martha's pancake makeup. She wasn't that good an actress.

With each tear, Casey felt her animosity dissolve. Martha was the only reason Art had been sober all these years. Casey hadn't been any good for him in prison. Her conviction was probably one of the reasons he hit the bottle in the first place. She rose and offered her outstretched arms to her sister-in-law. "I'm really sorry, Martha. This year must have been hell for you."

Martha shrank from her touch. "Hell because *she* came back, or hell because *you* did? I don't want your pity. *You* of all people!"

Casey backed off, stunned by the abrupt shift from sorrow to raw hatred in Martha's eyes,

"Yes, *you*! Jules was a shameless whore, but you're no better."

Crockett inserted himself between them like a referee. "Enough! Show me how Gabby escaped from a locked room," he demanded, steering Casey by the elbow toward the stairs.

"Let go, Crockett. I can show you right here in the kitchen." Crockett released her but stayed close behind as she led him to a walk-in pantry.

The room was packed with supplies: paper and cleaning products to the left, dried foods to the right. Shelves on the far wall were laden with bottled and canned goods. Casey knelt and ran her hand over the wall behind the cans on the bottom shelf. She pushed and jumped aside when the whole wall swung toward her like a door.

"Damn!" muttered Crockett. Before them was a windowless, bare room the size of a linen closet that had no ceiling. A metal pole ran vertically through the center.

"The armoire in Gabby's room is directly above us. It has a false back that slides to give access to the same pole. See this?" Casey pointed to a leather handle on the inside of the moving wall. Crockett leaned forward, but she waved him back. "Just grab the handle, jump, close the door, and ride. Watch!"

For the second time, Casey rode the pole to the cellar, landing inside the clubhouse. Quickly, she picked up a dishrag from the floor to wipe her fingerprints off places she might have touched when she'd come to get Martha's handwriting.

Something stunk! She threw the rag to the floor, but the stench of vomit remained on her hands. She cast about for something else to wipe down the hilt of the sword. Heavy footsteps lumbered down the cellar stairs. *No time!* She dashed out of the room and met Crockett and Martha at the foot of the stairs.

"Show me where you landed," Crockett ordered.

Casey led them to the corner room. "This was our clubhouse."

Crockett fingered the broken tape and swore under his breath. "You were in here, *too?*" He cast an accusatory glance at Casey.

Crockett's anger surprised her. "I was trying to find Gabby. How was I supposed to know where it happened?"

He instantly eased off. "What the hell's this?" He pointed to the cat's eye symbol on the door.

Casey ignored his attempt at distraction. "Do you mind if I walk along the side of the room, *Chief*? To show you where I landed." Before he could respond, she entered and snatched the Sword of the Spirit off the wall and brandished it in the air.

She cocked her head to listen as she tapped the ceiling with the tip of the sword. The sound changed abruptly from blunt to hollow. "Trap door," she stated. "Pole." She struck a metal pole that looked just like the other support beams in the cellar, and then handed the sword to Crockett, hilt first. Might as well add his fingerprints to it. "Slaves took the pole to escape bounty hunters."

Crockett studied the trap door for a few moments before examining the sword. "These scripture references?"

Martha cut in. "That's the Sword of the Spirit. We made the swords in Bible School. When we could recite a passage from the Bible from memory, we wrote it on the blade." Martha spoke to Crockett, but she glowered at Casey. Casey wrinkled her nose, baiting Martha, remembering how it used to infuriate her. The childish act brought the current situation crashing back. Jules. Out of the corner of her eye, Casey saw Martha stoop to pick something off the floor.

"What'cha got there?" asked Crockett.

He doesn't miss a beat, thought Casey.

"Just a stick," Martha said. "Looks like Ralphie had a go at it. Gabby liked to play down here. The dog followed her everywhere and chewed on everything. The blanket Jules was wrapped in is Ralphie's blanket."

She tossed the stick to Crockett.

"Great. Now we've touched *every* object and surface in the room. Surprised you could find anything left on the floor." He turned to Casey and explained. "Martha tidied up earlier this morning before calling the police." He rubbed his fingers over the deep indentations on the stick. "Wouldn't think the little digger had teeth this big." He toyed with the stick before asking Martha his next question. "You think Gabby saw Jules?"

Martha nodded.

"How'd she get from here to the barn without anyone seeing her?"

"I have no idea."

Casey explained. "Under the desk, there's an opening to a tunnel that leads to the well in the courtyard and then out to the barn. Slaves either climbed the metal spikes inside the well to get out, or continued through the tunnel like Gabby did. They'd climb the ladder to the hayloft and hide in the hay. If a bounty hunter climbed up to the loft, there's a rope hanging from a pole in the hayloft window. Jules and I used to jump from the window, grab the rope, and slide to the ground."

Clunk!

Casey and Crockett jumped in unison.

"What the—"

"Relax. That's the spin cycle," Martha explained.

"You're doing a wash?" Crockett stared at Martha.

Martha shrugged. "Jules threw up all over—"

"Jesus, you're *washing Jules' clothes*?"

"Yes, I am. She took them off and dumped them in the corner before she put on the choir robe." Martha pointed to another black robe hanging beside the door. "Casey and Jules stole the robes from our church. I didn't know I wasn't supposed to touch anything, and besides, why leave her filth all over the place? Captain Watson agreed that she was an overdose."

"May never know," Crockett muttered. "No fingerprints on wine glasses or bottles, no clothes. Rinsed out, thrown into the dumpster and smashed to pieces, or in the washing machine. A clean sweep."

"I was only doing what I thought—"

Crockett talked over Martha's whine. "Accident, overdose, homicide. Nothing untouched but the body to tell the story." As he spoke, Martha picked up the dishrag, holding it from a corner as if it were the tail of a dead mouse.

"Goddamn it! Drop it!" Dread registered on his face as he looked at the rag. "You didn't touch the body..."

"I just wiped her off where she'd been sick, and straightened her hair a bit."

"Give her a manicure? Hate her guts one minute, wash her up the next—" Crockett fumed.

Martha could barely contain her venom. "It wouldn't help the child to know that her mother was a drunk, a drug addict and a *whore*!" She stormed up the stairs. Seconds later, the Kenworthy door slammed.

Before Crockett could ask more questions, Casey patted the Bloody Cats Eye symbol on the clubhouse door and followed. She hesitated at the back door for a look around Jules' kitchen. It hadn't changed all that much. They'd added a dishwasher and a few new appliances.

Keys hung on a pegboard next to the door. The large key on the right opened the door to the Loveland mausoleum. No one would miss it until the funeral. Casey was dying to know what Jules had hidden in the mausoleum the day she and George were in the cemetery. She snagged the key and left.

Chapter Twenty

Crockett sank into the warm leather seat of his cruiser and lowered the windows to release the heat. He called the station from his car radio. "Anything on George?"

Jenny responded, recognizing his voice. "Nothing from the conference or the State Police."

"How about Art?"

"No. Sorry. Why are we looking for him?"

"A personal thing. Want to make sure he's okay."

"How's the little girl?"

"She's with her grandma for now." Crockett didn't try to disguise his distaste for Mrs. Loveland. "Gabby saw her mother in the cellar, but no way to tell what she understands. Alcoholics pass out all the time. Pretty freaked though. Casey found her hiding in the barn with her dog."

"Poor kid."

"Anything else?"

"Connolly was looking for you." Crockett heard the reluctance in Jenny's voice. "He's on the telephone now. I could cut in if you want me to, but if not …"

"Thanks, Jen. Rather not."

Finally, he was alone with his thoughts. Before Gabby had left with her grandmother, she asked Martha if her mother was awake yet. He summoned up the image of Casey and Gabby in the barn. Madonna and child in the manger. With a little dog. He retrieved the chewed stub of wood from his pocket. A little dog with big teeth.

He doubted that forensics would find anything. Not much in the cellar that hadn't been scoured, dusted, or screwed over by Martha and Oberlin's finest. Jules had probably taken her own life—either by accident or by design. Either way would be hard to prove, but he was bothered by so many loose ends and strange behavior. How deep into the layers of ugly truths would he have to dig to find out what really happened Friday night?

What had he expected? The cast of characters had been mixing it up for years. Brothers and sisters, teammates, friends, lovers. They were all connected, some in multiple ways. Take Art. He was Casey's brother, Martha's husband, George's friend, and was hopelessly in love with Jules. And Crockett had protected him in school from Ron and Dougie.

Today, Crockett was struck by the phony smiles, nervous chitchat, and outright lies. Casey didn't seem surprised that Jules had died, just frantic to find Gabby. Think she'd show some emotion. She and Jules had been thick as thieves. Well, they *were* little thieves. But who could expect Casey to mourn the woman who ran off with her man? Even so, Casey's behavior was bizarre, jumping down the pole, whirling like a dervish waving that crazy sword.

And Martha, Mrs. Clean, "tidying up" the corpse and throwing in a load of laundry. The change in her appearance from washerwoman to elegant housewife had been truly amazing. Her tears were genuine, but they were for Art's binge and her own loss. Her attack on Casey had shocked him. "Jules was a shameless whore, and you're no better!" Did she mean Casey was a shameless whore, or an ex-con, or both?

Even those missing were acting strangely. Art on a bender after so long sober. George unaccounted for since Friday afternoon. You'd think a man with a drunk for a wife and a small child would leave a number where he could be reached. Crockett rubbed his sore knuckles and wished he'd pasted Watson instead of the wall. Would have been softer and a lot more satisfying.

Could be he was overreacting. Maybe Art had had a bad night, and Martha was protective. George had a flat tire, and Casey was … well, he didn't know what to make of Casey.

He wanted to go home and hug his wife and little girl, but first, he had to check George's phone for possible messages. Reluctantly, he returned to the Kenworthy back door, but when he turned the knob it was locked. Mrs. Clean was efficient. He trudged to the Cavendish door, knocked, and waited for Martha to answer.

"You again, Crockett?" She didn't ask him in.

"I need the Kenworthy key."

Martha took a key from a pegboard inside the door but, instead of handing it to him, she marched across the patio and unlocked the door. Inside the Kenworthy apartment, she followed Crockett down the hallway to the telephone in George's study. No blinking lights on the answering machine. Crockett hit the "Replay" button, but all old messages had been deleted. George sure wasn't making this easier. As they left, Martha re-locked the door and marched back to the Cavendish entrance.

"Art back yet?" Crockett asked.

"He'll be back when he gets hungry. Or runs out of booze."

Crockett said a prayer of thanks for Leila. If Art were smart, he'd keep on going. "I'll be back in the morning. If George or Art come home, give me a call. And thanks for taking care of—"

Martha closed the door before he could finish his sentence.

Once again he sank into the warm leather seat of the cruiser. Still light outside. Days were getting longer. So were his hours. "Let it go, JoJo." Closing his eyes, he focused on the muscles in his neck and shoulders where he stockpiled tension. He inhaled and exhaled slowly, listening to the air entering and leaving his body and to the steady beat of his heart.

He pictured himself trudging through a dark forest carrying a heavy pack. As the trail descended to lower elevations, the aroma of pine needles in the soft cushion underfoot changed to the sweet decay of oak leaves. At the edge of the forest, he came upon a clearing flooded with golden buttercups dancing in the sun. A large pirate's chest sat amidst the blossoms.

In his mind's eye, Crockett eased the burden from his aching shoulders and transferred each one of his troubles from the pack to the chest. He locked the chest and lay down among the flowers. His troubles wouldn't go away, but he could lock them up for a little while and think about life's small miracles. Like Gabby when she whispered, "JoJo."

It still hurt that the little girl seemed to cringe from him, and it took him a few moments to channel his sorrow and anger. His high school football coach had shown him a useful trick during the last championship game. When an opposing player had taunted him with racial slurs, Crockett reacted and bumped him aggressively. After the next tackle, the jerk bumped back and they came nose to nose with words. The referee pushed between them in seconds.

Coach yanked Crockett out of the game and led him out of earshot of the bench. "You ever learn? You fell for it when Swain baited you in practice. Now that piece of white trash wants you thrown out of the game. You wanna win, you gotta play. Take two seconds for control. Two. Smile at that asshole for two seconds. Then catch the ball and run like hell.

On the next down, the player upped the ante with an insult to Crockett's mother. Crockett pretended to take the bait, counted off two, focused his rage, caught the pass and sprinted into the end zone. It worked. A few seconds was all he needed. Just this morning, two seconds allowed him to deflect Gabby's terrified reaction. Then again, he'd almost pasted Watson. Only worked with motivation.

A motion off to the right broke Crockett's reverie. A lone figure slowly hunched toward the Gourd. Crockett turned the key in the ignition and the car rolled forward. At the sound of the engine, the figure whirled about. Crockett pulled alongside.

"Hey, Art," Crockett called quietly. "Where you been?"

"I thought you'd be gone by now, Crockett," Art replied.

Chapter Twenty-One

"Ride with me a minute." Crockett reached across the front seat and pushed open the passenger door. "You look like hell."

Art slid in. "And a gracious good evening to you, too. In truth, I just awoke." Art drew a small bottle from his pocket. "Do you mind? Hair of the dog, you know." He took a long pull.

"Sleeping?"

Art drained the bottle. "In the back of Elmer's truck, my home away from home." He nodded toward a derelict vehicle in the Gourd parking lot. "I'm sorry to disappoint you, but I was *non compos mentis* most of the day." He raised the bottle in a mock toast, remembered it was empty, and caught himself just before he pitched it out the window.

"Appreciate it if you tuck that little baby right back in your jacket."

Art shrugged and jammed the bottle into his pocket. His wry smile quickly faded. He reeked of cigarettes and alcohol.

"I loved her, Crockett. I always loved her. Always will."

Crockett kept his eyes on the road. Nothing he could say. He knew Art had been in love with Jules for years, but he had assumed it ended when Art married Martha.

"I tried everything. Denial. Alcohol. Drugs. Even marriage. When Jules returned, I was able to behave myself, but at a dear price. She was so unhappy. It broke my heart to watch her destroy herself. And Martha—"

"Did Martha know?"

"Of course. She's no fool." They rode in silence for a little. "Martha patched me together after the accident and…all the rest. It was pretty bad. I wouldn't have made it through that time without her. Oh, hell, you don't want to hear all this."

Art held his right arm up and examined a jagged scar on his wrist. He'd fallen from a ladder while changing the storm windows on the second story of the Gourd. Glass severed his dreams as a piano virtuoso along with the tendons. What Art had omitted, Crockett already knew. Within a year of the accident his mother died, Casey was arrested, and Jules ran off with George. Art stayed and drank.

"Luckily or not, depending on one's perspective, Jules and I were never more than 'friends.' But I could see her every day. Could always dream." Art bowed his head. "No more."

Gently, Crockett put his hand on Art's shoulder. He felt the tremors in Art's thin frame. Crockett's policeman's eyes scanned likely trouble spots as they rode, but his ears were tuned to Art's sobs. As they made another lazy circuit around the perimeter of town, the streetlights came on, illuminating the darkening sidewalks.

"Time to go home," Art said softly.

"What's that?"

"When the streetlights came on, Casey and I had fifteen minutes to get home to the Gourd."

"Casey helped find Gabby this morning."

"She should have been Gabby's mother. God, how we mess things up!" Art must have sensed Crockett's worried glance, because he added hastily, "I'll be all right, old man. Or I will be, once I replenish my supply."

"When did you start?"

"Last night. Jules was a bit in her cups at the bar, so I walked her to her door. She opened a bottle of wine. I gallantly finished it off so she wouldn't kill herself mixing alcohol with…Christ! Listen to my pathetic excuses. If I stayed with her, she'd be alive now, but I hauled my butt to the bar." They lapsed into silence, lulled by the sound of the tires.

As they passed streetlights, Crockett caught Art's expressions in sporadic freeze frames. Even as a kid Art had reminded him of Fred Astaire with his long, droll face and cultured manners. Art had been a runt when Crockett met him in seventh grade, an asthmatic egghead who might've weighed a hundred pounds soaking wet.

Crockett was walking toward the school cafeteria when he noticed Art trotting by his side. The kid had shadowed him all week.

"I could help you in English," Art offered, craning his neck to watch Crockett's expression.

"Why'd you want to do that?" Nervy, thought Crockett.

"Because I'm smart. We could help each other."

"What you want from me?"

"See those guys—the big kid and the fat one next to him?" Art nodded toward Ron and Dougie. "If you weren't here, they'd pound the crap out of me."

"Why's that?" Crockett was amused by Art's language until he saw the fear in his eyes.

"They hate my guts. And they want my lunch money."

"So, you're smart, and I'm big, that it?" Crockett slowed his gait so Art could keep up without wheezing. He looked down at the long, pinched face. Crockett didn't need a reason to dislike Ron and Dougie, but he sure could use some help in English. "Deal," he said.

"Are you taking me home, officer?"

Art's sudden question brought Crockett back. "No other place to go, except the station. Haven't done anything wrong, have you?" Crockett jested, but his eyes searched Art's face.

"The atmosphere might be more hospitable there," said Art, "but I don't suppose you serve the type of refreshment I'll need to see me through the night. I may be the only one to mourn her passing."

He spoke too soon. When they pulled up to the Gourd, the old inn had joined Art in sorrow. The blinking stars in the tavern's sign had been turned off and the drawn window shades gave the building a melancholy expression, like a veil over its eyes. An unnatural stillness replaced its normally rowdy, Saturday night voice.

"If you are off duty, you might join me in a last toast to Jules—for old time's sake. And, if you want any further discourse with me, you'll have to come inside. I left my butts there."

"They'll kill you, Art."

"Not soon enough. C'mon. We'll go in through the restaurant and avoid the Gorgon." Art led the way, turning on the muted lights behind the bar.

Instantly Martha's voice penetrated the walls between the kitchen and the bar. "It's about time you got your little pansy ass home and put your story together. Crockett will be back tomorrow. He's not as dumb as—" Martha gasped as she barreled through the swinging kitchen door and caught up with her voice.

"A vote of confidence for our Chief of Police," announced Art, "delivered by—"

"Oh, hush." Martha turned to Crockett. "I wasn't expecting you, just my sod of a husband."

Recovered fast, thought Crockett, studying Martha. All made up, she was quite a looker. Until she opened her mouth. Revlon hadn't invented vocal makeup.

"I believe you mean 'sot,' m'dear. 'Sod' is British slang for sodomite."

"Whatever." Martha switched on the fluorescent overhead lights on her way back to the kitchen.

"Jesus, have a heart!" Art yelled after her. He walked to the kitchen door and hit the light switch. He grabbed two Buds and then flung himself into a booth across from Crockett.

As if on cue, Martha reappeared with a platter of finger sandwiches that must have been intended for the evening's canceled party. She flipped the light switch on again as she passed the doorway.

"Goddamn it! We're closed in mourning."

With a disdainful smile, Martha turned off the lights and then surprised Crockett by sliding into the booth next to Art, placing the sandwiches in front of him.

Art pushed the sandwiches across the table.

"Don't mind if I do." Crockett palmed a sandwich. "Expecting a crowd of little people tonight?"

Martha didn't smile.

117

"Got to thinking, slow as I am," he continued, snagging another spurned delicacy, "You and Casey didn't seem too broken up about Jules this morning. 'Specially surprised me with Casey. They were that thick growing up." Crockett snapped his fingers.

"Come on, Crockett!" Martha snorted. "What would you expect? Just hours after she was arrested, Jules sat right over there in the corner booth, holding hands and making eyes at the loyal George."

This morning Martha and Casey had circled one another like cats. Now Martha spoke in Casey's defense. Of course, he wasn't the only member of the audience tonight. He glanced at Art, whose skeptical expression suggested that he wasn't buying it either. "Didn't like Jules much, did you?" he asked, hoping to provoke an honest response.

"No. Although I was taken in by her charms, just like everyone else." She cast a wry smile Art's way. "It took me a long time to see under the glitter and glow. I worshiped her as a child, but she grew up to be a vain, greedy woman. She pushed too far and took more than her share. She was a drunken slut."

Art lit a cigarette, took a deep drag, and blew the smoke to one side, his idea of smoker's etiquette.

"Any idea where George might be?" Crockett asked, suddenly turning to Art.

"No. And frankly, I don't care. I'm about as fond of George as Casey was of Jules. For many of the same reasons. We both lost our best friends when George ran off with Jules."

Martha leaned forward and snorted. *"Friends?* You and Casey lost your—"

"Did you see Jules Friday night?" Crockett asked Martha.

Martha leaned back and took her time answering. "Sure. Just about everyone in town saw her. She waltzed into the kitchen around six o'clock or so, piecing."

"Piecing?"

"Yes. She'd help herself to a piece of this and a piece of that. Jules thought the world was her oyster bed, and she deserved every goddamned pearl."

"Look at the situation from a different perspective," Art interjected. "Jules owns this oyster bed. In her kitchen, she can do whatever she wants."

"Not anymore." Martha's mouth twisted into a sardonic smile. Martha grabbed the empty platter and walked to the door.

Art blew a lazy smoke ring after her. "Jules was alive long after six. She paid a second visit to the bar around eleven. Lots of people saw her then."

Martha couldn't slam a swinging door, but she flipped the light switch one last time.

Art cursed and hurled an empty beer bottle at the offending overhead light. The bottle broke on impact and the light flared and popped just before the building went dark.

"Mommy!" Gabby's plaintive voice howled from above.

"Nice work." Martha's sarcasm trailed after her up the stairs.

Chapter Twenty-Two

Crockett closed the front door of the Gourd softly, checking to make sure the lock caught. A gentle breeze washed away the cloying cigarette smoke from the bar, replacing it with the spring scent of moist soil and new grass, still warm from the day. His faithful cruiser waited for him in the Fire Lane.

Time to go home. Sit in the big chair and let Jackie jabber and climb over him, while Leila made gravy for the pork roast she'd promised this morning. Her parting kiss had promised more than a roast, if he could stay home long enough to collect.

Jenny's voice blasted out of nowhere. Instinctively, Crockett reached through the car window for the microphone. *No, damn it. Go home. You're not on duty.*

"Crockett, if you can hear me, Connolly and Drucker want you at the station. Please call in, sir. Connolly says it's an emergency."

He looked at the radio as if it were a hissing adder, puffing out venomous fangs. Strangle it? Crush it in his bare hands? Or just unplug the sucker and save himself an embarrassing expense report.

Calm down, JoJo. He grabbed the neck of the offending machine and growled. "Crockett. On my way, Jen."

He had hoped the meeting could wait until Sunday, but Connolly and Drucker were already twisted up in their underwear about graduation. Jules' death might push them over the edge. So, what was so important that they wanted him to come in late in the evening on his day off?

Tonight the town was deserted, but next week at this time it would be a madhouse. Baccalaureate, graduation, and class reunions took four days. Parents of undergraduates would arrive to gather up their progeny. Cars heaped with student belongings, Oberlin's version of low riders, would create a traffic nightmare.

Last year a few enterprising graduates rotated the street signs at the corners of Tappan Square. After a full day of complaints from lost out-of-state drivers, some wizard figured it out. The press had been quick to point out the irony of getting lost in Oberlin.

Plans for graduation included plays, concerts, parties, receptions, symposia, and a flurry of weddings. And now, if Mrs. Loveland had her wish, her daughter's funeral on Saturday. Half the faculty and most of the county would turn out to pay their last respects to Jules.

Crockett braked as a gray squirrel dashed into the street. Illumination night promised to be a security nightmare. The police were supposed to protect hundreds of well-to-do families and notables as they strolled across thirteen acres of town green, lit only by the glow of Japanese lanterns. Connolly had given Crockett clear orders: the police were to be omnipresent but invisible. Any disturbance was to be handled with the utmost discretion.

Despite dawdling under the speed limit, yielding the right of way to squirrels, and waiting patiently for a yellow light to turn red, Crockett found himself on Main Street, a block from the station. He stifled a yawn. He was bone aching tired.

"Aw, Jaesus." The *Oberlin News Tribune* van was parked in a Visitor space in front of the building. An amateur camera crew of Oberlin College students pushed lighting equipment to and fro, testing for the most auspicious angles. A small group of curiosity seekers hovered on the outskirts, waiting for action.

Connolly and Drucker must be holed up inside. Just leave them there. Tempting as the prospect was, Crockett rolled past the encampment and left the cruiser behind the Texaco station.

Maybe the crew wouldn't recognize him out of uniform. In the rush to get to the Gourd in the morning, Crockett had thrown on a sweatshirt, jeans, and a leather jacket. He turned up his collar and sauntered toward the press van in a slow, rolling walk. Passing the van, he glared inside at the student reporters with enough heat to melt their pencil leads. The crew averted their eyes and busied themselves with stray wires and light meters. *Vultures.* As soon as he was behind the building, Crockett vaulted the stairs to the rear entrance.

Jenny mouthed a silent welcome and pointed to the interview room where two other vultures were feeding. Connolly hunched over the remains of a pizza, picking at pepperoni carrion. His shirt was rumpled and stained. In contrast, the fastidious Drucker pecked at a wedge of pizza on a paper plate. A napkin protected his silk tie.

"Good of you to show up, Crockett." Connolly wiped his mouth with a paper towel saturated with tomato sauce and grease.

Crockett forced his eyes away from flecks of oregano left under Connolly's chin and nodded to Dean Drucker, who was too busy mouthing silent messages across the table to notice Crockett's good manners. Crockett felt like an extra in a silent movie.

Finally Connolly grunted, claiming the floor. "I suppose you saw the little party outside?" He didn't wait for an answer. "Just *how* did the student newspaper hear about Mrs. Kenworthy's death?" Connolly's *modus operandi* was never to say what he could insinuate.

"Police haven't issued a statement to the press. How did *you* hear about it?" Crockett lobbed the grenade back across the table.

Dean Drucker straightened to performance posture, drew a deep breath from his diaphragm, and folded his hands over his stomach, like a tenor preparing for his grand entrance. "The world will be watching Oberlin during this last week of graduation ceremonies. We must wear our Sunday best, especially now that we will be mourning the loss of a beloved faculty wife. As I'm sure you can appreciate, Mrs. Kenworthy's death will be a matter of great interest to the press. You know the fourth estate. Scandalmongers.

"We're here tonight to help assist you in the preparation of a brief, yet sensitive statement about the tragedy. Our objective is to inform the public while maintaining a suitable atmosphere of privacy and decorum for the bereaved family."

The Dapper Dean's well-modulated delivery negated any trace of sincerity. He corralled a few errant crumbs into a neat mound while he edited the syntax of his next paragraph.

"You worried about me being 'brief' or 'sensitive?'" broke in Crockett, unable to listen to another second of Drucker drivel.

Drucker's eyes involuntarily darted to a piece of paper in front of Connolly.

"Never mind." Crockett snatched the paper and scanned its contents. "A few changes, sir, it'll be perfect." Crockett snagged Drucker's Lamy pen and changed "accidental death" to "sudden death." Farther down, he corrected "tradgedy" to "tragedy." He added a second "t" to "Crocket," signed it and shoved it back to Connolly. "Thanks," he said. "Nice feel to it." He tucked the pen into Drucker's pocket and turned to leave.

"Sit down!" Connolly's command was punctuated by spittle-tinged sauce. "You know how people read 'sudden death.' It's a euphemism for 'suicide.'"

Crockett stopped but didn't sit.

"Watson said Mrs. Kenworthy's death was clearly an accident. From what he reported, there is *no doubt in our minds* that the poor woman died without deliberation."

"May be right, sir. May have been an accident. Or, could be suicide. Or foul play. All we know for now is 'sudden.' Autopsy will tell the story."

"*Foul play? Autopsy?* Are you out of your fucking mind?" Connolly lurched forward. "You are not hearing me. Jules Kenworthy's death was an accident. There will be no autopsy."

Crockett shook his head. "Sorry, sir. Law is firm about procedures in an unattended death. Medical Examiner's got the body. He'll be discreet. And thorough. Should have word by Wednesday. Thursday, the latest." Crockett hesitated, and then added, "Gotta be done by then. Mrs. Loveland wants the funeral Saturday."

Both men exploded, but Drucker's voice training won.

"*No!* The funeral will have to wait. The world will be watch—" Drucker's smooth tenor broke into squeaky fits and starts.

"Don't worry, Dr. Dean. Truth is, most folks would rather watch league bowling than hear the late-breaking news from Oberlin, Ohio." Crockett's voice mimicked Drucker's unctuous tone. "Doubt anyone will talk about the deep bruise on Mrs. Kenworthy's face, or the cocaine and wine bottles, or the strange scene in the cellar where she was found in a choir robe wrapped in a blanket. Far as I know, no one's asked about the whereabouts of the missing husband, Professor Kenworthy."

Drucker's eyes threatened to pop onto the table. He turned to Connolly and raised his eyebrows.

Instantly, Connolly assumed a chastened pose. He steepled his stubby fingers, and turned down the corners of his mouth in remorse. "I'm sorry if we offended you. I guess the pressure's getting to us. This is a very grave matter. We had hoped that you could appreciate the delicacy of the situation." Connolly waited for acknowledgement from Crockett.

When no response was forthcoming, Drucker took over, almost whispering. "We drafted the release to help you out, Joseph."

Crockett stood stock still for a full minute, his left hand cradling the balled fist of his right, his eyes fixed on the paper between them. Finally, he mustered a token smile. "Call me 'Crockett,' 'Chief,' 'Chief Crockett,' or 'Mr. Crockett.' Lots of options." He paused for emphasis before delivering his response. He began in a Drucker whisper. "I am cooperating fully. Even helped with spelling." His smile faded, and his voice hardened as he walked to the door. "We will investigate. It's the law."

Chapter Twenty-Three

Casey swung back and forth on Mae's front porch, listening to the church bells call parishioners to Sunday Services. Martha would be in church listening to her father, Reverend Swain, rail at the few good souls in the community, while the sinners like her drunken brother slept off their transgressions in peace.

She toyed with the tin cup she'd found on the clubhouse floor. At breakfast, Mae said the cup had been part of a soldier's mess kit from the Civil War. Art found it while playing in the tunnel from the cellar to the well. He'd treasured it for years and used it to collect bar tips. How would he explain the migration of the cup from the bar to the clubhouse floor if Crockett asked? The cup could be a problem, but with luck, Crockett hadn't seen it.

The church bells stopped their nagging. Time to go. Casey rode her bicycle to the back courtyard of the Gourd. She pressed the doorbell and cursed her brother. How could someone so smart be so stupid? He'd been sober for so long. Now he could be in big trouble.

Answer the door, damn it!

It must've been hell for Art when Jules moved back to the Gourd. Or as close to heaven as he could get. Pathetic. Both of them. *All of us*, she corrected herself. Mooning over high school crushes. Jules never got clear of Ron, Casey had awakened at the crack of dawn, hoping for a phone call from George, and no one ever got over Jules.

Casey pounded on the door. "Art! Open up!"

When they were kids, Art would turn crimson if Jules looked his way. Was he in love with her then? Knowing how Art felt about Jules, Casey had been dumbfounded when he began dating Martha. One day Casey screwed up her courage and asked him what he saw in her.

"She's not so bad. Rather pretty, actually. And we both needed a date," was his reply. When Art's world had fallen apart, Martha patched him together.

Casey put her ear to the door, listening for sounds of life. Nothing. She looked about for pebbles to lob against the bedroom window. Slim pickings. She smiled as her eyes returned to the well.

The old stone well was topped by a traditional, peaked roof. A water bucket was still attached to the rope that threaded through a hole in the hinged wooden cover. They'd nailed down the cover after the scare with Gabby, and Martha had placed a new pot of pansies on top. The little flower faces watched Casey, nodding encouragement.

She knelt beside the well and probed the smallest stones close to the bottom until one moved. She pried it loose, freeing up a larger, round rock. Her fingers explored the secret nook that the rock had protected. Yes! Still there after all these years. She withdrew a small brass key, replaced the rock, and then repositioned the smaller stone to secure it.

The Cavendish key on the west side of the well, the Loveland key on the east. Casey let out a deep sigh. Memories of childhood with Jules had flooded her consciousness. Part of Casey had died with Jules—that part that shared youthful dreams, secrets, embarrassments, and triumphs. To distract herself from maudlin thoughts, she poked around the Loveland side of the well, wiggling a few stones before one gave way. Inside, her fingers searched for another key. No key. Instead, she touched a smooth surface.

She gasped and dropped a plastic bag filled with white powder. It wouldn't be sugar in a hiding place Jules knew about. She wiped the bag with the bottom of her shirt. Holding it between folds of cloth, she poked it back into the shallow cavity and replaced and wiped off the stones. She backed away from the well. Her instinct was to run as fast and as far as she could. Then again, if anyone had seen her, her goose was already cooked. She might as well talk with her brother.

Just as she turned the key and entered, the door to the upstairs Cavendish apartment opened and Art slouched through. The moment he saw Casey, he motioned to her to stay downstairs.

"Let's get some coffee in the Gourd. Our larders are empty," he muttered, tucking a wrinkled shirt into his jeans. Bare ankles were visible above his loafers. She doubted that he'd bothered with underwear. An aura of stale smoke and booze engulfed him. She grimaced at his ruined eyes. His mouth drooped at the edges, exaggerating the slope of his thin face.

"Don't even start, Sis," he growled.

She wasn't about to lecture him. Nothing she could say would help unless he decided to sober up. They maintained an uneasy silence as he unlocked the Gourd kitchen and made a pot of coffee. When the death rattles of the machine signaled that the coffee was ready, he filled a cup for Casey and then wiped down every possible counter, before taking a seat opposite her at the help's table. He concentrated on his coffee, slurping slowly to lessen the burn of the hot liquid.

The family slurp gene. As Casey waited for the small belch that invariably followed the dual intake of liquid and air, she took Art's tin cup from her pocket.

"'Scuse me," he burped, looking up. "Hey, where'd you find that? I've looked all over for it." He reached for the cup, but she held it away.

"Bet you have."

"What's that supposed to mean? Give it here," he demanded, holding out his hand.

She rocked back on her chair and fixed him with a level stare. "Where did you last see it?"

"What the hell?" Art rose and leaned toward her.

"*Sit down.*"

"What's this about? I thought you wanted to see me."

Casey slammed forward, her voice metallic. "I said, sit down."

Art aggressively poured himself another cup of coffee.

"I found the cup on the floor of the clubhouse Saturday morning."

His eyes shifted from her to the cup. He sank into his chair. "In the clubhouse," he repeated as if in a trance. After a few moments, he looked at her through red pools of pain. "I swear to you, I don't know how it got there. Last I saw it was at the bar."

"Suppose you tell me what happened Friday night." Casey kept her voice neutral, even cold. She refilled her cup to give Art a chance to compose himself. She didn't believe he'd killed Jules, but he'd need to be able to recount his movements in case Crockett's investigation suggested foul play. She listened while Art retraced the painful events of Friday night.

"Jules was wearing Mom's ring?" Casey exclaimed. She thought for a moment. "The service was closed casket, so we never saw…all this time. She had the ring all this time."

Art continued, telling her about the cocaine, drinking the wine, and finally about Jules' nearly incoherent words. "'I told them Charley made a mistake, but no one believed me. Casey set me up, but Charley got the wrong bike.' I don't know what she was trying to say."

Casey shook her head, stunned. "Unbelievable. She was talking about when I was busted. I've said over and over that it was a mistake. I borrowed a bike that was just like the one Jules rode. Charley left the cocaine in the pouch of the wrong bike. She said she told the truth, but no one believed her? I wish she'd been more convincing. Cost me ten years."

Casey shook her head again and looked at Art. "I didn't set Jules up. I wouldn't have done that. I didn't hate her then."

After a long moment, Casey returned to the current problem. "So, you left her and went to the bar. Did you go back? After you'd kicked back a few? Did you return for Mom's ring and find Jules in the cellar?" Casey hated the way the questions sounded, but she needed to know how he'd respond. "You emptied the bottle. She might have gone downstairs to the wine cellar for another."

"I honestly don't know. I have no memory of leaving the bar."

"Could you have gone back?" Casey persisted.

Art was quiet for a moment before answering. "I could have. When I was drinking before, I lost whole days. I'd wake up with no idea how I got home or what day it was." He drew his fingers through thin hair. "It's possible. I could have gone back." His voice cracked, but Casey pressed on.

"You loved her. But Friday night she was screwing around with Ron. Out of her mind on wine and cocaine. Wearing Mom's ring. Did you love her Friday night?"

"I remember thinking I'd do anything to help her, I loved her so, and then later, being so angry I wanted to—" He held his chin high in the air and held his breath. "She begged me to stay. I could have saved her, but I left." He buried his face in his hands.

Casey placed a hand on his shoulder. "Sorry. I know this hurts. Believe me, there was nothing more you could have done for Jules Friday night, and there's no way you could have killed her. I think Crockett wants to believe Jules died of an accidental overdose. From the way you looked Saturday morning, I can swear that you drank a whole bottle of Scotch and passed out."

She tossed the cup to Art and headed for the door. Damn! He'd never hold up under questioning.

Walking across the patio to her bike, Casey looked around carefully. The feeling of being watched had to be her overactive imagination. The coke in the well wasn't a trap for her. No one was setting her up, because no one—including Casey—knew she'd be poking about in the well this morning.

And yet, the sense of eyes on her back was pervasive. She shuddered and tried not to look guilty. As she rode toward Mae's, the sky darkened behind her with the threat of a spring storm. Halfway home, the wind whipped up, and moments later a few heavy, warning drops hit her cheeks.

Her knuckles tightened on the handgrips. Jules stole her mother's ring. Casey loved that ring and would have worn it in memory of her mother. But her mother had asked to be cremated with the ring so her ashes would meld with the token given her by a man she had dearly loved. Casey had reluctantly complied. A block from home, the rain fell in earnest, drenching her.

Where was it now? How could she ask if Jules was found wearing the ring in the clubhouse without letting on that Art had seen Jules wearing the ring late Saturday night? What was Jules thinking wearing it in front of Art? Maybe she was too drunk and drugged up to give a damn. One thought tripped over the next. Drugs. Jules' words.

As Casey dismounted and approached the house, the nylon curtain in the front window fluttered. Mae was waiting.

"Yoohoo!" Casey hollered, rushing toward the bathroom to discourage conversation.

"Yoohoo, yourself! Where've you been?" Mae intercepted her. "Dinner is at six, and nothing's been done. You're sopping wet! What's for dinner?" The words poured from Mae as if a tap had just been opened.

With the Gourd closed, Mae had rescheduled the family dinner for Sunday night so that Casey could attend. Casey slowed long enough to allay her aunt's fears. "Martha's bringing the food, probably some remnant from the restaurant. All you have to do is eat and keep it down until they leave. All I have to do is clean up." Casey glanced at the telephone.

"No calls. Who did you expect to call?"

Clearly Mae wanted to talk, but Casey couldn't face it. "Gotta take a shower."

She raced to her room, cast off her wet clothing, and stuck her face directly under the pelting pressure of the shower, waiting for the water to wash away the new hurtful images. Wrapping her head in a towel, she scurried naked across the hall to her room and curled under the comforter. She'd close her eyes for a few seconds before dinner.

But her mind raced. Why hadn't she heard from George? Where was he? In Casey's dreams, all had been solved without Jules. But now that she was dead, the real nightmares had begun.

Chapter Twenty-Four

Art poured himself another drink. He was relieved to have shared the story with Casey, but shamed by his weakness at the same time. He'd wanted to tell her about the dream, but couldn't. She had no idea how depraved he was.

The dream was so vivid, so real. When he awoke Saturday morning hungover and smelling of sex, he was surprised he could remember all the details of a wet dream to beat all wet dreams.

God strike him dead, but he loved it. He moaned as the top of the honey gold head moved rhythmically, feeling her lips and tongue slide up and down on him, teasing him with gentle bites to keep him from climax. He shuddered with pleasure when she took the length of him into her mouth, moving and thrusting in response. She reached under him and pressed lightly just behind his balls, causing his whole body to arch and writhe. He pushed her head down harder signaling his growing need. He wanted to ram her to China, hard, hard. But she had sensed the change in him and abruptly released him to fly in the wind.

"Who would have guessed what a stallion you are, Arthur!"

Something seemed wrong, but he couldn't focus. She laughed and pushed him gently back on the bed, and then crawled on top of him, straddling him with her legs. Ever so gently and slowly she lowered herself over him. When her softness encompassed him, she began to rotate, rocking back and forth and side to side, using his hardness to give herself pleasure.

Her hair covered his face as she bent forward to offer her breasts. He cupped and fondled them gently at first, then sucked as he felt her respond, harder and harder. When he felt his final motion begin, he released her breasts and pulled her buttocks to him roughly.

"Jules, Oh God, Jules," he howled, pumping what was left of his soul into her body.

Could he have returned on Friday night? Or was it a dream? Usually, dreams eluded him the moment he tried to remember them. Not this one. It was so real.

He couldn't talk to his sister, and he couldn't look at his wife. All he could do was hope for another dream.

Chapter Twenty-Five

When there had still been no word from George on Sunday morning, Crockett decided to take a closer look around George's study for an address or phone number of someone he could contact. Once again, Martha met him with a key, but this time with Gabby in tow. Martha was decked out in simple mourning finery, a slim-line black jersey dress, modest veil, and practical black pumps, required staples in the wardrobe of any pastor's daughter. The dress clung to curves that he had never noticed before, and dark stockings silhouetted long, shapely legs. Crockett realized he was staring and was thankful she couldn't see him blush. He watched her walk to the Cavendish rear entrance.

"Shit!" Martha barely kept her balance when one of her heels turned on a cobblestone. She ripped off her shoes and stomped across the remaining stones.

Crockett was relieved at the return of the Martha he knew and disliked. Ought to watch her mouth in front of the little one. Crockett unlocked the Kenworthys' door. As he entered the kitchen, a wave of Pine-Sol and ammonia brought back the macabre events of yesterday.

From the kitchen, Crockett followed a hallway past a bathroom and laundry and a family room. A polished mahogany table with a tall vase of wilting flowers dominated the dining room. A sofa, love seat, and priceless old family chairs lined the perimeter of a formal living room that was obviously never used. Crockett admired the grandfather clock and the portrait of the family patriarch, Abe Loveland, builder of the Drinking Gourd. He imagined the room blocked by a red velvet restraining cord with a sign instructing visitors to look but not touch.

George's study was the last room at the front of the building. Crockett almost lost his balance when his foot rolled over something on the old oak floorboards. When he stopped to look for the object, little footsteps drew up short behind him. He continued toward George's desk and stopped suddenly. Once more, small feet stopped abruptly behind him.

"Seems I have a little shadow. Strange. Big man with a little bitty shadow. Every time I move, my shadow moves." He walked forward two steps and stopped. Gabby moved behind him and giggled. Then she picked up her errant crayon and sat in a child's rocking chair in the corner of the room. The tap of even smaller feet announced Ralphie, but the little dog settled just outside the study door.

Crockett didn't speak directly to Gabby, remembering her terror the day before. Instead, he gazed at three walls covered with floor-to-ceiling bookcases and a set of portable, mahogany library steps used to reach the top shelves. Some rows were packed two-deep. Others had books tucked horizontally atop other books, jammed in every available crevice.

In the corner at floor level, the books changed from fat reference works to tall, skinny books. Gabby's library. Must be thirty little books, all lined up, with a couple of titles sideways just like her dad's. An open wooden crate housed toys and games, crayons, and coloring books. Gabby watched him from her little chair. When he looked down at her, she scolded the crayon for not being in its box where it belonged, watching out of the corner of her eye to gauge his reaction. He smiled, turned his back, and approached an old oak desk facing the front window.

Sitting in the wooden swivel chair, he imagined George watching people come and go, their images distorted by the small wavy windowpanes. The cinnamon fragrance of deep purple petunias in the window box wafted through the open window.

Books piled on the floor next to the desk had numbers on their spines. Library books. Crockett leafed through the top book. It smelled musty. George was probably the only one to crack its cover in a hundred years. The date due slip inside the back cover indicated that it was due two weeks from Friday. Several bookmarks tagged items of interest.

On the desk, a smooth oval stone, hand-painted with a white daisy and the words "Pick me" anchored a stack of pink While-You-Were-Out slips. The top message read, "Please call," the next, "Call before noon," and the third "Urgent. Call before you leave." All were dated Friday, May fifteenth, the day Jules died. Only the last message had a telephone number. All were from Renee.

The same telephone number appeared on a small scratchpad, along with letters and numbers and what looked like times. Two sets were scratched out; the third set was circled. A large arrow filled in with a heavy lead pencil pointed toward the circled figures.

"Mustn't touch," said Gabby. Startled, Crockett dropped the pink slips. He imagined the agreement between father and child. You can play quietly in the corner, but you mustn't touch anything on the desk. "Okay, but I need to look." Crockett retrieved a pad from his shirt pocket and copied down the information on the scratchpad.

Side drawers held everything one would need to work at home—paper clips, staples, pencil leads, erasers, scissors, tape—but no address book, no calendar, no appointment book.

Two file cabinets, one at each end of the desk, were filled with neatly arranged tabs. Crockett leaned closer to see the photo on top of the left cabinet. "Well, I'll be—" He caught himself at the last minute. The Four Horsemen, George, Crockett, Ron and Dougie, stood with arms around one another looking mean and triumphant. Football league champions. Art had dubbed them the Four Horsemen of the Apocalypse in the *Oberlin News Tribune*, but luckily only the Four Horsemen part had stuck. Athletics had thrown George and Crockett together in high school, but they had nothing in common these days. When their paths crossed, the interaction was friendly but a little awkward.

In a smaller photo, four children posed by the well in the back of the Gourd. Art's long, serious face was a giveaway. The taller, golden-haired boy must be George. Sitting on top of the well were two young girls, one with dark hair in braids, making a face at the camera, and another with honey-colored locks flirting with the photographer.

Nostalgia was not helping him find George. Crockett picked up the last pink slip. 212 area code: Manhattan. He dialed the number. After four rings, an answering service informed him that he had reached the Yale University Press and informed him to call back during business hours during the week.

Gabby pretended to read a book in her chair in the corner. She had crossed one leg over the other at a right angle.

"Does your mama have a desk, too?" he asked.

"Yup." She continued to turn pages.

"How 'bout you show me where?"

"Okay." She returned the book to the bookcase and led the way into the hall. Ralphie abandoned his vigil at the door and joined them as they climbed the stairs to the second floor. Crockett looked down another long hallway. Directly above George's study was a room decorated in early Americana. Guest room.

Across the hall, they entered the master bedroom and bath. Crockett glanced at the disarray—the rumpled, unmade bed, clothing draped over chairs and piled up on the dresser. A bra and panties strewn on the floor. No sign of George in the room. The room smelled of cigar smoke. George didn't smoke.

"C'mon. Mommy's desk is in her other room." Gabby led him into a large room crammed with women's clothing. Shoe racks and shelves lined the walls. Crockett opened a closet, gasped, and backed away from two sets of blank eyes that stared at him from dismembered heads.

"Mommy's hair," announced Gabby, "for when she's late and has to look pretty."

"Right," muttered Crockett, catching his breath. The manikin heads sat on a shelf above the clothes, each displaying a honey-colored wig, one with short hair, one longer.

Eager to leave the heads behind him, he examined a curious dresser with twenty, inch-deep drawers. He pulled out a drawer. Jewelry. On the wall, a mesh screen displayed pairs of pierced earrings.

Against the side wall a padded stool faced a small table with an oval mirror. Crockett stared in awe at a cosmetician's dream of brushes, bottles, atomizers, lipsticks, nail polish, eyeliners, mascara, nail files, creams, balms, lotions, and puffs.

Gabby led him to a small desk in the corner where Jules kept her papers: notes, old bills, a car insurance contract, receipts. Evidently, Jules took care of the personal finances. Crockett leafed through a stack of bills neatly marked paid and the date. He looked closer at a recent payment. At first, he thought it must be a restaurant account, but then he remembered that Martha kept the Gourd records. This was a personal account, a whopper of a payment to a company called GFS. Where the hell did George get money to pay bills like this? He reminded himself that he was here to find George, not investigate his finances, but he made a mental note to add GFS to his Snowballs list.

"You have any idea where your daddy is?"

"Nope."

Crockett poked around further, but there was nothing to indicate where George was staying.

"I saw Mommy," the small voice behind him announced.

"Mommy?" he whispered to match her voice.

"She smiled at me."

Crockett took a deep breath and turned to face Gabby. The last time he'd seen Jules, she was staring at the ceiling. She had looked surprised, but her expression was definitely not a smile. He knelt to speak with Gabby at five-year-old level. "When did you see Mommy?" he asked gently.

"When I was clouding. Mommy's in heaven." Gabby spoke in a matter-of-fact tone. "Daddy told her to go to hell, but Martha said she was in heaven. I saw her in the clouds this morning. She's so pretty."

Crockett breathed a sigh of relief, but it was premature.

"How long does she have to stay there? I want her to come home."

Crockett recognized the plaintive note, the precursor to tears. He wished he could kiss her hurt and make it better. "I'm sorry, honey. I'm just looking for a telephone number for your daddy." He watched Gabby's face fall and then change to hope at the prospect of calling her father.

"C'mon," she said, taking his hand and leading him down the hallway to a storeroom at the end of the hall. "Daddy's room." She led him through a maze of boxes piled ceiling high to a clearing in the corner where they found a futon on the floor and a reading lamp. Stacked next to the futon were a few of the inevitable books that trailed George everywhere, but no phone numbers or clues to his whereabouts.

As Gabby led him out of the room, Crockett peeked into the closet. Shirts, slacks, and jackets hung neatly in a row. Folded underwear and socks on the top shelf, shoes paired off on the floor. Jules luxuriated in the master bedroom like the Queen of Sheba, while George hunkered on the floor in a corner like a monk, surrounded by a wall of boxes.

Finally, they poked their heads into Gabby's room. Crockett saw it the day before, but he didn't want to give her room short shrift.

"Didn't eat your vegetables," he said, eyeing the remains of her dinner.

"Peas. Yuk."

"I don't like them either. Why do you eat in your room?"

"I eat here when Mr. Ron comes."

Crockett paused to keep the astonishment out of his voice. "Mr. Ron was here?"

"Yup."

Gabby's matter-of-fact tone told him that Mr. Ron's visits were a normal part of her life. Crockett shook his head. After a decade of police work, he wasn't sure about "normal," but he did know that Ron smoked cigars.

Crockett retraced his steps to the master bedroom. Martha had removed two wine glasses from the room in her Saturday morning cleaning spree, but maybe she missed something. The smell of smoke was strong. As he knelt and raised the bedspread, he spied an ashtray that had been shoved under the bed. He took a tissue from a box on the bedside table and wrapped it around the stub of a cigar.

"Shouldn't smoke," Gabby said behind him.

"You're right," he agreed as he followed her out the room to the hallway.

Gabby stopped suddenly bringing him up short behind her. She looked down to the right and whispered, "I have a shadow. Big shadow for a bitty girl." She giggled and dashed down the hall to the back stairs.

Crockett laughed and followed. About halfway down the stairs, he stopped smiling. Gabby had no idea how the events of the weekend would change her life.

Ralphie's sharp yip startled him. He had forgotten that the dog was part of the parade. Ralphie's nails slid and scratched as he struggled to gain traction in his headlong dive down the back steps. He flew past Crockett and Gabby barking in earnest.

The back door slammed. Ralphie yipped in excitement, toenails dancing on wood.

"Hi, puppy. Where's my girl?"

"Daddy!" squealed Gabby, running down the steps as fast as her little legs could go.

Chapter Twenty-Six

Crockett allowed time for the father and child reunion before asking to speak with George alone. George put Gabby down for a nap and then returned to the kitchen.

Either George hadn't heard of Jules' death before he walked in the door, or he was a damn good actor. After Crockett recounted the events of Saturday morning, George looked as if he had aged ten years. Maybe he had. He sat at the kitchen table, shoulders slumped and eyes staring at nothing, stunned. Crockett kept a professional distance, but his instinct was to reach out and comfort his old teammate.

"I was looking around the house for a clue to your whereabouts," Crockett probed gently.

"I went to a Civil War conference this weekend."

"Tried there. Found your hotel room, but you weren't at the sessions."

"I don't bother with those. I spend my time with the vendors in the exposition hall. They've got all the good stuff."

"Anyone who can vouch for your whereabouts Friday night?"

"Why on earth would I have to vouch—"

"Protocol. Reconstructing the events of Friday night for the paperwork. Young woman dies alone under strange circumstances, we have to complete a detailed report: condition of the deceased, scene of death, and the whereabouts of significant others when she died."

George's head moved side to side as if he were waging an internal battle. When he finally spoke, his expression was sheepish. "In that case, I have to admit that I've been misleading you a little. I didn't think there was any reason to complicate things, because it would hurt others needlessly. So I simplified a bit."

Crockett leaned back in his chair, shifting his initial sympathetic response into neutral. He watched George with new eyes. Now he'd have to explore the lie and whatever ugliness it covered. "Not a good idea to protect an officer of the law from the truth."

"Yes. Well," George hesitated, "I had a last minute change in plans."

Crockett waited for him to continue, but George seemed distracted. He could be in shock, or he could be stalling while he constructed a new story. Crockett tried again. "You had a number of 'Urgent' telephone messages last Friday afternoon."

"Renee." Again he let the conversation lapse.

"Renee?"

"My editor. I've been writing a book. Renee was upset because I'd asked for another extension." George rubbed his hand over his face as if to dispel cobwebs, and then began anew. "I found some new material that strengthens my manuscript. The book was already two months late, so Renee wasn't thrilled about last minute changes. We argued and she finally agreed, but only if I'd deliver the changes to her in person this weekend. A little emotional blackmail."

George's expression quickly changed from irritation to confusion. "This is unbelievable. Why was Jules in the cellar?"

Crockett backed off a little. "I know this is painful. When did you leave?"

"Friday night. Eleven o'clock, Continental Air Lines." He poked about in a leather satchel and pulled out a planning calendar stuffed with papers. He sorted through the papers twice and then checked his jacket pockets before throwing up his hands. "I guess I didn't keep the boarding passes. Renee booked the flight, round trip from Cleveland Hopkins to LaGuardia. The airline will have a record of who was on the flight."

"New York hotel receipt will do."

George shook his head. "I stayed with her. It's a long story." He wrote a telephone number on a slip of paper and pushed it toward George. "Call her if you must. She'll vouch for me."

"I have the number."

"So, if you already knew where I was Friday night, why all the questions?"

"Lies annoy me." Crockett hadn't known George's whereabouts, but he wasn't about to yield his advantage.

"Give me a break, Crockett. Before this thing came up with Renee, I really did intend to go to the conference. I kept the hotel room because Jules would have gone ballistic if she found out I'd gone to New York and stayed with Renee." George paused a second before forging on. "Actually, Casey probably wouldn't be too pleased, either." George looked up with a sheepish expression. "This is just between us, right?"

Damn! George's statement gave credence to Watson's gossip about George and Casey. Crockett unclenched his fist and took a few long breaths. It wouldn't help for the Chief of Police to pound the crap out of the grieving husband. Amazing how one lie could instantly taint a relationship. Now he wasn't ready to let George off the hook. "Maybe. Depends on what the Medical Examiner has to say after the autopsy." Crockett regretted his harshness at George's sharp intake of breath. All the color drained from his face.

Crockett waited for George to regain his composure. Despite his desire to punish the philandering SOB, George and Casey were none of his business. No matter what George's recent relationship with Jules had been, he'd loved her once, and she was the mother of his little girl. This had to be a painful time. Crockett shuddered. He couldn't imagine anyone telling him they'd have to do an autopsy on Leila. The idea of slicing and sawing, weighing, and measuring was barbaric.

"Is that absolutely necessary?"

Crockett nodded. "When no one else is present, it's called an 'unattended death.' Law requires an autopsy."

"'Unattended death,'" George repeated hollowly. "Do you suspect foul play?" He shoved back from the table. "Someone could have killed her?"

"More likely an accident or suicide. Any reason she'd take her own life?"

George relaxed a little. He ran a finger around the rim of his empty coffee cup. "If you were upstairs, you've seen our living arrangements. We live a lie. Well, more like a truce. She goes her way; I go mine. I'm satisfied with teaching, research and, of course, with Gabby. Oh God, Gabby." He looked to the stairway leading to Gabby's room.

Crockett shifted in his chair.

George's voice continued in a monotone. "Jules was bored. She was always a party girl, but she never drank during the day until we came back here. I probably should have paid more attention, but frankly, she was only interested in what she couldn't have. She liked the thrill of the chase. We were on again, off again over the years. It may be hard for you to believe, but I loved her. I've always loved her."

They were both quiet, the air heavy with unspoken thoughts.

"How? How did she look?" George spoke slowly, as if he were unsure that he wanted an answer.

"She was wrapped in a blanket. Martha said she'd been sick. She wore a choir robe and had a nasty bruise on her cheek."

George shook his head. "You know, it just doesn't make sense. Jules was unhappy. She might even have been screwed up enough to take her own life, although that would *really* surprise me. But I can't imagine her letting anyone find her looking like that."

"Martha said the same thing."

George's eyes widened in dread. "Did Gabby see her?"

"Afraid so. She scared us Saturday morning. Martha and I couldn't find her, so I called Casey. She found Gabby and the dog hiding in the barn."

"Oh, my poor little baby." Tears streamed down his cheeks.

Chapter Twenty-Seven

Voices gradually invaded Casey's consciousness. Pots banged and drawers slammed. Casey sighed. Martha was in the kitchen. Time for the Cavendish family dinner.

The only saving grace at a dinner with Art and Martha was watching Mae work Martha. They were both information brokers, but Mae was the master. Tonight Mae would troll for every detail about Jules' death.

Casey was sick of hearing about Jules. *Out, out damned Jules!* But now that Jules was out, the stain remained. Casey remembered when she and Jules had tried to remove the third drop of blood from under the Cats Eye symbol on the clubhouse door. Martha's blood. Another stain that wouldn't go away.

Casey'd fallen asleep with a towel wrapped around her head. Now, looking into the mirror, a punk rocker stared back at her, hair at all angles. Her new look? She pulled on a funky caftan with slits up the sides and slid into sandals. No stockings. She wanted her rose tattoo to show. She'd purchased a tattoo kit in the drug store to shock the Scowlies, but it would work equally well with Martha. Was the ankle bracelet overkill? Nah. She dabbed patchouli behind her ears. Let the games begin.

"Quit your fussing, woman!" Mae's voice carried an edge. Martha was already under her skin. Her aunt had planted herself at the end of the dining room table. As Casey entered the dining room, Mae's eyes widened at Casey's choice of evening apparel. "I see you dressed for dinner, too."

Too? Casey's silent question was answered when Martha appeared with table linen.

"Take that end," Martha ordered as she unfurled a tablecloth.

Casey breezed past Martha to the kitchen noting Martha's black dress, dark stockings, and heels. Fire engine red fingernails and lipstick provided dramatic contrast against Martha's pale skin and mourning dress.

"Why, hello to you, Martha," Casey called over her shoulder. "What's for dinner? No, wait. Let me guess…" Casey sniffed the air.

"Oh, shut up," Martha hissed as she returned to the kitchen for silverware. "Nice of you to wake up in time to eat. You could at least help with—" Martha stopped mid-complaint to stare at Casey. "Would you look at what the cat threw up!"

"Casey, would you bring my glass?" Mae called from the dining room. "It's on the table next to my bed. There's still a drop left, and my olive. And start calling your brother. He's on the porch smoking and taking a nip."

Casey wrinkled her nose at Martha and took off to do Mae's bidding. She found Art on the front swing.

"Hey." Casey sat next to him. After a few moments, she leaned her head against his shoulder. They listened to the old chains groan under their weight, comforted by each other's presence, knowing they didn't have to talk. They had always been able to be quiet together.

After a few moments, Art gave her a sad smile. "Hey, yourself. Nice hairdo." He ruffled her hair and reached for a flask on the porch floor. Casey snatched it before he could protest, and then surprised him by taking a long pull. She gasped and rolled her eyes as the liquid burned a path to her stomach.

"Panther piss," he explained.

"Casey?" Mae's querulous voice pierced the air.

"Is it time?" Art nodded toward the door.

"Relax. She wants her martini."

"Coming!" she hollered back. She replenished Mae's martini and added another olive from the half-sized refrigerator next to Mae's bed. Before returning to the dining room, she looked out the window and admired the petunias she'd planted in the burnt-out teapot garden.

Martha bustled into the room and placed salt and pepper shakers in the center of the table between the candles. She frowned at Mae's glass, but made no comment and returned to the kitchen.

Mae sipped her drink and then, with a secret smile, moved the saltshaker an inch to the right. Martha came back with tartar sauce and oyster crackers. Apparently, they had been talking about Jules, because Mae's next question belonged in a series. "Why was she in the basement?"

"She was after more wine." Martha cast her eyes down. "It's all so sad. A tragedy. I'll miss her." She pushed the saltshaker back into place and surveyed the table.

Miss her? Since when? Casey raised an eyebrow at Mae, but Mae was way ahead of her. "I didn't realize you and Jules were close."

"We had our differences growing up. But when she came back, she was so unhappy and lonesome. She needed a friend to confide in, and someone to help with Gabby."

Jules and Martha? Friends? Jules pouring out her heart to Martha Swain? Impossible. Could Jules have been *that* unhappy? She couldn't let the remark pass. "I'm confused. Yesterday you condemned Jules as a whore and an unfit mother." Casey let the statement hang to encourage a response.

Martha gave Casey an all-suffering smile and then spoke deliberately and softly. "Yes. I know. She wasn't perfect. Far from it. There were times I asked the good Lord for help, and He showed me how to channel my negative thoughts into understanding and acceptance. I've learned a lot from Jules."

"Oh, gag!"

Mae intervened. "What have you learned, Martha?" She nudged the pepper ever so slightly to the left.

Martha smiled sweetly, set the knives, forks, and spoons in proper formation, and realigned the pepper. "Well, for one thing, I found out that George was up to his old tricks. That's why Jules hit the bottle."

"Old tricks?" Mae asked. But Martha was off to the kitchen again. In frustration, Mae castled the salt and pepper.

Martha reappeared with four plates. "You *do* know why George and Jules had to come back, don't you?" Martha paused for effect, using the silence to distribute the plates. "Professor Kenworthy got caught with the wife of his department head at Yale."

"Jules told you that?" Casey blurted, her mind reeling. Could it be? Tonight she might get sick *before* eating Martha's entrée. Martha's hand stopped in midair and hovered over the salt and peppershakers. She turned and glared at Mae. Mae's head was down, her mouth set in a little smile, her fingers toying with the properly laid silverware.

"No." Art entered and slouched against the doorjamb. "Martha read about the sordid details in Jules' private journal. That is, until Jules locked her out."

"I only read a few pages to try to help her. She spent hours in the cellar, drinking and writing. Gabby and Ralphie would cuddle up beside her. So sad."

"But Gabby told her mother that Auntie Martha had done a *'Don't touch,'* didn't she?" Art prodded.

They took their places around the table. Ignoring Art's question, Martha turned on Casey. "Thanks for all your help tonight. I'm sure you won't mind serving." She shoved a platter of fish into Casey's hands. Then she responded to Art. "Why must you put the most negative interpretation on things? At the beginning of the journal, Jules wrote that part of her therapy was to express her emotions in writing. I read on only so that I could understand her better."

"Jules told me she locked the filing cabinet and hid the key where you would never find it." Art chuckled, as if pleased at the thought.

But I found it. Casey concentrated on serving the fish.

Martha took to the offensive. "From what she wrote, the last straw was George's affair with her best friend."

Casey almost dropped the platter. *Just a kiss in the cemetery, not an affair.* She began serving the peas. *But, there was intent.*

"You should have seen George's face this afternoon after he learned—"

"George?" Casey started and missed the plate. *George was home, and he hadn't called.*

Martha tilted her head to the side with a cagey glint in her eyes. "Didn't you know? George came back this afternoon. Crockett was snooping around at the Kenworthys' and gave him the awful news. He said George took it pretty hard. He'd been off visiting Renee."

"Renee?" What was Martha talking about?

Martha assumed a look of wide-eyed innocence. "Surely you know about Renee?" she whispered.

Casey shrugged. "His editor."

"Renee was Jules' *other* best friend, the one at Yale, the wife of the department head."

"Let's get this dinner over with," Mae interrupted.

Casey, stunned by the turns in the conversation, actually put a forkful of fish in her mouth. She gagged instantly and reached for some water.

"Very funny." Martha was not amused.

But Casey wasn't acting. She coughed discreetly, parking the offending mouthful into her napkin.

Mae deftly covered her fish with pieces of lettuce. "I'm as confused as Casey. Wasn't Jules fooling around with your brother, Ron? Weren't they a hot item even in high school?"

"I wouldn't know. Jules did sink back into some of her old habits. It's so easy to do." Martha looked pointedly at Art, and then fixed Casey with a knowing smile.

"Are you referring to Art's backsliding, Jules' drinking and drugging, or something else?" Casey challenged.

"Well, let's just say that you are not one to cast stones in the drug department, my dear."

Casey stopped all pretense of eating, tossed her soggy napkin onto her plate, and rose to clear the table. She responded to Martha in measured tones. "I am not—and never will be—your 'dear.' I've never had a drug problem. Jules did. Your new *dear* friend, the all-suffering, misunderstood Jules, let me take the fall for her and spend ten long years in prison. You're lucky you didn't become best buddies with Jules until *after* she died. She ruined everyone else who knew and loved her."

Casey stopped her diatribe when Martha bowed her head. Could she be praying?

Martha sighed audibly and shook her head. When she spoke, her voice was in a lower register. "What terrible, terrible things to say about the person who was your best friend for so many years. She loved you. Even when you were a convicted felon, she still loved you. Enough to name her daughter after you."

Casey stopped mid-stride, balancing plates laden with remains. "What are you talking about?"

"Gabriella *Cassandra* Kenworthy." Martha stole a glance at Casey to make sure she'd scored. "You heard me right," she whispered. "*Cassandra*. She named her firstborn after you."

This time, Casey found it easier to maintain her composure. After all, she was the one carrying a stack of plates. As she neared Martha, Casey's toe conveniently caught on a chair leg, and she lurched forward. "Oh, no!" she gasped and watched with satisfaction as Mae's cleverly concealed fish slid off the top plate into Martha's lap.

"Shit!"

"Serves you right," Mae hissed. "Go home. There will be no dessert."

Minutes after the front door slammed. Casey's shoulders slumped and she fought to control her sobs. She hadn't known. Gabriella Cassandra.

Chapter Twenty-Eight

A t eight o'clock on Monday morning, Crockett pulled into the "Visitor" space in front of Swain Construction, a gray brick building in an industrial park on the east edge of town.

As he walked toward the entrance, Crockett caught his reflection in the polished surface of Ron's BMW. He turned his head for a profile shot. Mean mother. He rolled his shoulders and flapped his hands to loosen up. Just an informal call on an old teammate. Short and sweet. See if Ron could shed any light on Jules' death.

Crockett knew that Ron had done well since he returned from the Marines, buying out a small construction firm and building it into a successful business. He had a corner on municipal projects and was at the top of the college's favored contractor list.

A perky blonde greeted Crockett in the reception area. "Good morning, Chief." She flashed him a smile. "Ricki" had decorated her nameplate with a smiley face.

"Mornin'. Here for a word with Ron."

Ricki pushed a button and announced his presence and then offered him a seat in the reception area.

While he waited, Crockett examined a display table with scale models of Swain Construction projects, many of which he recognized. On a second table, a heavy green drop cloth covered the lumps and bumps of a large project. He couldn't resist a peek. He lifted the cloth and whistled. A brass plaque identified the model as Emerald Acres but gave no additional information. As he raised the cloth higher to admire the detailed touches,

Ron's familiar baritone boomed behind him.

"Crockett!" Ron stopped short and extended a large, meaty hand, forcing Crockett to move forward to shake hands. "Hold my calls," Ron instructed. He ushered Crockett into his office and waved him into a chair next to a round table.

Leather creaked as the chair yielded to Crockett's weight. Scents of expensive cigars and British Sterling cologne permeated the room. Pictures of English hunting scenes completed the image of a country squire's den.

"What brings you here so early?" Ron adjusted the creases in his light wool slacks and settled into the chair opposite Crockett. Despite his tailored shirts and buffed nails, Ron looked like a well-dressed thug with the bull neck and muscular thighs of an all-league running back.

Crockett ignored Ron's question. "Impressive models in the lobby. Recognized most of them except Emerald Acres. Where did you build it?" He shifted in his chair and wondered what made him uneasy.

"We haven't built it yet. We're still negotiating with landowners and subcontractors. I thought I'd closed a deal last week, but the owner balked. It's a tricky business. Gotta get all your ducks lined up and then give it your best shot." Ron shouldered an imaginary rifle and picked off sitting ducks one at a time.

Crockett didn't smile at his performance. Curious. Crockett was taller than Ron. That was it. Ron had screwed his chair up higher. Dominance trick number two. Subtle, but effective. Could be Ron was born with an extra testicle. Even the seating was planned so that Crockett had to squint into the morning sun. He rolled his chair around the table until the sun was out of his eyes. "Thought you might have some thoughts on the events at the Gourd last Friday night."

"Jules' death." Ron swiveled in his chair to reach a small, wooden humidor on a sideboard guarded by an ebony swan with a graceful arched neck. The feathering detail was meticulous, and the wood gleamed with polish. Two pictures sat beside the swan, one of Mariko, Ron's wife, and the other, the much-publicized photo of the Four Horsemen.

Ron selected an Excalibur. "Smoke?" he asked, offering the box too briefly, snapping the lid closed to discourage acceptance of the offer.

Crockett let the silence hang while Ron clipped the end of the cigar, wet it between his lips, and lit up, pulling slowly until the tobacco smoldered. Finally, Ron spoke. "Who would've thought." He paused, yet another control mechanism meant to signal Crockett's next question.

Crockett played along. "Thought what?"

"Thought she'd take her own life. True, isn't it?"

"Too early to call. Still reconstructing events of the evening. Reason to believe you paid Mrs. Kenworthy a visit Friday night."

"And what might that be?" Ron took a hit on the cigar and then rolled it in a long alabaster ashtray.

Crockett withdrew a plastic bag from his pocket and placed it on the table. Inside was the stub of the cigar he'd found in the ashtray under Jules' bed.

"Well, no shit, Sherlock. You're becoming a first-rate spook," he paused, "or, is that the CIA?" His mocking tone left no doubt that a slur was intended. "Sure. George must have told you I was there. I wondered if he saw me leave."

Crockett masked his surprise by shifting his weight in the chair. "Tell me about your visit."

"There's not much to tell. She was unpacking a bag when I arrived. Kid came home from a sleepover unexpectedly, so Jules couldn't go with George to his conference. We had a few drinks and retired to the bedroom." Ron flashed Crockett a conspiratorial, man-to-man smirk. "She was all loosened up before I got there. Ready."

Ron drew his fingers through his short hair and licked his lips. "Practically blew the top of my head off, y'know what I mean. We were lying there, sweating, when the garage door opened and that yappy little mutt went crazy in the girl's room." Ron pulled on his cigar. "Georgie-poo was home. I suggested we surprise him, but Jules had me leave by the front door while she intercepted him in the garage."

"That the last time you saw her?" Crockett heard the disgust creep into his voice.

"Yeah. But I had no reason to think it would be the last." Ron's voice carried an indignant overtone, as if Crockett's disdain impugned his manly rights.

Crockett backed off a bit, stretched, and offered Ron a slow smile. He then nodded toward the stunning studio portrait on the sideboard. "Beautiful. Marianne's her name?"

The photographer had captured Ron's wife in a magical moment of ambivalence between delicate sensuality and child-like innocence. Exquisite cheekbones and a long, graceful neck provided dramatic contrast to the enigma of her eyes. Her lips curved suggestively at the corners, leaving the viewer to wonder if her next move was a growl or a blush.

"Mariko." Ron corrected. He looked at the picture with obvious pride and then turned it so that Crockett could no longer see her.

"None of my business, but what do you need with Jules when you have such a lovely wife?"

"You're right. None of your business." But Ron couldn't let the implied criticism go unchallenged. "If you saw a hundred dollar bill on the ground, would you walk away from it?"

"Even if you knew who it belonged to?" countered Crockett.

"I figure, somebody dropped it, that's his problem."

"And if you're already rich?"

"You can never get too much, or be too rich. I told you years ago that I'd be good and rich someday," Ron laughed, referring to his middle name, Goodrich.

Ron's watch beeped the quarter-hour, letting Crockett know that his time was up. Dominance trick number four. Crockett leaned back. He wasn't rushing off. "Anyone who can vouch for your whereabouts late Friday night?"

"What the hell, is this a criminal investigation?" Ron leaned back and folded his arms across his chest.

"Might turn out that way."

Ron shook his head and then raised a hand and dropped it. "OK, yeah, sure. Lots of folks saw me Friday night. After my little visit, I was late for dinner, so I hightailed it home. Actually, I stopped at the jeweler and the pharmacy first and then went home. The wife and I had a couple of drinks with the Watsons, ate dinner, and then took in the band concert on Tappan Square. Ricki—at the front desk—is also our babysitter. She can vouch for when we got home. Wasn't that late. Hell, I was wasted."

Crockett nodded and rose to leave.

They didn't shake hands.

Crockett drove slowly back to the station. He hadn't spoken ten words with Ron since high school. The camaraderie suggested by the photo of the Four Horsemen was a photographer's lie. He despised Ron. The feeling was mutual.

Still, if Ron's story was true, there was another part of Friday night that George had failed to mention.

Chapter Twenty-Nine

Casey unlocked the Children's Room and entered but didn't turn on the lights. No one would expect her on her day off, and with luck, no one would notice her presence.

She took two samples of Martha's handwriting from her book bag: Martha's Cats Eyes oath from the clubhouse and a letter she wrote to Casey in prison. Too bad she didn't have a current sample of her writing. For class, the prison letter and the childhood oath would have to do. Barbara Roman wouldn't expect a report on the assignment so soon, but Casey had studied graphology in prison and was eager to apply her skills.

First, she focused on Martha's childhood writing, comparing the graphological evidence from her handwritten oath to her own perceptions of Martha as a girl. No surprises there. She was insecure, selfish, jealous, and childish with a combination of traits that could suggest dishonesty, or at least a tendency to bend the truth.

The sharp jangle of the telephone broke her concentration. She glanced at the clock. Eight-thirty. Someone forgot the Children's Room was closed. Or, possibly George? Because she wasn't supposed to be there, Casey let the answering machine click in.

"Damn. I forgot you play hooky Mondays."

Casey grabbed the receiver. "Crockett?"

"Meet me for coffee tomorrow morning?"

"Sure." *What did he want?*

"Still have those sketches you talked about?"

Casey relaxed. "Yes, but why do you need them? You've already identified

Bear and Dumbo."

"Could show the sketches to a few students."

"OK, I'll bring them." With relief, she hung up and returned to her analysis.

After writing up her findings from Martha's Cats Eyes' oath, Casey tackled her adult writing. Casey's jaw tensed just looking at it. She traced over the letters to get a feel for the motion, and, by extension, for the writer. After a paragraph, she stopped and shook out her hand to relax the cramped muscles. The tension was palpable, suggesting the pent-up anger Barbara had mentioned. Two hours later, she finished her report.

She placed the report in her book bag and picked up the Civil War conference program George had left with her and the page she'd swiped from Jules' journal. In the past week, Casey had read and reread the two samples.

She scanned the journal page and rested on the third paragraph.

"I'd take off with Gabby tomorrow, but it would break her heart to leave her father. It would break his heart as well, but at this point, I don't much care. He got us into this mess, screwing around. Besides, where would I go?"

The entry added credence to Martha's comments about George's dalliance with Renee. Was he a philandering SOB, or was he miserable in a failed marriage and seeking solace elsewhere? There were always two sides to a story.

"I'm so sorry, Casey. For all of us, believe me, I'm sorry. I made a terrible mistake," George had said. Which terrible mistake: screwing around and losing his job at Yale, or marrying Jules? Or could it possibly be leaving Casey?

Another line at the bottom of the page confused her: *"God, I'm walking a tightrope, robbing Peter to pay Paul. If he figures out what I'm doing, there will be all hell to pay. I can't keep this up much longer."*

What was Jules doing? The image of her entering the Loveland mausoleum last Thursday flashed into her mind. Casey reread the passage. Who was "he?"

She studied each curve and space as if it were an ancient hieroglyph resisting translation but couldn't see any overt patterns that would signal dishonesty or deceit. No little ticks or screwy loops, blotches, or smears. No hesitation or irregular spacing. Just the opposite. Good rhythm, form, and speed. Some muddiness and tightness in the last entry and a few worry loops. So, Jules was indulgent and insecure, but who wasn't? Casey turned the writing upside down. A few words drooped below the lines on the paper suggesting lack of energy or depression.

She turned to the back cover and studied the hasty note from Jules. Casey shrugged. Why not? If it worked for Martha, why not for Jules? She placed the tracing paper over Jules' signature and slowly, painstakingly, re-created the image. Even after her practice with Martha's writing, it was harder than she had expected.

The *J* dominated all of the other letters. She wrote the letter over and over, filling the entire page with *J*'s, working slowly at first, and then developing speed. Then she tackled the smaller letters, little *u, l, e, s*, all connected. They were somewhat rounded, leaning to the right. *"ules ules ules ules ules"* she wrote.

Bookie had draped himself along the windowsill, his tail switching back and forth. With a cavernous yawn that displayed every tooth, he stood, stretched, and circled before resettling. Good idea. Casey got up and walked around the room.

Maybe it was time for a different tack. To write like Jules, she'd have to think and feel like Jules. Casey re-traced the name and pictured Jules. Tall, confident, leggy Jules with swinging, caramel hair. Casey tossed her hair to the side the way Jules did.

"Jules," she signed. Better. Jules as a coed flying across campus on her bicycle, the object of desire of every male she passed. Flirty, carefree "Jules." Every time she wrote the name she said it aloud. Laughing "Jules." "Jules," with the smokey eyes.

Prom queen "Jules." Clever, careless, impatient, selfish "Jules." She wrote faster. Thoughtless "Jules." Mean, catty, greedy "Jules." Best friend, tramp, betrayer, Judas "Jules!" Snap!

Casey jumped. She'd broken the pencil lead and gouged a hole in the paper. She threw the pencil on the floor. Bookie jumped from the window and batted it about. When Casey didn't respond to his antics, he stomped to a spot in front of her and glared.

Casey scooped him up into her arms, nuzzling her face in his fur. "Sorry, fella. I didn't mean to upset you. How about a snack?"

Bookend squirmed loose and hit the floor walking toward the bookcase. He leaped to his new feeding spot and nudged her hand as she filled his bowl.

"Hey, it isn't all bad. I've got you, you old hairball. And I'm Outside, for now, anyway." She stroked Bookend and returned to her desk.

She pictured herself sitting at the Kenworthys' kitchen table, wine glass in one hand, pen in the other, listening to sad music, and began writing in large, loose letters. She was getting the hang of it. Big deal, what good did it do? Nothing. But maybe she could help Art. His drunken recall—or lack of it—would never stand up to questioning. He looked guilty falling off the wagon the night Jules died. Casey could write a simple "so sorry" note from Jules.

What was she thinking? That would be forgery.

But she knew firsthand how facts could be twisted to railroad a suspect. In college, she'd worked and studied hard, making money for room and board and books. Industrious Casey—driving students to the airport at school breaks; selling sandwiches at night to hungry rich kids in the dorms; shelving books in the stacks on Sunday afternoons, and working two meals a day as a waitress. She also tutored Charlie Crockett after school twice a week.

During her trial, the prosecution used her industry to create a drugging scenario. She knew the airline curbside check-in people by first name, and a few of them had been linked to drugs. She spent afternoons with Charlie Crockett, known cocaine user and runner. She roamed the dorms late at night under the guise of selling sandwiches. Worst of all, she knew the stacks intimately, and they were practically lined with cocaine. The nail in the coffin was the bike she'd "borrowed" because hers had a flat and she was late for class. The trial had been held at the county seat where jurors didn't know that "borrowing" bikes was a townie tradition in Oberlin.

None of these facts were proof of her dealing, but for that they had the coke in the bike she was riding. The seriousness of the drug problem in town and two overdoses in the college ensured a stiff sentence.

The only time Casey had seen Jules during the trial was when the prosecution called her as a witness. Jules cried and appeared reluctant when she was asked if she'd ever done drugs. "I tried it once with Casey," she whispered. Well, that was true. Jules had taunted her and challenged her to join her just once in a line of coke. Against her better judgment, Casey tried it, but she didn't like the loss of control. But, of course, that was the reason Jules liked it.

So, goody-goody Casey got ten hard years for borrowing a bike and snorting onc linc of coke. Since her return, she'd been the model worker and student, her only transgressions a stolen kiss or two. Maybe it was time to cross the line. Walking the line sure hadn't done much for her.

You're justifying. Damn straight. She looked at Jules' script again and then took out a clean sheet of paper. This would be practice: she could write it again later wearing a pair of Mae's gloves. Even then, she wouldn't have to use it.

A shadow darkened the page. Casey sniffed. Scowlie Circulation breath. Casey covered the paper and rolled backward quickly, colliding with something solid.

"Damn! Watch what you're doing!" Circulation howled.

Casey bit her lip. "Oh, Mrs. Edwards, I'm so sorry. I didn't expect you to be standing *directly behind my chair* in the dark." Casey kept her voice sweet.

"I wondered who could be in here on a Monday. The room is closed, you know."

"I guess I should know that, since I work here." Casey was pushing it, but she didn't care.

"So, what *are* you doing here at this hour on Monday?" Within one sentence, Circulation traversed the spectrum from indignation to suspicion.

Casey backed out of range of the lethal breath rays. "Finishing up my last college paper. Mrs. Palmer lets me use supplies for my studies." Casey dished up the lies cheerfully. As she spoke, she repacked her book bag.

"Actually, I'm glad you're here."

"You are?"

"We need help logging in and shelving returns. That is, if you're finished with your paper." She glanced meaningfully at Casey's packed bag.

Casey groaned. All year long, students blew off overdue notices, but at the end of the year when the college threatened to withhold their diplomas, they coughed up a mountain of books and paid the fees.

"Well, as you know, it's my day off," Casey demurred.

"We'll pay, of course."

"I'd have to miss my last class." She'd miss the last American History class, but George wouldn't be teaching it anyway.

"Overtime."

"Okay." Casey grabbed her bag and followed Circulation upstairs. She could earn extra money and return the books she'd checked out for George.

Chapter Thirty

Tuesday morning, Casey slid into a booth opposite Crockett.

"Two coffees," Crockett ordered as she approached.

No banter today. A muscle jumped in Crockett's jaw. He hunched over his empty cup like a tightly wound spring. "Watcha got for me?"

He'd forgotten he invited her for coffee. No matter. She had plenty on her mind. "It may be just a coincidence, but—"

"Don't believe in coincidence," snapped Crockett.

Casey flinched.

"Sorry. Don't mean to bite your head off. Go on."

"Everything I touch turns to powder." Casey described visiting Art on Sunday, and how she'd found the bag of cocaine in the well.

"Might have more to do with the Kenworthys than you. Jules had a nose full of cocaine when she died. There's a packet of powder in an old Loveland hiding place in the well at the Gourd. And the book McPhee used in the stacks to exchange money for coke was the Buckmaster book you couldn't find, last checked out by George."

Casey's jaw dropped. She composed her face with effort before speaking, aware of Crockett's watchful gaze. "There's one other thing. Friday, when I was riding my bike in the cemetery, I saw Jules enter the Loveland mausoleum. I wondered why she'd visit that musty old place unless she was up to something. As kids, we used to stash our more 'objectionable' treasures there."

Crockett nodded, but changed the subject. "You tell Art about the baggie in the well?"

"No. He had enough worries after the trauma of the weekend."

"Still in love with Jules?"

Casey drew in a sharp breath. If he knew, why ask? "Yes, he probably was. I remember wishing someone would look at me the way he looked at her. He knew it was hopeless, but that didn't help."

She chose her next words carefully. "We talked about Jules for a while on Sunday. No way to avoid it. It was painful for both of us." She waited a few seconds before changing the subject. "Oh, I almost forgot." She pulled a sketchbook from the depths of her book bag and showed him her quick sketches of McPhee and Bear.

Crockett studied the pictures. When he turned back a few pages and chuckled, Casey leaned forward and saw it was a picture she'd drawn of him.

"Handsome dude." He handed back the book with a wide smile.

Casey's cheeks warmed. She busied herself tearing out the pictures of Danny McPhee and Bear. She studied Crockett's picture for a moment, and then reluctantly ripped it out and slid it across the table.

When she jammed the book into her book bag, the cover caught on the drawstring, sending it skittering across the floor. As Crockett picked it up, a folded loose-leaf page fell out and wafted toward the floor. Casey blanched and dove for it, but Crockett was quicker.

"Oh no! Don't!"

Crockett's face registered shock, anger and then melted into pain. He touched the page and closed his eyes, as if he were trying to make contact with his little brother. He bowed his head.

Casey had captured Charley's cocky smile as he waved at her from Tappan Square across from Peters Hall. She'd drawn the picture in Marysville, to record her last image of him before he was crushed beneath the police cruiser.

Casey stretched her arm across the table to connect with Crockett. "I'm sorry, JoJo. So sorry. I forgot it was in the pocket." She stopped. Nothing she could say that might diffuse his anguish.

Crockett raised his head. His eyes were moist as he smiled bravely at Charley's image. "Truth? *He* was the handsome dude in the family." Suddenly, Crockett frowned and grabbed Casey's retreating hand.

"Mean," he exclaimed. "Where'd you get that?"

When she'd reached across the table, Casey's sweatshirt had drawn back, revealing a jagged scar on her forearm. Hastily she pulled down her sleeve, but he wouldn't release her hand.

"Marysville."

"*Knife* fight?"

"Self-defense."

"That why you didn't get out early?"

"Partly. I was an 'unrepentant and dangerous felon' because I wouldn't confess, was in a knife fight, and wouldn't name my attackers."

"That it?"

Casey hesitated. "No. There was a rumor that the drugs dropped in the Oberlin bust were only part of a larger shipment earmarked for northern Ohio that had gone missing. Some inmates and guards were convinced I knew where the mother lode was. I didn't. After the fight and a few interrogations, they transferred me to the hard time unit."

Crockett whistled softly. "Rough place. All black and Hispanic, right?"

"Luckily, my cellmate LouAnne believed me and took me under her wing. She's a black Amazon nobody messes with."

"What she in for?"

"Murder."

Crockett drew back and his eyes widened.

"She caught her husband molesting their little girl."

Crockett signaled for more coffee. After their cups were refilled, he switched gears again. "We never talked about the arrest and how Charley died."

Casey stared at a saltshaker on a nearby table. "I was the first one out of Peters after class. I had a million things to do before George arrived." Casey hesitated, but Crockett nodded for her to continue. "Charley hollered and waved to me as I hopped on my bike. He was across the street. I couldn't make out his words, so I just waved back. Then all hell broke loose."

Tightness spread across Casey's chest. She couldn't get enough air. She dug her middle fingernail into the flesh of her thumb. LouAnne believed the brain could only process one pain at a time. But no matter how hard Casey dug at her thumb, she was overwhelmed by the howling sirens closing in as she mounted her bicycle. The deep voice of the bullhorn. Flashing lights. The squad car careening over the curb, Charley running and looking over his shoulder, the car smashing into his body—

"Casey!" Crockett was beside her in a flash. He pushed her head between her knees and told her to breathe slowly. She tried to focus. Her palms and temples were moist.

Crockett dunked his napkin in water and pressed it against her forehead.

The waitress and then the manager of the restaurant appeared beside the table. Crockett reassured them that she was OK.

"Take it slow, girl."

Casey's breathing gradually returned to normal.

Crockett spoke gently. "That day changed both our lives. But I wasn't there. You were." Gently, he righted her and wrapped the napkin around her bleeding thumb.

She turned so he couldn't see the tears well up in her eyes. "That day changed the lives of everyone I loved."

Crockett filled in a few blanks. "The cops must've watched Charley make the drop, and then waited until someone took possession before moving in. But why would Charley stick around? Doesn't make sense. He should've been long gone."

"He would have been, but I ducked out of class ten minutes early."

Crockett nodded.

"When I talked to the girls in Marysville, they were amazed at the amount of coke in the drop. Who would need that much dope?"

"Don't know, Casey."

She let out a deep breath. "I hate to see you hurting so. That's why I've never talked about it. I don't know about you, but I've had enough tears. I'm sick of feeling like a victim. I wake up some days feeling like I'm covered in

164

gray prison dust, invisible and automatically guilty."

Crockett took her hand and pretended to examine it for dust. He gave her a sardonic look, and examined his own hands. "I best be on my way before my woman hears her black boy's been holding hands with a gray girl."

Chapter Thirty-One

In Tuesday morning's staff meeting, Crockett suggested showing the sketch of McPhee to the students who'd been in the basement of Barrows for a possible identification. Connolly nixed the idea and explicitly ordered him to stay clear of any college contact until after graduation. When Crockett pointed out that students would be gone by then, Connolly had responded, "That's the idea."

Connolly also told him to wrap up the "Kenworthy tragedy" as fast as possible. As far as Jules' death, there was no question in Crockett's mind what Connolly wanted, but the circumstances surrounding her death were too weird for him to ignore. Everywhere he poked, ugly emerged. With friends and lovers like hers, he could easily entertain the notion of suicide or foul play.

As he drove toward the Gourd, Crockett reviewed Sunday's conversation with George. By the time he arrived, he'd decided to play bad cop. Good cop sure hadn't worked. George hadn't mentioned seeing Jules Friday night. He hadn't just omitted facts, he'd been purposefully misleading. Crockett slammed the car door and strode toward the Kenworthy front entrance, his jaw set in a hard line. He ignored the bell and beat on the door.

A little face peered out from George's study window. "JoJo! JoJo!" Gabby sang out as she ran to the front door.

Crockett forced an instant attitude adjustment and managed a smile. Kid was wrecking his act.

"So it's 'JoJo' now." George emerged from the study. "Kids sure make friends fast. Come in." He gestured for Crockett to enter, raising his eyebrows in a mute question.

Crockett answered with a cold stare.

"Gabby, honey, JoJo and I have some business to talk about."

"I'll be quiet," Gabby promised, sensing his next words.

"No, sweetie. You scoot up to your room and draw me a picture. I'll be up in a little while. I'll bring you some ice cream."

Gabby's lower lip shot out, but she did his bidding. Crockett heard slow steps of protest as she climbed the stairs.

Crockett had the sensation of déjà vu as they took the same positions at the kitchen table they'd occupied two days before. George waved at a counter laden with dishes of food. "What'll we do with all of this? There's enough here to serve Sunday brunch at the restaurant. People don't know what to do, so they bring food."

"Seems you left out a few facts about Friday night. Care to refresh your memory?"

George's shoulders slumped. When he spoke his voice was quiet and strained. "I was hoping some of the ugliness wouldn't have to come out. It'll be hard enough for Gabby to grow up without a mother. I didn't see any reason for her to know what a slut she was. Does all this have to be public?"

Crockett crossed his arms over his chest and tilted his chair back on two legs. "Talk to me."

"I'd been planning to attend a conference. Well, you know about that, and the trip to New York."

"You and Jules were going to the conference, but your plans were interrupted when Gabby returned from her sleepover."

"No. Jules never planned to accompany me. Civil War stuff bored her blind."

"So why was she unpacking a suitcase when Ron arrived?"

George frowned and shook his head. "I have no idea. I didn't see any suitcase. When I came home for a few things I'd forgotten, Jules met me at the garage door in a housecoat. She reeked of alcohol. And sex. She tried to block me, but I pushed past her and saw Ron leaving by the front door.

"She followed me to the study. I couldn't believe her. She'd thought I'd already left and was angry when I interrupted her little party. I told her she could party all night for all I cared—just to get out of my way, I was late.

"Then she was interested. 'Late?' she asked. 'Who is she? I should've known. We've had a long dry spell, and you're no monk. At least I don't think you're a monk.' And then she came on to me. Unbelievable! Standing there dripping with another man's semen, trying to seduce me. When she put her arms around me, I called her a whore, told her I wasn't into gangbangs, and pushed her away."

He hesitated, but Crockett nodded for him to continue. "Her balance wasn't very good with all the alcohol, and she fell backward. She hit the floor and her face must've hit the doorjamb. Frankly, I don't think I pushed her that hard. I offered to help her up, but she kicked and spat at me. Then she called me a few choice names, struggled to her feet and staggered down the hall. I figured she couldn't be hurt too badly.

"I gathered my bag and left. I didn't know Gabby was upstairs. I'm not surprised she didn't come down. She always made herself scarce when Jules and I fought."

"Anyone who can confirm any of this?" asked Crockett, giving him a leveling gaze.

George paused again. "No."

Crockett rose to leave. "Could have told me this before."

"How could I expect you to understand? We were...the 'Golden Couple.'"

"All walk on the same ground. No more sudden trips to New York, OK? Stick around 'til we get all the loose ends tied up." Crockett left George at the table and walked out the front door.

He sat in the cruiser, heavier with the burden of George's story. Once again, he felt relieved to be leaving the place.

"Crockett! Crockett! Come back here!" George hollered from the doorway. He waved a paper in the air. "I found this in the freezer. It's a note from Jules."

Later in the afternoon, Crockett sat in his office and stared at the note encased in a protective plastic bag. George had opened it before Crockett could reach the kitchen, fouling it with his prints.

Dear George,

Take care of Gabby.

I'm sorry—Forgive me if you can.

I love you both,

Jules

The note was what Crockett had hoped for. He understood why no one had found it earlier. Who'd look in the freezer? But Jules knew George would find it when he got ice cream for Gabby.

Even with the note, Crockett had a hard time picturing the night Jules died. She was drunk early according to both Ron and George. But she had to be sober when she wrote the note, or at least not falling down drunk. The note was written in a steady hand. That meant a planned suicide. She'd written and placed the note in the freezer before her party began.

She was sick in the cellar. She had to have swallowed the sleeping pills after she was sick for them to have taken effect. She could've gone back upstairs, taken the pills and returned to the cellar, but if she was so vain, why not change clothing and clean up a bit upstairs? Why wear a choir robe?

Another scenario. She went to the cellar for wine. She was sick. She stripped, put on the robe, washed down the pills with a bottle of wine, rolled herself up in a blanket and died. But that meant she had to have the pills with her. There was no pill bottle on her, in the trash, or in the house.

He rewound his mental tape to the kitchen scene Saturday morning. There were three wine bottles: one on the table, one in the trash, and one upstairs in the bedroom next to Jules' bed. There were two wine glasses in the bedroom, and a single glass on the kitchen table. No glass or bottle in the basement.

Speculation was getting him nowhere. He called Barbara Roman and asked what she'd need for a handwriting analysis of the note.

Chapter Thirty-Two

D r. Dundee, the Medical Examiner, kept office hours in the clinic attached to the county hospital. Crockett followed the receptionist down a corridor lined with examining rooms. He steeled himself for the interview and entered the doctor's immaculate office.

Dr. Dundee's freewheeling autopsy style had earned him the moniker "Max the Ax." He delighted in traumatizing interns, slicing and hacking with seeming abandon. Despite his penchant for drama, his surgical technique was flawless, and his track record as a medical examiner, unblemished.

Dundee tilted forward in his leather swivel chair as Crockett entered. "You're here for Kenworthy, right? Let's make this quick. I'm running late."

"Waiting room's empty," Crockett said as he settled into the straight chair facing Dundee's desk.

Dundee shrugged. "Golf, my man, golf. One must keep one's priorities straight."

Dundee retrieved a file from a tidy stack on the corner of the desk. The man reminded Crockett of a praying mantis, over six feet four with skinny arms and legs. His complexion had a grayish cast, and his cheeks were pocked with acne craters. But his most prominent feature was a pair of bulging bug eyes that he could twirl independently behind coke bottle glasses.

Crockett could never figure out which eye was the stray, making it hard to know where to look when talking to him. The nurse told Crockett that Dundee could focus when he wanted, but he enjoyed playing ocular pinball for its effect.

"You'll get all this in the written report. In simple terms, she died of a combination of alcohol, sleeping pills, and cocaine. The sleeping pills were secobarbital, which are unusual, but not unheard of, nowadays. Seco got a bad rep as the suicide pill of choice a number of years back. Now doctors prescribe phenobarb, which isn't as lethal. Anyway, the little lady had herself quite a party. Did I mention she'd had intercourse?"

"My best estimate for time of death is between eleven in the evening and three in the morning. She'd just begun to stiffen with *rigor mortis* early Saturday morning. As you know, *rigor* usually sets in between one and six hours after death.

"Must've been one strange woman." Dundee opened the file. One eye tracked his pencil down the page, scanning the transcription of his verbal autopsy. He flipped to a page of lab results.

"Here. Traces of unusual chemicals in her stomach fluids. Not enough to kill her, but certainly not what you'd expect. In addition to asparagus and meatloaf, coconut and cream, there was diethylene glycol butyl ether, surfactants, perfume, and colorant." Both eyes focused on Crockett expectantly, as if he were about to deliver a punch line. "No idea? The lab guy said it was a cocktail of Lemon Fresh Pine-Sol and Tilex. Must've been trying to clean up her act." He brayed at his little joke.

"You saw the bruise on her cheek, but there's another thing. She had little slivers of wood and abrasions on the inside of both cheeks at the back of her mouth. My guess?" He looked to Crockett, who nodded for him to continue.

"This part is pure speculation. Remember in the old westerns when the hero jammed a stick between his teeth and bit while his sidekick pulled the arrow out of his chest?" Dundee pretended to chomp down on two fingers to illustrate his point. "Maybe she bit on wood so she could knock back the cleaning cocktail. It didn't work, because the chemicals made her retch." He lurched forward as if he were throwing up.

Crockett recoiled. "Got it. Anything that would make you suspect foul play?"

"You're going to have to make that call. She'd had a busy night: booze, drugs, sex, pills. She could have been hit or the bruise could have been caused by a fall. Personally, I'd think anyone who dressed up in a black robe and drank cleaning fluids in the cellar was out of her mind. Throw in alcohol and drugs, and you have the classic scenario for an overdose or suicide."

"But?" Crockett could tell the doctor had more to say.

The doctor tapped his pencil on the report and then shoved himself back from the desk as if distancing himself from the written word. "Well, the sex and the bruise suggest the interaction of a couple of people during the earlier part of the evening. A lovers' quarrel that takes a very nasty turn? The stick could have been forced into her mouth." Dundee paused and closed the folder. "Another thing has nothing to do with the autopsy, but I thought it was awfully strange. Here, I'll show you."

The doctor jumped up and rushed out the door, returning in seconds with a paper modesty sheet used to cover patients during physical examinations. He spread the sheet out on the floor, and then, to Crockett's surprise, lay down on one side of the sheet. Gripping the edge with one hand, he rolled over, wrapping himself cocoon style in the sheet.

"This cloth isn't big enough, but you get my point." He extricated himself from the sheet and got up.

The bizarre demonstration supported a question that had been nagging at Crockett all week. Why didn't Jules just curl up in a corner and draw the blanket over her?

"It's hard to imagine someone in her condition having the coordination to roll herself up in a blanket like a rug on moving day." Dundee glanced at his watch. "You'll get the formal report soon. Sorry I couldn't be more definitive, but she died under very strange circumstances." With that, he swapped his white coat for a jacket that hung behind the door and was gone.

Crockett stared at the sheet on the floor. The blanket bit had bothered him, and now there were strange chemicals and splinters of wood.

Chapter Thirty-Three

A letter addressed to Casey in Lou Ann's distinctive writing had been placed in the center of her desk instead of in her mail slot. She turned it over. Taped shut. The Scowlies weren't even pretending they weren't reading her mail. The return address, "The Ohio Reformatory for Women in Marysville" had been crossed out and replaced with "Saint Mary's Home for Naughty Girls." A red stamp across the front said "State Prison."

In the note, LouAnne announced that she would get out of prison in a week.

"Head for the Rox, lay low, check it out, you know. Get laid, no one watchin or listenin! Smoke a whole one myself. Keep clean, Girlfren. Got a room for you here— XOX, LA

Not much, but it buoyed Casey's spirits. LouAnne would return to Roxbury, Massachusetts, where she'd grown up. It had taken Casey six months to write to LouAnne and even then, she wasn't sure she wanted a response. She was Outside.

Now, with Art drinking his dinner, Martha spewing venom, Crockett acting funny, and George giving her the silent treatment, she missed LouAnne's honesty and her direct, crude, free spirit. She wished she could just lie back on the top bunk and pour out her soul—as long as she didn't have to stay.

Sometimes she was so lonely she talked with LouAnne at night, imagining her friend's response. But today, Casey was rehearsing lines for a conversation with George using Bookend as her audience. At first, the cat had responded, but by the third round he tired of the game, yawned, and curled his head under his paws.

Casey had written out her main points. Why haven't you called? When will I see you? How is Gabby? During the last iteration, she revised the order and changed the tone. How are you holding up? How about Gabby? Was she eating? Sleeping? I miss you. Rather transparent, but it was eleven-thirty, and she wanted to get to his office before he broke for lunch.

She hopped on Mae's bike and took a shortcut past the faculty lot. Good, the Civic was still there. He must know she'd see the car on her way to the library. Why couldn't he pick up the telephone and put her mind to rest, one way or the other?

"This limbo freakin' sucks." She smiled at LouAnne's voice.

Casey threw Mae's bike at the rack and watched it buckle and crash. Instantly, she felt a wave of remorse. The trusty wheel lay in a jumble, wheel upturned, handlebars askew. "Sorry," she muttered as she pulled it upright.

"Casey girl, get a grip!" Crockett's voice.

Was she losing it, talking with cats, hearing voices, and apologizing to a bicycle? Slow down. Casual was the ticket. "I thought I'd drop in to see how you're holding up," she practiced, entering the building and crossing the lobby. "I'm worried about Gabby. How is she?"

Casey caught the alarmed eye of the department secretary and swallowed the rest of her monologue. Downstairs, George's office door was closed, but the overhead light inside illuminated the glazed glass panel in the door. She raised her hand to knock, but the image of Renee's pink slips flooded her vision. She barged in.

"What the—"

"Why haven't you called?" Casey demanded.

George rose quickly and walked around his desk. Instead of a hug, a peck on the cheek, or even a handshake, he skirted her, closed the door, and leaned against it.

"Afraid I'll embarrass you?" Casey walked behind George's desk and sat in his swivel chair, skewering a speechless George with accusing eyes. She resisted the impulse to spin. "Cat got your tongue? Let me help. You're delighted to see me. You've missed me, but were too shy to call. You were in an accident, and your short-term memory was blown all to hell."

"Casey, calm down." George let out a long, audible sigh. "I thought *you*, of all people, would understand." He sighed again, eyes downcast. "Actually, I was counting on it. This has been a very difficult time. For me. For Gabby. And, I suppose, even for you. I happen to be dealing with a motherless child and some grief of my own."

Casey cringed, chastened, and embarrassed. There was no hole to crawl into. She waited for George to fill the silence.

"I've thought about you every day. You've got to believe that. It's just—" George broke off and bit his lip.

Casey felt a weight on her chest, like a dentist's radiation blanket. "I'd hoped you would call Saturday, or Sunday at the latest, as you'd promised." She forced herself to continue. "Today's Thursday, and I still wouldn't be talking with you if I hadn't forced my way into your office."

"Jesus, Casey! What do you expect?" George turned away and threw his hands in the air.

Stupid. Stupid. She never should have come. She rose and headed for the door.

George's hand on her shoulder stopped her. He turned her to him and drew her chin upward. Casey refused to meet his eyes.

"Sit for a moment, Case. Please."

She didn't sit, but she didn't leave, either, paralyzed by indecision.

"I couldn't call. There just wasn't an opportunity on Saturday. Sunday—well, you know, Sunday was impossible. And ever since then, Crockett's been nosing around asking questions, and a patrolman has been watching the house. I think Crockett suspects something. He knows we've been seen together. I think he's got you figured for the drugs, and the two of us—"

Casey shook her head in denial. Only days ago, Crockett had held her hand and listened to her tell about the packet of coke in the well. They'd talked about the drug bust and Charley's death.

George ignored her reaction. "He asked me repeatedly where I was on

Friday night. Not just for the time we were talking on the porch, but later on as well. If the police are watching me, or Art, or Martha, or you, they could also be listening to our telephone conversations. I thought it best to steer clear for a while."

"You can't be a serious suspect, George. Surely someone at the hotel or conference can vouch for your whereabouts. Why are you worried?"

George paused before answering. "Frankly, I'm more concerned about you. Who can vouch for you later Friday night?"

George hadn't responded to her question, and now she didn't respond to his. "Did you know that Jules used a book you'd checked out of the library for her drug drop? She gouged a hole in the center for the coke and gave it to one of Swain's construction goons to shelve in the stacks."

"No, Casey." George spoke slowly as if she were a child. "Ron gave Jules the drugs. She only got stoned on the nights when I was out and he showed up. She wasn't a dealer, and she wasn't half as bad as you'd like to believe she was. She did it to punish me. But once she got going, especially when she mixed alcohol and drugs, she didn't know how to stop."

George rubbed his hands in a washing motion. "I'm only telling you these things for your own good."

"Spare me the lecture, Professor."

George pulled back and pursed his lips. "You needn't be sarcastic. It's time to let bygones be bygones. Just as you paid a price for what you did, Jules paid the price for whatever sins she committed—against you, or me, or Art or anyone else who feels wronged."

He never believed I was innocent. Casey felt like she'd been kicked in the stomach. She barely heard his next words.

"As I say to Gabby every night at prayers, 'Remember how much she loved us, and how dearly we loved her.'"

A protective numbness engulfed Casey. When she spoke, her voice was ice. "You're wise to maintain a safe distance. I can see that now."

"I have a six-year-old child to protect, and a teaching career I can't afford to jeopardize."

"She's five. Don't worry. I hear you, George." Casey wrenched herself from his magnetic field. "Every word."

"I need time to sort things out. Can you understand that?"

"Oh, yes. Time is something I understand. Very well." She backed until she hit the door.

"What do you expect me to do?" George followed, grabbing her arm. "Tell me," he demanded, tightening his grip. "What should I do?"

For a moment Casey stood mute before the angry stranger crowding her. But then LouAnne's voice came through, pure and simple. "Pound sand."

She made it to the Ladies' Room before throwing up. She retched until nothing was left and then, unable to stop, continued with dry heaves, purging herself the only way she could.

When her breathing returned to normal, she doused her face in cold water. She looked in the mirror at the red splotches on her eyelids and cheeks caused by the violence of her heaves. She opened a high window and gulped in cool, fresh air. From her vantage point she could see the faculty parking lot. George's Civic was already gone.

She clung to the railing as she mounted the steps to the main entrance. Halfway home she realized that she was using the bicycle to steady herself, wearing dark glasses to protect her telltale eyes from passersby.

Chapter Thirty-Four

When Casey walked into the house, Mae intercepted her. "Where've you been? You're late for lunch. Did you see the *News Trib*?" Mae ignored Casey's silence. "Why the dark glasses? You been in a fight?"

Casey chose the safest topic. "What's in the *Trib*?"

"See for yourself. It's on the coffee table." Mae's off-hand response belied the undercurrent of excitement in her voice.

Casey found the paper and flipped it to the front page and froze at a picture of George and Jules, dancing and laughing. He was giving her his look of extra-wide-eyed intensity, and she was clearly responding.

"Would you look at the nails on her? Disgusting. Where did the *Trib* dig up that picture?" Mae continued.

Casey looked at Jules' slender fingers and beautifully manicured nails. "Yes, Mae. I haven't forgotten: 'Only whores and rental car agents wear red nail polish.'" In the background, Leila wore the tiara of Oberlin High School's first black Homecoming Queen.

Behind George and Jules, Casey danced with Crockett, his large black hand on her bare white back. Next to them, Martha gazed dreamily into Art's eyes. He wore an amused expression, probably delighted that the girl in his arms had her mouth shut. Ron wasn't in the picture. He didn't dance.

Casey didn't doubt for a second that Martha had provided the picture. Crockett would lose points, dancing with the wild, white trash ex-con. But for a second it felt good to focus on the innocence of the picture. Paradise lost. Julietta Loveland, beloved jewel of Oberlin, and George, the golden boy. Crockett, tall, very dark, and handsome, and Leila, the Queen. And Art the musical prodigy with Martha, lovely in her moment of silence.

"I thought George was your date," Mae continued.

Amazing, the information Mae stored in that brain of hers. "He was."

"There's another picture toward the back," Mae said. But Casey didn't have the heart to read the continuation of "Oberlin Beauty Dies in Tragic Accident." She flipped the paper onto the coffee table. Time for her to leave— the job, the town, and, most of all George. He *"needed time."*

When Casey entered the library at five minutes past one, she was surprised to see Circulation and Reference huddled in the foyer, talking in low voices. She nodded but didn't stop. On her desk was a copy of the *News Tribune*. The nasty Scowlies probably wanted to see her reaction to the picture. But the paper was opened to Library News and School Lunches and had a note attached, "See me, Mrs. Palmer," partially covering another photograph.

The picture under the note featured Gabby with her mouth shaped in a round "O" of wonder, her hand poised to stroke a large black cat. Bookie's eyes were half-closed in a self-satisfied expression. It was a prize-winning photo.

Casey glanced at the windowsill to see if Bookie was waiting to be let in. No kitty, but then, he knew when to make himself scarce. She looked up, but he wasn't atop the bookcase either.

Neither was his dish. Or the plant. There was dirt on the floor beside the bookcase, as if Bookend had knocked the plant off the shelf. Seconds later, she found the broken cat dish, pottery shards and mangled plant leaves in the wastebasket. Full alarm sounded in her brain.

The door opened behind her. Wheeling about, she was sickened by Circulation's ghastly smile. "Mrs. Palmer has been looking for you."

"Where's Bookend?"

Circulation looked puzzled and then nodded. "Oh, you mean the cat. You were warned about feeding him."

"Where is he?" Casey demanded.

Circulation shrugged. "Probably the Veterinary Clinic. Two men came while you were on your extended lunch break. I've got to give that old cat credit. He gave them a run for their money. He bit one man all the way through his leather glove."

"They took my cat?"

"Mrs. P's instructions were to destroy the animal and donate the carcass to the biology department."

"No!" Casey howled. "Why? He wasn't doing any harm."

"Having feral cats roaming around the library would suggest we have a rodent problem. Mrs. P caught the others, but never could catch him. Not in the stacks." Circulation smiled. "Never would have caught him if you hadn't fed him down here." She turned to leave and then added, "I almost forgot, the police were here looking for you."

"Crockett?"

"No."

"Dougie?"

"'Captain Watson' to you."

"Dougie," Casey repeated, but she didn't have time to spar with Circulation. She had to rescue Bookend. She turned her back, grabbed the phone, and dialed Information.

"I'd be cleaning out my desk, if I were you," Circulation advised on her way out.

Casey hit Redial. Seven tones, three rings, and a click later she was dumped into answering machine hell for the fourth time. "You have reached the Oberlin Veterinary Clinic. Our hours of operation are..."

She waited five minutes and tried again.

"You have reached the Ober—" Casey slammed down the receiver.

The clinic was two miles east of town. She could go home and get Mae's car, but she wasn't sure it would start. Then she'd be three miles from the clinic. She called the Town Taxi, only to be told that no cabs were available because of the rain. Nothing else she could do but bike to the vet.

Outside, rain hit the pavement in heavy spring splats. As she rode Mae's wheel across Tappan Square, the skies darkened behind her. By the time she reached the center of town, the heavens opened and pouring rain matted her hair and rolled down her face, soaking through her clothing.

She pushed on. Cars whipped past, splashing her with sheets of water, mud, and debris. Casey strained to see the random potholes scattered like land mines in the road. To avoid a large body of water, she signaled to move left to the car behind her. Instead of giving her room, the driver pulled alongside and forced her into the water. She felt the rush of air as the car passed within inches.

She was about to make an internationally recognized hand signal, but swore under her breath instead when she saw the car was a police cruiser. She squinted. The driver was white. Not Crockett.

Suddenly the bicycle plunged forward and stopped abruptly in a large cavity. Casey bailed just in time to avoid flying over the handlebars. Standing mid-calf in water, she righted the bicycle, cursing the driver and the universe. When she remounted, she'd lost the power in her legs and could barely move the pedals even though there was no incline. She looked down. The front tire was flat.

With a mile to go, she abandoned the bike and ran. At the edge of town, the sidewalks disappeared, forcing her to slosh through the deepening river at the side of the road.

As she ran, Casey conjured dark schemes of vengeance for Palmer and the Scowlies. First, she'd declaw them without anesthesia. Slowly, one nail at a time. No use spaying them—they'd dried up years ago. Unless, of course, some intern needed practice. She'd feed them bat dung and dorm food and forget to clean out their cages. Later, she'd offer the carcasses to a research institute.

She had tried hard to please Mrs. Palmer, but she realized now how much she despised the woman. Bitter, cold, mean—formaldehyde coursed through her veins. Damn! Casey's mind was back in biology lab where denuded specimens of frogs and cats soaked in fluid. She picked up the pace and whispered a prayer to the powers that be to spare her kitty.

Rain plastered clothes to her skin. She shivered despite the heat of exercise. A flash lit the blackened sky, followed by a deafening crash of thunder. "The gods are angry," she muttered. Or bowling. What the hell did they care what happened to her or her cat? She spotted the veterinary clinic ahead and began her final sprint.

The parking lot at the clinic was full. Casey followed a Labrador retriever and its owner through the door, causing an eruption of howls, yowls, and curses as pet owners within struggled to control their animals.

A prominently displayed "Help Wanted" sign on the front desk ensured lousy service. One woman fought with a jammed copier, while the other talked on the phone, leafing slowly through an enormous appointment book. A bank of red buttons on the telephone blinked on hold.

Casey pushed forward, ignoring the angry objections from those queued up before her. "Is this where they bring the strays?" she gasped, still out of breath.

The woman covered the mouthpiece of the phone, "You'll have to wait—" She looked up at Casey and instantly changed her tack. "Yes. The animal warden brings them here."

Casey released a sob of relief. "Thank God! I've come for my cat, Bookend. He's a big black tom with battered ears."

"Harry—" the receptionist hollered to someone in the back room. "You still got any of them cats?" She turned back to Casey. "Usually, it's just dogs, but he came in with a passel of cats today." She returned to the person on hold, and with exaggerated patience, explained that there were no openings until the following week.

The woman behind Casey cleared her throat with enough volume to startle the dogs in the room into temporary silence. The receptionist ignored both of them, and penciled in an appointment time, followed by the owner's name and telephone numbers at work and at home, the dog's full name, nickname, and for all Casey knew, his Social Security number.

"Excuse me." The woman behind Casey prodded a finger into Casey's shoulder. "You can't just barge—"

Casey whirled and bared her teeth. The second receptionist abandoned the copier and rushed to intercede. "Harry left already."

"I don't need Harry. Give me my cat."

The women at the desk exchanged a glance, and then the first one spoke softly. "If Harry's gone, he's taken the cats with him. We can't keep them here. We only keep the kittens."

The second woman joined in. "If the cats have a tag, he'll call the owners but if not, well, they're euthanized."

"*Euth...* You *kill* them?" Casey's voice rose to a wail. "My cat had a collar and a tag. No one called. Where is he?" she shouted. Every human, canine and feline eye in the room focused on her.

When the first receptionist leaned forward to whisper, the whole room leaned forward to listen. "As I said, we call on tagged animals immediately and keep them until we locate the owner. I don't think he left any of the strays today." When Casey didn't budge, she continued, "You can look out back if you like."

Casey barreled through the door leading to the rear of the building. She was greeted by barks, wails, and whines from the caged animals in veterinary purgatory. She bumped into an old man mopping the floor. "Harry?"

"No'm. I'm the custodian."

"I'm looking for my cat—a big black tom—who was brought in today."

"Sorry, honey. Only strays we got left are the kittens by the back door." He pointed the tip of his mop toward the door and then walked the mop backwards in a graceful, swirling motion.

"They killed him?" Casey could barely speak.

"Have to ask the girls at the desk 'bout that," the custodian muttered, turning his full attention to the mop.

"Where are the cats they put down?" demanded Casey. "I want my cat. To bury him." She choked on the words.

The man stopped mopping and looked at her with sorrowful eyes. "Healthy ones go to the college. Others, the landfill."

Casey burst out the back door howling and was instantly joined by the pets left behind in a communal wail of protest.

She should never have fed him. He'd been safe for years, prowling the stacks. In his element, Palmer was no match for him. But exposed in the Children's Room—cornered—Casey howled again. He must've lost his collar in the fray. Or they took it off him out of spite for biting. She cursed herself for her stupidity, Palmer for her hatefulness, and Circulation for her vindictive glee.

She walked slowly, oblivious to the rain that mixed with her tears. The same police cruiser plowed through a deep trough of water by the curb, drenching her as he passed. Dammit! That was intentional. She took a moment to wipe mud off her blouse and face. Halfway to town, she picked up Mae's wheel, and began the long push to town, weeping for her poor, brave kitty, her soul mate and companion. *Oh, Bookie.*

Chapter Thirty-Five

C asey reached the center of town, exhausted and chilled to the bone. She pushed the heavy bike down an alley next to the hardware store to the bicycle repair shop. The repairman said the tire wouldn't take but fifteen or twenty minutes if she had some shopping to do.

With a little time to burn, Casey wandered the aisles of the hardware store. Hell, she didn't even know why she was fixing the bike, but she felt a strange loyalty to Mae's old wheel. Mae would never ride it again, and Casey couldn't take it with her. Because she had to go. Her best friend had been euthanized. *Oh, Bookie, I'm so sorry*. Fresh tears streamed down her cheeks.

Her numb fingers randomly picked up and discarded a screwdriver, a paintbrush, and a drill bit. She mentally developed her own personal *Clue* game: Mrs. Palmer in the Children's Room with a wrench; Circulation in the Ladies' room with a toilet plunger; Reference in the stacks with a doorknob.

In the kitchenware section, Casey found a teapot with a whistle spout for Mae. She was about to check out when she spotted the perfect item for the Children's Room. Although not as dramatic as a wrench, plunger, or doorknob, it would send a message.

Aw, Jesus, she was going to miss that cat. She would never be able to work in the Children's Room again. The room and the kitty had been an oasis, a place she'd made her own, where she felt inviolate. Now the police were tailing her, George was a loss, and the sour old dishrags at the library hated her so much they'd murdered her cat.

After charging her purchases, Casey picked up Mae's wheel and headed home.

Casey closed the screen door slowly and tiptoed down the hallway toward her room.

"Casey, is that you?"

She halted mid-sneak. Old people should be deaf. Mae attributed the loss of her sense of smell and taste to Martha's cooking, but her hearing and eyesight could challenge a hawk.

"Casey?"

Casey stood stock-still, waiting for the acute listening period to pass. The last thing she wanted was to share her horrendous day with her great aunt. Her clothing clung to her like a wetsuit. She needed a hot shower and a hole to crawl into to lick her wounds and plot her revenge.

"Casey?" Mae's voice quavered slightly.

"Hi, Mae. I'm home," she called back, compelled to respond by the needy undertones in the feeble voice. "I'm soaked to the bone. Gotta take a shower." Before Mae could object, Casey was down the hall and into the bathroom. She turned the shower on full blast, covering any guilt-spawning response from her aunt.

For the second time in as many days, she faced the hot blast of water and released gut-wrenching sobs of loss and betrayal. Sharp needles of water melded into a numbing rush. Steam fogged the room, shrouding the mirror and creating a protective wall around her.

Thump. Mae's cane. Thump. Thump. Mae was scolding her for using up the hot water. Casey thrust her head under the nozzle to drown the noise in the roar of the shower. Thump. Thump. She felt the vibration in the floor. Usually Mae quit pounding.

She turned off the water, wrapped herself in a towel, and opened the door, releasing a cloud of steam. "Mae, are you OK?"

No answer. Casey sprinted down the hall and burst into the front room. "Mae?"

Mae lay atop the hospital bed, covered by a knit afghan. Her eyes were closed, but she was breathing.

"Mae, what's the matter?" Casey ran to the bedside.

Mae opened one eye. "Nothing's the matter. Where've you been?"

"Taking a shower," Casey snapped.

Mae opened the other eye. "Sit, Casey." She patted the bed. "What's the matter, dear?" Her bossy tone melted to concern.

Casey opened her mouth to speak and then broke down in great long, heaving sobs. Images of Bookend crowded her mind: batting paper balls, back talking her in double syllables, offering his tummy for a soothing scratch. After she regained a little of her composure, she looked out the window. "It's Bookie, my kitty," she whispered.

Once again she broke, seeing Bookie's ratty fighter's ears, switching tail and his long stretch of a body as he peered down on her from his perch, camouflaged by the ivy plant. It was too much. She couldn't stand it.

He hadn't done anything wrong: he was just a wonderful old cat. The image of him skating across her desk on a manila envelope clearing everything in his glide path before leading her to his dish released another flood of tears. Maybe she shouldn't have fed him. Speaking in fits and starts and hiccups, she told Mae about what Mrs. Palmer had done. When she finally stopped, she was surprised that Mae's eyes were misty and that her old claw was holding her hand.

Chapter Thirty-Six

Halfway to his morning dentist appointment, the flickering warning light on the dashboard of Crockett's cruiser escalated to solid red. He glared at the light, but it didn't back down. Oil. Damn. He'd need the car over the weekend for graduation. Crockett turned on his strobes and made a U-turn. The perks of a police officer.

On his way to the Texaco station that serviced the police cars, Crockett called and canceled his dentist appointment. He left the cruiser, bought a cup of coffee, and walked across the street to the police station.

Inside his office, he eased into his chair and swiveled until the early morning light warmed his face. When the coffee was the perfect temperature, he drank it in a few long gulps. He dug his Bombs and Snowballs list from beneath the blotter and crossed "Housemaster" off the Bombs side. The housemaster at Barrows had positively identified McPhee from Casey's sketch of Dumbo and said McPhee was a frequent visitor to one of the seniors, the fat boy who had stood vigil the night Cam overdosed. When Crockett asked the housemaster to ring the boy's room, the man had hesitated and then said the boy had gone out, and suggested Crockett leave a note.

Next, he crossed off Dundee and added "seco" to the bottom of the list. Max Dundee said the sleeping pills Jules had taken were rarely prescribed. Most families had whole medicine cabinets crammed full of prescription and over-the-counter drugs, yet no drugs of any variety were found in the Kenworthys' house, suggesting someone had made a sweep of the place before the police arrived.

Near the bottom of the list was "CC." For a split second Crockett wondered why Charley's initials were on the list, but, of course, the CC was for Casey. While he was thinking of Charley, he scribbled "Mannon, Oberlin Nursing Home" on the Snowballs list. He looked at the name for a moment and then reached for the phone book, located a number, and dialed.

The phone rang three times before a tired old woman's voice answered, "Oberlin Nursing Home, how may I help you?"

"Chief Crocket, Oberlin Police. Like to speak to Oliver Mannon."

"I'm sorry, Chief, but Ollie don't talk on the phone. He gets all confused when he can't see a face. You have to come by, you want a word with him. Have to warn you, his mind's not what it used to be."

Crockett asked for the visiting hours before ringing off. He could drop by before he went to see Barbara Roman about the note George had found in the freezer. Outside his office, Jenny hummed as she took off her coat and unlocked her desk. Seconds later he heard the tapping of light fingers on a typewriter.

When Crockett reviewed his list, he noticed an ink blur next to CC. Curious. He examined the paper more closely. Beside each item was a small dot, as if someone used a pen to guide his eye. Watson. Every paper Watson ever touched was marked with his annoying little polka dots.

Crockett's thoughts were interrupted by the sound of the Dot Maker himself, grousing up the back steps to the station. Moments after the door slammed behind Watson, Connolly blustered through the front door.

"Coffee ready, Jen?" Connolly hollered from the conference room. "Did you get the videotape player?" he added.

"One thing at a time," Jenny muttered. "Coffee's coming. The player's in the captain's room," she called back

She drew in a sharp breath as Crockett appeared in his doorway. "Scare me to death!"

Crockett took the coffee pot. "Relax." While he measured out the coffee, he explained the car situation and then nodded toward the conference room. "What they up to so early?"

"They're viewing the tape from the library surveillance camera."

189

They turned in unison at the rumble of heavy equipment rolling down the hall to the conference room.

"Who called the meeting?" Crockett asked softly.

"Captain Watson."

"I'll drop in after I read my mail. You see the Kenworthy file?"

"Watson signed the release late yesterday. They needed it to cremate her remains. Watson said it was okay, since he was the officer of record for the call."

"What did he put for cause of death?"

"'Accidental death.'"

In the past week Watson's resentment had taken on a sharper edge, and his resistance to command was just shy of insubordinate. Crockett decided to forego his mail.

As he opened the door to the conference room, the momentary flash of light silhouetted Watson and Connolly huddled before a screen. Crockett settled into a seat at the far end of the conference table. Watson and Connolly exchanged glances. Watson shrugged. The three of them stared at a dark, empty aisle in the library stacks.

"Just about there," Watson said, checking the counter on the machine. Moments later Casey pushed a two-tiered cart laden with books into the aisle. She looked behind her, left and right, and then walked to the aisle where McPhee had left the drugs. The video clearly caught her profile as she shelved three books. She glanced down the aisles again before leaving, pushing the cart before her.

Crockett couldn't object. He'd ordered the surveillance. He was surprised to see Casey back in the stacks when he'd told her to stay clear. What was she thinking?

Watson flicked on the overhead light. "Thought you were at the dentist."

"Guess not," Crockett replied.

Watson postured like a well-fed pit bull on his home turf. "My library source reports that Professor Kenworthy was the last person to sign out the book we been watching."

"And who is this 'source'?" Crockett asked.

"My aunt works Reference." Watson puffed his chest and addressed Connolly. "Casey and the Professor were getting it on. She had access to the book used for the drug exchange. She told you that she'd been in the aisle during the drug deal to cover her tracks in case someone saw her. Now we've got her on tape returning books to the same aisle. Casey and Jules used that gouged-out-book trick to pass notes in high school."

"There's more?" Connolly asked Watson. He didn't acknowledge Crockett's presence.

Watson produced an envelope and shook out a few photographs. He gathered them in a deck and dealt them to Connolly. Crockett leaned forward to see the images. The first two were shots of Casey and George kissing. The Loveland gravestone placed them in the cemetery.

"You're tailing Casey?" Crockett blurted.

"You have a better lead?" challenged Watson.

Connolly turned to face Crockett for the first time. He wagged the remains of a jelly donut in Crockett's direction to punctuate his speech. "I ordered it because Casey is a friend of yours. I thought it would be better if you weren't involved."

Watson dealt the last few pictures. "We figured you have a lot on your plate already, with graduation, and the dentist and all."

Crockett's mind recoiled. What was this "we" stuff with Watson and Connolly?

Watson pointed. "That one's the best." In the photo, Casey knelt beside the well at the Gourd holding a plastic packet.

"My aunt reports that she's getting mail from her old cellmate in prison. Could be her source. After all, Casey's a convicted felon who did time for dealing."

Connolly was eating up Watson's case as fast as the second doughnut he had stuffed down his craw.

Crockett couldn't let Watson ride roughshod over Casey with nothing but circumstantial evidence. "Might be another possibility," he suggested. When neither Watson nor Connolly responded, Crockett forged on. "Jules is your dealer. She knows McPhee. Has access to the book George took out of the library. Knows the trick of carving up a book to pass messages. She was on the scene—and was a known substance abuser—during the bust when Casey was arrested."

Connolly shook his head but didn't bother to stop chewing long enough to verbalize his disagreement.

Watson objected. "Why would Jules need the money? Lovelands are loaded."

"Maybe once. No more," Crockett countered. "The Lovelands passed along a heavy load of debt when they turned over the Gourd to George and Jules and bought into the retirement place. College teachers don't earn big money."

"You know all this for a fact?" challenged Connolly.

"Still checking the numbers."

Connolly shot Watson an expectant glance. When Watson shrugged, Connolly let loose a low belch of doughnut dyspepsia. His fingers drummed a sticky march on the table.

Crockett continued. "I agree that McPhee's the other connection. The Housemaster at Barrows said McPhee was the boyfriend of the fat boy at the recent overdose. Haven't reached the kid yet to confirm."

Connolly erupted. "Do you have any idea who the 'fat boy' is?" His voice cracked like a teenager's.

"You mean, 'who the fat boy's *father* is'?" baited Crockett.

"I told you to keep a lid on it through graduation. Only four days to go. I thought you could handle that. If Drucker finds out you've been anywhere near that boy, there will be hell to pay." Connolly shook his head and stood, passing behind Crockett's chair. "You don't take direction very well, do you?"

Crockett waited the requisite two seconds for control, easing his eyes into half-mast. "Last I checked, I was Chief."

"Chief means you answer to me. You can't accuse a faculty wife of drug dealing without proof. Or call the son of the Chairman of the Board of Trustees a faggot and a druggie. The poor woman is dead, and the boy is just about to graduate."

CHAPTER THIRTY-SIX

"Even more reason to talk to him before he leaves town."

"*No!* You hear me?"

Crockett's voice was an octave lower and deadly calm. "Far as I'm concerned, Casey's just trying to graduate, too. You've got nothing but circumstantial evidence on her."

"You listen to me, Crockett." Connolly pointed a stubby forefinger in Crockett's face. "We've had complaints about you from townsfolk and from the college. You better straighten up and fly right."

Crockett pictured bending the finger backward but it was too sticky and disgusting to touch.

Watson entered the fray. "'Circumstantial' isn't much different from 'coincidence,' is it? I thought you didn't believe in coincidence."

Cunning little shit. Crockett ignored Watson. "Who's complaining?" he asked Connolly.

"Swain claims you're harassing him. He says you're trying to embarrass him by making a scandal about his personal life." Connolly continued with insulting slowness. "You've got to be impartial to be a good Chief, Crockett. Swain is one of our most successful and influential citizens. He's so upset he may build his new retirement complex somewhere else. We'd lose jobs and tax revenues and a place for our elders to retire just because you have an old grudge to settle." Connolly threw his jacket over his shoulder. "I've got another meeting."

Halfway out the door, Connolly turned. "Take the rest of the day off and think about your attitude and professional behavior. Be in my office tomorrow morning, nine o'clock sharp." The door slammed hard enough to rattle the glass.

"Whatcha want me to do about the girl?" Watson called after Connolly.

Crockett turned the full force of his glare on Watson. "Leave Casey alone."

Watson smirked and hitched his pants but decided against the last word.

Crockett returned to his office, more in defiance of Connolly's order than anything else. He sat in the dark, reviewing the meeting. Clearly Connolly and Watson had planned it for a time when Crockett would be out.

He'd been operating under a number of faulty assumptions. First of all, just because Watson was fat, illiterate, and disgusting didn't mean he was stupid. The evidence Watson had compiled against Casey made a straightforward and convincing, if circumstantial, argument. And he'd been clever enough to gather the information without alerting Crockett's suspicions.

Watson might not be stupid, but he wouldn't risk anything without Connolly's encouragement, which brought Crockett to consider his second assumption: that Connolly was his supporter. Connolly may have needed Crockett in the last election, but his recent behavior resembled an airport windsock with a strong gust blowing from the college. Connolly had to show both the Town Council and Drucker that he was on top of the drug situation and that there would be no further investigation into the death of Dr. Kenworthy's wife.

The miserable little doughnut-eating-nose-slime was probably making a proposal to replace him to the Council this afternoon. Connolly would use Swain's complaint and the attempt to question the fat boy as evidence of Crockett's refusal to take direction. He'd cite Crockett's lack of objectivity and cooperation in the pursuit of a suspected drug dealer.

Something didn't ring true about Swain's complaint. Swain was a locker room braggart. Screwing around with Jules would only add to Swain's swagger. Ron hadn't hesitated to tell Crockett about what a good lay Jules was.

Now, he was complaining about Crockett and threatening to build his retirement facility in another town when, just days ago, he'd told Crockett the Emerald Acres plan had fallen through while shooting imaginary ducks out of the air. Crockett pictured the detailed model of Emerald Acres in Swain's lobby. There was a lot invested in that project. The model was too detailed to be a flash in the pan.

Maybe Ron was just supporting his old buddy Watson. Dougie and Ron had been friends growing up, and they still had dinner together. If Watson were making another move for Chief, Swain could be an influential supporter. Anyone in construction could use a friend in the police department.

Crockett threw down his pencil. Listing bad assumptions was getting him nowhere. If he didn't think of something soon, he'd be out of a job, and Casey would be under arrest. Hell, his problems were mild compared to hers. She could do big time for a second offense on drugs.

If you started with the assumption that Casey was guilty the first time, then her involvement the second time made sense. But what if she weren't guilty the first time? What if she was just in the wrong place at the wrong time as she claimed?

Crockett remembered the look of horror on Connolly's face when he'd suggested Jules was the dealer. Crockett could build a circumstantial case against her without stretching the facts. Not as strong as the tape and Watson's pictures, though. Unless he could beef up the financial angle. According to George, he and Jules were making a hefty payment every month because Jules' parents had poured a pile of money into a retirement home instead of paying off the renovations to the Gourd. How much money were they talking about?

He picked up the phone and called Olmstead Manor and asked to speak with the Marketing Director.

"This is Mrs. Frank. How may I help you?" A honeyed matron's voice came on the line.

"Chief Crockett, Oberlin Police. I'm looking into placing my mother into your facility, and—"

"I'm sorry. At present all of our units are occupied. I'll be happy to put your name on our waiting list and call when there's an opening."

When someone dies. Crockett gave the woman his home telephone number, but just as she was about to ring off, he asked "Maybe you could give me an idea of how much a unit costs."

He sensed a slight hesitation in Mrs. Frank's response. "Well, it depends on the size of the unit. You'd be looking for an efficiency, I assume?"

"Actually, I was thinking more along the lines of what the Lovelands bought."

The pause was more pronounced. "Do you know the Lovelands, sir?"

"Yes. Yes, I do," Crockett replied honestly.

"Well then, you must know that they merged and renovated two of the largest apartment units here."

No, he knew no such thing. Crockett assumed a folksy attitude. "Well, my mother probably won't need two apartments. One would do."

"Why don't I just send you our brochure? It provides the detail on the units, the clinic, and also our selection process."

"Selection process?"

"We have a number of people on the waiting list. Our selection is based on an assessment of how the individual will fit in with the current residents. We have a very tightly knit community. Would your mother have friends here?" The honey in Mrs. Frank's voice was considerably watered down.

"No. Don't believe so."

"We recommend that the elderly select places where they have friends or family and will feel most comfortable."

Crockett almost laughed aloud. "You have any black residents?"

"Not at present," Mrs. Frank responded carefully. "Have you considered the Oberlin Nursing Home?" A touch of honey returned with this suggestion.

"The old Children's Home?"

"Well, yes. I was just trying to be helpful."

"No need to send a brochure, ma'am," Crockett purred.

Mrs. Frank released a sigh of relief.

"I jes' drop by when I be in the neighborhood." Crockett tossed the receiver toward its cradle, pleased with the accuracy of his aim and with the image of Mrs. Frank wincing as it crashed into place.

He stuffed the Bombs and Snowballs list under his blotter, grabbed the folder on Charley, and locked his door.

Jenny looked up as he approached her desk. "Your car's ready."

Crockett nodded. "Know anything about this special Council meeting?"

"Just that Dean Drucker called in really angry and demanded it. I asked Connolly what it was about, but he wouldn't say." Her forehead pursed in premature worry lines.

"Town's 'leading citizen,' Ron Swain, and the Chairman of the Board of Trustees at the College calling for my head. Drucker wants me tethered and muzzled for the big weekend."

"It might be a good time to lay low," Jenny suggested.

Crockett broke into a wide smile and looked down at his chest. "Hard to hide." His smile faded. "You probably heard, I'm off. May pay me a visit to Officer Mannon. *That* you didn't hear." He grinned down at Jenny and sauntered out the front door, sporting bravado he didn't feel.

Chapter Thirty-Seven

After the scene at the station, Crockett was in a sour enough mood to drop in on Mrs. Frank at Olmstead Manor and stir up a little arrhythmia in her blue blood. He pulled into a long, curved drive leading to the entrance. Turning on the strobes, he parked behind a stretch limo purring in the Fire Lane. Olmstead residents were pampered with every luxury piles of money could buy.

He entered a marble foyer and a reception room enhanced with soft lavender scent and strains of chamber music and followed a discreet sign pointing the way to Admissions. A plush Oriental runner led down the hallway to Mrs. Frank's office.

He knocked and poked his head into a light and airy room filled with shiny plants that reflected in the high gloss finish of the mahogany furniture. Mrs. Frank sat behind a wide desk, dressed like a full figure model for *Modern Maturity*. She looked up from a stack of papers and frowned. "Deliveries in the rear," she said, returning to her papers.

Crockett knocked a second time and entered. "Chief Crockett. I called earlier about my mother."

Mrs. Frank spoke as if she had a severe case of lockjaw. "Yes, Chief. Our brochures are at the front desk." As she nodded toward the front of the building, she noticed the cruiser's flashing lights. "What's wrong?"

"Limo in the Fire Lane." Crockett gave her a slow smile.

For a split second, Mrs. Frank was confused. Then she nodded, opened a drawer, retrieved a brochure and price list, and handed them to Crockett. He pocketed the papers and returned to his car.

Two blocks farther down the street, Crockett pulled into a Visitor space at the Oberlin Nursing Home. A rusted-out Chevy was the only car in the lot. Someone had tried to slow the progress of disintegration with shots of Rust-Oleum. It looked like a leopard. The trunk was wired shut, and a crease across the front bumper gave it a rakish smile.

He opened Charley's file and re-read the end of the police report. Officers Heiser, Bradley, and Mannon had been involved in the bust. Heiser had a fatal heart attack, and Bradley was killed in a high-speed chase a few years later. Besides Casey, Mannon was the only person alive who was involved with the bust. He was the officer who chased Charley across Tappan Square and crushed him under his cruiser. Sporadic reports about Mannon's health suggested he'd been retired within months of the incident and drank himself into a stroke.

Crockett gazed at the sorry building before him. Years earlier the Oberlin Nursing Home had been the Children's Home, a county orphanage. A disgrace then, it was utterly derelict now. Heavy raindrops ran down the windows in grimy rivulets, making the building look as if it were crying.

He reached the entrance in four giant steps. Entering, he was accosted by a blast of naphtha and ammonia. Strong as the cleaner was, it couldn't disguise the pervasive odors of sour old people and urine. Long window shades blocked out all natural light. He squinted to get his bearings, shivering at the cold and dank surrounds of the foul cave. His sleeve brushed against the leaf of a fake philodendron, releasing a small mushroom cloud of dust.

"Afternoon, Chief," a heavy, black matron called from the reception desk.

Crockett approached and smiled down at the woman. "JoJo to you, Mrs. Johnson. You lookin' fine this afternoon. How you doing?"

"Can't complain, and if I could, ain't nobody listening." Mrs. Johnson laughed, wiped her hands on an apron, and thrust her hand out to shake. She had shiny, round cheeks, a round face, round body, and a warm, welcoming smile. "Call me Maude, JoJo, honey. C'mon, I'll show you to Ollie...Officer Mannon." She looked at the wet splotches on his shirt. "Guess the rain started up again. Mother Nature's car wash. Not so's you'd notice by my old dump."

Maude kept up a friendly patter as they passed through a living area dominated by an old console TV. An elderly black man in a wheelchair stared at the flickering images on the screen, his face devoid of expression. The sound was turned off. A woman sitting next to him held his hand and talked, but he paid her no mind. Her sound had been turned off as well.

Crockett followed Maude down a long hallway with doors off to the left and right. Room after room was vacant.

"I put Ollie in a bigger room in the corner. Might as well live it up. Only five residents left. I figure we got a half year before we shut down. Owner's got two other homes over to Elyria in better shape. He could transfer these folks, but he's too cheap, an' this place is good on the taxes. Lots of rooms, no patients. Big loss."

Crockett shook his head. The Board of Health must have winked at this place.

Maude entered first to announce their presence. "Ollie, honey, you got a visitor."

The slight figure slumped forward in restraints in a wheelchair bore no resemblance to the overweight cop that lived in Crockett's mind, the cop with a florid face out for a little sport, chasing down his brother who was fool enough to run.

Maude turned Ollie's chair toward Crockett. She daubed a thin line of drool that wagged from Mannon's lower lip and checked his eyes. "Say hello to Chief Crockett, Ollie."

Tiny eyes were all but buried under loose folds of flesh that draped Mannon's eyes and cheekbones like clothes hanging on a line. Mannon couldn't weigh more than a hundred pounds. Maude touched his arm to get his attention. The skin stayed where she pushed it. In contrast, his fingernails were long and healthy, with an ivory cast. Crockett felt an odd impulse to clip them.

"Ollie goes for the layered look," Maude said, tucking a wool blanket under Mannon's legs. The old cop wore multiple layers of clothing and blankets. "Hard to stay warm without any fat," she explained. "Like a Coke?"

To Crockett's surprise, Mannon grunted agreement. Crockett nodded and Maude left to fetch the drinks. Crockett didn't know where to begin. Pathetic little man couldn't have much to say if he could talk. Crockett wished Mannon were in better health. Be so much easier to hate.

Maude returned, fitted Ollie's drink in a holder on his chair, and popped in a straw. "Mash that buzzer, you need anything. I'm the only one on duty."

"You alone here?" Crockett couldn't hide his surprise. Only five residents, but Maude was no spring chicken.

"Yep. Boss don't waste a dime on help. I told you, this place is a write-off. It'll be knocked down once the last of 'em shuffle off."

Maude talked as if Mannon had one foot in the grave. Crockett didn't know where to look. He didn't want to embarrass Mannon, but didn't want to ignore him either. His eye caught on a pair of light blue, fuzzy slippers on Mannon's feet.

"Free," explained Maude, following his gaze. "Booties made by the Eastern Star ladies. We make do, right Ollie?" She grinned and patted Crockett's shoulder as she left the room. "Needn't squirm, JoJo. We talk a lot about death here. We be all the same, old and poor."

One side of Mannon's face smiled. The other remained inert.

Crockett felt strangely chastised. Maude had the heart to adopt Mannon, knowing full well what a mean bigot the man had been. Reluctantly, Crockett pulled up a chair.

"Your brother's death changed my life."

Crockett almost dropped his Coke. Mannon's voice echoed in his hollow chest before exiting the side of his mouth. Despite the reedy, whispered quality, Crockett had no problem understanding him.

"Changed his, too." Chastised or not, Crockett wouldn't give ground for pity. The man had run down his brother.

Mannon nodded and was silent for a while before picking up the thread. It was difficult for him to speak, but he was determined. "Usually, you do something wrong, you can fix it. Take back words. Apologize. Make it up to the wife. Whatever." Mannon paused and rattled in a breath. "Nothing I could do to bring your brother back. His life was over. So was mine."

Mannon turned his head sidewise and addressed the blank wall, offering

Crockett his living profile without the distraction of the paralyzed side. "My fault. I was too close. Couldn't stop. Honest to God." Mannon's good hand clenched his inert one.

Crockett waited while Mannon took a long pull on the straw and wiped away a new trickle of fluid from the unmoving part of his mouth. His head bowed until his spare chins met and rested in his chest cavity. Crockett listened to the tortured whistle from his bent esophagus for a few minutes before pressing the buzzer.

Moments later Maude appeared. She raised Mannon's head and looked into his eyes. "Anybody home?" she asked gently. She fumbled for a pulse and then turned to Crockett. "Sometimes, he plays possum. Others, he's out, like now. Like his battery needs charging."

Both of them jumped at Mannon's voice. "Crockett wasn't supposed to be there." Maude left quietly as Mannon continued. "Way we planned it, he'd make the drop, and we'd wait for the dealer. Pick him up later."

"Charley was cooperating?" Crockett's was genuinely surprised.

"Nah. The tip came from Elyria. When Charley saw us rolling, he shouted to the girl and then ran. That's why I chased him."

"Nothing about a tip in the report." Crockett tossed the report on the bed.

"Lot of things aren't in a report. You know that. You're a cop."

"Tell me things I don't know."

"Tip was on Solly's Oberlin foreman."

"Solly–Solomon Gram?" Years ago, Solly was the boss of a drug ring in Elyria that distributed drugs to northern Ohio through construction crews.

Mannon nodded and then convulsed in a coughing spell that wracked his body. "We had to let the foreman go. Didn't have anything on him that would stick, but he gave up Charley."

"I thought the bust was a local deal," Crockett interjected. "Who was the foreman?"

"No reason to name names. Solly was a cunning old fox. Whenever a link was broken, Solly'd wipe out the whole chain. Foreman was lucky he got away." Mannon wheezed and coughed up a wad of phlegm that hung on his mouth.

Crockett wasn't about to clean him up. Instead, he turned his head parallel to Mannon and stared at the same place in the wall. "Why do you think the Oberlin bust had anything to do with Solly?"

"No one'd dump that much stuff in a public place. Solly was sending the Narcs a message with their own stuff." Mannon chuckled and then succumbed to another round of chest-wrenching coughs.

Time to leave the crazy old cop to his delusions. He wasn't making sense, and talking exacerbated his emphysema. How could Charley's drop be a message from Solly to the Feds? Crockett chugged the rest of his Coke and pushed back. "Thank you for your time, Officer." He made it to the door before Mannon's voice challenged him. "Don't believe me, eh?"

"Think you blowin' smoke, Sir," Crockett acknowledged, but his voice was kind.

Mannon hesitated. A cagey look crossed half his face. "Hell, what can they do to me? Try to use this, I'll deny every word." Mannon looked at the wall again and continued his story.

"The Feds couldn't crack Solly's operation. They'd get a runner once in a while, but they couldn't join up the links. Then they intercepted a shipment of coke in Lorain. They laced it with a trace chemical and then released it to track the distribution chain. Solly let the Feds know he was onto their game by dumping it right back in their lap in the Oberlin bust. He was smart, though. Offered the Feds a sacrifice, the Oberlin cell, so's they could save face."

"You prove any of this?" The story was just crazy enough to be true, but Crockett held onto his skepticism.

Mannon turned to face Crockett. Anger and paralysis distorted his features. His voice came out in a forced whisper. "The drugs confiscated in the bust had the trace." He coughed up more phlegm. "The Feds wouldn't confirm it, but rumor had it we only recovered half of the drugs."

Crockett was stunned. Casey had mentioned the same rumor. None of this was in the public record. "How about the student, Casey Cavendish?"

"What about her?"

"She went to prison for dealing."

"Well, she must've been a regular drop, or Charley wouldn't have left the coke in her bag."

"Regular drop, meaning a user, but not a dealer?" Crockett probed.

"One or the other. Hell, all them kids at the college were snorting, smoking or shooting something."

Crockett crushed his Coke can. "So, dealer or not, you figured Cavendish got what she deserved."

"She was convicted by a jury of her peers," Mannon countered, unwilling to yield the point.

"But you just shot down your own argument. The size of the drop had nothing to do with her, just made her look like a dealer."

Mannon made a production of fitting the straw into the side of his mouth and then finished off the drink in long, slow drags.

Crockett backed off, hoping for more information. "What happened to Solly?"

"Feds got him on taxes. He didn't last but three months in jail. Far as I know, the rest of the marked dope never showed up. End of story."

"All's well that ends well," Crockett muttered. "Charley died. Cavendish went to prison. The cops and college solved their drug problem. Feds were saved from public humiliation." Crockett paused for a beat. "And you retired on full disability."

A momentary flush of anger swept across half of Mannon's face, but seconds later the old cop looked as if he were going to cry. "I didn't mean to hurt the boy. I was just having me some fun." He studied his yellowed nails and shook his head.

When he looked up, he cast his eyes around the room, and then looked directly at Crockett without a flicker of recognition. "Maude! Maude? Snap open a cold one for me, will ya?" he hollered. "And bring one for my friend here," Mannon hesitated, confused.

"Crockett. No thanks." He rose as Maude entered with two more cans of Coke. "Appreciate your help, ma'am," he said, refusing the Coke. As he walked down the hall, Mannon's voice followed him. "What'd that cop want?"

Pathetic as Mannon was, the image of him chasing Charley across the campus for a little sport tempered Crockett's compassion. The cop may have volunteered the information about the bust in the hopes that Crockett would forgive him, but he also knew there was no way Crockett could use it.

Casey was telling the truth. Charley made a mistake. Left the drugs in the wrong bike. And Jules never said a word, or if she did, no one had listened. Nothing he could do to prove any of it. They were just pawns in a much bigger game.

The common links between the past and the present were Jules and construction. Could Jules have been dealing using McPhee as a runner? Where would she get the cocaine? Crockett made a mental note to have the coke from the Barrows overdose tested in the unlikely chance that it could be the part of Solly's coke that had never been found.

Although they hadn't caught McPhee on the surveillance tape, he might talk if he thought they had. Crockett called the station and left a message for Watson to pick up McPhee for questioning.

Chapter Thirty-Eight

C rockett left the nursing home and drove south to Wellington, a small town every bit as charming as Oberlin, but without a college. The storm had passed over during his visit with Mannon, leaving deep puddles in the road.

He'd asked Barbara Roman to analyze the note George found in the freezer and compare it to samples of Casey's writing. As he drove, he decided that if Barbara's analysis indicated Jules wrote the note, he'd agree to Watson's conclusion of "accidental death" despite all of the weird circumstances. He pulled into an unmarked gravel driveway and parked beneath a buckeye tree that shaded a tidy red bungalow with white shutters.

Barbara greeted him at the door and led him through the house toward her study. She unlocked a file cabinet beside her desk and pulled out a manila envelope of handwriting samples and a baggie containing Jules' suicide note. "I wish I had more definitive news. As I mentioned on the telephone, I have a professional conflict because I've met Casey, and a personal conflict because I've become quite fond of her." Barbara paused to let her words sink in.

"Believe me, I don't want to hurt her either. But you're a document examiner, and I'm the law."

"This is a personal favor, so I won't write a report, I won't accept payment, and if it comes to that, I won't testify." She waved down Crockett's objection. "I examined the writings with your questions in mind. I'll address them individually." She put on a pair of half glasses, instantly aging herself ten years, and picked up a sheet of paper with Crockett's questions.

Her voice assumed the deliberate, professional tone that Crockett had heard her use in the courtroom. "First question: 'Was the suicide note written by Jules Kenworthy?'" Barbara chose her words carefully. "I could easily convince a jury that Jules wrote it.

"Second: 'Could it be a forgery?' It's possible.

"Third: 'Could Casey have written it?'" Barbara paused before answering. "Maybe. I'm torn by this one."

"But if you had to stake your reputation on it—"

"I stake my reputation every time I analyze a writing." Barbara softened her tone. "I know you're in an awkward spot. If I didn't know Casey took advanced correspondence courses in graphology in prison, I'd say there is a strong argument that Jules wrote the note. But Casey is very good. There's a chance she wrote it."

"Good enough to stump the expert?" Crockett's surprise showed in his voice.

"Well, here. See for yourself. She did a brilliant study of Martha Swain's writing." Barbara flipped through stacks of papers next to her desk, found a thin, bound report, and handed it to Crockett. A handwritten note from Casey on the outside thanked Barbara for letting her attend the last few weeks of her class.

Crockett leafed through the pages. Conclusions preceded evidence for two separate sections: Childhood and Adulthood. He scanned the Childhood section.

"*As a young girl, the subject was spoiled, self-centered, and weak with tendencies toward deception.*" Evidence for the above conclusions included mention of a "victim *t* bar."

"What's a 'victim *t* bar'?" Crockett asked, hoping to neutralize Barbara's defensive posture.

Barbara drew the letter *t* with a bar crossing the vertical shaft that made the letter look as if its arms were reaching toward the heavens in supplication. "She felt the world was dumping on her. She was the victim. She couldn't control what happened to her and therefore didn't feel responsible for her actions."

"How's that mean she's a liar?" Crockett was confused.

"It doesn't. Alone, it isn't enough to signify dishonesty. But when you find it along with a nest of other ugly traits, you've got trouble."

"So, Martha was a nasty little kid." Crockett wasn't surprised.

"Yes, but her adult writing is picture-perfect, as if she had gone through a metamorphosis that washed her soul clean of her dirty little secrets."

"Born again?"

"More like fearful that she wasn't good enough. She created a shell that made her *look* perfect, although she knew, inside, she hadn't changed."

"Why's that fearful?"

"Because she's afraid for others to see the real Martha. There is no way to tell from the writing what she's hiding."

Crockett pointed out words in Casey's writing. "Casey's got the same victim *t* bar. That mean she's a bad seed, too?"

"Not necessarily. There's a difference between *feeling* that you're a victim, and actually *being* a victim. Casey swears she's innocent of any drug crime. If she is, then she was punished severely for something she didn't do."

"No way to prove otherwise now." Crockett paused and rubbed his forehead. "Drug runner and Jules are dead. No living witnesses 'cept an old cop in a nursing home whose mind is gone."

"How'd the runner die?" Barbara asked gently, watching Crockett closely.

Crockett winced. "Accident. He tripped, and a cruiser ran him down."

"You knew him." It wasn't a question.

"My brother." Crockett looked down and then away and then rose to leave.

"Does Casey have a reason to want Jules' death to look like a suicide?" Barbara asked as she led Crockett to the front door.

"Could be protecting her brother, Art Cavendish, or George Kenworthy, Jules' husband. Both men saw Jules the night she died. George even struck her." Crockett hesitated. "Also a chance Casey's covering her own tracks."

At the door, Barbara put her hand on his arm. "The writing can't give us the answer this time. I'm sorry about your brother."

"Was a long time ago."

"Some wounds don't heal. Take care. Go punch a tree, run ten miles. You look like you're about to explode."

Chapter Thirty-Nine

Early Friday morning, Casey unlocked the door to the Children's Room. She flicked on the overhead light and looked around the room slowly. No trace of the mangled plant. No broken dish. No dirt on the floor. Even the cat food was missing. The floor was polished to a high gloss.

She removed the envelope of photos from the "S" volume of the children's encyclopedia. At her desk, she cleaned out her personal effects. With great care, she arranged the little gift she'd purchased at the hardware store, covered it with a tissue, and pushed it far back in the drawer where she usually kept her latest studly photo. Before closing the drawer, she pocketed the mausoleum skeleton key that she'd mixed in with the pencils.

Finally, she polished off a short letter of resignation. *Yes!* Casey felt like dancing a jig around her desk. She glanced at the clock above the tall bookcase and her bubble of euphoria popped. Bookend should be sprawled out for his nap behind the plant. No plant. No kitty.

Casey cast one last look around. The children's mats were rolled up behind the stool where she'd read stories on Saturday mornings. She patted her rear pocket for her Children's Club ID card and her front pocket for the skeleton key, grabbed her book bag, and closed the door.

After shoving her resignation into Mrs. P's mailbox, Casey left the library and rode toward the Gourd. She had to return the skeleton key to the mausoleum while George and Gabby were out greeting guests at the funeral home. The funeral director needed the key to unlock the mausoleum for the internment of Jules' ashes.

The key taunted her. How long would it take to check out the mausoleum? Ten minutes? Fifteen at most? She'd never have another opportunity to find out what Jules had been up to. Casey's curiosity turned Mae's wheel toward the cemetery. As she entered, the quiet beauty of the dogwoods and flowering crab apple trees enveloped her. The loudest noise was the crunching of bicycle tires on cinders.

When she reached the mausoleum, she glanced behind her to make sure she hadn't been followed. As an extra precaution, she walked the bike around the building, leaned the bike against the back wall, and returned to the front.

She looked across the path to Abe Loveland's aboveground monument. Had Jules seen them when she drove up the other day? It no longer mattered.

The skeleton key turned in the lock. The grate complained bitterly as metal scraped over cement. Inside, coffin vaults lined the walls to her right and left, stacked four high on each side. Beside each vault, a brass plaque identified the sealed remains. Casey walked across an oriental rug to a beautiful old cherry rocking chair where visitors could sit awhile and visit.

In front of her was a niche sealed by a glass frame screwed into the wall. Inside were funerary urns and boxed-up relatives who had passed away after Uncle John died. Casey wished it weren't so dim so she could see better. The lovely ceramic urn would be John Loveland's wife, Lucetta. Cousin Ephraim and wife Joanna were ensconced in plain wooden boxes. They weren't among the favored. She squinted but couldn't make out the names on the other containers.

Casey sat and rocked in the old chair, bitterly disappointed. She'd been certain that she'd find something, but whatever Jules had been up to, there was no sign of it now. Get over it. Time to return the key.

But what if she had it backwards? Casey replayed her mental tape of Jules entering and leaving the mausoleum. She was carrying something in the bag when she left. Casey couldn't remember if there was anything in the bag when Jules entered. She returned to the glass frame and peered at the urns and boxes again. Curious. Despite the protective window, a fine layer of dust coated the urns. Was there a slightly cleaner place to the right of

Lucetta? She couldn't be sure.

The still air was broken by the hum of an automobile engine drawing near. Casey crouched, waiting for the car to pass. Silly, no one could see inside the darkened room. If they could, they would notice a chair rocking slowly without an occupant.

She waited another moment until the car disappeared. She checked her watch. Time to return the key.

Chapter Forty

Crockett's morning meeting with Connolly had been moved to the conference room. When he entered at precisely 9:00 AM, he understood why. Two members of the City Council flanked Connolly on each side like bodyguards. He'd recruited backup for this morning's carnage.

"Gentlemen," Crockett nodded, taking a seat. Conversation ceased. The five men across the table nodded to him as one.

Connolly waited until all eyes were upon him before speaking. "I thank you all for coming here this morning. I know how crazy your schedules must be at this time of year." He walked to Crockett and placed a hand on his shoulder, as if to soften the blow of the words to follow.

Crockett flinched at the touch but managed to control the expression on his face. He studied the somber Council members. Couple more and it'd look like the Last Supper. He had no illusions about the purpose of the meeting.

Connolly launched into his prepared speech. "You know I supported your nomination as the first person of color to head the force. And I've been pleased with the work you've done up to now."

Nothing Crockett could do but endure the little man's drama.

"Clearly you're over your head with this crime wave. One dead college student, a bunch of overdoses, and drugs everywhere: in the library, on the streets, in the dorms, at the Drinking Gourd. It's out of control."

Just as Connolly drew breath to continue, Dean Drucker burst into the room, all smiles, handshakes, and apologies for being late. Connolly acknowledged Drucker's tardy entrance with a dark nod and a glance at the clock and waited once more for full attention. "It was a very difficult decision, but we have no choice. Our responsibility is to the people of the town and to the college." Connolly bowed his head for a few seconds and then raised his eyes to the heavens. "I'm sorry, Crockett. Be prepared to brief your replacement Monday morning."

Members of the Council studied their cuticles and toyed with pencils. Crockett looked at each member in turn before rising. Connolly seemed to be waiting for him to say something. Did he expect him to grovel? Beg for another chance? Make a farewell speech? Fuck 'em. Crockett squared his shoulders and walked the length of the table, forcing each person to acknowledge him and shake his hand. Few returned his direct gaze.

Watson burst into the room and addressed Connolly. Watson's stage whisper reached every ear in the room. "Couple of students found a guy with his throat cut in the Arb."

Crockett turned to Connolly. "I'm Chief 'til Monday?"

Connolly hesitated.

"Yes or no?"

"Well, technically, yes, but Watson here can—"

"Drive." Crockett finished Connolly's sentence, grabbed Watson's elbow in a pincer grip, and ushered him out the door.

Watson drove to the Arboretum in surly silence. Crockett rode in a stunned silence of his own. Why hadn't Connolly just fired his sorry ass on the spot? Why wait until Monday? *Because this was graduation weekend.* Damage control. Drucker and Connolly would avoid negative publicity at all costs. They'd announce his replacement on Monday *after* the spotlights had dimmed.

Watson pulled up behind two black and whites and an ambulance. He slammed the door and led Crockett down a well-worn path into the Arboretum.

About fifty yards into the forest they came to a clearing cordoned off with yellow tape. A police photographer's flash lit McPhee's skinny frame that had been shoved under bushes at the side of the clearing. Dundee had already completed his preliminary examination of the body, and the crime scene experts were sweeping the area.

"When was this called in?" asked Crockett.

"A while ago. I held off disturbing you, knowing you had a meeting."

Crockett pictured his fist slamming into Watson's nose. "How'd the kids find him?" he asked in a neutral voice.

"Jogging. One guy went behind the bushes to pee. When he looked down, he was pissing into the wide-open eyes of a corpse."

"You get my message last night to pick up McPhee for questioning?"

"Yup, but he wasn't at home, and he didn't show up for work this morning."

The EMTs positioned a body bag on a stretcher next to the corpse. As they lifted him, Danny McPhee's head lolled to the side, connected to the body only by the spinal cord. The motion exposed the deep gash that had all but decapitated him. Crockett let out an involuntary low whistle and looked away. The two-second-control rule worked for shock as well as anger, but this time Crockett gave himself a few extra seconds.

"Whoever did this was one mean fucker," he said, more to test his voice than to make an observation. But he was talking to air. Watson was retching into the bushes. When he returned, he looked sheepish and smelled of vomit. "No wallet or identification, but no question it's McPhee." Watson talked to cover his embarrassment. He wiped his mouth on his arm and then sniffed his sleeve. "Must've been sudden. Or he didn't feel threatened. Never pulled his knife. The M.E. found a stiletto in one boot and a packet of coke in the other."

As if on cue, Dr. Dundee joined them. "When you said there was a body in the forest, I expected a messy decomp job. But this body's still nice and fresh. Probably happened in the last twelve hours, maybe less. If it weren't for the obvious neck wound, I'd say he died from terminal acne." Dundee brayed and grabbed his bag. "I know. I know. Time of death to the nano-second." He turned to the EMTs with a big grin and a wave. "Meet you at the morgue, guys."

"Man enjoys his work," grunted Crockett. "Time to call on Swain."

Ricki greeted Crockett and Watson like clients as they entered Swain Construction. "Mornin', Chief, Captain. Have a seat while I round up the boss."

Crockett resumed his earlier examination of the scale model of Emerald Acres in the reception area. He pushed the cloth aside revealing an ell-shaped building divided into two sections, a pharmacy/food mart and a restaurant. For the first time, he noticed a sign on the side of the building, "The Underground Shoppes." To the right of it, was a long, two-story residential building with parking spaces next to individual units. He was impressed by the size of the project and the level of detail that included shrubbery and footpaths between buildings.

Ricki returned and joined Crockett. "It was a dynamite plan, but it fell through. That's why it's covered." While Watson cleaned himself up in the bathroom, Crockett took the opportunity to speak privately with her. "Captain Watson says you work for Ron on the weekends as well."

"Oh, yes, I babysit for Ron's boys often. They're adorable. You know their mother's Japanese?"

"Did you babysit for them last Friday night?"

"Why, yes, I did. I remember because they came home so late that night. It must've been twelve or twelve-thirty before Mr. Swain drove me home." She giggled and explained, "Mom expected me home by eleven."

Ron strode from his office and pulled the green cloth over the model. "What brings you back so soon, Crockett?" He didn't offer to shake hands. "Ricki, honey, bring some coffee."

Watson returned and the three of them were seated in Ron's office. Crockett watched Ron's face closely as Watson informed him of McPhee's death. Ron's eyes widened at the description of the wound, but settled quickly into a noncommittal expression. He grunted, reached for a cigar, and then thought better of it.

"Not too torn up over the news," Crockett observed.

"No great loss to mankind. Or to Swain Construction. McPhee was always shining up to students, never where he was supposed to be. I came close to firing him a couple times, but you know how it is. You can't afford to let anyone go these days, unless he's a complete loser." He looked pointedly at Crockett, offering a condescending smile.

Crockett refused the bait. "We'll need to know McPhee's full name and next of kin."

Ron hollered for Ricki to bring McPhee's personnel file. "McPhee was such a little maggot. Why would anyone bother to kill him?" He reached for a cigar and this time completed his clipping, wetting, and lighting ritual.

"Scumbucket like him, could be any number of reasons," said Watson. "The guy was a flaming faggot, buggering every—"

"Here it is, Mr. Swain." Ricki pranced in with McPhee's file.

"*Homosexual*. Watch your mouth, you want to work in this town."

Watson turned on Crockett with a sly smile. "Watch my mouth till Monday, anyway."

Ron handed the file to Watson. "Make a copy." Watson took the file from Ron and stalked to the door.

When he was out of earshot, Crockett stretched out in the leather chair. "Looks like you planned to build Emerald Acres—and the Underground Shoppes—on the Gourd property. You talked with the Kenworthys?"

Ron rose and walked to the window, adjusting the blinds. "Plural? No. Jules? Yes." The silence hung on the cigar smoke between them. "I guess there's no harm in telling you now, since it will come out sooner than later. Jules was suing for divorce. She'd already talked with a lawyer. He told her if she got cleaned up, she could expect to be awarded her girl and the Gourd.

"As you know, Jules and I go back a long way. We had plans to develop the property." Ron's voice took on an almost dreamy quality. "The project was designed to provide much needed retirement housing, plus the draw of shops in an historic setting."

"Sounds like a commercial."

Ron examined his buffed nails and his expression turned sour. "Looks as if Georgie'll get what he wanted after all: his little girl, and his historic monument. And I lost a multi-million dollar deal and one of the best lays I've ever had. All I can say is, I hope you nail the bastard."

"Make it sound like George was involved in Jules' death."

"No shit. They were at each other's throats. Possession is nine-tenths of the law, and neither was willing to move out of the Gourd. Let's just say her death was convenient." Ron spat out the last words. He pointed his cigar at Crockett. "And don't give me any of your high moral ground bullshit. Jules was looking out for the future of her kid. She had a right to a life like anyone else."

Watson entered the room with copies of the personnel file.

Crockett addressed Ron as he rose to leave. "Surprised you didn't get the word from Watson. Jules' case is closed: 'Apparent suicide.'"

Watson hitched his pants and followed Crockett out the door.

"Shut the fuck up." Watson hadn't said a word, but Crockett wasn't taking any chances.

Chapter Forty-One

Crockett walked from the station to Rexall Drug, headed to the counter at the rear of the drugstore, and greeted the pharmacist, Kristin Lombard. She was a tall brunette with a bubbling laugh that raised his spirits a few notches.

"Have a hypothetical question for you. Would you be able to fill a prescription for secobarbital?"

"Sure, but doctors mostly prescribe phenobarb these days. Are you having trouble sleeping?" A look of concern washed over Kristin's face.

"Nah. I sleep standing up. This is business. Need to find out which doctors still prescribe the old stuff, secobarbital."

Kristin shook her head slowly. "I wouldn't be able to give out patient information without a court order."

"I don't want the patient. I'm after the doctor." Crockett made it sound as if he were hunting a malfeasant physician.

"Well," Kristin hesitated, "even for that, I'd still have to do a search of patient prescriptions."

"Sorry." He turned to leave. "Got no business putting you on the spot."

"Crockett, get back here. I have a question of my own."

Crockett obediently returned to the counter, bemused by her bossy tone.

Kristin's voice lowered to a confidential tone. "Word has it Watson will relieve you on Monday." She tilted her head to the side and raised her eyebrows.

"True. Shoulda come here instead of the station. Rather hear it from you." Crockett couldn't disguise the irony in his voice. "Got the word this morning. Wouldn't have tried to pull this little stunt if I had more time."

"Stay right there." Kristin disappeared behind the counter. Crockett picked out two birthday cards and a graduation card while a full five minutes passed.

Finally, Kristin returned with a victorious smile. "Now, if I had your question," she engaged and held his eyes, "I'd focus on a few internists in town, you know, doctors like, say, Preston or Bates."

Crockett thanked her and returned to the station for his cruiser. Could be a complete waste of time. Other places to get drugs in northern Ohio besides Rexall Drug in Oberlin. And anyone with half a brain would have thrown out any remaining pills. But he had nothing better to do except clean out his office. Last thing he wanted was to spend his remaining time on the force around Watson or Connolly, and one of those pricks was bound to be there.

Earlier in the week, Crockett had scratched Art and Martha Cavendish off the list when Martha produced a bottle of phenobarbital prescribed by Dr. Preston. Ron had an alibi. That left George and Casey. He drove slowly toward Mae's house. Wasn't looking good for Casey if he couldn't defend her against Watson and Connolly. They'd railroad her into another stay in Marysville. Nonetheless, he had a job to do.

Or did he? He slowed to a crawl. Bag it. Hell, they bagged him. Crockett braked and stared out the windshield at nothing in particular. A few moments later his eye caught a motion in the rearview mirror. An old man in a Buick was waiting patiently behind him. How long had the man been sitting there afraid to toot his horn? Crockett swore softly and pulled into Mae's driveway.

He walked up the steps and pressed the doorbell. While he waited, Crockett looked around. Casey'd done a remarkable job cleaning up the yard. He especially liked the teapot graveyard ablaze with flowers. He rang the bell again and waited. Maybe the bell didn't work. He pounded on the door.

"Who is it?" an old voice cawed.

"Chief Crockett, Oberlin Police Department, ma'am."

"Don't 'ma'am' me, Crockett. I know who you are."

The door opened slowly and Mae glared up at him, tilting her head like a bird. Crockett was shocked at how much she'd shrunk. She clutched the front bar of a walker to steady herself. Turning, she aimed the aluminum contraption toward the living room.

"Casey's not here, so what is it?" She turned around and fell backward. Crockett jumped to catch her. She cackled as she landed in her chair.

The room smelled of talcum powder and medications. The once graceful living room had a hospital bed, two sitting chairs, and a portable potty. The top of a half-sized refrigerator was covered with plastic bottles of prescription drugs.

"Won't keep you. Just a few questions."

"Police always have questions. People don't always have answers." She challenged Crockett with a rude stare.

"Who is your family doctor?"

"None of your flipping business."

Crockett rocked back and laughed, and to his surprise, saw the beginnings of a smile on Mae's lips.

"Dr. Winifred Preston. Presto. The woman sucks your blood, scans your heart, pokes your privates, and runs your credit card through the machine in five minutes flat. She's Casey's doctor too, if that's your next question. Why?"

"Do either of you use sleeping pills?"

Mae's face closed down. "I do. Not Casey." Her eyes flickered involuntarily to the top of the refrigerator.

"Mind?" Crockett examined the vials. Here it was. Phenobarbital. Not secobarbital. Crockett let out a sigh of relief. Stealing a glance at Mae, he was surprised at how her eyes were riveted on the bottle in his hand. He read the prescription date and dosage, and then counted the capsules inside. "Where are the rest?"

"Some missing?" Mae reached for the bottle.

Crockett ignored her outstretched hand. "Quite a few. Any idea where they might be?"

"My, but aren't you nosey today." Mae toyed with a ring that was too loose for her bony finger but wouldn't pass over her enlarged knuckle. She drew a comforter over her legs. "Must be time for my nap."

"Pills might be important in an investigation."

Mae stared wide-eyed at Crockett, as if she'd just been doused with a bucket of ice water. "Jules," she whispered. "You think Casey...? Oh, damn it to hell!" She lurched to her feet, balanced with the walker, and shuffled to the bay window. Grasping the hem of a grayed nylon curtain, she held it out to Crockett, eyes moist.

"Why?" Crockett asked as he made out the slight bulge of pills in the hem. But he knew the answer.

"Well, my time's coming soon." She held out a shaking hand. "Gets worse by the week. I'll need the pills and my bottle of courage," she pointed to the refrigerator, "to see me through the last patch. Casey would take care of me, but I can't let her. She's had enough trouble."

Crockett opened the refrigerator. Dry vermouth, vodka, and olives. "You know alcohol and sleeping pills don't mix, don't you?"

"I'm counting on it," Mae whispered. Crockett leaned forward to make out her next words. "Please, Crockett. Don't tell Casey. She'll take them away. I don't want to be a vegetable." Mae worked her way to the bed.

Crockett offered his hand to Mae as he rose to leave. "They're the wrong type of sleeping pills, ma'am." He squeezed her cold hand gently. "Those pills won't help. Drug companies make them weak these days so people can't use them to commit suicide. If you take *phenobarbital* with alcohol, you'll be a vegetable for sure. Besides, it's not your time. Casey needs you. She loves you, you know."

"She's a young fool." Mae nodded slowly and placed her shaky hand atop his, her eyes brimming over. "Thank you," she whispered.

Chapter Forty-Two

After her visit to the cemetery, Casey rode to the Gourd. She leaned her bike against the far side of the barn. As she passed the barn door, she started at motion above her. The rope she and Jules had used to slide down from the hayloft was swinging in the breeze. Relax.

She ran across the cobblestones and flattened herself against the building. George probably wouldn't be home from visiting hours yet, but there was no reason to announce her presence to Martha or Art. No sounds from the kitchen, but she hadn't expected any. The Gourd wouldn't open for business until after the funeral.

Old wood shrieked overhead as a window was opened on the second floor. "I've got to make an appearance at the funeral home. You stay here with Gabby," Martha ordered. "She's in her room." Martha's voice faded as she turned from the window.

Casey didn't wait to hear more. If Gabby was in her room, the Kenworthy door would be unlocked, and she could quickly deposit the key and be off. She sidled across to the Kenworthy steps. The door opened without a sound, and Casey slipped inside. Again she listened but heard only the rush of water running through old pipes. Martha in the shower.

She hung the key on its assigned peg and turned to go. She should leave, but the door to the cellar pulled her like a magnet. Probably not a good idea. George would be home soon. But he wouldn't look in the clubhouse; he wouldn't know she was there. All she needed was a few minutes to read the last entries in Jules' journal.

She opened the cellar door and counted the stairs as she descended. At the bottom, light from the coal chute windows made the going easier. The clubhouse door was still open and had been re-crossed with crime scene tape. Casey ducked under the tape and headed for the Sword of the Spirit.

She unscrewed the hilt and shook out the key to the file cabinet. Again, the lock popped and the drawer opened with a low rumble. She reached into the back and pulled out the last notebook. On the top right-hand corner was a date, followed by a dash. Casey sat and leaned against the wall beside the high window for light, and opened to the last entry:

It's now or never. I can't do this anymore. I told him I'd been to a divorce lawyer, but I haven't. He's surprised we've been able to make the payments.

"Mommy's story."

Casey almost departed her skin. Gabby was lying in the corner. "What the heck are you doing down here?" Casey forgot to whisper.

"Shhhh. This is a quiet place." Gabby wore a choir robe that matched the one Jules had been wearing when she was found. She closed her eyes and clasped her hands across her chest as if she were in a coffin.

"What are you doing?" Casey whispered.

"Going to see Mommy. She's in heaven."

Evidently, the key to Gabby's upward journey was the place her mother's body had been before it was removed. Gabby's sneakers made little bumps a third of the way down the robe. Another lump lower down wagged rhythmically.

"I think you have to be a bit older to go to heaven, honey." Casey didn't want to burst the bubble of hope, but this was just too weird.

Gabby's face fell, her disappointment registering in the length of her lower lip.

"I bet Mrs. Cavendish is wondering where you are."

Gabby pulled a face and then peeked at Casey. "Read me Mommy's story."

"Mommy's...?" Casey's voice caught. Gabby stared at the notebook in Casey's hand.

"Read about the little girl in the garden and her dog and how she sings to the flowers."

"Wouldn't you rather read upstairs where it's warmer?"

Frown. Wrong answer. "We read the books here. Then lock them up. Then the treat." Gabby stood, raised the robe so she could walk, and plopped down next to Casey.

Reluctantly, Casey opened the notebook. "Once upon a time, there was a little girl named…" Casey squinted at the page. "I can't read her name."

"Alice," Gabby said impatiently.

"Alice, of course." Casey scrolled her finger down the page with a frown of her own, as if she were looking for something. "I don't know the story," she hinted. "What's the little dog's name?"

"Shiner. He's white with a big black spot over one eye. Shiner follows Alice everywhere."

Casey nodded. She pretended to read. "Alice looked out the window. The sun was bright and warm. Beside her, Shiner wagged his tail. Without a sound, Alice dressed. She put her finger to her lips. 'Shhh. We don't want to wake anyone up.' Quiet as mice, they tiptoed down the hallway to the back door. The door creaked, *cccrrrrrreeeeeeekkkk!* They stood still as statues. No one came. Alice closed the door quickly, but it still made a little *creeeeek.*"

Gabby giggled and snuggled closer. Her arms were cold. "Ralphie, bring the bankie." Ralphie walked to the corner, picked up his blanket, and dragged it to them. Casey stared. Could it be the freshly laundered blanket that Jules had died in?

"Read."

Bossy little thing. But Casey obeyed. "Free! Alice skipped in the sunshine with Shiner trotting beside her." Casey hesitated. The actual text where her finger stopped read, *"I don't know how much longer I can keep going. I have enough for the rehab program, but it will be hard to leave Gabby that long. How can I explain to her that it's the only way we can be together in the long run?"*

Gabby squirmed. "Read about how she sings," she demanded, grabbing for the book. Casey teased her by holding the book out of reach. "'Alice loved the flowers. She sang pretty songs to them to make them happy. Every tune was different, because every flower was different. She sang to the pansies first, and when they smiled at her, she—'"

The Kenworthy back door banged open.

225

"Uh oh." Gabby's owlet eyes registered trouble. She put her finger to her lips. "Secret? Promise?" she whispered.

Casey nodded, and mouthed, "Secret."

Gabby shrugged off the choir robe, ducked under the tape, and vanished. The click of Ralphie's toenails was drowned out by a second set of footsteps overhead and a lower man's voice. "Be better for us to talk alone for a minute. Thought you might shed some light on a few loose ends. Where do you think Jules got the sleeping pills?"

Crockett!

Silence.

"Jules didn't use sleeping pills. No reason to. After drinking enough wine, she'd just pass out."

"Autopsy report said Jules died from a mixture of cocaine, alcohol, and secobarbital."

"I couldn't bear to read the report. What is seco—?"

"A sleeping pill that doctors don't use much these days. Report also said there were trace chemicals from cleaning fluids, but not enough to kill her. Who was her doctor?"

"Dr. Markowitz. We all went to him. And no, I don't use sleeping pills."

"Drug cabinets didn't even have aspirin."

"OK. I was worried about Jules. Afraid she might do ..." George hesitated, "what she did." There was a long pause and the sounds of chairs scraping on the wooden floor. "So I cleaned out all the drugs one night after we'd had a particularly nasty argument, and I'd said a few things I probably shouldn't have. I told her if she continued to whore around with Swain, I'd sue for divorce and get Gabby. No judge would give an alcoholic slut custody of a child. 'Over my dead body!' she yelled at me. 'But maybe that's what you want. Then you can screw around with Renee, or Casey or whoever it is this week.'"

Casey stifled a sob.

"You were getting a divorce?"

"No. I'd never leave Jules. I loved her. I just didn't like her very much. I think I told you before that Jules and I had a gift for hurting each other."

CHAPTER FORTY-TWO

I was the one you told. In the cemetery. Casey wished she could disappear.

"You might as well know that Jules emptied her personal bank account and cleaned out her papers and jewelry from our safe deposit box Friday morning."

Mom's ring.

"She didn't touch our joint account. I just found out this morning when I went to the bank."

Crockett spoke slowly as if to emphasize his next points. "Jules didn't use sleeping pills. She didn't go to a doctor who prescribed secobarbital. She died from a combination of alcohol, coke, and *sleeping pills*. She withdrew jewelry, papers, and money. You still think her death was an 'apparent suicide?'"

No answer.

"She planned to take off?" Crockett pressed.

"I thought about it all morning. I can't believe she'd leave Gabby."

Chairs scraped again followed by the sound of footsteps.

"Crockett?"

The steps halted.

"What do you make of all this?"

"She tried to leave."

"And?"

"Someone stopped her."

"Jesus," George whispered. "You don't think that I..."

"Doesn't matter unless I can prove it." The door creaked on its hinges. "But, no. I don't think you killed her."

"What changed your mind?" A note of petulance crept into George's voice.

"I called Renee. She said you slept in her bed Friday and Saturday nights."

No! Casey's mind reeled. She's his editor! He stayed at the hotel. He had hotel receipts to prove it. Didn't he? Casey gulped. Had she spoken aloud?

Silence from above.

After a long moment, George spoke. "Who does that leave?"

"Martha. Ron. Art." Crockett hesitated. "And Casey."

"You think Casey could have done it?"

"No. But she wrote the note. Did a number of foolish things to protect Art…and you. Looks like her trust was misplaced."

"Meaning?" Petulance was laced with anger.

When Crockett didn't answer, George filled the silence.

"You're asking about my intentions with Casey. I don't have anything to apologize for. We took a walk to the cemetery and kissed for old times' sake. I shouldn't have encouraged her, but everywhere I turned, there she was. And you've gotta admit, Crockett, she's tempting. Or are you above such temptations?"

Casey's face burned.

Silence.

"Casey knows I could never marry an ex-con. The faculty would never accept a dealer."

"Still don't get it, do you? *Jules* was the one doing drugs in college. The drop at the bust was intended for Jules, not Casey. And now, there's reason to believe Jules was dealing through McPhee."

"Jules." Much of the life had drained from George's voice. "That would explain how she made the payments. But how? Where would they get the drugs?"

"Daddy! Daddy!"

"There's my girl!" George shouted.

The patter of small feet was followed by hysterical giggles and a long squeal. Casey imagined George twirling Gabby over his head. She used the commotion overhead to re-file the journal and cover the sound of the filing cabinet drawer rolling shut. She punched in the lock and replaced the key in the hilt of the Sword of the Spirit.

"JoJo!"

As Casey ducked under the tape, Crockett called Gabby a little monkey. Casey followed in Gabby's footsteps, making her way across the cellar, past the old furnace to the Cavendish stairs. She ran up the stairs, cracked the door, and listened for a second before slipping out and dashing to her bike. She'd thought she couldn't feel any worse. She was wrong. Wrong, heartsick, and angry.

Chapter Forty-Three

Casey stood at the back of the large group of mourners, waiting for the funeral director to open the Loveland mausoleum. The church service had been standing room only, and, although suitably solemn, it didn't have as much to do with the celebration of Jules' short life as it did with the manner of her death. With tears flowing down his face, Art had played the church-appropriate variations of Jules' favorite songs on the organ. One line from the James Taylor song haunted her: *"I've seen fire and I've seen rain, but I always thought I'd see you...one more time again."*

Even the interment of Jules' ashes had an impressive draw, the best show in town on Saturday afternoon of Commencement weekend. The crowd arranged itself in a semi-circle around the entrance to the mausoleum, layered in tiers: first row, immediate family and relatives, next, close friends, then associates from the town and college, and finally, curiosity seekers. Casey should have been in the inner sanctum, mourning the friend who had been like a sister to her. Instead, she observed from the outskirts, strangely detached one moment, and overcome with emotion the next.

In front, George held Gabby's hand and bent to talk to her. How could he explain burning up her mother's body and putting her ashes in the box that he cradled under his arm? How did a little girl feel about locking her mother in a dark mausoleum, never to return? Casey rocked back and forth on her heels, staring at the box of ashes.

She shifted her focus to Crockett at the back of the crowd and nodded as their eyes met. Beyond, a long line of parked cars stretched back to the entrance of the cemetery.

Ron stood off to the side next to his car. Compared to the townspeople's Sunday best and the faculty in academic tweeds, he looked the dandy in his tailored Italian suit. Bear stood behind the black BMW, watching the crowd with a sweet smile.

The now familiar complaint of metal grate upon concrete brought Casey's attention back to the mausoleum. The funeral director led George and Gabby down the steps into the stone building with Dr. and Mrs. Loveland close behind. Seconds after they disappeared into the building, Mrs. Loveland's shriek pierced the air. "Where is Uncle John?"

"*Shhh!* Keep your voice down." But the stone walls broadcast every whispered vowel to the startled crowd outside. George calmed his histrionic mother-in-law. "It was probably just a teenage prank. Who on earth would want Uncle John?"

"Don't make light of it. It's not funny!" Mrs. Loveland exclaimed, her voice rising in indignation. "We can't leave her ashes where it isn't safe."

The funeral director burst from the building and scanned the crowd until he spied Crockett who was already making his way forward. A ripple of murmurs arose from the crowd. Necks craned to see the action.

Crockett spoke a few words with the director and then ducked into the stone building. He returned almost immediately followed by George, Gabby, and the parents. George still carried the box. The pastor announced that the interment would take place later and asked all present to bow their heads in a final prayer for the deceased.

Casey watched Bear shuffle from the periphery over to Watson. The two retreated from the crowd, heads together. Then, feeling Crockett's eyes upon her once again, she obediently bowed her head.

Jules *had* been hiding something in Loveland after all. Casey pictured the lighter place next to Lucetta's urn where Uncle John's remains had been. When Jules left the mausoleum, she'd carried Uncle John in the bag. Casey had little doubt that Uncle John's box was stuffed with white powder.

The persistent song easily wormed its way back into her head and overwhelmed the pastor's drone. *"I've seen fire and I've seen rain..."* She'd never see Jules again. You can't make new, old friends. As her eyes brimmed, she fought off tears by calculating how much a funerary urn of cocaine would bring on the street. *You almost made it. Who stopped you? Who hated—or loved—you enough to kill you? Or was your death drug business? What should I wish for you, dear friend? To rest in peace, or to roast?*

Chapter Forty-Four

"Dust to dust. Ashes to ashes."

Art let out an involuntary moan, unable to reconcile his image of Jules with the ashes in the box under George's arm. He closed his eyes and willed himself to think of her as a young girl with straw in her hair, winking down at him from the hayloft. Jules as Juliet to his Romeo in the high school drama club. Jules strutting her long legs and little white boots before the marching band. Jules the Queen. Jules of his dreams.

When did he start loving her? He didn't know. But he had never been able to turn it off. He knew she was promiscuous and hurt people he loved. But she was just so alive. He groaned at the irony. He tried everything to escape her spell. Nothing worked. Maybe death would release him.

"Amen."

Observers in the outer circles melted away, while those closer waited to say a few words to the bereaved. Art and Martha paid their respects quickly. He held Martha's arm to keep her heels from sinking into the moist grass. Aware that she would be in the limelight, she had worn high heels that showed her legs to advantage. Under her veil, he could make out the suggestion of rose lipstick, blush, and even the hint of perfume, a floral scent that reminded him of Jules.

He helped her into their car and gave her the admiring look she expected. He leaned over and brushed her cheek lightly with his lips. "You look lovely." Martha lowered her eyes demurely and then, without raising her head, looked up with a shy smile. He backed off, recognizing the move as a Jules rip-off.

Art drove toward the Gourd, thinking about Martha's futile efforts to be sexy like Jules. One morning when Martha thought he was asleep, he'd watched her practice the Jules flirtation move before her make-up mirror, rehearsing it over and over and over before she was satisfied. So what? The labor involved in perfecting the gesture should increase his appreciation, not incur his disdain. Hell, he practiced the piano for hours at a time to learn the right moves. What was the difference? Clearly, he wasn't Bach. But she pretended to be Jules, and she was a fake.

"I can't believe my brother and his goon showed up today. He's got brass balls."

Art winced at her language. He chose his words carefully. Martha called Ron every name in the book, but she would brook no slur on her brother from the Cavendish clan. "Why do you think he came?" Art asked, noncommittally.

"Came? *Came?*" Martha snorted. "She poisoned him the same way she poisoned all of you. She created a sexual vacuum, sucking you all in." Martha's hand became the snout of a vacuum cleaner seeking imaginary dust balls. "Thhhuuuup! Thhhuuup! Thhhuuup!"

Art braked at the unexpected sound, causing a hiccup in the line of traffic behind him.

"Ron was special, though, and he knew it. He was her first lover." Martha paused. "And hopefully her last."

"What's that supposed to mean?" Art was immediately on the defensive, wondering if she knew something about the night Jules died that he couldn't remember.

"Nothing." Martha's voice was nonchalant. She looked out the window and drummed her freshly painted fingernails on the armrest.

Art concentrated on driving, opting for a brooding silence over further exchange.

"Well?" Martha demanded when she couldn't stand it any longer.

"Well *what*, Martha?" Sometimes Martha went too far. "Do you think you could muster a charitable thought for once? Jules has just been buried, for chrissake."

"She wasn't buried. She wasn't even shelved." Martha giggled. "Don't be such a flaming hypocrite. You like it well enough if it smells of Jules."

Art accelerated and wrenched the steering wheel to the left. The car spun sidewise into the Gourd parking lot, throwing Martha against the passenger door. She looked into his eyes and awarded him her nastiest, *gotcha* smile.

Art slammed the car door and strode to the Gourd. As he stomped up the stairs to their apartment, he regretted yesterday's decision to pour all that beautiful amber liquid down the drain. He loosened his tie, kicked off his funeral shoes, and threw himself across the bed. No, this would never do. Martha would be on him in seconds. He jumped up to change his clothes.

The bedroom door flew open. Art hung up his suit and rummaged around the closet floor until he found a sweatsuit composting in the corner. He pulled on the pants and jammed his feet into a pair of running shoes with broken heels. Martha hadn't spoken or moved from the doorway.

He eyed the vamp posturing before him. He should consider himself a lucky man.

"Nice buns, Artie." Martha lowered and softened her voice.

So damn contrived. She just couldn't be herself. Even called him "Artie" like Jules did. He hoped he could get away without a scene. He waited for her move. She shifted her weight to one foot, grimaced, and tossed a high heel past him into the closet. When she reached for the second shoe, Art lunged for the door, fending her off as she tried to block his progress. Caught off balance, Martha fell backward onto the bed. Quick as a cat, she rolled and then crouched, crawling across the bed toward him, thinking she was sexy. Jesus, she misread his push as an *invitation*.

Art flung himself down the back stairs. He opened the door and let it slam shut without exiting. He stood still and listened. When he heard Martha's steps above him, he snuck back down the hallway and entered the Gourd kitchen. In the dark, he felt his way through the swinging doors to the bar, grabbed a glass and a bottle of Jack Daniel's, and slid into a booth.

"Here's to you, Jules, m'lady."

Aah! The blessed fire of the first one going down. He must learn to address Jules in the past tense. He poured another. A few more hits and time and tense wouldn't matter one whit.

Chapter Forty-Five

As the mourners paid their respects, Crockett watched Casey kneel and speak with Gabby and give her a kiss. She said a few words to George but never touched him.

Casey joined Crockett. "Hi, JoJo. Sad day." They were quiet for a moment, taking in the scene. She looked beyond him. "I see you've lost your ride."

Crockett had come with Watson to minimize the number of vehicles in the funerary caravan. He followed Casey's eyes as the cruiser disappeared beyond the first bend in the winding cemetery road. "Little shit." Crockett noticed the bemused expression in Casey's eyes. "One more day on the job, say what I think."

"What will you do, JoJo?" Casey's eyes searched his face.

"Don't know. Thought this was the job for me. How about you?"

When no reply was forthcoming, Crockett continued. "Got a strange complaint from the Circulation Librarian. Something about assault with a mousetrap."

Casey suppressed a grin. "Time for me to start fresh someplace they don't have a rodent problem." Her somber expression returned. "Where the police aren't trying to frame me."

"I told Watson to lay off. He still after you?"

Casey nodded. "What do you think of the missing box?"

"Same thing you think. Full of dope."

"I think I was followed again yesterday."

Crockett looked directly into Casey's eyes. "Be a good time to lay low. Watson may have enough for a warrant."

"When I left Marysville, Oberlin was the place I wanted to be. Now I want to leave, but I sure as hell don't want to go back to Marysville." Casey glanced over at George. "It's as if we all took a 'time out,' because we were naughty. But when we returned, we picked up where we left off. Except now, the games are for real." Casey's voice quavered. "I didn't steal Uncle John, JoJo."

"I believe you. Just can't prove it. This town's no good for you. If I were you? I'd leave."

Casey looked stunned for a minute, then gave him a gentle rabbit punch and moved away.

Crockett turned his attention to the line of mourners offering condolences to the family. Gabby stood silently at George's side, her little hand raised to his, eyes fixed on the box that George tucked into his torso like a football.

He waited ten minutes until the line thinned before moving behind George. He bent forward to speak, "Have a question—"

"Jesus, Crockett, this is a funeral," George hissed out of the side of his mouth. "Can't your damned questions wait until we find a spot for her ashes?"

Crockett backed off, while George shook more hands and finally spoke to the Lovelands. Mrs. Loveland gave George a perfunctory hug and patted Gabby on the head as if she were a little dog. Gabby pulled away, tugging at her father's hand. Mrs. Loveland continued patting the air for a moment and then allowed her husband to give her his arm and walked away.

Crockett approached again and spoke quickly. "No questions. I need a ride to the station. You could fill out a missing per—" Crockett hesitated, "a theft report."

Although he had put on a fresh shirt and a charcoal suit, George's tie was askew, and his hair ruffled as if there were a breeze. His eyes looked as if he hadn't slept in a week.

"Sure. We'll drop Gabby and the ashes off at the Gourd." The three of them walked in silence to the Civic. George handed the ashes to Crockett and buckled Gabby into the back seat.

"Who was Uncle John?" Crockett asked as the car inched toward the cemetery entrance.

"Dr. Loveland's uncle. John was the first of the clan to be cremated. When they got a full house of coffins, John was too cheap to build another mausoleum. Instead, he created the niche for funerary urns. Jules' mother was so pis—" George glanced quickly in the rearview mirror at Gabby. "Uh, so angry at John, I was surprised she got upset today."

Crockett turned his head, aware of a small sound from the back seat. Gabby was holding a quiet but animated conversation with herself. He shifted his attention back to George who was speaking.

"Someone went to a lot of trouble to break in, unscrew the protective plate, remove the box, and then replace everything. But why? Why would anyone want to take Uncle John?"

"'Cause he was cold." Gabby's voice was a little louder, as if answering George's question.

George spoke quietly to Crockett. "She's been asking why we're putting Mommy in 'the cold place.' She's got some notion that the mausoleum is cold and damp."

"Put Mommy in the warm place." Gabby still pretended to talk to herself.

George raised his voice. "Where would you like to put Mommy's ashes, honey?"

"Next to Uncle John."

George nearly rear-ended the car in front of them. "Sorry." George and Crockett exchanged glances.

Crockett turned in his seat to face Gabby. "Do you know where Uncle John is?"

"Uh huh."

"Will you show us?" Crockett asked softly.

"Yup. He's behind the furnace. Mommy said it was a good place, 'cause it was cold in the stone house. He's happy now." She smiled.

Minutes later, they turned into the Kenworthy driveway. As soon as Gabby was unbuckled, she took command. "You carry Mommy," she ordered her father. "You come, too, JoJo." She marched through the garage into the house.

Ralphie greeted her at the door, dancing and yipping his welcome. His tail gyrated like a rotor, threatening to lift him off the ground. Gabby led the parade down the stairway into the old cellar. She passed the ancient coal burning behemoth and halted beside a modern furnace one-third its size. To the right, four shelves lined the stone foundation. Canning jars coated with dust crowded the top two shelves. The third shelf was jammed with trowels, pots and work gloves. The bottom shelf held boxes of chemical fertilizers, rose dust, and an opened bag of potting soil. And behind everything, in a plain wooden box with a lock, Uncle John.

"Well, I'll be—" George caught himself again and just stared.

"Mommy said she put him on a shelf to keep him dry."

"You helped Mommy?" Crockett asked to keep the patter going.

"I surprised her. Katie broke her arm, so I came home early."

"Last weekend?" asked George, suddenly attuned to their conversation.

"Dunno when." Gabby shrugged and frowned at the floor. "When I was s'posed to sleep at Katie's."

"It's all right, honey." George reassured her. "You surprised Mommy. Did she have Uncle John when she came home?"

"Yup." Gabby eyed the shelves. "Put Mommy here." She tugged the bag of potting soil off the shelf. The bag split, spilling fresh dirt on the floor. "Uh oh," she said, looking quickly up at her father.

"It's OK." George carefully placed Jules' ashes on the space cleared by Gabby. "But I think we'll have to return Uncle John to Grandma and Grandpa." Before Gabby could object, he added, "I bet they have a nice warm spot for him in their basement."

This seemed to appease her, because her attention shifted to her mother's ashes. "Ralphie, get the bankie," she ordered. He obediently trotted from the room. Gabby didn't seem fazed when George picked Uncle John off the shelf.

Ralphie returned, hauling his ratty old blanket. Gabby patted him absently and walked to her mother's box. She touched it gently. "You be warm here, Mommy." Carefully, she covered the box with the blanket and tucked her in.

George led a reluctant Gabby upstairs. Crockett heard him explain that he had to leave her with Martha for a few minutes while he drove JoJo to work and returned Uncle John. She responded with a tired whine that quickly developed into tears.

While he waited, Crockett called the station and was surprised when Watson answered.

"Where's Jenny?"

"Her console's all lit up with calls coming in about an accident with injuries on Route 10."

"I'll be there in fifteen minutes."

"No need. We can handle an accident without you."

Crockett ignored the remark. "When she gets a free moment, ask Jen to get the locksmith."

"As I said, we're busy here right now. Whatcha need him for?"

"We found Uncle John's cremains, but the box is locked."

Crockett heard a click and a dial tone.

Chapter Forty-Six

Art awoke slouched in a booth with a half-empty bottle of whiskey. He lit a cigarette and took a long drag, watching the end glow red. It was dark in the bar with the curtains drawn. How long had he been here? What time was it? What did it matter? He pulled on the cigarette and cursed. How long would it be before the desire for a drink and a cigarette—and for Jules—would finally die?

He ground out the cigarette and reached for another. When the match flame touched the tip of his cigarette, he knew he wasn't alone. With a familiar metallic clink and plunk, the ancient jukebox on the far end of the bar came to life, emitting an amber glow like a spaceship. The figure silhouetted against the machine had long legs and a short skirt. Blonde hair radiated in a halo of golden light.

Christ, was he dreaming or still drunk?

"Craaaazy." The voice of Patsy Cline haunted the air. Jules turned and raised her arms to dance with an imaginary partner, moving gracefully with the music.

"Stop!" he screamed. "Stop it!" Covering his ears, he staggered to his feet, knocking over the bottle of Jack Daniel's. He steadied himself with his left hand. "Shit!" His hand flew to his mouth. No dream. The cigarette had burned his palm.

Jules twirled closer. She wore a fuzzy blue sweater and black leather skirt, her legs sheathed in fishnet tights.

"Hi, Artie. Wanna dance?" Jules slurred slightly.

Perspiration beaded Art's forehead despite the cool, damp air in the bar.

He squinted, straining to make out her features. "Go home, Jules. Party's over." How many times had he said those words? *But she was dead. He was talking to a dead woman.* He had to be dreaming, but he couldn't wake up.

When the song ended, Jules did a double twirl and bent backward as her imaginary partner lowered her in an ending dip. But she didn't come up. Wood splintered and snapped. He rushed forward.

"Goddammotherfucking chair!"

Art stopped cold. Unmistakable. Martha struggled to disentangle herself from pieces of wood. No dream. A living nightmare.

"Let me help, Martha. You okay?" He extended his hand.

"Jules. I'm Jules," said Martha, brushing herself off and righting Jules' wig.

Art smelled the wine on her breath, and her eyes were glassy. A marriage made in heaven, the two of them.

"OK, Jules. I'll take you home. Easy now." Martha draped her arm around his neck, and he held her around the waist. They staggered through the bar in the dark, bumping into tables and chairs until they reached the kitchen. He led her to the stairway to their apartment where she balked.

"I can't carry you up the stairs, Martha."

"Not my house. Take me home."

"Enough. Quit playing games. You're drunk, and I can't carry you up the stairs."

"Going home." Martha lurched toward the back door, opened it, and fell down three stairs to the cobblestones below. "Fuck!" she howled.

Art rushed to her side and helped her to her feet. "Okay, Jules. I'll take you home." They wove their way toward the Kenworthy back entrance. When they entered, Martha swayed and put a finger to her lips. "Shhhhh. Don't wake Gabby."

"Gabby's here?"

"I put her to bed when I got dressed for the evening. I'm really not a bad mother, you know." She gave Art one of Jules' most endearing smiles. With the makeup and the wig in the low light, she was Jules.

Art heard a small bump followed by clicking toenails and then rough scrambling and barking. Ralphie plunged down the stairs in full attack mode. "Whoa, Ralphie." Art offered his hand to sniff. He seemed to pass muster, because Ralphie's tail began its rotor action.

"Okay, let's go."

"Need a nightcap," slurred Martha in a very convincing Jules' voice.

"I'll bring you one once you're settled in." Art gently steered her toward the steps and buttressed her from behind, supporting her slow progress up the stairs.

As they passed Gabby's room, Art peeked in and was relieved to see a child-size little mound in the bed. Ralphie trotted into the room, jumped onto the foot of the bed, circled three times, and curled up against the mound.

"Quiet now, Ralphie. Don't wake your mistress." Just before Art closed the door, Ralphie jumped down again and ran out. "Coming with us?" Art asked, reaching down to scratch the dog behind his ears. Ralphie snarled.

Art recoiled, bumping into Martha, but Ralphie wasn't paying attention to them. He sniffed the air. His growl deepened and his hackles rose. He gave one sharp, nasty bark and ran to the head of the stairs.

Chapter Forty-Seven

Casey sat on Mae's bed and described the church service and the scene at the cemetery. Mae listened carefully while she unloaded her worries about finding drugs and being followed by the police. "What do you plan to do?"

"Crockett asked me the same thing. He said the town's no good for me, that I should take off."

Mae considered this information for a long moment before speaking. "Crockett's right. I've loved having you here with me, but you've got to leave and start afresh somewhere else. As soon as you can."

Casey's mind whirled. She stared at Mae in stunned silence. She'd thought about leaving, but always at some vague, later date. Now, Mae was practically pushing her out the door. Mae and Crockett were right, but that didn't make it any easier. She thought about Watson's vendetta and George's mortifying words and had to agree. "But what—?"

"What will I do? You don't have to worry about me."

Casey started to object, but Mae overrode her. "I've already put a down payment on an efficiency unit at the Manor for when the shake gets worse. It's a snobby place, but I'll be damned if I'll live with Martha." Mae spat out the name with a venom Casey hadn't heard before. "There's a suitcase in the armoire in the hallway. Take my car."

"Thank you." She gave Mae a long hug.

In the armoire, Casey found a small worn leather suitcase with straps and buckles. Tears streamed down her cheeks while she packed her few belongings. Too much. Too fast. She didn't want to go and couldn't leave soon enough. Just as she tightened the straps, the doorbell rang. She imagined her life-changing scene interrupted by a solicitation from the Avon lady. She dashed into the front room where Mae peeked out from behind the curtain.

"Police," Mae whispered. "Got your things?"

Casey nodded.

"Back door," Mae ordered. "I can hold him for a good five minutes. Godspeed, dear."

Casey kissed her aunt on the cheek, grabbed the bag, and bolted for the back door. Behind her, Mae's walker clumped slowly to the front door. "Who is it?" she challenged.

Casey flung open the back door and skidded to a halt.

Watson's bulk filled the doorway. "Going somewhere?"

Casey glanced past Watson to the driveway. One swift kick and she could get past Watson to Mae's car and freedom. But Mae's old heap was no match for the police car blocking the drive. She glared at Watson and considered kicking him anyway, but that would be assaulting a police officer.

"You're under arrest." Watson's smile showcased his bad teeth.

"Show me the warrant," Casey demanded.

Watson pushed her roughly against the wall, grabbed her wrists, and handcuffed her.

"Dammit, is this necessary?"

"Nope, but it'll give the neighbors somethin' to wag about." Watson prodded her down the driveway toward the cruiser. The patrolman who'd rung the doorbell held the back door of the car open.

Casey waved her shackled hands at Mae on the front porch.

As they rode downtown, Casey didn't try to open the door in the back seat, knowing from experience it would be locked. No more options, but she'd be damned if she'd go down without a fight.

245

Chapter Forty-Eight

The back door closed followed by heavy footfalls on the kitchen floor.

Ralphie barked in earnest and plunged down the stairs.

"Shit! Get off!"

Ralphie growled and snarled.

"God damn!"

A high-pitched howl. Thump. Whimpering. Silence.

Art put a finger to his lips and beckoned Martha to follow him down the hallway.

"It's OK, silly. It's probably Ron." She laughed Jules' bubbling laugh and called out, "Ron, honey, leave that little dog alone."

Footsteps pounded up the back steps.

Gabby's door flew open. "Ralphie!" She ran for the stairs.

Bear scooped her up as she tried to pass him. "Slow down, missy." He tucked her squirming body under his arm.

"No!" she screamed and kicked. "Ralphie! Let me go!" She sank her sharp little teeth into Bear's side.

"Fuck! Everything bites!" Bear shook her hard.

"Noooo!" Gabby bit his hand and he dropped her. She scrambled to escape, but then froze, staring owl-eyed at Martha dressed in her mother's clothes and wig. She shook her head and backed into Bear.

Bear shoved her into her room and slammed the door and turned toward the apparition. "Well, well. Looks kinky, Martha—or Jules?"

"Jules," Martha breathed. "I wasn't expecting you. Artie was just helping me with Gabby."

Sensing Bear's confusion, Art circled his temple with his forefinger and mouthed "Martha."

Bear's cupid lips curled as he eyed Martha. "Lookin' good, sugar."

Martha leaned against the doorjamb and rewarded Bear with a Jules smile.

"You want to be Jules, I can do Jules. Always wanted to do Jules," Bear growled.

Startled, Martha backed away.

"I came for the girl, but I can come for you, too."

"That's enough!" Art moved between Bear and Martha.

Bear backhanded him, sending him crashing against the wall. Art crumbled into a heap. Bear kicked him viciously in the side before turning back to Martha who'd begun to whimper.

"You hurt Artie."

Martha moved toward Art, but Bear grabbed her and pinned her arms behind her back, forcing himself against her. "C'mon, Jules. You saw what happened. Little shit attacked me." Bear backed her down the hall, laughing as she struggled. "Ron said you liked it rough." He shoved her into Jules' bedroom.

Art rose to his knees, blood streaming down his face. He crawled after Bear. He saw the boot coming but couldn't dodge fast enough.

Art moved his right arm and a lightning bolt of pain shot down his side. He groaned and wheezed. *Turn. Can't breathe.* He moved his arm again and pain seared through his midriff. *Can't see. Something in my eyes.* The side of his head felt like a smashed pumpkin.

Other way. Over. Better. Slow. Slow. He took long rasping breaths. The intake was excruciating, but he had to breathe. As he waited for the pain to subside, he heard a low moaning from Jules' room. *Oh God, Martha!* He grasped the doorjamb to pull himself up to a standing position and cried out as another bolt of pain ripped his side. His eyes blurred and he slumped to the floor. Using the wall to guide him, he crawled inch by inch toward the pitiful sound.

Martha was sprawled face down on Jules' bed, arms bruised, wig askew, sobbing. Bear was nowhere in sight. Bile rose in Art's throat. He leaned against the side of the bed. "Martha," he gasped.

"Jules," she whispered. "Help me. Bear—"

"You're safe now, Martha." He struggled to maintain consciousness as he stroked her cheek. But Martha was gone. This was Jules.

She talked into the pillow, oblivious to his words. "He took Gabby."

Art held her hand. His eyes fixed on the aquamarine ring on Martha's finger.

"Bear took my little girl," Martha sobbed. "Call George. Tell him to take Uncle John to Loveland or we'll never see Gabby again."

Jules was wearing the ring the night she died. Oh. Sweet. Jesus. No.

"Artie? Artie!"

Art's eyes lost focus as he yielded to blessed darkness.

Chapter Forty-Nine

George and Crockett drove in silence toward town. More pieces of the puzzle had begun to click into place for Crockett at the cemetery. Jules had been on the run. She'd planned her escape to coincide with George's conference but postponed it when Gabby came home unexpectedly from a sleepover. She'd emptied her safe deposit box and taken Uncle John's funerary box, undoubtedly full of cocaine.

Jules and Danny McPhee were both involved with drugs, and both were found dead within a week. Crockett shuddered, remembering the slash in McPhee's throat. He didn't believe in coincidence. Jules, not Casey, carved out one of George's library books for the drug exchange, and McPhee made the drop in the stacks.

The scenario made sense until both were killed. Why wipe out a successful drug operation? Why was Jules running? Were Jules and McPhee caught skimming and selling on the side?

At the station, the bustle of activity pushed Crockett's speculation to the back burner. He greeted Jenny and scanned the call report. A fender bender, an elderly man having trouble breathing, and a concussion in the college alumni lacrosse game. He frowned and whistled at the accident on Route 10. A semi had jackknifed causing a three-car pileup with injuries. "How bad is Route 10?"

"Three ambulances. The Staties closed the road. The semi was a double, driving empty, over speed. The driver swerved to avoid a creeper without brake lights. The rig buckled and rolled across two lanes squashing the first car. Cars behind plowed into the side." Jenny looked down for a moment. "Family of four and a car of teenagers." The console lit up. Jenny swallowed hard and took the next call, speaking into her headset with deliberate control.

"Watson on it?" Crockett asked after she cleared the line.

"No. Can't raise him on the radio. After you spoke to him, he made a few calls and then left. Nothing much he could do at the site anyway, but we sure could use another car here."

"Good thing we got extra ambulances for Commencement."

"They're all out now. I called for backup from Elyria, just in case." Jenny turned to the console for another call.

Crockett ushered George into his office. He handed George a pen and the forms to fill out to report the theft of the ashes.

"Why do this when we've already found the ashes?"

"My money says Uncle John is still missing, and this box is stuffed with cocaine. Know for sure when the lock guy opens it."

While he watched George fill out the paperwork, he listened to the familiar bustle around him and realized how much he was going to miss it.

Might as well pack up his personal items while he waited. He wrapped the family photos in newspaper and put them in a box along with his coffee mug, extra tie, aspirin, Girl Scout cookies, and a few other personal items. He almost tossed the picture of the Four Horsemen, but tucked it into the box at the last minute. Not that many years ago, Swain, Watson, Kenworthy, and Crockett had pulled together as a team, winning the league championship.

In no time, the office was stripped of his presence. Finally, he withdrew the Bombs and Snowballs list from under the blotter. All the Bombs were checked off, but there was still one Snowball left: GFS, the initials on the large invoice he'd seen in Jules' papers.

George signed the report and handed it to Crockett. He shook his head in disbelief. "This is just so far from anything—" He seemed to lose his place. "I had no idea what was going on."

"What's GFS?" Crockett asked.

"The company that holds our mortgage. I called yesterday, but got the answering machine. I don't know how we'll make the payments unless we can renegotiate the note. They could foreclose, but it wouldn't be in their interest." He drew his fingers through his hair.

"Even with all the renovations Jules' parents made, it still needs a lot of work. The property has all kinds of zoning conflicts. They had it on the market for two years but couldn't find a buyer. Just aren't that many people around here with money to pour into a business and a residence. Maybe some developer could—"

Crockett pounded his fist on the desk. "Damn! One Snowball left, and it's a Bomb." He crushed his list and threw it into the wastebasket.

"What the hell—?"

"GFS." Crockett pulled the *Oberlin Telephone Directory* from the bookcase and flipped to "Mortgages" in the Yellow Pages. The ad at the top of the page featured a sleek black swan. Crockett pounded the desk a second time. "Remember how Swain bragged he'd be good 'n' rich someday?"

"Yeah. So?"

"Goodrich is his middle name: Ronald Goodrich Swain."

"I fail to see what—"

"GFS. Goodrich Financial Services. Swain holds the note to the Gourd. He planned to develop it into a retirement facility with shops, but couldn't get his hands on it while Jules made the payments." Crockett rose to close the door for privacy, but stopped short when he heard Casey's voice.

"Take your hands off me."

Crockett was out the door in two strides. "What's going on?"

"I brought in your friend for questioning. Just in time, seeing's she'd packed a bag for a trip."

"Take off the cuffs."

Watson ignored the order. "I see you've already got the other lovebird."

Crockett grabbed Watson's shirt and slammed him against the wall. "Take. Off. The cuffs," he demanded, piercing Watson with a white-hot glare, before releasing him.

"Okay, okay!" Watson unlocked the handcuffs and threw the keys onto the counter.

Jenny's hand shot into the air, the signal for emergency. Instantly the room quieted. She pretended to cough into the headset. "Excuse me. Please repeat your name." She punched the speakerphone.

"Jules. Jules Kenworthy. Please help me," a weak voice pleaded.

Crockett and George moved behind Jenny at the console.

"Take it slow, Mrs. Kenworthy. Where are you?" Jenny maintained her calm, modulated voice.

"I need to find my husband. He could be there with Crockett. Please hurry."

"Mrs. Kenworthy, where are you?"

"I'm at home. The Gourd. Please find George."

Casey waved her unfettered hands for Crockett's attention and mouthed, "Martha."

Crockett put his hand on George's shoulder and gently guided him forward.

"Jules?" George whispered. "Jules? What's the matter?" His voice regained its normal timbre as he spoke.

"Bear took Gabby. He—" Jules faltered.

"Talk to me. What about Gabby?"

"Bear took her to Loveland. He hurt Artie."

Crockett held up his hand to prevent Casey from speaking.

"He said to bring Uncle John to Loveland by nine o'clock, or we'll never see her alive again."

"It's OK, Jules," George reassured her. "Crockett and I have Uncle John here with us. We'll get Gabby back."

"No! You can't tell Crockett! Bear said he'd slit Gabby's throat if he sees a uniform. Please, George. No police. Get Gabby."

"What about Art? You said he was hurt."

"He's breathing, but Bear kicked him in the head. Send an ambulance. Hurry. Get Gabby." A sob was followed by a clattering sound.

"Jules? Jules, talk to me! Jules?" George shook his head.

Quickly, Jenny dialed the number on the console display. Busy. She dialed twice more with the same result.

Crockett strapped on his shoulder holster. "Watson, take the cruiser to the Gourd." Watson didn't answer.

"Hear me, Captain?"

"Yeah, yeah. I hear you. I'm looking for my damn keys."

"Get back here after the ambulance arrives. Casey, you—" Crockett stopped mid-order. "Casey?" he hollered.

But Casey was gone.

"Won't get far, she's on foot," muttered Watson, searching the floor by the counter.

"Doubt it." The strobes of a police cruiser flashed by the front window and fishtailed into a barely controlled right turn. Crockett picked up Uncle John and nodded to George. "Take your car."

"No police," George objected.

"Go alone, you and Gabby are both dead. Bear's killed once, maybe twice. Move!"

Chapter Fifty

C asey had never driven a car with such power and so many toys. When she accelerated and made the right turn out of the station, the backend of the car slued sideways. Metal creased metal as the car sideswiped a U.S. Post Office box. She righted the wheel, over-compensated, and came headlight to headlight with a pickup truck. She laid on the horn and pulled to the right, missing the truck by inches.

Bucking and swerving, she ran lights and stop signs with abandon. By the time she reached the Gourd, she had easily broken every traffic law on the books, but she was beyond caring. If it weren't for the circumstances, she would have reveled in her little joy ride. As it was, she almost sped past the Gourd. She hit the brakes. The cruiser spun, jumped the curb, and stalled out on the front lawn. She left the strobes flashing and ran to the house.

She took the stairs two at a time to the Cavendish apartment, calling for Art and Martha. No answer. She poked her nose into each room, ending in the room that was her old bedroom. No one.

"Jules" had made the call. Had to be at the Kenworthy apartment. The fastest way there was to use the storage passageway that connected Casey's old room to Gabby's room. She walked to the chest of drawers against the wall. Putting all her weight against the chest, she shoved it aside, opened the door to a low storage way, and crawled in. Seconds later, she burst into Gabby's room. She stood perfectly still in the dark, listening. Sobs came from the front of the house.

She found Martha in Jules' bedroom bent over on the side of the bed. Art lay on the floor beside her, breathing in shallow, tortured rasps. Casey knelt beside him. "Jesus god, what happened?"

"Artie's hurt bad," Martha sobbed.

With blackened eyes from smudged mascara and Jules' wig at an angle, Martha looked like a deranged hooker. She had a nasty scrape on her knee. *Artie.* Martha would call him Arthur. This was Jules speaking.

Casey stroked her brother's forehead. "Hold on, Art," she whispered. "The ambulance will be here soon. Just hold on." Casey continued to stroke his forehead while Martha told her what had happened. Martha's mastery of Jules' intonation and mannerisms was so complete that Casey had to glance up occasionally to confirm that it was Martha, not Jules, speaking.

After what seemed like an eternity, an ambulance screeched to a halt in front of the Gourd, and Watson and two EMTs piled out. "Up here!" Casey hollered from the second-story window. Watson glared up at Casey, surveyed the scene, hitched his pants, and sauntered to the cruiser. He drew his hand along the crease in the side and looked up again. He'd arrest her the moment Art was sent to the hospital. But to her surprise, Watson got in the cruiser and peeled off.

The EMTs moved quickly, strapping Art onto a stretcher, hauling it downstairs, and loading him into the ambulance. Martha climbed into the back.

As Casey was about to close the door to the Kenworthy apartment, she heard a mournful whimper. She stopped and listened. There it was again. The whimper became a high keening wail.

Casey rushed inside as the ambulance pulled away. She followed the pitiful sound until she found Ralphie, shaking in a little heap under a chair in the kitchen. She cooed softly, calling his name. He tried to rise but yelped and fell to the floor in pain. Casey saw blood on the floor where his nose rested.

"Stay quiet, Ralphie. I'll get help." She wrapped him in a towel and rushed for the telephone. She knew the number by heart.

She cradled Ralphie in her arms until the veterinary van arrived and took him to the clinic.

Chapter Fifty-One

"Drive slowly. Give me time to get in place before you reach the mausoleum," Crockett instructed. "When you get there, do what Bear tells you. Make the swap. Get Gabby." Crockett waved George forward. A block later, the Civic turned into the entrance to the cemetery.

Crockett ran behind the car until the taillights disappeared around a curve. The last of the evening light penetrated the canopy of leaves overhead, creating strange moving shadows. The result was perfect for cover, but difficult for navigating the twists and turns of the road.

Crockett ran along the cinder path as fast as he dared, uncomfortable in his dress shoes. At this rate, he'd be no help at all. He picked up the pace, trying to visualize the route to the back of the cemetery. His foot turned on a stone, and he pitched forward, catching his fall with his hands in the cinders.

He slowed at an unexpected split in the path. Which way? He'd lost his bearings. In the fast-fading light, everything was foreign. Left or right? He couldn't just stand there. Choose!

He cast around for something familiar and spotted a small mausoleum in a clearing across the road. Couldn't be the Loveland mausoleum, so it had to be the Fairchild building. If so, he was in the middle of the cemetery, halfway to Loveland.

He ran to the monument. Yes! He made out the raised letters spelling Fairchild carved into the stone lintel above the door. His elation was short-lived. He was in the center, but which way did the mausoleum face?

Crockett circled the building as darkness settled in, considering the paths from every angle. Which way? A wrong choice would doom George and little Gabby. He threw his arms to the heavens for guidance.

And there it was. The Drinking Gourd. The Big Dipper with stars in the bowl pointing north. The Loveland mausoleum was on the rear south corner of the cemetery. He turned and ran. No time now for the road. He dodged the larger gravestones and jumped the lower ones. He'd never forgive himself if something happened to Gabby.

As he crested a low rise, red taillights moved off to the right. The car was still rolling. He was in time for the swap. He loped behind the Civic, staying beside the road in the grass and the shadows.

Suddenly, headlights flooded the scene. Crockett hit the ground and rolled behind a gravestone. The Civic jumped forward, stuttered, and stalled. Seconds later, George got out of the car, shielding his eyes with his hand.

A deep voice boomed from behind the bright lights of Bear's truck. "Hold the box in front of you. Don't try nothing cute. I got the kid."

"Where is she?" George demanded.

"Safe. Put the box on the hood and step back."

"Not until I see Gabby."

Crockett inched backward out of the swath of light. He darted from headstone to headstone until he was behind the mausoleum and crouched next to a large slab less than ten feet from the building.

The silence of the night magnified the metallic grating as the mausoleum's heavy gate swung open. Flickering light illuminated the interior. Moments later Bear emerged holding Gabby at arm's length, gripping her hands over her head in one massive paw, a flashlight in the other. Her wrists were tied with twine, and he'd gagged her with a bandanna.

"It's okay, honey, I'm here now. I'll take you home," George called out. He retrieved the box from the passenger seat and placed it on the hood.

Crockett elbowed through the grass to the back wall of the mausoleum like a Marine in basic training.

Bear released Gabby. She ran to her father as fast as her little legs could move, her whimpers muted by the bandanna. George rushed forward and scooped her into his arms, making soothing sounds while he untied her.

Crockett reached the front corner of the mausoleum.

Bear walked to the Civic and grabbed Uncle John. Placing the box on the ground, he withdrew a gun from under his belt in the small of his back.

Crockett unsnapped his holster.

Bear smashed off the lock with the butt of the gun. Removing the lid, he stared for a moment in disbelief. "Fuck!" he spat. "Dirt!" He grabbed the metal box and heaved it at the Civic and then bashed it into the car, over and over. The side window of the Civic shattered, and the box came to rest on the driver's seat. Breathing hard, Bear glared at it for a long moment and then laughed. He picked up his gun and shot out the car tires.

Bear whirled around and aimed at George.

"I swear I didn't know—" George began.

"Shut up, Professor. Move." He waved the gun toward the mausoleum.

"Let her go," George pleaded.

"Not a chance."

George walked slowly, carrying Gabby in his arms. Bear followed, his mouth curled in a small smile.

Crockett angled for a clear shot, but George and Gabby were in the line of fire.

At the mausoleum, Bear suddenly raised his leg and kicked George in the back, sending him sprawling on top of Gabby. Bear raised his gun.

Bear's gun exploded as Crockett slammed into his body.

Chapter Fifty-Two

Casey figured out why Watson hadn't re-arrested her. He'd wait until Monday when he'd be Chief and wouldn't have to face Crockett's rage. She shuddered, remembering the fury in Crockett's eyes when he'd pinned Watson to the wall.

She grabbed the kitchen telephone and called the station.

"Oberlin Police Department. How may I help you?" Jenny answered.

"Jenny. It's Casey. Have you heard from Crockett?"

"No, but before he left he asked me to call you and tell you to stay put at the Gourd. *Not* to go to Loveland. I'm sure he'll call as soon as he can. He and George left in the Civic, so they don't have a radio. I'll let you know the minute I hear from him."

Casey dialed Allen Hospital. All she could learn was that Art had been admitted. She called the Oberlin Veterinary Clinic and got a recording informing her of the hours of operation. She hung up and pounded the wall in frustration.

As she paced, images shot through her brain. Art's bloody temple. Martha's crazy behavior. Bookend's broken dish. Gabby's owlet eyes peering out from beneath the straw in the barn. The vet's assistant carrying Ralphie's little body wrapped in a towel. She thought about George and the mortifying words she'd overheard the day before.

Finally, she thought about Jules. *Fire and rain...* Jules must have realized the game was up if she'd been on the run. She'd taken Uncle John out of the mausoleum, closed her bank account, and emptied the safe deposit box.

George and Crocket had Uncle John, but where had Jules hidden the rest of her stash? She stopped pacing. She had to do something or go crazy with worry. What would Jules have done? Jules had "hidden" Uncle John in plain view on a shelf in the cellar, but Casey suspected that her papers, money, and jewelry would be much harder to find.

She started the search on the second floor, methodically working her way through the rooms, examining every hiding place she and Jules had ever used. For the second time that day, she crawled through the storage space between Gabby's room and the Cavendish apartment and back. Nothing.

In Gabby's room, she opened the tall armoire, removed the lower bar of Gabby's clothing, and groped until she found the false plate that opened to the pole. Nothing along the sides or the back. She slid her hands up the pole. Her hand hit something soft taped to the side. Pay dirt! Of course, she'd missed it when she slid down the pole earlier. Jules was taller.

She peeled off the bundle carefully. It was a scarlet velvet purse with tie strings. Attached to the string was a small tag. "To Gabby, All my love, Mom." She loosened the ties and shook the contents of the purse into her hand. She drew in a sharp breath at the sparkle of diamonds and emeralds.

Carefully, she returned the jewels to the purse and re-taped it to the pole. Jules knew Gabby would find it when she was a little taller while she played in the secret passages of the Gourd.

The first floor was easier because the rooms were either for show or occupied primarily by George. She examined the kitchen and pantry with extra care, poking into each likely crevice and cranny. With reluctance, she turned on the light and took the stairs to the cellar.

Behind the new furnace, there was fresh dirt on the floor. Exploring, she discovered an opened bag of potting soil next to a funerary box partially covered by Ralphie's blanket. She unwrapped the box and read the brass inscription on the side: *Julietta Loveland Kenworthy.* With a lump in her throat, she rewrapped the box in the blanket and completed her tour of the cellar.

Finally, she ducked under police tape and entered the clubhouse. She should have known that the search would end here. A few rays of light from the bald bulb in the center of the cellar seeped through the wooden slats, providing just enough light for her to make out the pole, the desk, and the filing cabinet. She retrieved the candle, matches, and saucer from the top drawer of the desk.

When she lit the candle, the short wick sputtered and flickered, causing her shadow to dance as she made a circuit of the room. Walking slowly, she touched everything and examined anything that moved. Aware of the lesson from the mausoleum, she thought about what could be missing, not just what was there. The choir robe was nowhere in sight. Gabby had left it in a heap when she ran to greet her father yesterday. Martha must have tidied up.

Casey unhooked the Shield of Faith and examined the back. Nothing. But Jules could have removed the front aluminum plate and placed documents behind it. Casey retrieved a dime from the pencil drawer of the desk and turned the small screws that fastened the plate to the wood. She and Jules had hidden one of the two skeleton keys to the mausoleum in a gouged out hollow beneath the symbol of Saint John, but now there was neither a key nor any of Jules' papers.

She laid the shield on the floor and approached the file cabinet and desk. No reason to search there. She'd already explored the contents earlier when she read the journal.

That left the tunnel. She groaned. It was the logical place, but she'd hoped she wouldn't ever have to crawl through that tunnel again. She put her weight against the end of the desk and pushed it to the left, revealing the crude hole at knee level. Holding the saucer and candle before her, she entered the tunnel, inching forward on her belly through the narrow passage. The ground was cold and damp, slick to the hand; the air smelled like a summer camp mattress. Pooled wax spilled onto her fingers. She swore when a sharp rock dug at her side as she made slow progress through the seemingly endless tunnel.

A freshening in the air signaled the approach to the well. The tunnel opened close to one side of the well. A crude wooden plank spanned the distance over the water on the left side to the continuation of the tunnel on the far side. Metal rungs fixed into the stones provided handholds while walking the plank and also a ladder to reach the top.

Her heart thumped and perspiration beaded her forehead and ran down her face, stinging her eyes. As a child, she'd had a recurring dream where the satanic, gaping maw of the well abyss rose up, encompassed her, and sucked her under.

She drew a few long breaths and felt the edges of the plank. At most, it was six feet across. She needed to go out on the plank far enough to reach up to a recess in the wall. If Jules could do it, so could she.

The plank was unstable on the rough ground. No way she'd stand and walk across the way Jules used to do. Balancing the saucer and candle as far out on the plank as her arms could reach, she straddled the plank and pulled herself slowly forward. Just as she reached the middle, the plank shifted and the saucer slid sideways. The flame extinguished and the saucer fell into the water below.

Pitch dark. She raised her left hand, feeling the contours of the round stones on the side of the well until her fingers dipped into a recess in the wall. Abe Loveland had created it to store supplies for fugitive slaves in case they had to hide inside the well for any length of time. She reached in timidly, wary of what might be living in the hole. Empty. She sat on the plank, stymied.

Jules knew about her fear of the plank, and how she'd glue herself to the wood and creep across. Jules took the plank in two long steps with balance beam grace. She'd stop and tease Casey before leaping like a cat onto metal rungs and climbing up to the mouth of the well.

Now the well was sealed, the cover nailed down after the scare with Gabby. But the wooden bucket still hung from a rope, about five feet above the plank in the center of the well.

She and Jules had exchanged their top-secret Bloody Cats Eyes notes in the bucket: Casey from above, Jules from below. Jules would balance on the plank, hold onto a rung with one hand, and snag the bucket.

Casey lit a match and raised it overhead. The bucket dangled out of reach above her head, taunting her. She stared at it until the match burned out. *Damn!*

Ever so slowly she rose to a standing position, using the stones on the side of the well for balance. Just as she reached her full height, the plank tilted again like a restaurant table with a short leg. She clawed the stones to steady herself.

Forcing herself to be still, she explored the slimy stones with her fingers until they touched a metal rung. Grasping it with her left hand, she waved her right arm in widening arcs over her head. On the third try, her hand hit the rough outside of the bucket. She drew it to her.

Casey felt around the lip of the bucket and then inside. Her fingers connected with a heavy cloth surface. Gotcha! She grasped an edge and tugged, but the bundle was surprisingly heavy. She tugged again. Must weigh four or five pounds. On the edge of the bundle, she found a cloth handle. She gripped it and yanked.

The bucket tilted, freeing the pack. The sudden weight shift threw her off balance, and her right foot slipped off the plank. She held onto the rung for dear life, teetering over the abyss, but the pack's weight and momentum pushed her backward against the wall. She lowered herself to the plank, crawled to the tunnel opening, and collapsed inside.

When her hands quit shaking, she lit a match to see her prize. It was a Gabby's backpack made of heavy denim, decorated with yellow ducks and purple bunnies. Inside, a fat manila envelope confirmed that she'd found Jules' stash and not Gabby's lifetime supply of candy kisses.

She crawled back to the clubhouse, dragging the pack behind her. Inside, she released a long sigh of relief and lit another candle before examining the contents. Sitting on the floor with her legs straddling the pack, she unzipped the back compartment. *Jesus, Mary and Joseph.* She withdrew ten one hundred dollar bills. A thousand dollars in pin money.

She dumped the money onto the floor and returned to the pack. The manila envelope held Jules' personal papers: birth certificate, Social Security card, stock certificates, passport, and a bank check for twenty thousand dollars.

Best to hide the pack for now and retrieve it later. She pulled the bag to her to repack the contents. Curious. It still seemed heavy. She patted the sides. Nothing. It was bottom-heavy. She turned it over and found a zipper that circled the base. She pulled the zipper and almost fainted at four cylindrical packets of white powder inside.

Omigod! If this was Jules' stash of cocaine, what was in the box George and Crockett had taken to the cemetery? She groaned, picturing the bag of fresh potting soil.

A door slammed. "Casey? Casey, where are you?" Jules' voice came from overhead, in the kitchen. Had to be Martha. Casey listened to Martha's footsteps as she walked down the hallway. They became softer as she mounted the stairs to the second floor.

Casey had to move. It wouldn't be good to be found in the cellar with a backpack loaded with coke and Jules' papers. She wiped off any surfaces she might have touched, zipped the bottom of the bag, and pushed it in front of the tunnel entrance with her sneaker. She wanted nothing to do with the cocaine.

The cash was another matter. She eyed the dismantled Shield of Faith on the floor by the wall. She stuffed the money into the manila envelope and placed the envelope against the wood backing of the Shield, covering it with the metal plate. Martha's footsteps descended the stairs to the first floor. Casey heard her bustling in the kitchen. What was she doing?

Working quickly, Casey inserted each screw in its hole and turned it clockwise with the dime. "Casey?" The cellar door opened.

No more time! She needed a diversion. *Think!* The answer was on the wall before her. Quickly, she re-hung the Shield and unhooked the Sword of the Spirit. She retrieved the key from the hilt and unlocked the file cabinet.

"Casey? Are you down there?" Footsteps clomped down the stairs. Just before the door to the clubhouse creaked inward, Casey yanked one of Jules' spiral journals out of the file cabinet and slid to the floor in front of the pack.

"Reading my story?" Jules laughed and stepped into the candlelight, shaking her golden locks.

Casey gasped.

"Surprised?"

Chapter Fifty-Three

C asey knew the figure before her was Martha, but Jules' laughter was so convincing it took her breath away. Martha wore the missing black choir robe and carried a tray before her.

"Martha, you look like Jules tonight," Casey said softly, hoping to dispel any animosity. "Jules is dead, Martha." Keeping her voice calm and firm, Casey continued. "You're beautiful, but you are clearly still my brother's wife, Martha Cavendish."

"*Agonies Dei cum laude in excelsis digitalis...*" Martha paused. She evidently couldn't remember the rest of the bogus Latin phrases Casey and Jules had strung together for their childhood initiation ceremony. Instead, she hummed a few bars of "Walking After Midnight" as she approached, her voice catching in the appropriate Patsy Cline manner. "I brought you a little cocktail."

The tray had a cup on it and an object Casey couldn't see covered by a napkin. "I already dealt with Martha. Now it's your turn."

Acting like a vain Jules, Martha had changed into a shorter wig and applied fresh makeup and Jules' favorite perfume. She was stunning, except for eyes that burned with manic concentration.

"How did you 'deal' with Martha?"

"I dressed her up to look like me and gave her a juicy little drink." Martha laughed. "You were there today when we tried to inter the miserable little snitch."

"But you, Martha, went to Jules' funeral this afternoon with your husband, Art." Casey tried valiantly to return to sane ground.

265

"Oh, George didn't mind me going with Artie today. He knows Artie will be lost without Martha. What he never knew was that Artie always loved me best. Ron was there, too, the devil." Martha laughed another Jules' laugh, and then her expression became serious. "But now we have a little ceremony to attend to." Martha's sculpted lips bent into a smile. "Can't leave any loose ends."

"Just like you, Martha, to want to tidy up." Casey tried to taunt Martha back to reality. She squinted and saw that it was Art's little tin cup on the tray.

"Too smart for your own britches. And such a goody-goody. *'No thank you, Jules. I don't do drugs. I can't afford them.'*" Martha mimicked Casey's voice perfectly. "Well, you can afford a sweet little cocktail tonight. This one's on me."

Martha placed the tray on the floor. With one hand she picked up the cup; with the other, she lifted the napkin, revealing the long stainless steel blade of one of Jules' carving knives.

Casey shrank from the knife. "Why get rid of Martha?"

"I never liked her, you know that. Besides, she discovered my plan." Martha moved closer with each word.

Casey's mind raced. She kept her eyes on the knife while she tried to untangle Martha's crazed logic. Martha must have uncovered Jules' escape plan. Martha was a natural spy, and Jules was her favorite subject. Could Martha have killed the real Jules and then become Jules in her mind?

"You, old friend, are a different matter. I can't let you wreck my marriage and break up our family."

Casey scrambled to her feet and backed away. "What's in the cocktail?" she asked, as if it mattered.

"Nectar of the Cat's Eye: Lemon Fresh Pine-Sol and Tilex, and, this time, a little dab of cocaine just for you. You should get high at least once in your life." Martha laughed and advanced.

"You forgot the sleeping pills."

"What sleeping pills?" In her confusion, Martha's voice slipped from Jules' register to her normal whine.

"The sleeping pills you put in the drink you gave to Martha."

Martha regained Jules' composure. "Oh, silly. I didn't need sleeping pills. I gave her the same cocktail I'm going to give you."

No sleeping pills? Now Casey was confused. If Martha didn't use sleeping pills, then she didn't kill Jules. But she could be lying. Hard to tell when you couldn't figure out who was talking.

"She puked all over her clothes. I had to clean her up," Martha said as she took another step forward.

"That's the point. The drink you gave her last Friday only made her throw up. *It didn't kill her.* She died of an overdose of alcohol, cocaine, and *sleeping pills*, not all-purpose cleaners."

Martha tilted her head to the side. She was silent for a few moments before refocusing on Casey. "Clever, Casey. You were always the clever one. But it won't work this time." She smiled demurely and stepped closer. "If you really believe the cocktail won't kill you, why not take a little sip for old time's sake?" She placed the cup on the floor in front of Casey.

Casey stared at the foul liquid. She made a quick feint to the right, but Martha was ready, fending off with her left hand, slashing with her right. The wake of the knife passed Casey's ear. She jumped sideways to avoid the next slash. She fell sideways and landed hard on her left elbow. She cried out in pain when she tried to straighten her arm. Useless.

Martha screeched with laughter, grabbed the cocktail, and closed in. "Just a little drink now, Casey. A little ceremony to mark your last day as a Bloody Cats Eye." She placed the cup on the floor and pushed it toward Casey with her foot. "You might as well drink it and drift off into an endless sleep. The knife will make a dreadful mess and will be much more painful." She nudged the cup closer.

It was Casey's turn to mimic. In her very best Martha voice, she repeated Martha's last words. *"The knife will make a dreadful mess,"* she taunted. "Only Martha would worry about the mess. *Jules* could care less. You're screwing up your act."

"Shut up and drink it!" Martha sliced the air with the knife.

Casey pulled herself into a sitting position and clutched the cup. She held her breath, raised the cup to her lips, and drew in a big mouthful. Lurching forward, she spewed the liquid into Martha's eyes. Martha screamed and flailed blindly with the knife. She wiped her eyes with the arm of the robe and moved in for the kill.

Casey grabbed the pack to fend off the blows. Martha's knife slashed through the bottom of the pack, releasing a puff of white powder. She raised the knife for another slice. Casey grabbed the broken bag of cocaine from the pack and hurled it at Martha. On contact, the bag exploded covering Martha with a cloud of fine white powder.

Casey crawled into the tunnel. She could no longer feel her left arm below the elbow. She'd have only one arm to hike and pull herself forward. Quickly, she hooked the strap of the pack onto her belt so that she could haul it behind her to protect her rear.

Halfway to the plank, she stopped to catch her breath. Martha cursed and grunted in close pursuit. Casey stifled a moan and forced herself forward. Her useless left arm brushed against the side of the tunnel, sending shockwaves of pain through her body. Martha was gaining ground, hauling her body forward with two good arms.

Just as the grunting was about to overtake her, Casey reached the well opening and felt the plank. Balance would be dicey with only one good arm, but she didn't hesitate, throwing herself toward the abyss.

"Dammit! Goddamit to hell!"

Pure Martha directly behind her. Martha's knife sliced through the rubber sole of Casey's shoe. Casey gasped at the searing pain in her instep. She reached the far side and collapsed in agony. The pain in her elbow was forgotten with the newer assault on her foot. Her shoe was soaked with blood.

The swearing behind her turned into a high wail. Casey listened, unable to move, as the wail turned to sobs. Martha had stopped at the plank. Casey turned and lit her last match. A crying clown's face peered back at her. White powder highlighted Martha's black eyes, and the front blond locks of the wig were matted into dreadlocks. Streaks of tears ran down to a pink mouth. She'd shed the robe.

Casey couldn't figure out who it was—the fastidious Martha, the crazed Martha who thought she was Jules, or some maniacal combination of the two. Whoever it was, she hadn't killed Jules. Martha didn't know about the sleeping pills. If Martha didn't kill her, someone else did, but Casey didn't have time for detective work. She had to move before she passed out. She dropped the match as the flame reached her fingers and forced herself to continue, now favoring her left arm and right foot.

"Where are you going? Don't leave me, Casey!" Martha cried.

"Crawl across the plank, Jules."

"Noooooo. I can't. Come back. Don't leave me!"

"*Jules* could walk across," Casey taunted over her shoulder. She made slow, painful progress, pulling with her right arm, pushing with her left leg. No way she could haul the pack along with her. She unhooked it and left it in the tunnel to create an obstacle for Martha.

When the upward pitch of the tunnel increased, she knew she could make it. Her hand butted into a board covering the entrance to the barn. She lifted the board and pulled herself through the crude opening into the barn.

Chapter Fifty-Four

Crockett crashed into Bear, toppling him backward, then rolled to his feet and fired wide, missing Bear's head by inches. Bear screamed, dropped his gun, and covered his head with his hands, waiting for the next round.

Whirling lights and the piercing wail of a siren cut the air as a police cruiser skidded to a stop in front of the mausoleum. Watson slammed the car door and drew his gun, rushing toward Crockett.

"Good timing, Watson. Hold him." Crockett ran for Gabby and George. They were lying as they had fallen, George on top of Gabby. Gabby's foot protruded from under George's body. Neither moved. As he rolled George over, Gabby's face appeared, blood running down her forehead. "No!" he cried, drawing her to him.

"JoJo! JoJo!"

Crockett almost dropped her. Quickly, he examined her. Only a few scrapes from the fall. Her little body trembled.

Behind him, George moaned and stirred, rubbing his forehead. "I'm OK. Just a knock on the head."

Crockett wrapped Bear's discarded bandanna around a cut on George's head to staunch the bleeding. "May not feel like it, but you're one lucky man."

"Crockett!" Watson yelled.

Crockett hauled himself out of the mausoleum and up the stairs. The strobes of the cruiser lit the scene like a disco floor, making Watson's body jerk as he approached. Watson blanched at the blood on Crockett's hands and shirt. He asked in a much lower voice, "Are they..."

"No. George hit his head. Gabby's just scratched some."

Watson let out a sigh of relief.

"Close call," Crockett commented. "Too damn close." He sank to a sitting position, thankful for Watson's presence for the first time in his life. He thought for a moment. "OK. You take Bear to the station. We'll take Bear's truck to the hospital. We're close." Crockett was on top of the situation again. He rose and headed toward the mausoleum. After a few steps, he realized Watson hadn't moved.

Crockett turned. Too late, he saw the revolver in Watson's hand.

"Ain't going to happen your way this time, Chief." Watson moved in slow motion. He raised the gun and pointed it at Crockett's chest. His hand jerked in the pulsating light.

"Put your gun down slowly," Watson ordered.

Crockett was too far away to make a move. He bent slowly and placed his gun on the ground.

"Back into the little house with your fancy friends."

Crockett inched backwards. "You're not a killer, Watson. Bear's crazy. Assault, kidnapping—"

"Shut up. Move!"

"Back him up, Bear. Watson may not have the balls."

Ron's voice. Crockett cursed. He should have known Bear wouldn't be alone. So, he was right. Ron was the dealer and undoubtedly Jules' killer. The only surprise was Watson. He'd figured Watson for leaking information, but not as an accomplice. "What's Swain got on you, Captain?"

"I said, shut the fuck up!"

"Worth killing for?" Crockett asked, backing down the stairs into the dark of the mausoleum. Behind Watson, he spied Bear's bulky silhouette shuffling toward them.

"Worth killing you." With a sudden upward jerk, Watson fired two quick shots.

Crockett recoiled instinctively, falling backward on top of George and Gabby. Watson walked forward, looked down at him and whispered, "Stay dead." Watson fired three more rounds, turned and strode back toward Bear.

"What the hell—" George mumbled, struggling beneath Crockett's weight.

"*Shhh!*" Crockett hissed.

They waited in silence.

Ron's baritone boomed. "Good work, soldier. Didn't know you had it in you. C'mon, give me a ride in your cop car. Bear, bring your truck. We'll pick you up in the Gourd lot." Car doors slammed and tires spit cinder as the cruiser and pickup roared off.

When he could no longer hear the engines, Crockett disentangled himself and helped George and Gabby up. His mouth tasted as if he'd been sucking on a penny. Pebbles embedded in his hand from his earlier fall scraped his face as he wiped the perspiration from his brow. He swore softly and rubbed his face with the back of his hand, like a panther washing its face.

George released his hand from Gabby's mouth. He cradled her in his arms, rocking back and forth. Gabby whimpered softly. "It's OK, honey. They're gone." His reassurances were Gabby's signal that she could cry in earnest. The headlights of the stalled Civic provided enough light for Crockett to locate his gun.

George and Gabby made slow progress toward the car. Gabby's voice was curious, although still quavering. "Why was Bear mad at Uncle John?" George's wan smile darkened when he saw the smashed window and flat tires.

"You OK to walk out?" Crockett asked.

George nodded.

Crockett handed his gun to George. "Just in case Watson has a change of heart."

"Where are you—"

"Casey's at the Gourd."

"Casey! God, I forgot—"

"Get help. Keep her safe." Crockett put his big hand on Gabby's head in a giant's caress, then turned and ran.

"Godspeed," George called after him, but Crockett was already enveloped in darkness.

Crockett unwound his long legs as if he were on a breakaway run for the end zone in a race he couldn't win. Too much of a lead. He settled into a lope that he could sustain for half a mile.

If Bear could have made a clean swap—the cocaine for Gabby—Ron could have gotten away with it by disposing of Bear. How would Ron's plan change with three supposed dead bodies in the mausoleum? First, he'd go for the coke. Then what? If he could stage a fatal showdown between Watson and Bear, there would be no one left to tell the tale.

As he ran, Crockett pictured the events of Friday night a week ago. After Ron visited Jules, he picked up pearls and a prescription for Mariko, undoubtedly secobarbital, on his way home. Crockett had crossed Ron off his sleeping pill list when he thought that Ron had an alibi with the babysitter. But he could have dropped off the babysitter and paid a *second* visit to the Gourd.

His lungs were afire. Sweat rolled down his temples and stung his eyes. He picked up the pace, knowing Ron was probably already at the Gourd. Quarter of a mile to go.

During Ron's first visit to the Gourd, he already knew she was skimming to pay the mortgage. She and McPhee worked together selling coke on the side to students. Jules told him she was unpacking a small suitcase because Gabby had come home unexpectedly, and that was the reason she couldn't go to the conference with George. But Ron knew Jules had no intention of going anywhere with George. He figured she was on the run. She'd become a liability, threatening his drug operation and delaying his construction plans. Good lay or not, she had to go.

But that still didn't explain the cleaning cocktail. Had Jules tried to commit suicide earlier? Maybe Jules really did write the note.

Crockett cut across backyards and fields, running as the crow flies. How did Ron get into the drug business? He had had enough money when he returned from the Marine Corps to buy a failing construction company. Did he inherit Solly's old drug network? No, the Oberlin cell was wiped out in Casey's bust.

The last item clicked into place. Hell, Ron worked construction after high school. He was the foreman in Solly's old drug network who ratted out Charley. Mannon said that the guy that gave them the tip immediately went into the service. *Semper fi.* But before he took off, Ron stored the other half of the marked cocaine in the mausoleum. He had a key for his trysts there with Jules. And Jules had the other key.

Crockett's legs pounded and his mind raced. Watson would have told Ron about the video of Casey in the stacks, and about the hollowed-out book. She'd played right into their hands. With Watson pegging Casey as the dealer, suspicions about Jules' drugging would dissolve, and with them, questions about Ron's involvement with Jules.

He thought of Casey alone at the Gourd and picked up the pace. Ron wouldn't leave anyone alive who saw him at the Gourd tonight. Clever as she was, she was no match for the three gorillas headed her way.

Chapter Fifty-Five

Casey waited for her eyes to adjust to the darkness. She was in the last stall in the back corner of the barn. When she tried to stand, pain shot up her leg from her wounded instep. She fell backwards against a wall, dislodging a heavy object that crashed to the floor next to her. Her fingers explored a long, wooden handle that ended in three metal prongs with razor-sharp points: the pitchfork for mucking out the stalls.

She was losing blood. No one would look for her in the barn. She had to get to the Gourd. Casey spiked the pitchfork into the wooden floor and used it to pull herself to a standing position. Loosening the tines from the wood, she leaned on the pitchfork like a crutch, making slow, painful progress toward the door.

With the weight of her body, she shoved against the heavy barn door. After initial resistance, it rolled to the side on greased runners. Outside, lights from the Kenworthy windows and the single Gourd kitchen light provided just enough illumination to see that the courtyard was empty. No sound. No movement. Where were George and Crockett and Gabby? They should be back by now. A sense of foreboding replaced the fragile hope that had propelled her through the tunnel.

A long, pitiful moan floated toward her from the center of the courtyard. Martha was still stuck at the plank inside the well. Using the pitchfork, Casey hiked across the cobblestones. As she drew closer, another high, reedy wail ricocheted inside the well. She'd have to remove the heavy pot of flowers, pry off the lid, and then convince Martha to crawl out.

Good Lord, what was she thinking? Martha just tried to kill her with a carving knife. Besides, she didn't have the strength.

Get to a telephone. Call for help. Let someone else rescue Martha. She turned around at the crunch of tires on gravel. A police cruiser bumped down the tractor path that crossed the pasture to the barn. "Crockett! Over here! Crockett!" she hollered at the top of her lungs. She hobbled and skipped, retracing her steps toward the rear of the barn.

He must have heard or seen her, because the car left the path and bounced toward her. They were safe! She waved her good arm, weak with relief. The car's bright lights flicked on, blinding her. The tines of the pitchfork glanced off the cobblestones, throwing her off balance. She fell sideways. Just as she hit the stones, the cruiser thundered past. A rush of air lifted the hair on her scalp. Casey gasped. Whoever was driving tried to hit her.

With a squeal of brakes, the car slid to a stop.

Casey rolled, grabbed the pitchfork, and forced herself upright. The cruiser's tires spun on the dew-moistened cobblestones before gaining purchase and reversing toward her. She lurched toward the well, but the car cut her off. She couldn't make it. She gripped the pitchfork like a bat in her good hand. At the last second, she jumped back and swung with all her might. She heard the crash of metal on metal just before the car sideswiped her. The impact threw her across the courtyard. She collapsed face down on the cobblestones.

Car doors opened and slammed. Footsteps.

Through bloodied eyes, Casey watched a man approach. Watson! She held her breath and closed her eyes, trying to ignore the blood running from her nose. When he reached her, Watson prodded her side with his foot.

"Get her?" Ron's voice called from across the courtyard.

Slower footsteps shuffled in her direction. Bear shone a flashlight up and down Casey's bloodied body. "Yup."

"Keep a lookout. Fire a shot if anyone comes."

"Where are you going?" Watson asked.

"Where do you think, Captain? To find dearly departed Uncle John. Get rid of her in case an honest policeman passes by."

"Help! Help me, please!" Martha's voice wafted upward through the well shaft.

"Sheeeeeeit! What the fuck's that?" Bear lumbered back toward the voice. "In the well!" he hollered.

"Down here! Help!"

"Sounds like my sister. Martha? Martha! What the hell are you doing down there?" Ron yelled.

Casey rolled over in agony. She couldn't play dead, because she'd cry out when Watson and Bear moved her body.

"It's Jules. Ron, help me out of here. Please."

"Get the lid, Bear."

Voices and the crash of the flowerpot covered the sounds of Casey crawling to the pitchfork.

"Jules? You OK?" Ron added honey to his voice. "Hold tight, we'll get you out."

Nails screeched against wood as Bear wrenched the lid off the well opening.

Casey crutched her bruised and bleeding body toward the barn.

"Jules, honey, do you have Uncle John?"

With the lid removed, Martha's voice was suddenly clear. "I hid him in Gabby's backpack. But Casey took it. She took it with her through the tunnel."

A heavy slam.

"No, Ron! Damn you! Don't leave me in here," Martha screamed, but once more her muted voice echoed with an ethereal quality. Moments later when she cried out again, she sounded like Jules at twelve years old. "Please, Ron. Don't hurt Casey. She's my best friend."

Bear grunted. "Where the fuck's Casey?"

"*Shit!*" Ron turned on Watson. "What's the matter, Dougie? No stomach for hardball?"

"Tell him, Bear. She was a bloody mess," Watson whined.

Casey slipped into the barn and hobbled down the center aisle using the stall walls and pitchfork for support. Her foot throbbed, and her left arm was numb and useless. She was dizzy and couldn't see. She had to stop. She leaned against the stall and struggled to think. Hide. But where? Couldn't go on. Couldn't barter with the cocaine. She'd left it in the tunnel to block Martha.

"In the barn. Get her Watson," Ron barked.

Trapped. The barn was a mistake. Couldn't use the tunnel. Martha still had the knife.

Casey turned and spiked her way back to the door. She leaned on the door, propelling it across the track. At the last moment, a hand shot between the moving door and the doorjamb. But this wasn't an elevator. The massive wooden door easily overpowered the hand. The fingers plumped like sausages, popped, and flattened against the doorjamb. Watson's screams pierced the air.

She gagged and turned and spiked away from the mashed flesh and bone. The hayloft. Get to the ladder.

The door rolled back and a hulking silhouette blocked the light. Bear pushed a weeping Watson aside. With his flashlight, Bear swept the stalls left to right, moving down the center aisle toward Casey. When he was less than ten feet away, the light shone into her face. She gasped. He shuffled forward with a sweet smile.

But she'd gasped in surprise, not horror. Martha had crawled through the tunnel. Casey shifted from one side of the ladder to the other to distract Bear, while Martha crept up behind him carrying Gabby's backpack. Martha whirled the pack over her head once to gain momentum and smashed it into the side of Bear's head. He dropped to his knees, stunned.

"The loft!" Martha rushed to the ladder, put her arm around Casey's waist. The pitchfork clattered to the floor. "Just like old times, eh, Casey?" Martha's voice had taken on a higher tone, as if she were the much younger Jules of childhood.

Casey looked into Martha's crazed eyes. No time for contradictions. Martha pushed from below, and Casey used her good arm and leg to pull herself up one rung at a time. Behind them, Bear grunted to his feet.

"Quit whimpering, Watson, for chrissake!" Ron entered and picked up the pitchfork and flashlight. "You'll have to bring the girls down, Bear. Watson's not worth shit."

Bear placed a foot on the first rung and then stopped. "I...I can't do ladders, boss."

Ron prodded Bear in the rear with the tines of the pitchfork. "Do it!" Ron prodded him again. Bear climbed.

Just as Martha pulled herself into the loft, Bear's hands reached the top rung of the ladder. Casey turned and screamed, kicking with her good foot, catching Bear in the face.

Bear's body jerked backward as he let go to protect his face. For a moment he hung in mid-air before falling, plunging down onto the upturned prongs of the pitchfork. The tines ripped through his back, skewering him like a roast pig. He gazed up at the loft with an expression of innocent surprise. Casey choked and turned away.

Watson retched.

"Won't have to worry about him spilling his guts." Ron laughed. "Pretty soon there won't be anyone left to tell the tale. Looks like it's just you, me, and the two birds up there."

What happened to Crockett? Gabby? George? "Noooooo!" Casey wailed.

"Watson, you've got the piece. Shut her up like a good boy." Silence.

"C'mon. We don't have all day." Footsteps strode across the planks followed by a loud whack. Watson's whimpers escalated to sobs.

"Gimme the gun. I'll do it." Ron's voice softened.

From the loft, Casey watched Watson withdraw the gun from his holster and hand it to Ron. Ron took a step toward the ladder, then whirled and turned on Watson. A sardonic smile disfigured his face.

"Shit for brains!" He placed the barrel of the revolver against Watson's temple. "Keys," he demanded. Watson moaned and fumbled for a moment, producing a key ring. Ron yanked the keys from Watson's hand. "Bang!" he yelled. Watson fainted.

Ron scanned the barn with the flashlight and then disappeared under the loft.

Moments later, Casey heard splashing sounds. Washing away the blood? No. Her nose gave her the answer. *Gasoline!*

"Martha...*Jules!*" she whispered. "Move! He's going to set the barn on fire! Now! To the hay window."

Watson groaned as he regained consciousness. "Ron, you're crazy. Your sister's up there!"

"An added bonus."

Chapter Fifty-Six

Halfway across the paddock, Crockett spotted the silhouette of a police cruiser parked at an angle in the rear Gourd patio. A low rolling sound followed by a man's piercing screams came from the direction of the barn. Closer to the barn he heard male voices and then a high-pitched "Noooooo!" Casey? Crockett couldn't be sure. He sniffed the air. Gasoline.

He reached the barn and peered inside. A flashlight resting on the floor lit a hellish scene. Bear lay at an odd angle, the glint of steel spikes protruding from his chest. Crockett grasped the doorjamb and turned from the sight, instantly recoiling from something wet and slimy on the surface. *Jeasus!*

Ron entered the path of light, directing his voice to someone crawling away from him. As he approached Bear, he wiped a gun clean with a handkerchief. Hefting Bear into a sitting position, he lifted Bear's right hand, working to fit his thick forefinger through the trigger guard.

"Don't, Ron. I'm begging you. I always done what you told me."

"Don't get me wrong. I'm grateful. Just can't leave any loose ends. You first." He picked up the flashlight and pointed it to the loft. "Then the girls."

Crockett's eyes followed the light. A ghostly, Jules-like, white-faced clown with matted hair and a pink mouth leaned against a bale of hay. Had to be Martha. Something moved next to her. *No!* Casey's face and hands were streaked with blood.

Ron aimed the light toward the rear of the barn where Watson moaned and cradled a ruined hand. Ron balanced the flashlight on a bale of hay, lifted Bear's hand, and aimed the gun at Watson.

With two giant steps, Crockett launched himself at Ron. Ron wrenched the gun from Bear's hand just as Crockett's body collided with his. They crashed against a side stall and hit the floor, splintering wood beneath them. Crockett pounded Ron's gun hand against the floor, but Ron held on. Crockett rolled to the side and rammed his knee into Ron's chest. Ron grunted and released his grip, and the gun scuttled across the planks.

Crockett struggled to his feet. As Ron rose, Crockett slugged him in the solar plexus. Ron reeled backward but remained upright.

They crouched and circled like cats.

"Never get away with it, Ron."

"Nothing to get away with."

"Murder. Kidnapping."

"You got it all wrong. Bear killed McPhee. He took Gabby. Now he'll kill you and Watson, and we'll have a little barn burning."

Ron bent over suddenly, grabbed the flashlight, and hurled it at Crockett. Crockett ducked. The light smashed into the wall. Total darkness. And silence.

Watson moaned. Shuffling noises. Another moan.

A match flared lighting Ron's face and torso from below with an orange incandescence, like the devil incarnate. He stood just out of striking distance in the center aisle. He moved toward the front door of the barn. Behind him, Watson crawled across the floor.

"Match will go out soon, Ron," Crockett said, edging forward.

"Got a whole book. You wouldn't want the girls to go up in smoke now, would you? Be on your head, not mine." Ron nipped the flame between his fingers. Before Crockett could move, Ron struck another match.

"Bye, bye, Mr. Lucky," Watson croaked.

Startled, Ron turned toward the sound. A single shot ripped the air. Ron bent forward, grabbed his crotch, and dropped the match. With the whoosh of a wind tunnel, the aisle exploded, engulfing Ron and Watson in a wall of flames.

Chapter Fifty-Seven

Gabby pushed her baby carriage across the cobblestones of the Gourd courtyard toward Casey. "Wanna see my baby?" she asked. "Oh, yes," Casey replied, peering under the bonnet. "What's your baby's name?"

"Ralphie."

At the sound of his name, Ralphie's head emerged from underneath a blanket, and his tail thumped against the side of the carriage. His jaw was wired, and his front paw was in a cast.

"He's beautiful. You take good care—" but Gabby had already rolled on, leaving Casey standing alone beside the well.

A slight breeze offered the only relief from the oppressive humidity. Although the remains of the old barn had been cleared from the site, the moisture in the air brought up the scent of soggy ashes. Casey shuddered despite the heat. In her waking hours, she could control her mind and focus upon healing her wounds, but in the pre-dawn hours, the devils of the night danced over her, haunting her dreams with endless tunnels, pitchforks, popping fingers, and fire.

The image she would take to her death was Martha in the hayloft window, high-stepping in the flames like a crazed majorette. "Follow me!" Casey yelled as she jumped and slid down the hayloft rope to the ground. She turned and hollered, "Jump, Jules! Use the rope!" Too late, Crockett tried to turn Casey from the sight of Jules' wig bursting into flames and disappearing into the inferno as the barn imploded with a loud sucking sound.

She shook her head to dispel the image. Today, she planned to see her brother and then slip away. As well as one could slip away on a crutch with one arm in a cast.

She spied Art on the patio draped across a lawn chair under the shade of an umbrella. Casey lowered herself carefully into a chair next to him. "I understand Mae bought you a baby grand."

"Bribery," he said. "Speaking of which, I heard George gave you Jules' car to make amends."

"Too little, too late," she said, producing car keys with a smile. "But I'm not a total fool. You take good—"

Again, her advice was cut short. "Don't worry about me. You *are* stopping to see her on the way out, aren't you?"

"Yes, brother dear." Casey sighed with exaggerated, sibling patience. They sat for a few moments in companionable silence. Finally, she rose, kissed him on the forehead, and walked toward the car.

At the last moment, she turned and gazed at the Gourd once more, committing the details to memory. When she reached the street, she stuck the crutch in the jump seat of the yellow roadster and fired it up. Such a lovely purr! Casey welcomed the distracting pain of her bandaged foot on the clutch.

She parked in Mae's driveway and admired the garden of burnt-out teapots overflowing with petunias. Inside, Mae lay atop the hospital bed, covered by an afghan. She cracked open one eye and sighed, resting her hand on her tummy.

"Are you OK?"

Mae's stomach gurgled and rattled like a rusty pipe.

"Can I get you something?"

"We'd like our treat now, please." Mae's stomach heaved and regurgitated a large, black furball.

"Bookie! Omigod, Bookie!" Casey's voice broke. She scooped up the kitty with her good arm and buried her face in his fur. Casey swayed from side to side, dancing in place with her cat, saying his name over and over. Tears streamed down her face. Bookend placed a paw on each side of her neck and raked her cheek with a sandpaper tongue.

"How did—?" Casey began.

"Treat first," Mae demanded.

Casey kissed the top of Bookend's head and clumped to the kitchen. She prepared a tray with extra cookies and a glass of milk, and a bowl of cream for Bookend. She placed the tray on a serving cart and pushed it into the front room. With a proper butler posture, Casey served her favorite old cats their afternoon tea. After the snack and Mae's burp, Casey listened to her aunt's story.

"A man from the vet called and said to come get my cat. I told him I didn't own one, but when he read our phone number and the name 'Bookend' off the tag, I realized what had happened."

Of course! Casey had used the home telephone on Bookie's collar because she couldn't use a library number. "Why didn't they call earlier?" she asked.

"They did, but I stopped answering the phone when Watson was badgering you. When I didn't answer, the vet assumed I was away." As Mae talked, she stroked Bookie with a new pet brush, removing handfuls of fur. "Cats shed like crazy when they're nervous or excited," Mae explained, stuffing fur into a paper bag next to the bed.

"I had no idea you liked cats."

"I always had a cat. Problem was they died and broke my heart. After the last one, I swore I wouldn't get another."

"Here, I'll empty that," Casey reached for the paper bag.

"No! I'm saving it." Mae's eyes flashed and a smile of trouble began at the side of her mouth. She let the comment hang for dramatic effect before explaining. "It's for a Christmas present for Alice."

"You exchange gifts with Scowlie Palmer?" Casey was incredulous. Alice was Mrs. Palmer's given name. Next to Mae on the bed, Casey spotted heavy mesh material in a circular wooden frame and a collection of bright red, yellow, and brown threads. The outline of a rooster was printed on the material.

"At the Women's Club gift exchange, everyone puts in a present for a drawing. Alice will get the pillow."

"How do you know she—"

"Alice organizes it. She cheats. She won't pass up a throw pillow with a rooster on it. Her whole house is packed with stupid rooster knickknacks." Mae tugged a hairball gently from Bookie's side. He turned quickly to bite his objection, thought better of it, and resumed his energetic kneading. "Bookend has been helping me with the project."

"You do know Mrs. P is allergic—"

Mae awarded Casey with another secret smile and then quickly changed the subject. "Here, this is for you. I'm not going to cry or say goodbye. I have Bookend to keep me company. You're just going down the road apiece." Mae handed her a small paper bag. "I love you, child. Now off with you."

"Thank you, Mae. For everything." Casey scratched the top of Bookend's head, and bent and kissed a surprised Mae. "I love you, too," she whispered. She made it to the car before more tears flooded her cheeks. She peeked into the bag Mae had handed her and withdrew the hand-tooled leather case with Vernon Bathory's wedding picture, and an envelope. Mrs. Bathory's letter was still tucked behind the picture.

Casey gasped as she opened the envelope and found ten brand-new one hundred dollar bills. She unlocked the glove compartment and added the money to an envelope that already contained the thousand dollars Jules had hidden in the backpack.

She drove slowly through town, obeying the speed limit and most of the stop signs until she reached the edge of town. Then she stopped, put the top down, and headed toward the Ohio Turnpike.

With a single whoop of the siren and flashing strobes, Crockett pulled over the roadster. He walked to the little car, loomed over her, and glowered.

"Any idea how fast you were going, young lady?"

"Not fast enough," Casey responded, offering him a brave smile and wiping away tears.

"You'd leave without saying goodbye?" he accused, still scowling.

Casey nodded. "Too hard, JoJo. Just too damn hard." New tears welled up in her eyes and she turned her head away.

Crockett reached over and turned her face back to him. "That's better. I don't need to be the only one crying."

Casey looked into Crockett's eyes with an expression of surprise.

"Don't have to leave, you know. Mae and Art need you." Crockett hesitated. "Gabby loves you, and George—"

"You're not making it any easier, JoJo."

"That's the idea." Crockett shifted uncomfortably, reluctant to play the last card. "Mostly, I don't want you to go. Place won't be the same."

"The place is never the same. Just memories stuck in time. I need to make some new memories. I'm glad you decided to stay. It's a wonderful place for a family. Just not for me right now."

"Not going to win this one, am I?" Crockett looked away and was silent for a moment. "I understand. Times, I want to break free myself. Just go. Drive 'til I don't know the road. No worries. No responsibilities."

"No Leila, no Jackie," Casey interjected.

"Why I'm staying."

"So, you dream of going and need to stay, and I dream of staying and need to go. Too bad we can't meet somewhere in the middle." Casey gave him a wry smile.

"Guess that's what we be doing now—stealing a moment in the middle."

Casey surprised him by touching his lips with her fingers. "I have some good memories, too," she said softly. He drew her head against his chest and held it there a few seconds before releasing her. "Keep in touch, girl, and take care."

He returned to the cruiser, turned on the strobes, and gave Casey a police escort to the entrance of the Turnpike. Casey waved, took a toll ticket, and pointed the roadster north toward freedom.

287

Acknowledgements

Thank you, dear readers. You make my world go round.

Endless gratitude to members of my writers group: Mark Ammons, Cheryl Marceau, Frances McNamara and Leslie Wheeler, and former members Gin Mackey and Barbara Ross, for nursing along a short story which, over many iterations, morphed into a novel. Without your dedicated efforts and encouragement, there would be no story. Thanks also to Gerald Elias, Lynn Feller, Ron Kelly, Barbara Judson, Ellen Richstone and Susie Woodworth, who offered useful comments and critiques along the way. My appreciation for Graham Masiiwa, sensitivity reader, and for Barbara Harding, dear friend and handwriting analysis mentor, who provided graphological advice and counsel. Special thanks to Kate Flora, Barbara Ross and Hank Phillippi Ryan for their generous reviews, comments and support.

Sincere apologies to the real Oberlin College librarians who are truly professional, helpful and friendly, for their portrayal as "Scowlies" in the novel. As a townie and a graduate of the college, I love the place dearly, but the story needed an inept Dean of Students and a mean Town Manager, neither of whom are grounded in reality. Thanks to the late Jim Crockett, namesake of a key character, who helped me out of a dicey situation in a period of racial unrest in Oberlin.

For those familiar with the town, a shout out to Presti's, the real restaurant on the edge of town where I situated the fictional inn, the Drinking Gourd. For Oberlin grads and townies, you may also note that I took liberties with the dates when the Carnegie Library housed the Oberlin College reading room, reference room and stacks as well as the town's public library. Any errors or misrepresentations of the times, the college or the town are clearly mine.

Thanks to Level Best Books, especially Verena Rose and Shawn Reilly Simmons, as well as fellow Level Besters who constitute a vigorous, and vibrant community of authors. I'm also grateful to the members of Sisters in Crime/New England (too numerous to name!) who have been so very supportive over the years.

Most of all, bless you dear husband Jeffrey for your continued encouragement and love throughout the writing process. You're the best.

About the Author

Katherine Fast is an award-winning author of over 25 short and flash fiction stories. She was a former contributing editor and compositor for six anthologies of New England crime stories. *The Drinking Gourd* is her debut novel.

In her prior corporate career, she worked with M.I.T. spin-off consulting companies, with an international training firm, and as a professional handwriting analyst.

She and her husband live in Massachusetts.

SOCIAL MEDIA HANDLES:
Katherine Fast, Facebook and LinkedIn

AUTHOR WEBSITE:
Katfast.com

Also by Katherine Fast

Over 25 short and flash fiction crime stories.

CPSIA information can be obtained
at www.ICGtesting.com
Printed in the USA
JSHW020821090622
26862JS00001B/56